THE OBSESSED NOVELLA SERIES

BOOKS ONE - FIVE

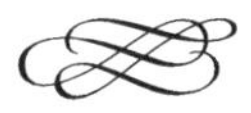

JEANNE ST. JAMES

Editor: Proofreading by the Page

Boxed Set Cover Art: EmCat Designs

www.jeannestjames.com

Sign up for my newsletter for insider information, author news, and new releases:
www.jeannestjames.com/newslettersignup

Created with Vellum

Warning: This book contains sexually explicit scenes and adult language and may be considered offensive to some readers. This book is for sale to adults ONLY, as defined by the laws of the country in which you made your purchase. Please store your files wisely, where they cannot be accessed by under-aged readers.

DISCLAIMER: Please do not try any new sexual practice (BDSM or otherwise) without the guidance of an experienced practitioner. The author will not be responsible for any loss, harm, injury or death resulting from use of the information contained in this book.

Keep an eye on her website at http://www.jeannestjames.com/or sign up for her newsletter to learn about her upcoming releases: http://www.jeannestjames.com/newslettersignup

Author Links: Jeanne's Blog * Instagram * Facebook * Goodreads Author Page * Newsletter Jeanne's Review & Book Crew * Twitter * BookBub

An Obsessed Novella

FOREVER
Him

USA Today Bestselling Author

Jeanne St. James

This is not just a love story, it's an obsession...

I can't keep my eyes off the tall, dark, and confident man who stops in the coffee shop every morning. I want this stranger more than I've ever wanted anyone before, even though I only know his first name. As an author, my imagination is my ultimate writing tool, men like Kane my muse. And the minute he leaves, I'm overcome with fantasies I can't control and my fingers fly across the keyboard ... until one day, I almost snap. My embarrassing outburst has me running out the door when he catches me and takes me to his home.

Though it's risky, I can't resist him. And with one kiss, he now owns me. This man will capture my sanity and trap it forever. He'll steal me one piece at a time until he possesses me completely. He'll ruin me for any other man. But I don't want anyone else, for it'll always be forever him.

Note: All books in the Obsessed series are stand-alone novellas. It is intended for audiences over 18 years of age since it includes explicit sexual situations, including BDSM.

CHAPTER ONE

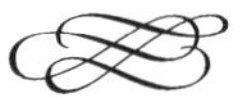

His name is Kane.
I will love him forever. He just doesn't know it yet...

The only reason I know his name is because every morning when he stops at the coffee shop for his large black coffee, the barista calls out, "Kane with a K."

Every. Single. Morning.

I assume the barista does it on purpose. Possibly to coax a smile out of him. But it never does. His expression never changes. It seems forever stuck in serious mode. He just grabs his coffee, throws money into the tip jar, spins on his heels, and leaves.

Maybe he's an important man. A busy man. A man with a lot of responsibilities on his broad shoulders. Maybe his mind is on what he needs to get done for the day.

But he never deviates from his routine. Black coffee. No cream. No sugar. No pastries.

Not once since I've noticed him.

I rarely pay attention to people coming and going from the shop since the mornings are usually busy. I sit in my corner with my laptop open, my brain spinning with ideas. Or not.

Sometimes I have severe writer's block. Those are the times my brain seems dark and empty. Nobody's home. I had it the first morning I noticed him. During those times, I stare off blindly while reaching deep into my head. Searching for… something. Anything. Begging for just a couple words to spur my creativity.

The front door with its delicate dinging bell usually never pulls my attention. Until that day. The day I happened to be staring at the door mindlessly, not paying attention to the influx of customers.

Until him.

He's tall. And broad. Not fat, no. Heavy muscles bunch under the dress shirt he wears as he pushes the door open and steps inside. His dark hair is super short on the sides, just a tiny bit longer on the top. A no-nonsense haircut. Like him… No nonsense.

His perfectly ironed, deep purple dress shirt is tucked neatly into his black slacks. His black leather belt is held together by a simple gold-tone buckle.

His eyebrows appear dark and heavy above eyes that make me blink. They are so light but I can't tell if they are gray or blue. No matter what, they're a shocking contrast to his skin color.

The only visible accessory he wears is a watch on his wrist. Even from where I sit, I can see it's quality. One I could never afford, and I probably wouldn't know the brand. But it screams *expensive*.

His legs are long and unmistakably solid, giving him a confident stride as he beelines to the counter.

Why does he stop here for black coffee? I'm sure he can afford a coffee maker. It isn't difficult to make. Some grounds, a filter, and some water. Push the button, wait, and voilà…

Ah, maybe he doesn't like to wait. But is it actually quicker to stop here every morning?

Maybe he doesn't like to clean up. Though, after studying him, my gut instinct says he can afford someone to take care of dirty dishes. Perhaps he even has a significant other who would be willing to do it. A wife. A husband.

A *lover*...

It doesn't matter why he stops each morning because once I notice him, I can't take my eyes off him. I can't concentrate.

I watch his lips move as he places his order. I wait for the corners of his lips to turn up as he talks to the barista. They don't. No eye crinkle, no smile, not even a nod of his head to acknowledge that he's speaking to a fellow human.

Nothing.

He never takes out a cell phone once while waiting for his coffee. I have never even seen him with one in his hand.

He would be the kind of person to think it rude to be on your phone instead of giving your full attention to the person serving you. Even if that attention is cold, lifeless.

He's consistent, and he always comes alone.

One day I switch from my regular table in the corner to a table where I can see his left hand. His ring finger appears bare. Though, that doesn't guarantee he isn't married. Or in a committed relationship. A lot of men don't wear bands.

I watch him every day. I learn the way he moves, that he's right-handed, that he takes fifteen strides to the coffee counter. That he always checks the lid on his coffee to make sure it's secure before pivoting to leave.

I turn into Pavlov's dog. When the bell rings at 8:02 every morning, I have to glance up. I can't fight it even if I want to.

After I watch him walk out the door, I spin fantasies about him. How he will look naked. How his face will twist when he comes. How his fingers will feel deep in my pussy, stroking my insides, making me wet.

How serious his kiss will be when he crushes me against him.

I can't escape my thoughts. My desires. My panty-soaking fantasies.

I think about changing coffee shops because I'm becoming obsessed.

I want to touch him. I want to see him smile. I want to make him laugh.

I imagine that something is missing from his life. Like me. I can solve all his problems. I can smooth his brow when it furrows after being overwhelmed at work. I can kiss away the tension. I can whisper soothing words in his ear to distract him from all the important tasks he's responsible for.

The only good thing about my obsession is it helps me write. Once the bell rings as the door closes behind him, my fingers tear across the keyboard. I no longer suffer from writer's block. Fantasy after fantasy pops in my head, and I squeeze my thighs together until I ache as the words spill out onto the screen.

He is my muse.

My inspiration.

His skin is dark, but I can't imagine him lounging by a pool. He seems too important for that. Or too impatient. He probably doesn't have time for fun. Life for him is about getting things done.

So, it isn't a tan. No, his skin tone appears natural. His heritage makes him dark. Brooding. Intense. Something lurks in his lineage that is far from middle America. Even *if* his driver's license classifies him as white, his family tree would say otherwise.

Kane with a K intrigues me.

I never sleep in anymore, but I don't have to set my alarm. My eyes pop open every weekday at the same time, my head already filled with him. I make sure I am at the coffee shop, in my usual spot with my laptop open, my chai tea fresh and hot in front of me by 7:50. Just in case he's early.

He never is. He's like clockwork. He has a routine, and sticks with it.

Every. Single. Morning.

I want to know what his last name is. What he does for a living. What kind of car he drives. Does he walk to the coffee shop? Does he live or work nearby?

When the tiny bell rings, I glance up. My eyes flick to the time in the corner of my screen, 8:02. Then they land back on him.

Today he wears a jacket over his light blue dress shirt, one that emphasizes the color of his eyes. His dark blue patterned tie is knotted perfectly, precise, tight to his collar. The cuffs of his shirt are visible over his hands. The correct length for a well-dressed man. His gold cufflinks flash as his arm swings in rhythm with his gait.

He's so out of my league, he never, ever glances my way. Not once.

I don't understand how he can't feel the heat of my gaze, the filthy sexual nature of my thoughts.

How can he not feel me undressing him?

Every. Single. Morning.

He has to wait this morning. Two people are ahead of him with much more complex orders than his usual large black coffee. The staff is short-handed today. His sharp gaze sweeps the space behind the counter before realizing the issue. He lifts his arm and checks his watch.

His toe taps. Most likely from impatience, not nervousness. His body turns as he surveys the shop. For once, he's noticing that there are other customers and things in the café other than just him, the barista, and his large black coffee.

I feel him, though he's not even close, not even touching me.

I sense the air shift with every breath he takes. I notice every blink. His long, dark eyelashes open and close like two Chinese fans.

Then his gaze bounces to me. Instead of continuing past, it stops. It stays. He stares. Possibly because I'm staring back. Maybe because my mouth gapes open and I'm breathing more shallow than normal.

I shift awkwardly in the hard, wooden chair as heat rises into my cheeks, and I'm mortified that I can't tear my gaze away from his.

His eyes narrow and his brows furrow, making his eyes appear darker than normal. They remind me of a stormy sea instead of the tranquil Caribbean Ocean.

My heart beats furiously as his eyes roam over my hair. I fight not to run a hand through it and hope it's all in place… because it usually isn't. I curse under my breath when his gaze drops lower to my mouth. I lick my lips before slamming my jaw shut, narrowly missing my tongue. His inspection of me is slow, thorough. Down my neck and then lower.

I'm glad I tossed on a V-neck cashmere sweater this morning and not an old sweatshirt. Never in my wildest fantasies did I think he would notice me.

Never.

His eyes roam smoothly to my cleavage and pause again. One second, two seconds, three seconds. Blood rushes to my head, and I squirm. Heat pools at my core making me wiggle in my seat.

God, just his gaze makes me want to come. My pussy throbs and I have an urge to touch myself.

All of those fantasies.

If he only knew.

He'd probably laugh and think I'm silly. That he's way out of my league. He would never be with someone like me.

But I want him to touch me. I want his fingers to rake through my hair, rip my head back. I want to feel his lips, his teeth, along the strong pulse in my neck. I want him to brush his thumbs over my hardened nipples.

I find myself light-headed and realize I stopped breathing. I'm waiting. Paused for him to make his move. To grab my hand, pull me out the door, to his house, his car, his office, where he could fuck me thoroughly and hard until he makes me explode into a million pieces.

I want to climb on his lap and spear myself on his cock, riding him hard until I'm slick, sweating, and clinging to his skin with my fingernails. I want to feel his teeth along the sensitive curves of my breasts.

I want.

I want.

I want him to touch me.

I need him to touch me.

I need his fingers, his hard cock, inside me.

And I'm as impatient as him.

I need it now.

I want him now.

Now!

I scream silently. A voice I don't recognize as mine yells, "Touch me, damn it! Touch me!"

Then I realize all customers' eyes are on me. Those words, that demand, were not contained in my head.

No.

I shouted it out loud. The rawness in my throat unequivocal proof.

My chair squeals as I shove it back and it falls to a clatter behind me. I grab my laptop, slamming the lid down. I tuck it under my arm and rush out of the coffee shop.

I leave my dignity behind, just like my chai latte.

My cheeks remain hot, my heart pounds, my stomach rolls. I'm about to evacuate the contents of my stomach.

I push through the front door and suck in fresh air, willing myself to breathe. In through the nostrils, out through the mouth. Slow, steady. Keeping the rhythm until my nausea subsides.

My back faces the store front, and cars with occupants, who are clueless to my recent life-changing outburst, whiz by. They don't know how crazy I sounded shouting to a man, a stranger, in the coffee shop behind me.

But I know.

And he knows.

I need to get away before the door opens, the bell rings, and he steps out onto the sidewalk. One we would have to share.

Because right now, the thought of sharing anything with him is too much.

I force my feet to move, my legs to function. I move forward blindly. Step by step.

Then a car horn blares, scaring me out of my stupor. And my whole body becomes a rag-doll.

CHAPTER TWO

Strong, long fingers firmly grip my upper arm, forcing me back onto the curb. My neck whips back and forth like a furiously shaken bobble head. A rush of adrenaline causes my stomach to flip, and my heart to skip a beat.

"Careful!" His voice sounds low, smooth, like warm honey. But it's firm, like a man who takes charge.

I haven't turned around yet.

Not yet.

I can't face him. Though he invades my personal space. "Are you okay?"

I can feel him inspecting me to make sure I'm whole.

When I don't respond, he continues, "Look. Can I buy you a coffee? I noticed you left yours behind."

Another reminder of my major malfunction.

I can't answer him, so I simply nod. I quickly gather my wits and tilt my head to the shop behind us and finally find my voice. "Not in there."

I'm so humiliated, I doubt I'll ever return to my favorite morning spot.

"No. Not in there," he agrees, and then chuckles.

His laugh resonates low and deep like his voice and sends shivers down my spine. I don't doubt his voice alone could melt me into a puddle at his feet. The amused sounds escaping him affect me more than I could ever realize.

And who knew he could even crack a smile, let alone laugh.

Strangely, I haven't faced him yet. I seem frozen in place. "Thank you for stopping me..." I hesitate, and he answers my unsaid inquiry.

"Kane."

My whole being knows his name. I hear it every morning when the barista yells it out. I nod and slowly turn around, dislodging his grasp on my arm.

"Kane." It rolls off my tongue as I repeat it. I realize I've never said his name out loud before. Even after all the weeks I've studied him while he waits for his black coffee. The name fits him.

He looks at me, a question in his eyes. But he doesn't ask.

"Lila," I offer. A delicate name for someone who's not.

"Nice to meet you, Lila."

My name on his lips sounds like he's sucking on a caramel. Sweet, sticky. It makes my toes curl, and my fingers clench.

"So, coffee?"

"Yes."

"I know the perfect spot."

I do, too... His bed.

I shake my head, squeezing my eyes shut, trying to knock my debauched thoughts from my mind.

"Are you sure you're all right?" This man who's never shown a smidgeon of emotion in all the minutes I have watched him, suddenly shows concern for a stranger?

And it hits me then. Kane with a K is a stranger as well. I shouldn't be going anywhere with him, should I?

He clears his throat as I stare up at him. "If you don't want to go..."

Of course, I will go with him. Because there's no other place I'd rather be than with Kane with a K.

If he ends up being some crazed serial killer, then hopefully I learn from my mistake. I snort out loud.

His eyebrows rise, and he stares deep into my soul.

"L-l-let's go," I finally stutter and then curse myself silently.

His brow smooths out and the creases at the corners of his amazing eyes crinkle. If I didn't know better, I'd think it's sort of a smile. Or a look of satisfaction.

He takes my elbow and walks me three cars down, pausing in front of a Mercedes sedan parked at the curb that's all blacked out. The paint, the windows, the wheels. It's bad ass. And looks super expensive.

He pulls the key fob out of his pocket and opens the door for me like a perfect gentleman. I guess I shouldn't expect anything less from him. I slide into the dark gray leather passenger seat and before I can say "boo," he shuts the door. The silence in the car during the time it takes him to make his way around to the driver's side makes me feel like I'm in some sort of luxurious, air-tight cocoon. I stop stroking the soft leather seat when he opens the driver's door.

Hell, I can't even afford a car. Ever since I quit my job to write full-time, I must make good use out of my two feet, and take advantage of public transportation.

But I'm happier, mostly. The downside is I've been lonely recently, since writing can be an isolated profession.

I sneak a glance at the man driving the car; he's probably never lonely. Instead, he most likely enjoys his alone time.

I look out of the windshield to see the direction he's heading through the city. As the street signs flash past, I realize he's heading west. To a better part of town.

No surprise.

"So, who were you shouting to back there?"

He doesn't know. Or maybe he's being polite and pretending not to know. Either way…

"I'm a writer. My characters have conversations in my head all the time."

He cocks an eyebrow but keeps his gaze on the road. It's the morning rush hour, and the streets are busy.

"I usually keep it under control, though," I assure him.

A smile creeps across his face. He gives me a quick sideways glance that says he doesn't believe me.

So, he knows.

Heat crawls back into my face, and I try to change the subject. "Where are we going?"

"It won't be long now."

Not an answer, but I turn to gaze out of the passenger side window. The businesses have turned into residences. Some large and stately, some smaller and well-maintained. The streets are tree-lined and litter-free. More upscale than where my apartment is. Just a bit.

"Don't you have to be somewhere?" I ask him. He's most likely never late to work.

"I do."

"And where is that?" I study his profile.

Since the traffic is lighter here in the residential part of the city, he turns his head to look at me.

No. It's not a look; it's a raking of his eyes over my face. I keep my expression blank; I don't want to let him know how he affects me.

But he does. My nipples pebble under his gaze and I squeeze my thighs together as the ache between them builds.

I fear he can make me come with only a look.

He returns his attention forward, and within a few seconds, he's pulling the large Mercedes into a driveway and then into a three-car garage. As the overhead garage door shuts behind us, I'm not sure what I should do. I'm now in a stranger's car, in a stranger's garage, at a stranger's house. And no one... *no one* knows where am I.

Smart move, Lila. You may end up being eaten with fava beans, or your skin may be worn as a coat. But, hey, he's hot, right?

"I... Uh..."

He doesn't wait for me to stumble through my concern. Instead, he gets out of the car and comes around to my side, opening the door and offering me his hand.

See? He's a complete gentleman. What serial killer has such good manners?

Fuck. Probably most of them.

My fingers squeeze tighter around the laptop I'm holding against me as I stare at his outstretched hand.

His fingers appear long, dark, and neatly manicured. Perfect to strangle me with. Why did I ever think it was a good idea to go with him to get coffee?

"Let me help you out, Lila. Take my hand." A demand.

Well, when he puts it like that... Okay.

I release one cramped hand from my computer and let him take it to help me climb out of the car. As he closes the passenger side door behind me, I turn and see two more vehicles in the garage. One looks like an old muscle car from the sixties. And the other isn't a car at all. The motorcycle, all blacked out like the Benz, looks fast and the emblem on the side belongs to BMW.

This man likes speed. Precision. Luxury.

Everything I'm not.

I'm a struggling author doing my best to make ends meet, having a hard time even paying my rent. I can't afford manicures, expensive clothes, regular hair appointments... or even a 1988 Ford Escort.

But I *am* a determined woman. And I have always been willing to work hard.

As he escorts me through a door into what I can only assume is *his* house, I feel determined not to be a murder victim today.

The hand that envelopes mine is warm, smooth, and very large, dwarfing mine. Now that I'm next to him, I realize how tall he actually is. In contrast, I'm not very tall at all. Only three inches over five feet. He must be a foot taller than me. Maybe not a whole foot, but it's close. Maybe six-one or six-two.

I glance down as we walk. His dress shoes shine, his pants are the perfect length. This man does not buy a suit from a rack. No, sir.

We travel down a long, tiled hallway and end up in a large, open kitchen. More tile, muted colors, perfectly clean.

And what do you know? A coffee maker sits on the counter in a corner under a cabinet. I get a sudden urge to run a finger over it to check for dust. I don't because he releases me and puts a hand along the small of my back.

The sweater I'm wearing is thin, and I can feel the heat of his palm on my skin. I try not to shiver since my nipples are hard enough as it is.

He guides me over to a stool at the center island and instructs me to "have a seat."

I do, and watch him shed his suit jacket. It's like watching porn as he slips it over his broad shoulders and down his arms. I can't pull my eyes away as he carefully folds it in half and lays it over a chair at the kitchen table.

"I guess you live here."

He runs a hand over his discarded jacket before turning, a crooked smile on his face. "No, I have no idea who lives here. I figured we could just borrow their coffee maker."

Oh, he has a sense of humor. I like it.

I like him.

From seeing him at the coffee shop, I never would have thought the guy had a personality at all. "You're a pretty good burglar then, since you memorized their alarm code."

"I don't forget things."

Strange comment. But, okay…

"Like you."

My eyes lock on his. His amazing blue eyes are such an odd color for his skin tone. "What does that mean?"

He ignores my question and moves around the kitchen pulling a bag of coffee out of the freezer. While he sets up the coffee maker, his back is to me and he asks, "Are you hungry? Do you want something to eat with your coffee?"

"Do you cook?"

"Only enough not to starve. What would you like?"

I shake my head but realize he's not looking at me. "Nothing. I'm not hungry, but thank you."

He glances over his shoulder at me. "Are you sure?"

"Yes, thank you." I'm not hungry, but I *am* curious. "Why do you stop at the shop every day if you have a coffee maker?"

He pushes the power button on the top-of-the-line appliance and turns to face me, leaning back against the counter. His eyes rake over me again, making me want to shudder under his gaze. "Because of you."

I frown because I still don't understand how him stopping for coffee every day has anything to do with me. "What about me?"

He pushes himself away from the counter and approaches. I'm watching him like he's a lion stalking his prey. This time I can't stop the shiver that trickles down my spine.

He leans forward, and I hold my breath thinking he will grab me, but instead he reaches around to grasp the back of the stool and spins it to face him. When he steps closer, my legs end up trapped between his.

He stares down at me with those eyes of his, and I can't release his gaze. I'm stuck. Frozen. Like a deer in headlights unable to avoid the oncoming car.

"Lila. I go in there every day to see you."

He's lying. He must be. Not once has he looked my way in all the days he's come in since I've noticed him. He must be making this up as he goes.

"I don't believe you," I whisper.

My gaze locks on his beautifully shaped lips as he says, "It's true."

I run a tongue over my own lips because suddenly I'm parched. The movement doesn't escape him, and he stares at my mouth.

"One day I was running late, and I figured I would just pop in there to grab my coffee, and I noticed you sitting in the corner, hiding behind your laptop. You had color in your cheeks, and your eyes had a soft, unfocused look. Your bottom lip was tucked between your teeth. You looked so sexy at that moment. I knew then I had to see you again."

When he speaks, his words sound beautiful, no matter what they are, no matter what the context. Just then I want to hear him say something offensive. A searing, obscene word. Like "fuck." The word fuck coming off his tongue would probably sound like doves crying and angels singing.

How bizarre. My line of thought is not a line at all, but a scribble. A messy doodle on a wrinkled piece of notebook paper.

"I was waiting for you."

"Waiting for?" I ask, now even more confused.

"You've been watching me for weeks," Kane says as he moves behind me. Not touching. He's simply there. A presence I can feel but not see. "Why?"

"Why..." My words trail off. I don't want to tell him why, I don't want to seem like a depraved soul. An obsessed stalker.

But he knows why. It hits me that this may be a game for him. He put himself in front of me daily until I noticed. Then once I did I fell right into his trap.

Was his approach some weird foreplay?

I shake my head slowly. My voice is low, breathless. "It was what you wanted, right? For me to notice you? If so, why didn't you ever speak to me?" Because the man certainly can't be shy, or an introvert like me.

He finally touches me, a finger sweeps my long hair off my shoulder, away from the right side of my neck. The air feels cool against my exposed skin. His body heat licks along my back as he leans close. Closer. Then he presses his lips against the curve of my throat. It's soft and delicate, like a butterfly landing on the center of a blooming flower.

"I've been waiting awhile to do that."

I still don't understand why he waited so long. Why not approach a woman you're interested in? "You never looked at me once, but you've been waiting to kiss my neck?" I murmur, not hiding the disbelief in my question.

"Yes," he says against my skin. "Every day I could see your body react when I walked in. You softened, you looked at me with heat I couldn't miss."

I shake my head only slightly, not trying to dislodge his lips which reminds me of silk brushing up and down my neck. Then the tip of his tongue draws a line along my spine.

"So, it was foreplay."

"I wanted to make sure you were interested."

"And my outburst cemented that."

His hands land on my shoulders and he squeezes them gently as he places his mouth to my ear. "Yes. You demanded I touch you."

That I did.

"Just how much do you want me to touch you?"

"How badly? Or how much?" I ask.

He releases my shoulders and moves around to stand in front of me, looking down once again. The man could intimidate without trying. "Both."

Heat creeps into my cheeks. Not from embarrassment this time. Instead, it's my burning desire fueling the flames.

I want him badly.

I want him a lot.

My body feels on fire.

"Don't make me guess, Lila. Tell me. Tell me what you want me to do with you. What you want me to do to you."

A simple answer would be "everything," but I doubt he'll accept that as an answer. He seems to be more detail-oriented than that.

Start simple, stupid.

"Kiss me." I struggle to keep my voice from lifting at the end. I don't want it to sound like a question, but more as if I know what I want.

"Is that all?"

I almost laugh at his question because we both know a kiss will not be enough. "No."

His smile widens, the corners of his eyes crinkle. He's amused. "Coffee first?"

"Oh, hell n—" Before I can finish, his mouth crushes mine, his lips moving, his tongue separating my lips, exploring my mouth with power and determination.

His fingers dig into the back of my head as he presses us closer. With a tilt of his head, he seals our mouths tighter together. A groan builds at the back of my throat. My eyes squeeze shut because I can't think of anything except what he's doing.

His kiss dominates me. Takes control of my body from head to toe. It makes the little hairs on the back of my neck stand on edge.

With one kiss, he now owns me.

He cups my face as he breaks the contact, moving only enough so I can speak. But still only a breath away.

Just a breath. I don't move. I can't. I open my eyes and meet his. His blue eyes make me shiver because they are shadowed, unreadable. And completely disturbing.

"Again," I whisper.

With a slight curl to his lips, he presses them against mine once more, this time more gently. Our tongues tangle, and I lay my hands on his chest. I place one directly over his heart so I can feel it beating under my palm. His races as fast as mine. Not a steady beat, but a pounding tattoo.

As he moves down my jawline, I tilt my head to offer my neck. His tongue, warm and wet, slides down the side of my throat making me almost purr. My nipples have turned into painful peaks, and I want him to touch them, suck them.

I don't even know this guy's last name.

But as his hands shift down to my shoulders, I realize I couldn't care less. His legal name could be Kane with a K, and I wouldn't give a flying fuck.

"What else do you want, Lila?"

Again with the questions. I don't want to tell him. I want him to know my needs. He's forcing me to think, to acknowledge that I want this stranger more than I've ever wanted anyone before.

This connection, this draw, makes no sense. It's heady, almost intoxicating.

He smells good. Dark spices, tangy. Right then, I know I need to taste him. Does he taste like he smells? Like an exotic dish that tantalizes my senses?

I inhale him deep into my lungs and say, "I want to take you into my mouth."

Without a word, he straightens and steps back from me. If I thought his eyes appeared dark before, they're even darker now. Dangerous and stormy.

He's no longer looking like a satisfied kitten who drank a dish of milk. He's back to that lion stalking his prey as he watches me carefully, cautiously.

Most men I know would have had their pants down and their cocks out before the offer was even finished. Not this man. He stands stock still and studies me, making me want to squirm.

Then suddenly one corner of his mouth lifts, and he offers me his hand. "We'll skip the coffee."

I ignore his hand and push myself off the stool and drop to my knees in front of him. Right on the kitchen floor. I reach for his belt buckle, and his hands fall to his sides as his stance widens. I glance up his body and see him watching me quietly. His expression unreadable.

I will see what I can do to change that. My fingers are trembling so I fumble a bit until I can unhook the buckle and unfasten his slacks. I slowly slide his zipper down and stare at the juncture of his open pants with anticipation. It's like Christmas morning.

I'm ready to unwrap my gift.

Since his stance is wide and his thighs are muscular and thick, his pants fall only past his hips. His boxer briefs are blue like his eyes and, from what I can see, he certainly is going to be giving me a very, very nice gift.

I swallow hard and try to control my breathing as I run my fingers down the cotton covering his bulge. I want to see him. I want to hold him, but I'm enjoying the anticipation of the unknown.

He doesn't move or make a sound as I cup him within my palm and feel the weight and heat of his balls tucked within his briefs. I glance up again. Still no reaction. I slide my fingers in and along the elastic waistband and slowly reveal what I've been waiting for.

My mouth waters at the sight of precum beading at the crown of his cock. I dart my tongue out to capture it. The salty goodness tastes like heaven, and my eyelids flutter shut. My pussy is wet and clenching, desperate to have his hard length, his thick girth within me.

He tucks a finger under my chin and lifts my face to him. "Look at me while you take me into your mouth."

I do. My gaze never wavers as I wrap my lips around the head. The only sign on his face is a slight movement, a very tiny twitch near his right eye. Not the reaction I'm looking for. But I've only just begun.

I wrap my fingers around the root of his cock and squeeze. I can't continue to look at him. I need to concentrate on making him break.

Deeper and deeper, I take as much of him as possible. My lips stretching, my tongue sliding, my mouth sucking. My eyes flick upward when I hear a noise. I didn't imagine it, but he still isn't showing me any reaction. He's keeping himself together, his control solid.

Now more determined, I run my tongue up the thick vein, capture the head in my mouth, suck harder, before lightly scraping my teeth over the most sensitive area.

My own actions make me ache for him, wet for him. Instead of stretching my lips, I want him to stretch me inside, fill me completely.

I take another pass from the root to the tip and his hips jerk. No, not a jerk, only a slight twitch. The man seems to be made of steel. Immune to the wet heat of my mouth, the softness of my tongue.

Another twitch, another sound. He's letting his façade slip. His hands dig into my hair, pulling it tight, making my scalp scream. I lift my gaze enough to see his eyes, now hooded, his lips slightly parted. His fingers clench and unclench in my hair following the same rhythm of my movement.

I slide my mouth up and down faster, and I finally hear his breathing become ragged, shallow. I want to smile my triumph, but I can't since he remains hard and long and thick within my mouth.

His thrusts start small, shallow, as he pulls my head towards him. I fight my panic as he bumps the back of my throat over and over. I swallow and breathe through my nose, my eyes water. I relax my throat, and I still can't take all of him. It's uncomfortable, but I want to see him break. I want to be the one to bring a look of unadulterated pleasure to his face. I want to hear him cry out my name.

As a tear rolls from the corner of my eye, I peek up at him again. His eyes squeeze shut, his jaw tightens, his lips press together. When a low moan escapes him, his eyes pop open, and he catches me watching him. His eyes darken as he holds my gaze, his chest heaves as my name escapes his lips.

And as his body tenses against me, he's about to fall apart. About to come undone.

"Lila... Lila... Lila," he chants on each breath. A raw sound escapes him, and then he grits his teeth and releases his hot, salty cum at the back of my throat. He still has a death grip on my head, holding me tightly as his cock pulsates on my tongue. And I accept all of him.

Because he's mine.

He just doesn't realize it yet.

CHAPTER THREE

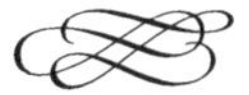

Kane leads me through the house to the master bedroom like he's escorting me to the prom... with a hand to the small of my back, his other hand holding mine in front of him. I feel as if we should waltz down the hallway instead of walk.

His is the only bedroom I've ever been in that has double doors. But beyond them is his domain.

The room is large, more like a suite, tastefully decorated in muted colors of tans and browns. The black furniture shines, and I can't imagine a piece of dust would last but a split moment on its surface in this household. No piles of clothes, no bottles of cologne or lotions in sight, not a stray sock or visible pair of shoes. The bedroom is as put-together as Kane with a K.

He might be a little shell-shocked if he saw my apartment. But now is not the time to worry about that. No. Right now, he directs me to the center of the room and releases me to circle as he inspects me up and down, like a filet mignon about to be devoured by a vegetarian sneaking a piece of meat.

My voice breaks as I ask, "Do you want me to get undressed?" Because why else would he bring me into his bedroom? For the actual cup of coffee I never received?

"No." He stops, and his deep voice behind me is like an aphrodisiac. I'm already wet from the blowjob I gave him. I'm already primed and ready for him to fuck me hard and deep and fast.

But he doesn't seem like the typical man. He appears to want to take his time, not rush. Appreciate the minute details.

"You're exquisite," he murmurs. His fingers rake through my long hair; then he suddenly grips a handful and forcefully yanks my head back. He presses his mouth to the tender spot where my neck meets my shoulder. Who knew that spot has the power to make me melt.

Maybe it's not the spot, and it's the man instead. It's possible that anywhere he places his mouth will make me come undone as he did in the kitchen. Though, I fear I'll shatter much faster than he did. I don't have his control… nor am I sure I want it.

His arms cross in front of me as he grips the hem of my sweater and pulls it up slowly. Up over my belly, over my ribcage, over my bra where the backs of his hands brush over my peaked nipples. I close my eyes at the sensation. He moves like molasses, and it's driving me mad. He continues, pulling the soft fabric over my head, my hair spilling around me once it's free. He leaves my arms in the sweater. I realize why as he slides the sweater down my arms, along my back. He leaves it tangled around my wrists. My hands end up bound behind me too easily. Simply with my sweater. My lips part and a shuddered breath escapes me.

He's hard against my ass, but there are too many layers of clothes between us. I make a noise of impatience, and I hear an answering chuckle.

"Lila, we have all the time in the world."

No, not true. I have a deadline, and he has somewhere to be. Even though I still have no idea where. He's a man that belongs somewhere doing something.

Though, maybe he answers to no one but himself.

I release a loud breath and twist my head to look at him.

"Face forward," he commands.

My first instinct is to argue with him. My natural reaction is to say no man tells me what to do.

But I know that's not the case. Not here. Not now. Not with him.

So I do it.

I stare at his large bed and wonder how soon we'll be on it. How soon he'll be completely naked. And, more importantly, how soon I'll be coming...

With my arms bound behind me, he nips lightly across my shoulders, at the base of my neck, down my spine, only stopping because my wrists are in the way. His tongue traces my spine all the way back to the top. With ease, he unfastens my bra, but it only falls forward until the straps catch my elbows.

He cups my breasts, lifting their weight, brushing his thumbs over the tight tips. Back and forth, back and forth, until my breasts are heavy with need. And that need is his tongue, his lips, his mouth.

"Beautiful," he whispers into my ear before tracing the outer shell with the tip of his tongue. He takes my lobe into his mouth, and I gasp that something so simple could be so erotic. I close my eyes as he sucks and his fingers capture both nipples, twisting, pulling, tweaking the nubs until my knees buckle.

He quickly releases my ear and catches me with an arm tight around my midsection. "Ah, you like that."

Like isn't strong enough. "Yes," I hiss.

One broad hand splays along my belly, the other squeezes and kneads my breast as his warm breath plays along my ear. "Perfect."

I'm not exquisite, beautiful, or even close to being perfect. But I'll wear his compliments like an outer skin because no one, not one man I've ever been with, has called me those things. Even if it's for a short time, I'll welcome his praise. He doesn't need to say those things to get me naked, and I know he's aware of that. So it makes me think maybe he believes what he says.

I feel good, desired. And I want him all the more, if that's even possible.

Kane takes my trapped wrists and turns me to face him. He appears a little undone. His dress shirt has been hanging free from his pants since the episode in the kitchen, his belt buckle dangles loose, his pants barely cling to his hips. His erection remains strong, the smooth bulbous head peeking above the elastic band of his boxer briefs as if reminding us not to forget it.

I don't think either of us will. I have the urge to lick it again, to fall to my knees. But I am at the point of needing more than that. I need some satisfaction of my own.

And my patience has long disappeared. "Get naked," I demand.

One of his brows lifts slightly, and his lips press together for a moment before he says, "I don't think you're in a position to demand anything."

"I can slip the sweater off my hands."

"I know you can, but you won't until I tell you to."

Damn. He's right.

I enjoy the power he has over me. It thrills me to my toes. This is more than sex. Because if this was just sex, he could have fucked me by now and had me halfway home.

"So far you've only asked for a kiss. And I wanted you to tell me what you want."

Once again, the word "everything" echoes through my soul. "I want you inside me."

He shakes his head slowly. "No." Not a *no* as in he will never fuck me, but instead, the one short word speaks volumes. He wants me to tell him to do things to lead up to that.

"I want your mouth on me," I tell him.

"I had them on your lips, your ears."

"More."

"Where."

I swallow hard. My pussy clenches. I want him there. My breasts ache. I want his mouth there, too.

I open my mouth, but nothing escapes.

He runs his hands along the outer curves of my breasts. "Here?"

I nod.

He slides them down my belly and over my jeans to the V in my legs. “How about here?”

I quiver at his touch. “Yes. There, too.”

His hands continue, traveling around my hips to my ass. He cups both cheeks and squeezes. "And here?"

I’ve never had anyone’s mouth there. The idea catches me off guard. It seems a more intimate place than my pussy.

“No,” I whisper, my voice catching.

“Who says you have a choice?” My gaze locks on his, and I know my eyes are wide, surprised. He gives me a slow, reassuring smile. “We will never do anything you don’t want to do,” he says, and I'm instantly overcome with relief.

Listen, I have an open mind. I’m up for experimentation. But I don’t know this man. *Yet.*

He slips his arms around me, almost in a hug, and he pushes the twisted sweater and my bra straps over my hands, letting them both fall to the floor behind me. “I have a better way to bind you.”

“I’ve never…”

“Never?” He lifts a brow as if surprised not everyone has been tied up during sex.

I shake my head. “No. Never.”

“Would you like that?”

“I don’t know…” The possibility excites me but scares me at the same time. The thought of not being able to escape if needed is intimidating though. My blood rushes through my veins, and my nerves stand on end. “If you bind me, I won’t be able to touch you.”

“Do you want to touch me, Lila?”

Oh, fuck yes. “Yes, Kane, I do.” My fingers find the top of my jeans and I fumble with the button.

He stops me immediately with a sharp, “Don’t.” He brushes my hands aside. “I will always undress you. I will take care of you. I will tend to you.”

The “always” part makes my head spin. That and the fact that

I've never had anyone take care of me or spoil me and it may be out of my comfort zone.

He pops the button of my jeans out of the loop and slides down the zipper. I grasp his shoulders for balance as he works the pants down my legs. I lift one foot and then the other as he tugs them off, stripping my shoes and socks at the same time. He is still fully dressed as I stand in the middle of his bedroom in just my panties. I'm not self-conscious because he's already told me I'm exquisite, beautiful, and perfect. And there's nothing better as an ego booster than that.

"Take your panties off, then sit on the bed, spread your legs, and show me where you want my mouth as I undress."

I take my time sliding my pink bikini-cut underwear down my thighs until they fall to my feet and I step out of them before backing myself to the edge of the bed. I sit and open my knees, hiding nothing from him. He remains in place, not moving a muscle, and I want to scream at him to take his clothes off. I want to see his body, I want him against me, I want to have his weight on and over me.

He finally moves so he's facing me directly with nothing blocking his view, and he reaches up to unbutton his dress shirt, slipping one button through the hole, then the next. He takes his time, not in a rush. He seems to be enjoying the view I'm providing. His eyes lock on my sex, and I slide my fingers down my belly until I'm right there, separating my folds, letting him see how slick and ready I am for him.

I circle my clit and press, and my hips jump in reaction. My goal of making him undress faster seems a failure. No matter how I play with myself, how many fingers I slide in and out of me, he continues to unbutton his shirt at the same pace.

It's maddening.

I need to discover a way to break his control.

"Let me see you come," he says as he finally slips his shirt off of his broad shoulders. He lays it over the back of a chair that sits in the corner, though his eyes never leave me, never leave my heated center, while he does so. He tugs his undershirt over his head and folds it neatly to place it on the chair's seat. He sits on the edge of the chair's cushion and unlaces his dress shoes. One then the other before sliding them off and tucking them and his socks under the chair.

His gaze has never once wavered. He watches my fingers strum along my pussy and my clit, my arousal increasing with each pass.

"I want to see you come, Lila," he repeats. He stands, now only in his dress pants. He yanks the belt free and instead of leaving it on the chair, he folds it in half and snaps it together loudly. The sharp noise makes me jump and my heart race. I imagine him striking my ass with it, making it pink and sensitive, hot to the touch. I close my eyes and thrust two fingers inside of me harder, faster. I rub my clit with my other hand just as hard and fast as well.

I'm close to coming, and he doesn't even have his pants off yet. My eyes pop open. "I need to see you."

With a sharp nod, he pushes his pants and boxer briefs down in one swoop. Folding them neatly, he places them with the rest of his clothes.

He nears the bed, though doesn't move to touch me. I fight back a frustrated scream, but I know what he's waiting for.

He wants to see me come.

I don't even have time to appreciate his nudity, his maleness, because I'm right there. Balanced precariously on that tight wire. Only seconds away from doing what he asked, demanded.

His watching me makes me lose my balance, and I fall. My eyes close, my hips rise, and my core ripples around my fingers. I cry out, gasping for breath. I haven't had such an intense orgasm in forever.

Now my forever includes him.

My climax only took a slight edge off my desire, but now I have the real thing in front of me.

He's built like a sculpted dark god. An angel in shadows. I can find very little softness along his lines and planes. His erection juts from his pelvis, long and thick. His hips are narrow, his thighs heavy with muscle. And once I reach his toes, I work my way back up, slower this time. Over the distinct muscles in his stomach, the curve of his firm pecs, his small, dark nipples, his wide shoulders, the visible veins in his hard biceps, the crook of his elbows, the powerful forearms, and then his long, elegant fingers. I realize at this moment… those fingers can wreck me.

They are capable of doing all kinds of things to turn me into a puppet. A play thing. They can control me.

When my gaze finally stops on his face, he smiles. It's a knowing smile. He knows I like what I see.

How could I not? He said I'm perfect. But he's wrong.

He is the one who's perfect.

And he is all mine.

He steps in between my thighs and lifts my now slack hand to his mouth. He slips the two fingers I had deep in my pussy between his lips and sucks them clean. His tongue swirls around my digits, and I swear I almost come again. It's one of the most erotic gestures I've ever witnessed.

"The appetizer was delicious, but I'm ready for the main course." He releases my hand and lowers himself to his knees between my legs. Wrapping his arms around my open thighs, he pulls me right to the edge of the mattress. I fall back onto my elbows, watching as his head lowers and his face disappears.

As with everything else, Kane takes his time, slowly stroking between my folds with his tongue. I open to his touch like the petals of a flower. A rush of pleasure overcomes me as he nuzzles my clit, licks it, flicks it, sucks it hard. My head falls back between my shoulders and my eyes roll in my head at the heady sensations his mouth invokes. A strangled moan escapes me as he separates my swollen labia with his long fingers, so his tongue can glide in and out of me. Heat builds at my center as he slides two fingers into my slick pussy, his tongue swirling around my clit now.

Fuck. I can't take any more. I'm wet, hot, and on edge. Getting dizzy and breathless, I lift my head and watch what he's doing to me as if just feeling it isn't enough. It's a heady sight, seeing the top of his head move in the same rhythm as his fingers. And as he sucks my clit hard, my heartbeat pounds in my ears, my body tenses, and then surrenders as a climax crashes over me. I cry out his name, this Kane with a K. And he stills as the last of the waves subside. He lays a gentle kiss on my now sensitive nub before pulling away and sitting back on his heels, studying me.

"That is the look I noticed when I first saw you sitting in the coffee shop's corner."

His soft words pull me out of my passion-induced stupor. Do I really look like I've just orgasmed when I write? Maybe I do while writing a steamy scene. I wonder how many other customers have noticed. I should feel embarrassed, but there is time enough for that later. Right now, I don't care.

I don't care about anything but Kane with a K and what he will do next.

As he pushes to his feet and stands over me, his eyes look intense, his lips shiny from my arousal, and his cock appears painfully hard. When it twitches under my gaze, I let a smile slide across my face.

"Where do you want my mouth now, Lila?"

He keeps including my name, and I enjoy hearing it come from him. It's like part of a game I'm willing to play. And want to play along, too.

I point to my mouth. "Here, Kane." Then I cup my breasts, pushing them together. "And then here."

He brushes his fingertips from my knees along the tops of my thighs, his hands meet in the center at my waist, his broad palms slide up my ribcage, but he doesn't climb on the bed. Not yet. He dips his head to kiss, lick, and nip a trail from my mound, over and around my navel, straight up between my breasts, across my chest. He lays a light kiss on my chin as his hands grip my cheeks, holding me still, then he pauses right above my lips.

I inhale my scent on him. It's intoxicating, and when he lowers his mouth to mine, I savor everything he tasted, my feminine flavor. Sweet and exciting. He slides his tongue along my parted lips and into my mouth, dipping in and out, making sure I taste myself completely. He captures my moan and swallows it, echoing it with one of his own.

When he breaks away, he presses his forehead to mine. "Lila," he whispers, almost as if he's in pain.

I'm in pain, too, because my ache for him is so deep. I need him inside me. I want to feel complete and I can't without him being a part of me.

He straddles my hips, and his cock lays hot and heavy on my lower belly. He moves his attention to my breasts, cupping them both, his thumbs brushing back and forth over the tight buds. My back arches as he kneads my flesh and lowers his head. As the edges of his teeth close around the delicate tip of my nipple, I still and hold my breath. I don't want to make any sudden moves because how he has me is dangerous. The tip of his tongue darts across the peak, flicking quickly back and forth. A rush of panic flows through me. One wrong move. One slip. That's all it would take to be hurt, possibly changed forever.

He widens his mouth over the areola, sucking my dusky pink flesh deep into his mouth. I relax and enjoy his tongue and lips as they play along my skin. He plucks one with his fingers, the other with his mouth. Over and over until I am lost once again, my eyes closed, only concentrating on how he manipulates my body. How he has command of my flesh, my being.

As with everything else, he takes his time; he's thorough and precise. Acting as if my flesh is something precious for him to appreciate, to worship. Once again, I'm overwhelmed with the feeling I've never been this wanted, this desired before.

Sweeping my fingertips over his head, I marvel at the texture of his short hair, the smooth skin along his forehead, the curve of his ears. His neck is thick and corded with muscle; his pulse beats strong and steady at his throat. I curl my fingers around his neck, but he slips away, his tongue blazing a trail back down my sternum to my belly. He rises for a moment, only long enough to turn me over, and he settles his weight again as he now straddles the tops of my thighs. With a sweep of his hand, my hair falls to the side, exposing the back of my neck and he begins again. His warm breath, his wet tongue, his firm lips, making their way from the edge of my hair, down my spine, along the valley of my back, only stopping when he reaches the crease between my buttocks.

My breath hitches and holds as I wait for his next move. He breathes along my skin causing goosebumps to dance over me. As he slides a finger between my cheeks, he asks, "And here, Lila? Do you want my mouth here?"

My pussy clenches at the image of him pleasuring my most secret spot. A mixture of desire and shock plays through my mind. I war with myself on how good it probably would feel, but I can't say yes. Not yet.

"No," I moan into the pillow. "You can't."

"Oh, I can. But I won't. Not until you're ready. When you beg me for it, I will introduce you to that incredible experience." He pauses as he runs his finger up and down the cleft of my ass. "But not until you want it."

I nod, my face hidden in my arms folded under my head.

"Make no mistake, Lila. I will let that go today, but nothing else."

But he had said—

"Nothing else," he repeats, the timbre of his voice dropping as if he knows where my thoughts lay. "I will never hurt you, but I don't want you to be intimidated by new experiences."

I squeeze my eyelids together for a second, then answer, "Okay."

CHAPTER FOUR

I wonder what I've gotten myself into as my arms stretch above my head, my wrists are bound and tied to a slat on his headboard. Two pillows prop up my hips as I lay on my belly. The rope feels silky soft, and I find nothing uncomfortable about it. He doesn't restrain me in any other fashion. My legs remain free, my mouth unencumbered, like he knows this is all new to me and he doesn't want me to be afraid.

I respect him for that, but it makes me curious about how kinky this man can actually get. He's gentle but firm with everything he does. I almost tell him I wouldn't mind him getting a little rougher.

Along with the rope, he gathered a handful of condoms and a bottle of lubricant, making me wonder how many condoms we will need. Hopefully, enough to leave me boneless and satisfied.

"Lila." Sometimes he just says my name. No rhyme, no reason. I think he likes to let it roll off his tongue. But I can think of better things for Kane with a K's tongue to be doing.

It surprises me to see the time on the clock by his bed. I've been here a couple of hours already, and we still haven't had sex.

Okay, I clarify to myself, we've been having sex, just not

intercourse. Not yet anyway. I know we'll get there. And I'm trying to remain patient because I'm sure it'll be worth the wait.

Being propped on the pillows with my legs spread leaves my slick sex and the seam of my ass exposed. I might not be ready for his mouth there, but I have a feeling he will introduce me to something I only write about in my novels but have never yet experienced.

It makes me pause and ponder if he actually knows who I am and has read some, if not all, of my books. Heat licks along my body, both from desire and a bit of embarrassment. If he's read even one, he may think me more experienced than I am. If so, he couldn't be more wrong.

My imagination is my ultimate writing tool, men like Kane my muse. They become the seeds of my dirty thoughts and desires. My unfulfilled fantasies.

If I give free rein to Kane, I'm sure he'd be willing to fill all of them. The thought makes me smile into the mattress. The only thing holding me back would be myself.

The mattress jostles as his weight returns to the bed. I know he's kneeling between my legs because I feel his heat. His body burns like a furnace. I twist my head just enough to see what he's doing.

My breath catches, my heart stops for a second then thumps faster, and my body trembles.

"I will not hurt you, Lila. I'll never do that."

Though he tries to reassure me, I can't pull my gaze from the belt in his hand. I've never been hit, or even spanked before. Not in pleasure, and certainly not in punishment.

"I'll only do what feels good to you. I'll only do what your body begs me for. You say stop, and I will stop. Understand?"

"Yes," I hiss as the cool leather of his dress belt slides along my ass cheeks and slips down the crack.

He pats the end without the buckle gently along my skin, and I hear his breath quicken and become slightly ragged. His tapping becomes a little firmer, and I bite my bottom lip, waiting for the sting. When it doesn't come, I release my breath and relax as he leans over to kiss the areas he touched with the smooth leather. Then his body rises, and his arm falls, the narrow belt smacking sharply against my flesh. I jump, but not from pain, more from surprise and a noise escapes me.

"Do you want me to stop?"

My heart thuds in my ears and I shudder. The initial surprise wears off quickly and, besides a slight sting, it doesn't really hurt. But the cool air feels soothing against my heated skin.

"Tell me to stop," he demands.

I roll my face back and forth on the bed, and groan, "No."

I jump as he strikes me again. This time the sharp sound filling the room matches the sting. I feel a welt rise on my ass cheek. He blows his breath along the heated, raised skin. And I groan.

Whap.

Whap.

Whap.

He avoids the same spot, always finding somewhere fresh. I cry out, but not for him to stop. No. Because this is something I've never realized I wanted, desired. Once I push aside the fear, I like his power over me, his power to cause pain, and then soothe it away with his kisses, his tongue, his pursed lips as he blows across my flesh.

"Your ass is red, Lila. Tell me to stop," he urges, and I can imagine him above me, his arm poised with the belt in hand, ready to strike again.

It surprises me to hear the tightness in his voice, the tension in his words. I'm now aware that using the belt as play makes him lose hold of his tight control. I find myself curious about what else will.

My skin now burns slightly, and I don't know whether to tell him to stop or keep going. If I have him continue, I might regret it tomorrow. And possibly the next day. But I want to explore this again, maybe not today, or even the next time Kane with a K has me in his control, but soon...

"Stop."

The bed shifts slightly with the lowering of his arm. I can't see his face to see if he's disappointed or relieved. After I hear the belt drop to the floor, I turn my head enough to check. He's still on his knees, and he's focused on my ass. Then he catches my gaze, and our eyes hold. No disappointment, no relief, no anything. His expression appears as if a blank slate.

But his eyes. Oh, those amazing eyes of his are dark, dilated, and hint at things I may not want to know.

Without breaking our gaze, he grabs the tube of lube laying near my hip and pops the cap. I sigh with relief because I will finally have him inside of me. Though I have no idea why he needs lube to fuck me since I'm wet enough that even a man of his size should have no problem entering me.

As the cool lube drips down the crease of my ass, I realize it wasn't intended for my original thought. Out of instinct, I yank at the ropes. Kane runs his finger lightly over my ass.

"Shh."

"Kane, I don't think—"

"It's not what you think. Don't worry."

Easy to say for him. It's not his ass propped in the air.

"I want to appreciate you everywhere."

"I get that, but—"

He keeps his voice low, soothing. "Lila, you can always tell me to stop."

There's that, but—

When his thumb presses against my anus, I stiffen. So many firsts today. I don't know how to feel about this new one. He brushes his thumb back and forth over my puckered hole, making it slick with the lube.

"Have you ever…" His voice catches.

Ah. More loss of control for Kane with a K. "No," I groan, shoving my face into the mattress. "No."

"Are you telling me to stop, Lila?"

"No." And, damn it, I'm not. With the light pressure he's applying, I'm discovering how sensitive, how stimulating, that area truly is. I suddenly want him to push harder, possibly even insert a finger completely inside of me. I'm willing to try something new.

He explores my virgin hole, gradually pushing and inserting his digit into me. Just the tip at first. More lube, more pressure. And he eases not his thumb, but a long finger inside. It feels strange though not unpleasant. He slides it to the first joint, stretching me. Then the second joint. He retreats.

"Are you okay?" he asks.

I'm not sure. Not good, not bad... Now, I'm just curious. And surprisingly willing to let this man do whatever he wants with me. That alone should scare me, but it doesn't. So far, Kane has done nothing to make me fear him but has only brought me pleasure. But it's clear this is only the beginning of what he wants to introduce me to.

And I'm ready to open my eyes to what he can offer.

"Yes. More, please."

His soft chuckle shakes the bed, and the low sound makes me smile into the bedding. "I like hearing you say please," he says as he slides not only one, but two fingers into me this time. Once again, he's careful and deliberate, easing himself deep within me.

"Then I will say it over and over again."

"I'd rather you not use it as a pleasantry, but while begging instead." When his fingers are fully seated, he works them in and out of my tight channel, and a sound I don't recognize escapes from the back of his throat. I groan at his unhurried motions; he's being too cautious with me.

"Faster," I demand.

"Beg me," he answers, much more demanding than me.

I inhale his scent which permeates the bedding deep into my lungs. "Faster... *please*."

"*Ah.* This, Lila? Is this what you want? Tell me."

As his pace changes, some of his caution does, too. He fucks me with his long, thick fingers over and over, and my pussy weeps for him. He hasn't touched it, and it needs his attention. It needs *him*.

It feels like I'm dripping, though I'm not sure if that's true. "I'm wet for you, Kane."

The deep rumble of his voice washes over me. "I see, Lila. I see how wet, how slick you are. How delicious you look. Is that all for me?"

"It's all for you. Only you."

"Do you want me to fuck you?"

"Yes, please, fuck me," I beg. My pussy clenches tight as he continues to work his fingers in and out of my anus, driving me completely mad.

This man will capture my sanity and trap it forever. He'll steal me one piece at a time until he owns me completely.

I will want no one but him. He will ruin me for anyone else.

But I don't care. I only care about here, now, and what he is doing… What he's capable of.

I cry out in both shock and relief when an orgasm rolls over and through me. Never in my wildest dreams could I believe I'd be able to climax with only that type of stimulation.

"Lila… Lila. You're so beautiful when you come. Like a blooming flower in the rain."

My muddled mind only registers some of what he's murmuring, and a distant thought of how he could write love poems flits through my head. But that's ridiculous, and I don't want someone who writes sonnets. I want a man who can make me scream nonsense. And can turn me inside out with want and need.

It doesn't need to be pretty. It just needs to be raw and real. And soon…

"Kane, please."

His breath hisses out at my plea.

"Please. Please. Please," I groan with each rock of my head back and forth.

He pulls away, and I'm suddenly empty, alone, as he moves off the bed and disappears. But he quickly returns, his weight heavy on the bed.

The tear of the wrapper sends a jolt down my spine and my back arches in anticipation. His heat sears me before he even touches me. His powerful thighs press against me, the light, wiry hair tickling along my skin. He grasps a fistful of my hair and pulls my head back, so I'm forced to look at the ceiling. A warm, wide palm slides along my back, over my shoulder blades, along my ribs, around the curves of my waist, and back again to my rear. As he positions himself against me, the round crown of his cock pushes against my slick, swollen folds. He slides his latex-encased head up and down from the top of my tight rosette all the way down to my sensitive nub.

I can't help but feel a little disappointment that I won't be able to watch him enter me for the first time. I want to study his face, his body, his response, and bathe in his pleasure at the same time.

Seconds seem like minutes, hours, eternities, as I wait, my breath hitching as it rushes through me, the fingers of my bound hands clenching into fists. All my breath escapes as he shifts forward, making me wetter, hotter, wilder, as he widens me, conquers me.

Finally, whispers through my head. My lips part and I tell myself to *breathe* as he fills me with excruciating slowness. He flows as slow as honey, a sweet torture. I must imagine the slight tremble in the fingers gripping my hip.

He adjusts the hold on my hair as he finally seats himself inside of me completely. I let out a mixture of a sigh and a relieved cry. He pulls my head back farther, stretching the front of my neck as he leans forward to whisper in my ear, "You're mine."

No, he's wrong. He doesn't know it yet, but he's mine. I buck my hips against him at the thought of him being mine for forever. It will be *forever him.*

With a slight turn of my head, I press my cheek against his luscious lips. His warm, damp breath wafts across my skin, his chest billows against my back, his hips press into me.

And he hasn't moved. He's stealing another piece of me. It's supposed to be the other way around. He's to belong to me. Not me to him.

So, I let him know my frustration by wailing loudly, thrashing against him. Anything, everything to make him move, to thrust, to pound me hard, deep. All my efforts have the opposite effect on him. But, instead, I make myself come again. My pussy throbs around him, the ripples squeeze him tight.

And he chuckles.

He's amused at the backfiring of my tantrum. "Patience, Lila. I will give you anything and everything you need. Trust me."

Trust me.

"Do I need to beg some more?" I ask. Before I even wait for him to answer, I scream at him to fuck me, to fuck me now, to fuck me hard, to fuck me until I don't know who I am anymore.

Please, please, please.

"Kane," I gasp as he tilts his hips just slightly. Then again. And once more as he blows out a breath and straightens up, releasing my hair. Now, both hands firmly grip my hips, pinning me down to the cushions.

"Are you ready, Lila?"

"Yes," I hiss, my eyes rolling back in my head. Now I want to kill him for making me wait so long, torturing, teasing me.

As his fingertips dig into the flesh around my hips, he braces himself and moves. I cry out as he gives me exactly what I've been waiting for. Heart-pounding, merciless, raw fucking. I grunt with each thrust as he pushes my body up the bed with the force.

"That's… it. Like that. Like that," I chant mindlessly. The room fills with the sound of my meaningless words, my grunts, my cries, our slapping flesh, his heavy, ragged breathing. Then he's repeating my name over and over in rhythm with his body.

I need to see you. I need to see you. I need…

I must have screamed that out loud, because he hesitates, his body heaves. He sucks his lungs full of oxygen.

"Please, I have to see you, Kane. *Please,* let me see you."

His fingers soften, release, and then he's gone. The cushions are abruptly yanked from under my hips, and he flips me over, leaving me flat on the bed, still tied at the top. But now I can see him. All of him. And he's glorious since his skin now has a sheen that emphasizes... every... single... muscle. The light plays off his body, making my mouth dry at the thought of how handsome this man is.

And I have no idea why he's with me.

But he is. And I fight myself from being self-conscious. I beat it back. I will not let it fuck with my head, to ruin this moment and the moments to come. I want to appreciate and enjoy what he offers, to bask in his desire. Now is not the time to question it, to question his motives, his thinking.

A corner of his mouth curls up. "Get out of your head, Lila. Stay here focused on me."

He's right. Right now, the most important thing in the world is here in front of me. The most significant person is looking down at me with a smile that steals my breath.

And possibly my heart.

Kane settles between my thighs, somehow his large frame fitting just right. No waiting this time, he makes us as one again. I release a sigh and gaze up into his eyes.

"Your body was made for me," he murmurs as he moves in a slow and steady rhythm. Gentle. Caring.

He pulls one of my nipples between his lips and sucks the peak roughly, his tongue flicking the tip. I squirm underneath him, my hips tilting upward, my back arching in an attempt to push my flesh farther into his mouth. He captures the other nipple between his finger and thumb and twists it back and forth. I squeeze my eyes shut as bolts of lightning run through me, down my limbs, landing in my core.

"No," he murmurs, a breath away from my damp breast. "You wanted to see me, so watch me."

My head rocks side to side as I stutter, "I... I..."

His voice gets firm. "Lila, do it."

And I do it. I open my eyes, and he's inches from me, staring into my soul, his eyes dark.

"That's it," he says before sinking his teeth softly into my collar bone.

His slow, smooth strokes quicken and he slides his hands under my hips, lifting me slightly. The angle is perfect for us to mesh, for him to bring me to the edge of the crashing waves.

As his pace increases, I don't care if he sees my contorted face, my reactions. I want him to see it all. My pleasure, my pain. I want him to see everything he's doing to me. I don't want to hide. I need him to know how he affects me.

Everything revealed in my face is because of him.

And he pounds me until I tumble into the waves. I gasp for breath as I get washed away.

CHAPTER FIVE

His strict instructions were not to leave the bedroom until he returned.

After he left, I wrapped his dress shirt around me and fastened a couple of buttons while inhaling his now familiar spicy scent woven throughout the fabric.

When the bedroom door knob turns, my breath catches. My pleasure and relief at his return scare me. How could I fall so fast for a man I've only watched from a distance and fantasized about?

I now know his body intimately, but nothing else. I've always had a good head on my shoulders, so why does this man make me lose it?

As he enters the room, I'm once again drawn to the magnetism that permeates from him, seeps from his pores. But I'm disappointed that he's dressed. Though, that can be easily rectified.

My mouth waters, most likely from seeing the two bags of food he carries, but it could be from the sight of him, as well. My stomach joins along and growls loudly as soon as the smell of the takeout makes its way across the room and hits my senses.

It smells as delicious as he looks.

"We're eating in bed?" I ask with surprise. His eyes rake over me, taking in the oversized shirt I'm lounging in. Hopefully he doesn't mind me borrowing his dress shirt.

"You're not going to eat."

I furrow my brows in confusion. So, I will sit here and watch him eat?

"I will feed you," he continues, a hint of amusement on his face.

Ah. That sounds even better than the food smells. Though, I now think I should keep a scorecard with all the "firsts" Kane is introducing me to in just these last few hours.

I pat the bed and then prop the pillows up against the headboard next to me. "Please, join me at my table, good sir!"

The deep rumble of his voice washes over me. "Do you prefer clothed or naked?"

"Oh, naked, of course. We wouldn't want to stain your clothes in case our food drops in say… your lap?" I wiggle my eyebrows at him, fighting my smile.

His own smile broadens, and he places the two brown paper bags on a nearby stool and slips out of the casual workout clothes he donned to run for the order. While he looks delectable dressed, he looks even better naked.

His blue eyes twinkle as he lifts his arms and circles slowly as if offering himself up like a piece of chocolate cake spinning in the dessert case.

Holy shit. This man…

He could easily become an addiction. I fear every minute longer I stay will make it harder for me to leave at the end of the day.

He rips the bags open and removes two covered plates. Actual real plates. These are no cheap, plastic takeout containers. "This place is the best in the area. I know the chef personally."

My eyebrows raise, though, it shouldn't surprise me. "So, you have some pull?"

"You can say that," he says, then laughs as he approaches the bed.

I tilt my head and look at him curiously. "Are *you* the chef?"

He laughs again, his teeth bright white against his dark lips. "No,

I'm definitely not a great cook. Remember? I told you I was passable."

"Tell me, Mr.—" It floors me I still do not know his last name. But then, he doesn't know mine either.

After placing the plates on the nearby nightstand, he pretends to wipe his hands off on his invisible pants, and, with a flourish, extends his hand. When I clasp his warm fingers, he bows, though his eyes never leave mine, and says, "McGovern."

"Oh, Irish! That's exactly what I expected your heritage to be," I exclaim with a twist of humor. He rises but doesn't release my hand, and I'm in no rush to pull it away. "Nice to meet you, Mr. McGovern. What part of the wee island of Ireland are you from?" I ask with a laugh.

He chuckles and ignores my question by asking one of his own, "And you?"

"Not from Ireland."

He shakes his head at me like I'm a naughty child. "You know what I'm asking."

"Flowers."

"Lila Flowers?" He cocks a brow.

I don't blame him. It's usually the reaction I get. And then it's typically followed by, "Why isn't your first name Lily or Lilac?"

But he's not typical, and he lifts my hand to brush his lips over my knuckles. "Beautiful name for an equally beautiful woman. A pleasure to meet you, Ms. Flowers."

"The pleasure is all mine," I retort. Definitely all mine. "Now that we have the formalities out of the way, can we get busy with our naked meal?"

He bows his head. "Of course." When he releases my hand, I start to remove his shirt, but he stops me. "Leave it. I like seeing you wear my clothes."

"But it may get stained."

"I have more," he reassures me as he gathers the plates and

carefully settles next to me, placing the plates on the firm mattress between us.

As he uncovers the dishes, I have a difficult time pulling my gaze away from the scrumptious sight in his lap and directing it toward the delicious food instead. But when I do, I'm shocked. It's all finger foods, but not of the tailgating variety. Oh, no. Colossal shrimp, some melty Brie cheese with crackers, strawberries, tiny pieces of toast topped with what looks like smoked salmon and red caviar. As well as crab cake sliders, and mouth-watering petit fours.

"Now *this* is a picnic," I murmur, looking at the variety.

He lifts a caviar hors d'oeuvre to my lips. "Have you had caviar before?"

I stare at the fish eggs on the tiny piece of toast. "No."

"Are you willing to try it?"

For you, I'll try anything, I want to say. Instead, I simply open my mouth, and he places the appetizer between my lips. I crush the crispy toast between my teeth, biting it in half. The smooth smokiness of the salmon, along with the salty creaminess of the caviar, combined with the crunchiness of the toast assaults my mouth. But in a good way. I close my eyes and chew, and when I finally swallow that heavenly bite, I open them to stare at him. He appears pleased. Probably because I didn't scrunch my nose and spit the mouthful out onto the hand he cups under my chin to catch crumbs.

"Wow," I finally say. He offers me the rest of the bite, and I take it greedily. As I'm chewing, and most likely rolling my eyes in ecstasy, he helps himself to one, popping the whole thing into his mouth. He then lifts a shrimp the size of a dinghy, and I gladly accept it. I have never tasted shrimp that sweet, succulent, and I groan. "I could get used to this."

This isn't your average shrimp cocktail with scrawny prawns surrounding a blob of jarred cocktail sauce. No. The sustenance he offers is luxurious, and with him feeding me bit by bit, wiping my lips with a napkin between bites, I feel like a queen. A spoiled rotten one at that.

Another first.

He takes turns between feeding himself and me. Until, finally, the first plate is empty and only two small squares of dessert and a half dozen plump strawberries remain on the second plate.

Though it didn't seem like much at first, I surprisingly find myself full, but still eyeball one of the petit fours.

As he brings one to my mouth, I open like a baby bird waiting to be fed by its momma. Instead of placing it in my mouth like the gentleman he is, he smears the cream center across my lips. I jerk back not expecting it, and he closes in, wiping me clean with his tongue.

Now, *that* is dessert. "Good?" I ask him, smiling even though there's still a little sweet residue left behind.

"Mmm. Sweet. Luscious. So edible," he whispers and does it again. This time I'm ready for it and my tongue darts out to taste the delicate creamy filling before he steals it all. He kisses the rest of it away and finally offers the dessert to me. I snag it with my teeth, purposely nipping at his fingers.

"Naughty," he fake scolds me. "If you bite my fingers off, how will I ever touch you?"

"You have other parts you can touch me with," I remind him, tilting my head towards his lap. Me nipping him seemed to stir something in him, the proof now growing before my eyes. "But you liked that."

"I did," he reassures me before enjoying the last dessert square. He raises a strawberry. "Berries are a great way to end our brunch. Come. Take a bite," he says and places one strawberry into his mouth, holding it between his lips.

I think I like this idea of his when I lean over and nip the tip off the berry. It's sweet and juicy, and a red drip rolls down his chin. He starts to wipe it away, but I stop him. "Uh-uh." And I lick from the bottom of his jaw up to the corner of his mouth. His erection is unmistakable now, jutting between us.

He plucks another berry off the plate. "Another?"

I nod, and instead of offering it to me, he bites the end off, then leans over to press his lips to mine. At the end of the kiss, he transfers the piece of fruit onto my tongue, and it's the best way I've ever eaten fruit. Hands down. Whether it's due to the quality of the strawberries or from him feeding them to me, it doesn't matter. Either way, strawberries are now my favorite fruit.

He removes the plates from between us and places them on the nightstand before turning back, holding another strawberry between his long, dark fingers. "On your back." Not a request, but an order.

I push away from the headboard and slide down until I'm flat on my back, his shirt bunched around my hips. With hardly an effort, he's straddling me, and I can't wait to find out how he will feed me this particular strawberry.

Starting at the top of my head, he traces the berry's pointed end over my forehead, over the line of my nose, across my lips, and down my chin. He skips it along my neck, across my collar bones, and in between my breasts until he's stopped by the first fastened button. Shoving the shirt to one side, he uncovers my right breast, and he draws circles around it, starting wide at the base, lifting and narrowing the rotation until he reaches the tip. I can't believe how erotic it feels to have him brush the berry back and forth across the hard nub of my nipple. My pussy pulses, ready for him once again.

He shoves the shirt to the other side and exposes my neglected left breast and creates the same wondrous sensations on that side, too. I've never loved strawberries so much as in that moment.

With one hand, he expertly slips the shirt buttons loose, revealing my stomach little by little. Within his fingers, he draws the strawberry down, dipping into my belly button, and then circling. He spreads the shirt wide open, and now, with the tip of his tongue, traces all the paths where the strawberry had wandered. His warm, wet, skilled tongue pulls a groan from deep down inside me. I cup his cheeks as he closes in on my mouth, crushing me to him. His kiss is so thorough it steals the breath from me.

Another piece of me gone. Another piece he now owns. When it is supposed to be the other way; he is meant to be mine.

As he pulls back slightly, we breathe each other in. He's my oxygen, and I'm his. His blue eyes hold mine, and my breath catches as a smile slowly spreads across his strikingly beautiful, but masculine, face.

I marvel at how I could be so lucky. I can't be. So, before I can stop myself, I ask, "Be truthful, did you really come into the coffee shop every day to see me?" Because I still struggle to believe this. Why would *this* man need to do this? And why me?

Kane frowns, his grip tightening around me. "I never lie, Lila."

He's clearly not happy, and I bite my bottom lip. Did I just make a fatal mistake by accusing him of being untruthful when he's been nothing but good to me?

I wish I could rewind to a few seconds ago when he directed his wide smile at me instead of his disappointment.

"I'm sorry," I whisper. "I just—"

"Do you honestly believe I don't find you fascinating? Even mesmerizing? You draw me like a moth to a flame, Lila. There's no reason to question it, just accept it as it is."

Silly me wants to say, I never accept things as they are. That's not my nature. I always need to know why, what makes people tick, what attracts couples to each other. It's the writer in me, the hopeless romantic, the curious soul.

I control characters' thoughts and feelings. I know my own. What I don't understand is Kane's. And I can't help but prod. But I remind myself, I have the rest of forever to discover his. I don't need to know him inside and out at this very moment. I can learn things along the journey.

But right now, I need to fix this.

"Kane," I start and take a deep breath before continuing. "I've never been popular, or 'one of the girls,' or even outgoing. I've always kept to myself and I use my imagination to create myself an exciting life. I've never been comfortable approaching men and I don't date often, but when I do… Let's just say, my options have been a bit lacking. Truthfully, I'm afraid I will turn into one of those crazy, old cat ladies." I find it weird I'm telling him all this since I never admit this to anyone. Not even family.

"How many cats do you have now?"

"None."

He tilts his head back and barks out a laugh. When he finally sobers, he looks down into my eyes. "Lila, you don't give yourself enough credit. When I walked into that coffee shop for the first time and saw you, I instantly knew there was something special about you. I don't know how or why, but I knew. And believe it or not, it wasn't until I had been there three mornings in a row you actually noticed me. And once you did…" He drifts off and smiles. "I was a goner."

A little bit of disbelief still niggles at me, but I push it away. I will not keep questioning myself—or him—on why he wants me. I'm just going to—like he said—accept it as it is. And enjoy myself. And him. Definitely him.

I trace my fingers over his brow and down his cheek. He snags them and presses the tips to his lips, kissing them, then sucks my middle finger into his mouth. As his tongue swirls around my digit, my eyelids lower while I watch his face and a shiver runs down my spine. You would think my finger was a luscious dessert or one of the ripe strawberries to savor.

I breathe out his name. "Kane…"

"You're delicious and I want to taste you again," he murmurs against the tip of my finger.

I know what he means, but—

He slides off the bed and disappears into the master bathroom. Within seconds I hear water running. He's drawing a bath. A dark and delicious scent wafts from the room and my nostrils flare as I try to recognize the scent.

Of course, it's him. Whatever he's adding to the water will make me smell like him, will mark me with his scent.

Moments later he strides to the bed, and I squeal when he scoops me into his arms. I loop my arms around his neck as he carries me into the bathroom. Once he sets me on my feet, he tests the temperature of the quick-filling tub. It's shaped like a curved triangle and large enough for both of us. It's not the typical tub/shower combination. A frosted glass shower stall is tucked into another corner of the oversized en suite bathroom.

He pushes his open dress shirt off my shoulders and it falls forgotten to the floor as he assists me into the jacuzzi tub. The temperature feels just hot enough not to burn my skin, but as I sink into the scented water, my muscles are soothed. I settle back with a sigh, and the water comes just high enough for my breasts to float. He motions for me to move up and when I do, he slips in behind me. As he lowers his weight, the water becomes dangerously high and threatens to sweep over the edge of the tub. In the water, I notice the contrast of his long, lean, dark legs hugging the outside of my lighter complexed ones. I slide my hands along the length of his muscular thighs, appreciating the contours and the strength contained within his flawless skin.

When he reaches around me, I notice he's reaching for a hair clip sitting on the edge of the tub and I can't help but wonder why he has it, whose it is. A former wife's? An old girlfriend's? Or does he keep them on hand for his coffeehouse conquests? I quickly forget all that as he sweeps my hair up to the top of my head and, with expertise, secures my hair to keep it from getting wet.

Before I can settle back against his chest to savor the soak, he brushes kisses down the side of my throat and around the bottom curve of my neck. I shiver fiercely. My nipples pebble painfully and the dusky pink peaks float just at the surface.

"Is the water too cold?"

"No," I assure him. It's he who gives me the goosebumps, not the temperature of the water. But the sight of my own breasts floating makes me slide slippery hands around them, cupping them, lifting, thumbing my own nipples. I lean back with my eyes closed as I play with myself. I know he's watching because he's still, quiet, only the sound of his breathing fills my ears. His cock is firm between us, growing quickly to its full girth and length. I wiggle back until I'm tight against him, his erection trapped between us.

"You touching yourself is a spectacular sight, Lila."

I play the game of innocent as I tilt my head, give him a light laugh, and say, "Is it?"

I pinch both nipples between my fingers and give them a little twist, crying out softly at my own actions. It feels like there is a direct line from the tips of my breasts to my pussy and I squirm a little against the smooth bottom of the tub. I squeeze my thighs together tightly because I want to come and I know it won't take much to get me there.

"Where else do you touch yourself, Lila?"

"Everywhere," I whisper, swallowing hard and leaning my head back against his collarbone. I lick my lips and inhale deeply as I feel my core burn hot for him.

"Show me," he says against the damp skin of my shoulder.

I continue to cup one breast while I dip my other hand under the water. I push my legs wider to make room and slide my hand into the apex of my thighs.

"Show me," he says again, his voice low and raw.

My lips part and a rush of air escapes me as I separate my plump folds and find my center.

"That's it, Lila. Come for me," he urges softly, his voice in my ear an aphrodisiac I never knew could exist.

I press and circle my clit until my hips jump and I finally slide two fingers inside myself with a gasp. With a last pinch to my nipple, I drop my other hand to assist. I play with my clit and I fuck myself, my hips dancing between his thighs. His chest now rises and falls at a quicker pace against my back and with a groan, he grips both of my nipples and twists them roughly. I cry out, arching my back. He pulls, pinches, and tweaks them with no mercy as I increase the pace of my hand, my fingers below the water. Waves rock back and forth, splashing over the edge of the tub and onto the tile floor. My breathing becomes short, ragged, and I move at a frantic pace. I'm right there, so close. I squeeze my eyes shut, concentrating on what his fingers—and mine—are doing.

He's whispering my name over and over. "Come for me, Lila. Come for me."

An explosive curse escapes me as my hips shoot up and almost out of the water. My core clenches with a ferocity I'm not expecting, causing my toes to curl, and my eyes to roll. I slam myself back into Kane and he takes the brunt of my action with a grunt.

I don't even pause to enjoy the afterglow of the orgasm. Before the sloshing of the water even slows, I'm twisting in the tub to face him and I impale myself on his erection before he can stop me.

"Lila," he cries out, stiffening, grabbing my hips with a grip that will leave marks. He holds me still and closes his eyes for a moment, fighting an internal battle. "No," he moans as he opens his eyes and looks at me darkly. "No."

"Yes," I tell him, not breaking his gaze. I pry his tight fingers out of my flesh and begin to move. I rock against him, my clit brushing against his pelvis as I work him in and out of me.

His head falls back and his eyes shut as he tenses beneath me, fighting the urge to just let go.

"Kane, Kane, you feel so good inside me. You fill me. You... complete me."

His eyes pop open and he levels his gaze at me. Something has switched inside him. He watches me with an intensity that coaxes another shiver through me. The tight buds of my breasts brushing against his warm, wet skin, sliding up and down as I move.

"What are you doing to me?"

Making you mine.

Before I can answer, he sinks his teeth into my neck and cries out against my damp skin. His hands find my waist and he holds me down as his hips rise. We grind together, unable to get any closer, though we try. And when I feel the strong pulses at the base of his cock, I come with him over the edge, until we both drown in each other.

And when it's over, I lay my head against his chest and he circles his arms around me, holding me close as our breathing calms, our thoughts return, and we realize the bath water is cooling and forcing us out and off of each other.

CHAPTER SIX

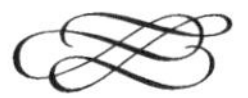

I am being punished because I've been bad. I took advantage of Kane's momentary weakness and we fucked without a condom. And now I must pay.

Once again, I find my arms stretched over my head, but this time I'm not on the bed. Oh, no. The soft ropes now hold my wrists overhead. My toes barely reach the carpet, but they do. And my world is currently dark.

Very, very dark.

Of course Kane owns a real blindfold and doesn't have to use a makeshift one. It covers my eyes completely, and it isn't going anywhere. The air shifts as he circles me, probably contemplating on what my penance will be.

I don't fear whatever he'll mete out. I certainly don't worry. Instead, I look forward to whatever plan he contrives.

More firsts, no doubt.

And more fodder for my books. Not to mention, my fertile imagination.

Something light sweeps across my ribs and over my belly. A feather, possibly, as it tickles along my skin. A brush here, a brush there. Over the hard points of my nipples, along the outer curves of my breasts. A brief touch to my lips, a stroke down my cheek. The only way I can describe it is *titillating* as he outlines the silhouette of my curves. From the top of my head all the way to my toes. If he missed an inch, I'd be surprised. I picture him in my mind's eye with an oversized peacock feather in brilliant purples, greens, and blues. A blue similar to his fascinating eyes. The lack of sight makes me long to see their exotic color.

When Kane tied me up, his instructions were that I was not to speak unless spoken to or asked a question. Otherwise, I'd be gagged.

The blindfold I didn't mind. The gag I wasn't sure about, so I agreed.

Now, as he sweeps the feather along the curves of my back, down the indentation of my spine, he tickles the crease of my ass and I do my damnedest not to giggle. I'm not usually ticklish, but being unable to see, and not knowing what he'll do next, makes me more sensitive than normal.

I gasp and he whips me with the feather at my outburst, which makes me want to giggle even more, so I bite my lower lip to prevent it. A feather whipping is the biggest oxymoron I can think of. It's no worse than a fly landing on me, though it actually feels so much better.

"Lila, the feather is only the beginning, remember that," his deep voice warns.

Sure, sure. What's next? A silk scarf?

However, I suddenly become serious when I imagine that a piece of silk sliding against my bare skin would feel very, very erotic. And now the joke is on me because I want that. It makes me ready for him to move on from the light teasing of the feather.

His warm lips press against the top of my spine and then he's gone.

My ears strain to hear his movements, to figure out what he's doing, to discover what's next. But his footsteps retreat out of the room.

Damn. He's left me alone suspended in the center of his bedroom. I tiptoe myself around and turn my body to face the door. I'm tempted to call out to him, but remind myself that he *very* firmly told me to stay quiet.

So I do.

I can honestly say I've never taken orders from a man before, not even my father, but Kane is no typical man. And, because of that, I fear I'd do anything he'd command. My intent was to make him mine forever. I am starting to believe he's quickly turning the tables.

My ears perk as his long strides eat up the real estate between him and I. A clinking in a glass catches my attention. Maybe he's thirsty since it's been a busy day.

I no longer know the actual time, but my body clock tells me it is at least late afternoon. The cup of coffee he offered me earlier now seems a lifetime ago.

I sense him standing in front of me. I hear him breathing. I imagine him smiling with anticipation of what he'll do next.

And what he does makes me scream in shock.

Cold. Burning cold makes me shudder. Kane swirls what can only be an ice cube in patterns over my skin, leaving a trail of moisture in its wake. I shiver again as my nipples become so erect it makes my breasts ache. And he hasn't even touched them yet.

He runs the ice over my belly and down to the apex of my thighs. He teases my clit with the slippery cube and he slides it between my hot folds. It melts to a sliver in his fingertips and I'm almost relieved it's gone.

Another clink and I groan, waiting for him to start again. He steps behind me and slides the ice cube down my back, over my buttocks, down my thighs, and then back up. He presses it against my clenched anus and holds it there until it melts completely.

Another clink and I jump as he cups my breasts, expecting the biting cold against my skin. But it's not there and I wonder what he's up to.

And when his mouth takes my nipple, I wonder no more. The

combination of the cold cube and my flesh on his tongue sends a shock-wave through me. I shudder violently and moan. The sensation feels extraordinary but I both hate and love it at the same time.

He sucks one nipple then the other, replacing the ice cube in his mouth when needed, until the tips of my nipples become practically numb. But as the last cube fades away, his mouth becomes hot, greedy, and he pinches, licks, and sucks me until I'm flushed, squirming, and biting my lip to keep from crying out.

When his teeth scrape each hard tip, I can't hold back any longer. I release a sound of frustration, but no words. I haven't broken the rule. Not yet, anyway.

But maybe I should…

I'm curious on what the punishment would be for breaking a rule during… punishment.

Maybe Kane with a K owns a cane with a C. I tremble at the thought. And as I imagine him lightly caning my back, the globes of my ass, my breasts, my core clenches fiercely in an orgasm. How can that be?

"Fuck, I just came," I cry out and then gasp at my outburst. *Shit.*

As he pulls away from me, my mind races with all the things he may do. Nipple clamps, whipping, paddling, gagging… I run out of options because compared to Kane, I'm so vanilla. I don't even know everything involved in kinky play.

Or he could dole out the worst punishment I can think of… refusing to touch me at all.

The last I could not bear. I will die without his touch. I will wither up into nothing and blow away like dust in the wind.

I want to apologize for breaking his rule, but I don't want to speak out of turn and make it worse. I wait for him to say something, anything, so I can respond. But he doesn't. I wish I could see his face, to judge his thoughts and mood, but I only see darkness.

If I tell him to stop, he will release me and remove the blindfold and I'd be able to drop to my knees to beg his forgiveness. But if I do that, he may very well steal the last part of me I'm keeping to myself, what I'm still holding onto tightly…

My free will.

Whenever he releases me from the ropes, I will want the power to walk away. Though I may not do it, I still want the choice.

However, he's supposed to belong to me. Not the other way around. I admit to myself that my powers of seduction must be severely lacking. The truth is, I'm the one held enthralled, not him.

He's good. He knows what he's doing. Me, apparently not so much.

I hear him move through the room, opening and shutting a door, and I hang there hardly breathing, my ears straining in an attempt to figure out his intent. My mind races at the possibilities.

But I could have never thought of what he does to me. Something cups my pussy. Not his hand. Something plastic with a rubber edge and shaped similar to an oxygen mask. He seats whatever it is tightly to my flesh, and then I hear a pumping sound —manual, not electric—and the air extracts from the cup around my mound. My skin tightens and my lips swell as if they're being pulled through a tight tube, though that's not exactly right. The more he pumps the plumper my pussy becomes, the wetter I become, the more sensitive my clit becomes.

If this is punishment, I'll take it any day.

I could consider my chastisement as him not having his fingers or mouth on me and just an impersonal piece of plastic. But the blood rushes to the surface of my skin as he pumps two more times and my flesh fills the cup. I feel and hear him unhook something—what I can only imagine is the tube and hand pump—and he disappears.

Literally disappears.

Out of the room. Gone. Not a word, not a whisper. Nothing. If I thought my mind was spinning before, it's now out of control like a Tilt-A-Wheel. My shoulders now ache from being stretched overhead and my pussy throbs fiercely with each heartbeat. And I hear nothing but silence.

He could invite in the mailman and there would be nothing I could do about it. He could take photos of me in this vulnerable position and post them all over the Internet. Or email them to my parents. He could be on the phone right this moment inviting a friend over to fuck me while he watches. Or, hell, a dozen friends.

Or he could be gathering sheets of plastic and his serial killer tool bag. And this might be the last I'm ever heard from again. Disappointment rushes through me at the thought I might never finish the book series I was working on this morning in the coffee shop.

Then I snort at my ridiculous notions. But it's true that my arms are getting tired and my pussy continues to get plumper within the confines of the contraption.

Seconds seem like minutes, minutes like hours. Even though there isn't an analog clock in the room, I hear an imagined ticking in my head as time slowly moves forward. When I'm about to give in and call out to him, he returns.

"Thirsty?" he asks.

He asked so I'm allowed to answer. "Yes." My voice sounds rough and raw. And before I can say more, I feel the press of a glass to my lips. Ice water flows down my throat and moistens my dry mouth.

"This will be my last reminder, Lila, that you can say stop at any time."

Once he lowers the glass, I shake my head. I say, "No," and envision a look of satisfaction and pride crossing his face.

"I want you to enjoy and appreciate everything I do to you."

"I am. I do," I reassure him. "But I'm ready to be released."

"Are you asking or telling?"

I think only for a second. "Asking."

"Then I need you to stay up there just a little longer. I'm certain you'll find it worth your while."

"Can I ask you a question?" And I realize I just did.

He hesitates before responding. "Yes."

"Would you ever let me do these things to you?"

Again, a pause, but longer this time. I start to think he won't answer when he does. "That would have to be negotiated. And, no matter what, I would need to school you on techniques first," came his low answer. Even though I can't see him, the sudden deeper pitch in his voice most likely matches the darkening of his eyes. I wonder what excites him more. The possibility of allowing me to do these sorts of things to him? Or the idea of him "schooling" me?

He runs a finger around the seal of the plastic contraption to break the suction and, if it were possible, my skin practically sighs with relief.

But even so, my folds remain swollen with every nerve ending alive and jumping.

"So luscious, Lila. You should see yourself. Beautifully plump and pink, shiny with your arousal."

He holds my hips as he sinks to his knees before me and slides his hands around to my buttocks and down the backs of my thighs. And, not expecting it, I squeal when he yanks me off of my feet. For a moment, almost all of my weight hangs from my extended arms. But before I can protest, he hooks my legs over his shoulders and takes the majority of my weight.

I cry out as his mouth finds me, and there's no mistaking the benefit of that pussy pump. I twitch at each stroke of his tongue on my clit, each lick along my labia. He sucks at my sensitive nub and I quickly climax with a gasp. But he doesn't let up, he continues sucking and licking, nipping and scraping, and his fingers slide around back to my ass. He separates my cheeks and plays along my crease, teasing my hole. And I can't take anymore.

I can't take anymore.

No more.

I yank at the ropes, wishing I could cup my own breasts, pinch my own nipples. And a strange mixture of frustration and satisfaction floods through me. Frustration at what he's not doing, satisfaction at what he is.

However, I know he can't be everywhere at once. This is where my own two hands could come in use, or even a friend of his. With that, my brain comes to a screeching halt at the latter. Ms. Vanilla is thinking very non-vanilla thoughts.

My smile turns into a grimace as his fingers play along my cleft and find their way inside me. Not just the two fingers in the front, but his pinky slides into my rear. And he works me into a frenzy, his mouth tight on my nub as he works his digits in and out of me without caution, without any sense of gentleness.

And I only want more.

More.

Instead, I scream, "Stop!"

Instantly, my legs slide to the floor, my toes find the carpet, and he's up and away from me.

The blindfold is swept off my face and I squint from the sudden brightness in the room. Kane stands before me naked, his long, thick erection jutting from his body.

"I'm sorry, Lila," he says, a look of concern on his face.

No. No. This is not why I want him to stop. "Release me," I demand.

He quickly picks at the knots of the soft ropes keeping me bound and I almost collapse when I'm finally free. He catches me and studies my face. "Are you okay?"

"Yes," I mutter. "Yes, I need you to fuck me, Kane. I want you inside me now." The thick sound of desperation coats my voice.

Relief slides across his face and quickly disappears, leaving a knowing smile in its wake. He sweeps me into his arms and deposits me on the bed, climbing up and over me. He straddles my body on hands and knees, staring down into my face. My eyes flick to the heavy erection hanging between his thick thighs. I'm not the only one ready.

"Lila, we didn't use a condom earlier. Do you want me to use one this time?"

A fleeting thought of how he will be the last man I'm ever with and that we'll be together forever so it's unnecessary, goes through me. It's risky, but we've—correction, *I've*—already fucked up and since I'm on birth control I'm not worried about that aspect of it. But still…

"No," I whisper, meeting his eyes. "I want nothing between us."

Something flashes behind his eyes before he closes them for a brief moment. And when he reopens them whatever it was has gone. "Tell me what you want."

"You," I simply answer.

"Tell me where you want me."

"Deep inside me."

"Tell me how you want me."

"On the bottom," I decide. And yes, I realize at that moment I need to be on top. He's had all the control up to this point. And I'd like to take a little of it back.

CHAPTER SEVEN

With a twist, he has me straddling his waist, his hands holding my hips. I study him as he lays underneath me in what I consider a more submissive position. Whether it is or not, remains to be seen. But for now, I choose to believe it is. With my hands free, I can trace his facial features and explore his body under my fingertips.

He lays still, only his eyes following my movements. His small, dark nipples are pointed and I flick them with my tongue. I get no other reaction than him tensing slightly. His fingers fist in my loose hair for a mere moment and then he rubs my long strands over his chest. As I work my way down his body, kissing, licking, tasting his skin, he once again grips my hair and when I reach my limit, my hair becomes like a leash and I can't go any further. And I want to. I'm only to mid-belly but want to go lower. With a yank, he forces me to look up at him. His eyes appear dark, dangerous. And as he tugs at my hair, I follow, moving my way back up his body until I gaze down into his face.

I touch my lips to his, slipping my tongue inside to explore his mouth. A moment later, he turns his head, breaking the kiss.

"Careful, or you may find yourself on your back again," he warns me thickly. My power to make him react leaves me a little heady.

"Not this time," I tell him, sounding a bit cocky.

He faces me again, his nostrils flaring, his eyes hooded. "Watch yourself."

"Or what?"

"Try me."

I make a noise at his "threat," not worried in the least. What can he do? Fuck me into oblivion? He's already spanked me with a belt. The memory from earlier makes my pussy clench tightly.

"I will gladly try you," I murmur, and sink my teeth into his shoulder. His body bows off the bed and his fingers dig into the flesh at my hip. His cock, nestled between my ass cheeks, twitches. When I release him, I swirl my tongue over the indentations I leave behind. "You like that," I whisper.

I see him grimace and his jaw tighten before I drop my head again, this time nipping him over his heart.

"Lila," he breathes. He tilts his hips and thrusts upward.

My laugh sounds low and sultry as I enjoy my power over him. I nip gently over his pecs and threaten to bite his nipples by scraping my teeth over the tips. But I don't bite that sensitive area, I move lower and this time he allows it. I move to straddle his thighs and take his hard length into my hand. I shoot him a quick glance before dropping my head to surround the plump crown with my teeth. I squeeze just enough so there's no mistaking what I can do, but I refrain from biting. My tongue darts out and captures the salty pearl of precum at the tip. I move down to his delicate sac, sucking him into my mouth, this time being very careful with my teeth. His fingers entwine in my hair as if he's ready to pull me away if I decide to do anything but be gentle with that precious package.

With a smile, I let him slide from my lips and I turn my head to nip his inner thighs. One side then the other. As I move my way back up, I catch his cock between my breasts and squeeze them together, working his length up and down between them.

"Enough," he chokes out, grabbing me under my arms and lifting me up.

I want to tell him I'll decide when he's had enough, but I don't dare. I really want to be on top and I think if I say that, I may find myself quickly on the bottom. Instead, I move up and over him, holding his cock in place as I slowly lower myself. As he stretches me, fills me, I watch him and he watches me.

His chest rises and falls a little quicker now and he brushes his thumbs over my taut nipples as I move in an ancient rhythm. I brace my hands on the smooth skin of his chest and I circle my hips as he kneads and squeezes my breasts. As I feel the pull deep inside me, my head drops back and my mouth parts. His cock fits me perfectly and strokes just the right spot. I grind my clit into his pelvis with each downward thrust.

Heat blooms into my chest and cheeks as an orgasm builds. I return my gaze to his. His breath hisses through gritted teeth, and when I'm just about to come, I pinch both of his nipples, giving him no mercy.

He bellows my name and I take flight as he drops me to the bed and mounts me with about as much mercy as I gave him. I wrap my legs around his thighs and draw him in as deeply as possible. He pounds me, our skin slapping, my still swollen and overly sensitive pussy taking every inch of him over and over.

"Come for me, Lila," he urges then grimaces, his body tightening, the veins in his muscles becoming more distinct, the cords in his neck popping. "Come for me."

"Tell me when you're going to come," I say raggedly. "Tell me when you're ready."

He drops his forehead to mine and squeezes his eyes shut. "I'm ready," he groans. "I'm going to come deep inside you."

His words are the push I need and I say, "Come with me."

He lifts my hips and slams into me one more time, crying out, "I'm coming."

My hips shoot up and out of his hands as I smash myself against him, the powerful pulses radiating out from my center. I can't even tell him I'm coming, too. But he can't miss the intense reaction my body has. My pussy beats as strongly as my heart, and I struggle to inhale oxygen. As I lower my hips back to the bed, he moves with me, not willing to break the connection. Not yet, anyway.

I can still feel an occasional twitch at the root of his cock.

"Did the pump enhance your pleasure?" he asks, holding his weight off me.

"Yes, that was intense," I answer with a smile. "And for you?"

"Absolutely," he murmurs and drops a kiss on my forehead. With a groan, he falls to my side and gathers me against him.

"So much for that being punishment."

He has my head tucked against his chest and his voice rumbles against my ear. "You will learn that my forms of punishment are more of a sweet torture. I don't want you to feel anything but pleasure."

"I hope you don't mind, but I don't think I can take any more of your *sweet torture* today." I'm feeling an ache below that's not from desire. Though I'm definitely left satisfied, I'd like to walk the next day.

His body shakes against mine as he chuckles. "I will let you recover since I need to as well. I'm not twenty anymore."

"Me, neither," I sigh. Twenty feels like a lifetime ago and as I look down his body, I realize no matter what his age, he's in better shape than most twenty-year-olds. And he's certainly more experienced.

"Dinner should be here shortly."

I glance at him in surprise.

He continues, "I ordered it when I got us brunch."

"You knew I'd still be here at dinner time?"

One side of his mouth lifts. "I just found you, Lila. Do you really think I'd let you go so quickly?"

"Well, I have to go home at some point."

He's quiet for a moment. "True, and I need to get back to my business. But it was nice spending a day playing hooky, don't you think?"

"Oh, yeah. You can play hooky with me anytime," I assure him.

"If you'll agree to spend the night, I can drop you off at home in the morning on my way to work."

This is no *wham-bam-thank-you-ma'am* hookup. Instead, this is a whole *keep-me-long-enough-to-want-you-more* scenario. To get me addicted, like I feared.

And he succeeded.

But I won't turn down an all-night cuddle.

"And I will pick you up for dinner tomorrow night. I will take you to meet the chef."

"Like an actual date?"

"Why do you sound surprised?"

I shouldn't be. We had a wonderful start to me loving him forever. And, of course, forever would include tomorrow night. And the next... "We can get to know each other better over a sit-down, clothes-on dinner," I joke.

He cocks an eyebrow. "*Ah.* You don't want me to feed you dinner in bed?"

"Oh, no, I do. Believe me. But aren't we doing this a little backward? Shouldn't it be dinner and conversation, and then you take me to bed?"

"You'd rather have things done traditionally." Not a question, but more of an amused discovery. "You're disappointed in how I handled things today?" Now I can detect a touch of humor in his voice.

"Oh, hell, no. Traditional is boring," I assure him, snuggling closer. And the sex today was certainly nowhere near traditional.

Gone are the days of wanting a man who only wants to fuck me missionary style. Kane has upped the bar until it's impossibly high. Not that it matters. Because he is my one and only now, anyway. Maybe I should let him in on my plans.

"That sounds promising," he says, smoothing his palm up and down my arm.

I want to purr like a kitten at his touch, but a yawn escapes instead. "If I get some food in me, I may end up snoring in your arms."

"I'm sure it will be a very sexy snore."

"You can let me know in the morning how sexy it is."

He cocks an eyebrow at me. "Will I have to smother you with a pillow so I can get some sleep?"

"Hmm. Possibly. You can roll me over if I snore too loudly."

He brushes a strand of hair off my shoulder. "Lila, if I roll you over, it won't be to stop your snoring."

"That sounds promising," I parrot him and give him a wink.

The doorbell interrupts our banter, and he leaves me amidst the wrinkled sheets to pull on his gym shorts once again. He's not gone long and on his return, the delicious smell of a hot meal precedes him into the room.

"Ooo. I can't wait to meet this chef." Sitting up, I stare longingly at the bags in his hands. I pat the bed beside me in a repeat of earlier. "I'll get fat if I never leave your bed and you keep feeding me all this good food."

"You were made to be spoiled, Lila."

As Kane settles in beside me, I think I could get used to him spoiling me. "By you."

"By me," he agrees.

"Only you."

The corners of his eyes crinkle. "Only me."

"Forever?"

"If that is what you'd like." He smiles widely then and I return the gesture.

Then he feeds me until I'm full and content. When he's done cleaning up, he slides back in between the sheets. He gathers me to him, holding me tight, brushing his fingers through my hair, laying light kisses along my cheekbones, my forehead, my lips. And, even though it's not late, I slowly lose the battle with my heavy eyelids. And I slip into restful sleep, my body intertwined with Kane with a K, my last thought being the morning's alarm will come too soon.

EPILOGUE

Beep. Beep. Beep.

I open my eyes to the sound of the alarm. But I'm not in Kane's bed which causes my heart to race as I panic.

My anxiety ramps to a new level as I see what looks like a doctor checking noisy machines surrounding me. Of course she's a doctor. She's wearing a white lab coat with the name *Emily Branson, M.D.* embroidered on it.

She smiles down at me, her hand patting my shoulder softly as if she's trying to reassure me. "You've been in a coma. We've kept you under to facilitate the healing of your brain. You've had major trauma, and your brain swelled from the impact." Her voice sounds soft, low, and soothing.

She leans by my ear, and I blink at her as she says, "There's someone here to see you." She tilts her head toward the open door. "He's been here every day during visiting hours." She gives me a knowing smile. "You're a lucky woman."

I can't say a word because I'm trying to process why I'm here, what happened. I watch the doctor push past a tall man, who wears a well-fitting suit, in the doorway and she pats the man's arm as she walks out of the door. "You can go in now."

He steps closer and smiles down at me, his teeth looking so white in contrast to his dark skin.

"When you ran in front of that car..." He trails off, his stunning eyes sad. He pauses to drag a chair next to the bed. He settles his long frame into it with grace. "I tried to grab you, but you slipped out of my fingers before I could—" His Adam's apple bobs when he swallows hard.

I shake my head. Slowly. Carefully. I don't understand what he's saying. I don't remember getting struck by a vehicle. Though, now that I'm awake, I feel like I've been hit by a truck. I look down at the needles and tubes sticking out of my bruised hand.

I may not remember what happened, but I remember him.

I will never not remember him. He seems to be a part of my being, my fiber.

I'm not sure why he's here, but I'm glad he is.

He carefully gathers my hand in his, and he leans back in his chair, holding it gently. He wears a serious expression on his face as he watches me with intensity. "By the way, my name is Kane."

Yes. Kane with a K.

I clear my raw throat in an attempt to speak. "Large black coffee."

Finally, his lips curve. "Yes."

"You saved me."

He shakes his head. "No. I attempted to," he reminds me. "I'm sorry I couldn't."

But wait. Everything that happened between us...

"But you took me home..." I start, but then drift off.

His brows furrow and his lips turn down at the corners. "No. The ambulance came and rushed you directly here."

"Do you have a coffee maker?"

His frown deepens because of apparent confusion. "Yes."

"Tell me. Why do you stop at the coffee shop every morning, then?"

His expression smooths out, and he gives me a gentle smile. "I think you know why."

Yes. I know why.

~

His name is Kane.

I will love him forever. He just doesn't know it yet.

An Obsessed Novella

ONLY *Him*

Jeanne St. James

This is not just a love story, it's an obsession...

Sydney:

Never in my life did I think my high school obsession would move right next door. I've never wanted anyone but him. Reid Turner is my ultimate fantasy. And I still want him. Badly. When he watches me through my bedroom window taking matters into my own hands, things suddenly take a turn...

And now that I have him, I'm not letting him go.

Reid:

I never knew she existed and now I can't get enough of her. She consumes me. When this night ends, there may not be anything left of me. She may own me completely. She my master and I her slave. In one way or another I will atone for never noticing her all throughout high school. I will gladly grovel at her feet to make up for what a fool I was.

Besides, who can turn down that luscious body of hers? Curves in all the right places, a mouth that could make a grown man cry. Super responsive during sex, and none of my twisted desires so far have made her bat an eye. And did I mention? She lives right next door. She may be the perfect woman for me.

Note: All books in the Obsessed series are standalone novellas. It is intended for audiences over 18 years of age since it includes explicit sexual situations, including BDSM.

CHAPTER ONE

SYDNEY

Holy fuck.

I peer around the curtain at the man carrying boxes from a rented box truck into the house next door.

My jaw shuts like a trap. What kind of fucking karma is this?

My fingers tremble as they grip the curtain. I must be dreaming. Never in my life did I think my high school crush would move... Right. Next. Door.

Right fucking next door!

My stomach churns and my pussy clenches.

I want to call someone. I want to run through the house screaming.

Reid Fucking Turner is moving next door!

Fucking pinch me.

I haven't seen him in eons. Hell, not since graduation. And that was so, so long ago.

But I know it's him. There's no doubt about it.

Every fiber of my being knows because I spent too many of my teenage years stalking—*err, watching*—him. I would recognize him anywhere.

His gait. His hair (though, it's cut much shorter now). His

shoulders (much broader than high school—the boy has matured into a man). Those thick thighs (they've always been muscular, due to him being a jock).

It has to be him.

My heart stops as he glances toward my window. I drop the curtain like it's on fire and pin my back against the wall. My heartbeat goes from zero to sixty in one second flat.

Holy crap, did he see me peeking?

The pulse in my neck throbs and it may jump right out of my throat at any moment. I clutch my hand to my chest while I try to slow my breathing.

Breathe in. Breathe out.

It'll be okay.

The guy never knew I existed in high school, so he probably wouldn't recognize me now anyway.

I've changed. *Matured.*

My thin, flat-chested body has definitely improved. My breasts might be bigger and heavier than I'd like and my hips curvy enough I can no longer squeeze into skinny jeans, but I've had no problem attracting men. No problem at all.

They seem to prefer something to grab onto when they're pounding into me, sweating all over me, grunting and groaning, and unfortunately, *most of the time,* leaving me unsatisfied and wanting.

And, *most of the time,* I can't wait for them to fucking put their clothes back on and leave.

Breakfast? No thanks. I'm on a diet.

But back to the subject at hand.

Reid Fucking Turner.

I peek out the front window again and wonder why he's moving his stuff by himself. I should head over and offer to help, shouldn't I?

Then I see them. A whole slew of buff, hot guys marching in and out of the house in a line like an army of ants.

Where does he find his friends? Studs 'R' Us?

Maybe they're all gay porn stars. I mean, our classmates *did* vote Reid most likely to succeed in high school. Porn stars are considered successful, right? They're *stars* after all.

I swipe at the bit of saliva gathering at the corner of my lip. *Fuck.* Gay or not, that is one hell of a man buffet. But how disappointing would that be? To find out my teenage crush turned out to dislike women?

Not only disappointing, but devastating.

I glance up at the ceiling and ask any deity listening, "Oh please, don't let that be true."

Reid has been my ultimate fantasy, my constant masturbation material, since the ninth grade when I first laid eyes on him.

Well, more like the day I bumped into him. The first time it happened by accident. The other dozen or so times over the course of our high school years were not so accidental. And one time I even *accidentally* brushed against the front of his jeans.

He felt warm and soft. But that night, I fantasized about him being hot and hard. And all mine. That ended up being a good night and I might have sprained a finger.

But no matter how many times I threw myself in front of Reid Turner, he never seemed to notice me. I had no cleavage, no shape. And I certainly wasn't a cheerleader, or even on the booster team or squad, or whatever the fuck it was called.

I was a nobody. Just another body *moo*-ving down a narrow, crowded hallway, going in and out of classrooms like herded cattle.

I'm not saying I never garnered *any* interest. Just not from Reid Turner and his ilk. Oh, I got kissed and fingered, and eventually my cherry popped, but none of it was worth writing home about.

And every time I found myself in some closet, the backseat of a car, the bedroom of some boy's house whose parents went out to dinner, I'd close my eyes and picture Reid.

That's how I had my first orgasm (one without doing it myself). If I'd squeeze my eyes shut really hard and pretend the guy was Reid, then I'd... *Yeah.* And the poor schmuck probably thought he had skills and most likely disappointed the next girl he fumble-fucked. And if he did, not my problem.

However, that ended up screwing me, too. Because no guy was ever good enough for me.

None of them were Reid Turner.

The fucker ruined me for any other man. And he never once even touched me.

Not. Once.

Whether he knows it or not (I'm pretty sure he doesn't), the man owes me a mind-blowing orgasm.

I snort as I imagine stomping over to his house to demand he make me climax. Wouldn't he shit a brick.

Though… Maybe I should give that some serious thought.

He may call the cops. Possibly apply for a restraining order. *Damn.*

I tap my finger on my chin as I contemplate all the ways I can approach him without getting myself arrested.

Then it hits me. He won't call the police. It's not because he's a criminal and wants to avoid the men in blue.

No, it's because he *is* the police. I forgot he's a cop. *Hot damn.* How could I forget that juicy piece of information?

I remember hearing about his career choice when I was at our lame five-year class reunion. The one I attended just to see him. Though, he never showed. And he never came to our tenth either. It was at that joyous occasion when I found out he had married his main squeeze in high school, Pamela Johnson. Head cheerleader, prom queen, voted most popular. Yeah, yeah, yeah. Blech.

So, that meant he wasn't gay. Or did that bitch turn him?

My eyes rake over the man meat carrying the heavy boxes and random pieces of furniture. No sign of her.

But that doesn't mean they aren't still together. Though, that might fuck with my fantasies.

Damn it.

And of course, his life choices are all about me. Right?

Right.

I pace my living room, wanting to know everything about his life *right now.* He leaves me no choice.

I'll have to do some recon.

~

I actually question my own life choices when I sneak around the outside of his house after dark. What have I been reduced to? I feel like I'm a high school stalker—*err, student*—all over again.

All those times I attended his wrestling matches, his baseball games, I'd sit in the bleachers and root him on. Not that he ever noticed, even though I was his biggest supporter. The ultimate fan.

But hell, at least he chose two sports where he wore tight outfits. Both, that snug onesie thing he wore in wrestling and those tight baseball stretchy pants. His round, muscular ass looked spectacular in both. But that unitard... No, I remember being scolded at one match by someone sitting nearby. It wasn't called a unitard, they called it a singlet. Didn't matter though, at least in that outfit he didn't wear a cup. I think all the females, including the mothers, noticed the healthy-sized Kielbasa link in his *singlet.* You couldn't miss it. In fact, I wouldn't doubt a few of our classmates' mothers hit on him. And possibly even scored. What teenage boy didn't want to fuck a MILF?

Anyway, now fifteen years later (give or take a year), I'm skulking around my neighbor's house like a freaking peeping Tom.

All because *Reid Fucking Turner* moved next door.

This isn't high school anymore, though. No. At thirty-one years old, I'm now dead serious about getting a piece of Reid. Especially since he owes me.

When I step on a stick, it cracks loudly under my foot and my heart, once again, goes into warp speed. I slam myself against the side of his house.

Holy fuck, if any of my other neighbors see me...

Screw them. This is all about me.

And Reid, of course.

I blow out a breath when I realize I might be a good candidate for the loony bin. I shake my head to clear it. I'm a freaking adult. What the hell am I doing?

How can the sight of this man reduce me to this crazy-assed behavior?

Fuck.

I drag myself back into the house, my head hanging in disgrace. I should be ashamed of myself. Maybe I should go over, knock on the door, and apologize for my bad behavior. Welcome him to the neighborhood. Invite him over for some sweaty sex.

I lock my front door and sit in my dark living room totally sickened by my actions.

Then I run upstairs.

CHAPTER TWO

REID

The new house is so quiet it's disturbing. I don't want to hear my own thoughts.

The guys only left an hour ago and I'm already lonely. Not that I'd admit that to anyone. I don't even like admitting it to myself.

But the last six months have sucked. The lies, the separation, the divorce. Moving from couch to couch, from spare bedroom to hotel room. Now that I've settled in my own place, I should be happy to move forward, to finally have a place of my own.

I open the fridge and stare inside. After work tomorrow, my first stop will be the grocery store. A man cannot live on beer alone. And the only thing staring back at me are a variety of six packs. Why? Because that's what my work brothers brought over when they helped me move. I grab one of the long necks and twist the top, letting the cool beer slide down my throat. It doesn't take but a minute to kick it and I grab a second one before closing the door.

Do I even know how to live alone? Hell, I practically married right out of high school. I went from my fucking parents' house to moving into an apartment with my high school sweetheart.

Sweetheart.

Right.

Fucking lying bitch.

I suck in a deep breath and try to push all that nasty crap out of my head. It's over. Move on.

I empty the second bottle, crack the fridge and grab a third before heading upstairs.

I don't even bother to turn on the light when I enter the master bedroom. I'm content to be in the dark. And without curtains yet, the moon reflects brightly into the room. It's peaceful, I try to convince myself. *Yeah, sure.*

I swallow another swig of beer, thinking I should be exhausted, but I'm not. Maybe the beer will help me sleep tonight—the first night in a new house. And if not, I can always rub one out.

Hell, I'm good at it now since my fist has been more loyal than my former wife. *Fuck. Move on, Reid. Don't let it eat at you.*

I sigh and move to the window, glancing up at the night sky and the almost full moon. I was lucky to find this house at such a great price. And with a fenced backyard I can finally get a dog. One of many things Pam would never let me have…

My bedroom window faces the side yard and my eyes rake over the neighboring house. I wish the houses weren't so close in this neighborhood. I like my privacy. But, once again, I bought it at a good price and it's in a nice community. So, I can't bitch too much.

A light turns on in the house next door. Which reminds me I should introduce myself to the neighbors this weekend. But for now…

Holy shit.

Holy, holy fucking shit.

I put my bottle down on the window sill and brace my hands on the frame, leaning in until my forehead almost touches the glass.

I love this house. It's the best house ever. The greatest house in the whole wide world.

Oh, please. Do not close your curtains. Do. Not.

Jeez, I could probably get fired for this. But at the moment, my cock and I don't care.

Cuff me, stuff me, take me away. But please wait until she's done. Do a man a solid.

I adjust myself in my jeans and focus my attention on the open window not twenty feet from mine.

Unlike my bedroom, hers is lit up. Her eyes look closed as she lies naked on her back, her legs wide, her knees bent. And, even better, her bed directly faces the window.

My luck is changing. Yes, indeed.

The woman's breasts are luscious, full but beautiful, the dusky nipples a perfect size. The perfect size for my mouth.

As she cups one breast, her other hand goes rogue. I have to swallow, which for some reason, isn't an easy task. I also must remind myself to breathe as her wandering fingers slide along her beautiful belly to dive between her legs.

Holy shit. I'm imagining this. Right? I dig the heels of my palms into both eyes and look again.

No, it's definitely real. This scenario reminds me of the porn we secretly watched as teenagers. This kind of stuff doesn't happen in real life. When do you look out your freaking window and see a hot woman playing with herself? You don't.

I can't see her expression clearly, but her lips are parted. And when her fingers pull at her nipples, I experience that pull myself, all the way into my balls. Since my jeans have become uncomfortably tight, I have no choice but to open them. I quickly unfasten them and shove them down past my hips, along with my boxer briefs. My cock weeps for her pussy, that I'm sure is slick with arousal by now. I swipe my thumb over the precum beading over the head and swirl it around the crown. My hips thrust forward as I fist my cock. But my palm feels dry and rough from carrying all the shit into the house today. And it feels nothing like her smooth, hot pussy would.

Damn. I need some lube but it's all packed away. It would take too long to find it. And I can't tear myself away from the window, anyhow. I fear I'll miss the best part of the show.

I squeeze the root of my cock and move up to the head, working along my length as I watch her.

Her hand blocks a clear view of her pussy, but what I see looks neatly trimmed. Her thighs are spread wide and her knees have fallen outward. The motion of her hand mesmerizes me, draws me in, turns my cock to stone, my balls tight. And I pretend it's my fingers invading her tight snatch. Sliding in and out, teasing her clit, fucking her relentlessly with my hand.

I need to hear her, so I pause only long enough to slide my window completely open. And for a second I listen carefully, my ears straining to catch any noise, whimpers, moans.

And I do hear them. The sounds that escape her make me grip my cock even tighter and tug harder, faster.

I match her rhythm, my hips thrusting forward as hers lift and fall. Her head rolls back and her neck arches when she cries out. Her hips shoot off the mattress while her hand moves rapidly and then stills a second later.

Holy shit. She came. She caught me unprepared, I wanted to come with her. I didn't expect her to get off so soon. I blow out a disappointed breath but continue to stroke my dick from the root to the tip. Squeeze, gather the precum, and repeat. My heart thumps violently in my chest as I watch her lay there quietly, her legs still apart, one hand lingering across her breasts.

Then, just when I think she's done and about to get up, she rolls onto her side and opens the drawer of her nightstand, pulling out something pink, long, and shaped like a—

Sweet Jesus.

The woman owns toys. As she falls to the bed again, I step back to ensure I'm in the shadows. I don't want to be caught with my pants down and my rock-hard dick in my hands.

I don't want to be caught being a depraved pervert.

The vibrator sounds so powerful I can hear a slight hum all the way in my house. I groan as she holds it against herself. And then the tone changes as she slides it along her pussy, pressing it to what

I can only guess is her clit and, once again, her hips jump off the bed.

She's killing me. This is so not fair. I should be sliding into her wet warmth not that battery-operated substitute.

I snort at my asinine thoughts. I don't even know her damn name and I'm jealous of a pink toy.

But as she slides the dildo inside of her, I no longer hear it. But I hear her. I see her rubbing her clit frantically with one hand and using the other to fuck herself with the vibrator.

My knees buckle and I brace a hand on the wall next to the window, fisting myself double time. I can't stop watching her. Her head rocks side to side and she cries out again. This time she's screaming out a name.

"Oh, fuck me, Reid. Fuck me, Reid. Fuck me!"

I shake my head because now I'm imagining things, since there's no fucking way she's calling out my name. I don't even know this woman.

"Reid, fuck me harder."

My strokes falter and I frown. But, look, I'm a man. I shrug that shit off and ignore the impossibilities.

And when she screams out she's coming, so am I. My cock gets even harder, I squeeze my eyes shut, and blow my load into my palm. Now, I'm the one crying out and I forget my window's wide open. When I lift my eyelids, we're staring at each other. And I wonder…

Am I wearing the same *oh-shit* expression as she is?

We both scramble. I drop to the floor, pressing my back against the wall. I still have one hand full of cock, the other full of cum. My heart is about to pound out of my chest.

Did she really say what I think I heard? Does she know me somehow? How is that even possible?

Was this a trap? Did my ex-wife set me up somehow? Could this have been planned? Maybe someone is outside taking photos of me jerking off to my neighbor. "Blackmail" echoes through my head. But if that's true, then the woman next door is in on it.

And now it only makes sense. Otherwise, how would she know my name?

I see my career going down the toilet, my pension disappearing. My finances drying up.

Fuck.

All because of whacking off. I slide up the wall and yank my jeans back up around my hips with my empty hand and I head to the master bathroom to rinse off the evidence.

I am a depraved fuck. I am no better than any other perv I've arrested for doing the same shit.

But again, maybe it was a set-up. As I stand over the sink, I study myself in the mirror. My own angry expression is reflected back at me. The more I think about it, the more pissed I become.

CHAPTER THREE

SYDNEY

The pounding on my front door makes my heart jump like it's just been zapped with an AED. I can't say I'm not panicking, because I am fucking panicking. I don't want to answer the door, but he knows I'm home.

Holy hell, does he know.

I didn't leave both the curtains and window open on purpose. Unless I did subconsciously. Maybe deep down inside I wanted him to watch me.

But I certainly didn't expect him to show up at my front door to confront me. I snag my black satin robe off the back of the bathroom door and wrap it around me, pulling the sash tight.

I don't know if I should go downstairs and answer it, or hide and hope he goes away until we both forget about what just happened.

As the pounding continues, I realize he won't forget anything at all. And neither will I.

"*Open the fucking door*!" His deep voice easily rises to the second floor, and he doesn't sound happy. Not. At. All.

If I don't answer the door, the neighbors will peek out of their windows, wondering what the ruckus is about.

And I'm already embarrassed enough.

I run down the stairs and skid to a stop at the front door, unlatching the dead bolt. As soon as I turn the knob, the door shoves open and I fall back from the force. He pushes into the foyer and slams the door behind him. His eyes look wild, but the anger behind them is unmistakable.

He leans back against the door and his chest heaves like he's out of breath. "*What the fuck*. How do you know my name?"

I open my mouth, but nothing comes out but a squeak.

Brilliant.

If I thought he looked hot this afternoon from a distance, he's blazing just feet from me. Especially with the cords of muscle and veins popping out in his neck. Anger becomes him.

"How do you know my name?" He pronounces each word slowly and carefully like he's talking to an obstinate child. "*Fuck*!" He drags a hand over his short hair and narrows his gaze in my direction. He pushes off the door and takes two steps toward me. "Answer me."

I'm sure I look like a fish out of water with my mouth opening and closing and no sound escaping. "I…" I clear my throat. "Why do you think I know your name?"

"Because you screamed it out when you came."

Heat rushes up my chest into my cheeks, partly from embarrassment and partly from irritation. His anger fuels my own. "Why were you watching me come?"

Now he's the fish out of water. I watch with satisfaction as he tries to formulate a reasonable answer. He has none.

"Your window was open," he shouts, like it's a valid answer.

"So was yours," I shout back.

"You should close your curtains," he says, more quietly.

"So should you," I answer, also losing some steam. I watch his anger suddenly dissipate into thin air.

He rubs a hand across his forehead. "That was fucking hot."

"It would have been better for me if I realized you were watching."

His expression tells me he can't believe I just said that. That makes two of us.

His hand scrubs his short hair again, this time faster, and he abruptly drops his hand and makes a fist when he realizes what he's doing. "Who are you?"

"I'm your neighbor."

He takes a menacing step closer. "Bullshit. How do you know who I am?"

I stand my ground, grabbing the ends of my sash and pulling it tighter. "Maybe I don't."

"You know my name."

"Maybe it's just a coincidence."

He hesitates and I can see the wheels spinning in his head. Then he shakes it and says, "No."

I arch an eyebrow. "You sure?"

He nods and steps close enough that I can smell a faint odor of beer on his breath. "Yes."

Unfortunately, I hate beer. But I love *Reid Fucking Turner*. So, you take the good with the bad. "It doesn't surprise me you don't know who I am."

His eyebrows furrow deeply. "You know my ex-wife? Did she set this up?"

What? What is he talking about?

I chose my words carefully. "I actually do know your ex-wife."

"You're friends?"

I laugh, though it comes out sounding a bit bitter. "Hell no."

"Then how do you know her?"

I lift a shoulder. "We went to school together."

He's now inches from me, staring down into my face, searching, trying to place me. "Were you a couple grades behind us?"

"No. I was a couple seats behind you at graduation." *Boom!* And I shut up.

His eyes rake over my face and he steps back enough to continue his inspection down my body. "Impossible."

I say nothing.

"What's your name?"

I stay quiet. He glances around, looking for some sign of who I may be. I know he'll find nothing. At least, not where we stand.

He suddenly grabs my upper arms and I wince from surprise more than discomfort. "Who are you?"

I give him a slow smile and he curses, releasing me.

"Fuck you, then." And with that, he spins on his heels and rushes out the front door, slamming it shut behind him.

Once again there's a pounding at my front door. I groan, roll over and eyeball the radio clock. 12:12. *What the fuck.*

I had fallen asleep in the spare bedroom, still only wearing my robe because I didn't dare go back into my bedroom with the window still open. I didn't feel like waving a greeting to my now angry neighbor, who just happens to be my lifelong wet dream.

Could it be him at the door again? Or did he send his cop buddies since he has this weird conspiracy theory that his ex-wife set him up? I knew Pam was a bitch, but really, was she *that* big of one?

What did he do to deserve that? Cheat on her? Is she a scorned woman looking for revenge?

Whatever. Not my problem. My problem is downstairs still knocking *very loudly* at my door.

I sigh, secure my robe and pad down the stairs. I can see the top of his crew cut through the high window panes at the top of the door.

"Open the door." Déjà vu all over again.

As soon as I flip the deadbolt, he's pushing his way in and shutting the door behind him. At least he didn't slam it this time. But I watch him secure the deadbolt. Okay, then. This isn't going to be a quick visit like the last one.

"It took me two hours to find this. It was buried deep in one of the moving boxes." He pulls a book from behind his back. My eyes widen when I realize what it is.

"Sydney Ryan. 'Syd Viscous' takes college prep courses and plans to attend State. Go State! She enjoys watching wrestling, baseball, and RFT. Her favorite food is pizza, and she loves chick flicks," he quotes from memory.

RFT. *Fuck.*

Reid Fucking Turner.

I put a shaky hand over my gaping mouth and my eye widen when he cracks the damn yearbook open to a page in the back.

He points to a picture. "Is that you?"

I lean in a little, just enough to discover he now smells more like whiskey than beer. He must have found his booze buried next to his high school memories. I look at a picture of him wrestling and, yep, in the background is me sitting in the bleachers with a lame lovesick expression on my face.

He flips through the pages and suddenly stops. "Is that you?" It's a picture of him in the batter's box swinging at a blurred baseball with me very clearly plastered to the fence behind him.

With a lame lovesick expression on my face. "Holy shit," I whisper.

He slams the book shut and stares at me. "Why don't I remember you?"

I gather my scattered wits, straighten up, and step away from him. "I don't know. Why don't you?"

He shakes his head and pushes past me to my living room where he drops the yearbook on the coffee table and sinks onto my couch. He plants his elbows on his knees and rakes both hands over his hair. It would work better if he actually had a head of hair like he did when he was younger, but he doesn't. His hair's so short that when he drags his fingers through it, it doesn't have the same effect.

But I like it short. It reminds me how mature he is now. And it's like he's *Reid Fucking Turner 2.0.* I decide right then and there that I will make him mine. All mine. (Cue the wicked laughter and the rubbing of my palms together.)

I've waiting a long time for this man to notice me. And now that he knows I exist, I plan on taking full advantage of it. I tug at the knot on my robe and loosen it slightly before following him. I move to the center of the room, keeping the coffee table between us.

I plant my hands on my hips, making sure the top of the robe gapes enough to give him a peek. And, like taking candy from a baby, his gaze beelines right to the cleavage I'm flashing and he licks his lips. He's on the hook and I'm about to reel him in.

When I finally speak, my voice sounds huskier than normal. "Reid, this was in no way a set-up and I'm not friends with Pam. Never have been, never will be."

"I realize that now."

His words make me wonder if I should be insulted. Apparently, I was never considered good enough to be one of Pam's friends.

I push the thought away. Who cares? *Reid Fucking Turner* is in my living room, right now, while I wear nothing but a satin robe. And I saw his cock just a few hours ago and I plan on seeing it again, but much closer this time. I actually plan on more than just seeing it.

Baby steps, I remind myself.

It's my turn to rake my fingers through my hair, which makes my nipples harden as they slide along the satin and I nearly flash a nipple.

His eyes jump from my almost nip slip to my face. "Did you stalk me in high school?"

I have two choices. One, I can lie. Two… "Yes."

"Why?"

"Have you seen yourself in the mirror?" I laugh lamely.

His eyebrows almost reach his forehead. "Have you seen *yourself* in the mirror? Why would you need to stalk anybody?"

My smile flattens. "I didn't look like this in high school. You just saw the proof."

"Yeah, but—"

I shake my head and hold out a palm. "When you have big breasted, blonde cheerleaders bouncing in front of you, fighting for your attention, the last thing you're going to notice is a shy, dark-haired girl who's as flat as a two-by-four."

"And look where that big breasted blonde bitch got me." He grimaces, pushing to his feet, and steps around the coffee table to stand toe-to-toe with me. That's when I notice he's barefoot and the top button of his jeans is unfastened. *Hot damn.*

He gathers a strand of my hair and winds it around his finger before watching it unwind. "I'm sorry I never noticed you. I'd like to make it up to you, if you'd let me."

Let him? I insist! I tilt my head and give him a smile. One I hope looks sexy, sultry. And not like a crazed loon. "What do you have in mind?"

He presses his finger against the indentation of my throat then slides it down until it reaches where my robe V's loosely. He hooks it in the fabric but holds it there. His eyes darken as he stares where his finger stopped and when he glances up, his nostrils flare.

His voice sounds husky and low when he says, "Anything you desire."

My knees weaken, but I lock them in place so I don't freaking collapse to the ground in front of him and kiss his damn bare feet. Not to mention, kiss the ground he's standing on. Because holy hell, I have waited my whole life to have sex with *Reid Fucking Turner*. And now the man tells me I can have anything I desire.

Just. Like. That.

If he sucks in bed, I'm going to just give up. I'll sew my pussy shut and never have sex again. Become a crotchety old spinster.

If he only knew what pressure he was under, he might have performance anxiety. So, I can't tell him that it's only ever been him for me.

Then I realize he needs to pay for making me wait so long. For making me want only him.

CHAPTER FOUR

REID

"I want to punish you."

At her words, the blood rushes through me and my ears ring. Did I hear her correctly? This night just keeps getting crazier.

My voice breaks as I ask, "Have you ever punished a man before?"

She shakes her head slowly. "No."

"And how do you plan on punishing me?" My cock is so fucking hard right now, I want to tear at my jeans and let it escape. It's like Godzilla wanting to smash some buildings.

But I need to hold off, let her express herself first. Give me a clear indication of what she wants to do to me.

Though, most likely, I won't say no to whatever she comes up with. I am the luckiest guy in the world right now. I never thought my shitty luck would turn around like this.

She has no idea how she'll punish me. None whatsoever. So, here's where I have to step in. Take control until I can hand it back over to her.

No matter what, I want to see her naked again. And this time, it's not going to be some latex or plastic vibrator fucking her. Guaranteed.

"Want some suggestions?"

Her eyes widen and she stares at me like I grew two heads. Then her expression changes as her mind processes the possibilities.

I like this woman. Oh yes, I do.

She's got potential.

I jump to my feet, raise a *wait-a-minute* finger, and rush to the front door. I yank on it and it doesn't budge. In my excitement (not to mention, a little worry she's going to change her mind), I forgot I deadbolted it. I unlock it with fingers shaking with adrenaline and sprint out the door, not even bothering to close it behind me.

My heart pounds as I burst into my house and take the steps two at a time. When I reach my bedroom, I glance around and find the cardboard box I'm looking for. It's marked "old pictures" in black Sharpie. I snort at my ingenious subterfuge, snag it, and fight the urge to slide down the banister in my haste.

I'm trying not to giggle like a little girl as I run back next door, now happy that the houses sit so close together. I slam her door shut behind me, flip the deadbolt again, and drop the box on the foyer floor. Then I bend over with a shooting side cramp. I press my hand into the pain and gulp oxygen.

Fuck.

When I finally catch my breath, I glance up and over into the living room and see she's still standing in the exact same spot.

I pick up the box, snag her hand to drag her upstairs and into her bedroom. I close the curtains (because I still wonder if anyone is out there spying) and then dump the contents of the box on her bed.

Her eyes widen in amazement and she exclaims, "Holy shit."

"I know, right?" I smile. Then my smile drops when I think maybe she's not so impressed. Maybe I just freaked her the fuck out with my enthusiasm. And with my box of "old photos" which really isn't a box of photos at all.

Nope.

It's my toy box. The one I kept hoping Pam would one day be

willing to play with. But she never wanted to. So, I kept my fantasies to myself.

And no man should do that. Well, unless the toys are illegal. But mine clearly weren't. You know, two consenting adults and all that happy crap.

I wave a hand over the bed. "You think you can figure it out from here?"

When her eyes light up and she glances up at me with a naughty smile, I'm relieved. When she answers, "Oh, hell yes," my whole body screams "Oh, hell yes," too.

Then she fingers an old pair of my handcuffs and the hair on the back of my neck stands up and my breath hitches.

"Do to me what you will," I tell her, my voice a little shaky.

"Get undressed."

Without hesitation, I grab the back of my T-shirt and yank it over my head, tossing it into a corner of the room. I rip my jeans down and kick them and my boxer briefs into the corner, too.

I stand before her naked, my cock jutting out from my body and I want to touch it but want her to tell me to. She inspects every inch of me. From the top of my head to my toes, then circles slowly around me. I imagine her tapping a crop against her thigh as she does it.

She suddenly transforms before me. Her spine straightens, her eyes harden, and she points to the floor. "On your knees."

I instantly fall to my knees, the impact making me grunt. I drop my gaze to the carpet, allowing myself to act the submissive I've always wanted to be.

I hear the ratchet of the cuffs as she spins them open and closed. The clicking sound of the metal teeth shoots lightning down my spine. My nipples harden to points and I only hope she can figure out some of the toys I've brought over (I say some, because if she uses them all at once, I might not survive).

She steps behind me and in between my legs. I automatically offer her my wrists and she clamps the cold metal handcuffs on me, tightening them enough so I can't pull free. My breathing shallows and my dick twitches in anticipation.

"What are you punishing me for?" I ask her as she moves towards the bed. I see her in my peripheral vision sorting through the stuff spread over the bedspread.

"For making me wait so long."

"What else?"

"For making me only want you and no one else."

I'm floored. I open my mouth to ask her more, but I almost stutter due to my surprise. I swallow hard and try again. "I'm sorry."

She steps in front of me and I level my gaze on her hands. She holds a candle and a lighter. She points the candle at me. "Is this for a romantic dinner?"

"No."

"What's it for?"

I hesitate.

"Anal?"

I shake my head but turn my gaze back to the floor. "No."

The sound of the lighter igniting makes me light-headed. And then I smell the wick burning.

"Look at me," she demands and I do. Her gaze flicks from me to the burning candle. The wax is already melting and rolling down the sides of the taper. "Lean back."

I shift my weight over my legs and she steps between my spread thighs. She stares at the flame for a moment, then turns the long, narrow candle to the side. Almost in slow motion, I watch the first drip of wax strike my body. It barely misses my right nipple and the burn against my skin makes me gasp.

She moves it over my left nipple, closer this time, and she hits her target, the drip of hot wax coating the tip of my nipple. I cry out and she pulls the candle away, righting it quickly.

"Do you want me to stop?"

"No." The painful pleasure is tolerable and I want her to

continue. My nipple tightens as the wax cools. I've wanted to try this kind of play for years and I'm not going to stop her now.

If she's willing to give, I'm willing to receive.

Just because I want to let her have the control this time, doesn't mean it will always be this way. But, I'm willing to let her punish me tonight. Because turnabout is fair play.

Being a cop, I must always remain in control while working and in my down time, I don't always want to be in control. Sometimes I want to be the one controlled, instead.

Another drip falls from the candle and lands on my chest. *It hurts so good* echoes through my head.

I close my eyes to avoid the anticipation of the liquid heat hitting me, instead I want to feel it as it happens. I groan when the wax completely covers one nipple, and she moves on to the other. A drip slides down my belly, but slows and hardens before reaching my cock. I breathe again in relief.

"You don't want to watch what I'm doing to you?"

"No."

"Why?"

"I like the anticipation."

"Ah," she murmurs. I hear her blow out the candle, the scent of the smoking wick burns my nostrils.

I open my eyes just as she slides a blindfold over my face. Everything turns black. She has taken away my choice to watch her actions. Now, I'm forced to use my imagination as she moves back toward the bed.

It isn't until she grips my cock that I realize this is the first time she's touching me. She's not gentle as she stretches a rubber cock ring over me and snaps it over the root of my hard-on. I grunt and fall forward a bit, but straighten up as she pulls my sac through the ring, too.

She may know more than she lets on.

She doesn't linger or try to give me any pleasure. She's gone quickly. The air shifts as she gets to her feet. I do a quick inventory of what's left on the bed in my head. And when I hear the smack of leather against her palm, I know what she's grabbed next.

My lips curve slightly as I picture her dressed in a black leather teddy, fishnet stockings, a thick leather dog collar with spikes, and high heels. If I wasn't wearing the cock ring, I swear I would come.

All I know is that I'm taking the woman shopping this weekend.

CHAPTER FIVE

SYDNEY

His lips part and he pants when I stroke the flat leather head of the riding crop down his cheek.

I feel as if I'm having an out-of-body experience. When I fantasized about having sex with Reid, I never imagined it like this. Not even close.

I tap his cheek lightly and slide the leather end of the crop down his throat and over the hard coating of wax dotting his chest and covering his nipples. As I continue down his sternum and over his abs, I wonder if he wants me to smack him with it. I can't imagine why else the item would be in his goodie box if he didn't want it to be used. I could ask him or…

I strike him on his thigh, the flat leather making a popping sound against his taut quadricep. His body sways but he doesn't cry out. I held back that time, and his lack of reaction gives me a little more confidence. I strike his other thigh sharply and his breath catches this time as he grimaces. A pink mark appears where the crop made contact.

His erection remains firm, extending out from his body. I brush the crop over his hard length and under his balls, which appear tight and dark due to the snug cock ring. I pause the riding crop at the bottom of his sac.

"Do you want me to hit you here?" I brush the leather end back and forth over the skin that contains the most delicate part of his body.

He groans. "No. Not there."

Now I regret blindfolding him and wish I could see his eyes. "Not even a light tap?"

He moans but doesn't answer me. I pull the crop away and he tenses as if he's expecting me to do it.

I don't. I can't do that to him. He would have to beg me first. Instead, I tap the crown of his cock lightly and he flinches but recovers quickly.

"How about there?"

"Yes."

I run the leather end up and down his length and tap the head at the end of each upstroke.

He grits his teeth but doesn't tell me to stop. Then, I realize I never gave him an "out," a way to tell me when things are approaching the limit of his tolerance, when the pain becomes no longer pleasurable or wanted.

I'm so out of my element, that I only know there are things called safe words. And I'm not even sure if we should be using them.

"What's your safe word?"

He shakes his head. "I don't have one."

I step back in surprise. "Why not?"

"I've never done this before."

And with that, my confidence just flies out of my open bedroom window. "What do you mean? You have all that stuff." I glance over at the various toys scattered over my bed. He must be shitting me. No one owns all kinds of kinky toys and restraints and has never used them.

I assumed he was a pro at this. Boy, was I wrong. I fight back a nervous laugh and look at the crop in my hand. I could hurt this man without even trying. We need to come up with a system if he wants to continue.

The game of Red Light, Green Light from my childhood pops into my head. "Green, yellow, red. That's what you're going to use." He nods and I'm tempted to rip off the blindfold to make sure he's listening. "I want to hear you or I'm stopping this right now."

"Yes. Red, green, yellow."

I really don't want to do anything to him where he has to yell "red" at me. I blow out a breath and study *Reid Fucking Turner* restrained in the middle of my bedroom floor, blindfolded, with hardened wax on his chest. A memory of the movie *Misery* flashes through me. I don't want to be the crazy lady holding someone hostage against their will. Which is silly, since I know Reid consents and it's his own toys I'm using on him. But still...

I don't know what the hell I'm doing. However, I'm wet and I'm enjoying this as much as he seems to be. And if he wants me to continue...

"Tell me a color."

"Green."

"Lean forward, put your forehead on the carpet."

He complies right away, using the strength in his abs to lower himself forward. His back curves, not giving me the access I need.

"Ass up."

He shifts his knees back until his body becomes a straight angle from his forehead on the floor to his ass in the air. His knees have to be hurting by now. But I brush that thought away and concentrate on my task at hand instead.

With a flick of my wrist, I bring the crop down across his back and I'm the one who flinches this time. He remains as solid as a rock, so does his cock as it hangs between his thighs.

"You like that?" I ask.

"Yes."

I hide my surprise. "You want more?"

"Please."

"What color?"

"Green."

I bring the riding crop down across his ass cheeks this time, the hardest I've hit him yet. I notice his skin swell to form a welt where I struck him. "What color?"

"Green."

Fuck. I don't want to hit him any harder, but I'm surprised how aroused all this makes me. I want to fuck him, not torture him. However, giving him the pleasure he desires makes me want him even more. I want to give him what he wants. Because I plan on him giving me what I need.

I strike him across the back of both thighs this time, narrowly missing his sac, and he makes a noise. "Color!" I yell a little panicked.

He hesitates for only a second. "Green."

Fuck!

I bring the crop down one more time across his ass and then quickly follow with another blow across his thighs again, then raise the crop one more time. "Tell me."

He sucks in a breath and his answer comes out ragged. "Green."

"No," I moan.

"Green," he repeats more firmly. As I stand above him, with the crop poised for another strike, he gets impatient. "Fucking green. Do it!"

I bring it down across his shoulder blades and his back bows as he cries out. I whip the crop across the room when I see a red line spring up from his skin.

"Sit up," I yell at him and he does, returning to sit on his heels. I rip off the blindfold and drop to my knees in front of him so we're face to face. I cup his cheeks in my hands and stare into his eyes, which are dark, unreadable.

I've loved this man almost my whole life. "I don't want to hurt you."

"You're not. Can't you see how hard I am?"

I can. But instead of answering him, I pick the dried wax off his skin carefully, noticing he winces occasionally.

His nipples appear red, irritated, and I kiss each one gently, before flicking them with my tongue. I kiss each red mark along his torso and when I reach his erection, I take him into my mouth. He murmurs something but I have no idea what. I take as much of his length as I can, though we're still in an awkward position on the floor. I can't believe I have *Reid Fucking Turner* in my mouth as I make him cry out with my lips, tongue, and teeth until he finally yells out the word yellow. I push myself back up and grab his face in my hands to finally kiss him.

I crush my lips against his, exploring his mouth, his tongue tangling with mine playfully before it becomes serious. And, holy hell, I'm kissing *Reid Fucking Turner.*

Finally.

I moan into his mouth, then reluctantly push away. "How do I get the handcuffs off you?"

He glances towards the bed. "There should be a key somewhere amongst the rest of the stuff."

I sure as hell hope so, because I want his hands all over me. And now I'm the one impatient. I stumble to my feet and rush over to the bed. I sweep my hand over it, looking for a key.

"It's silver, thin, and metal."

I roll my eyes, glad he can't see me. Like I don't know what a key looks like— "Wait." I hold up what may be a cuff key. "This?"

He nods and I sink to my knees behind him, trying to figure out how to unlock the cuffs. After fumbling and a few curses, I figure it out and release him. He lets out a sigh and rubs his shoulders and wrists but when he goes to move, I stop him. "Don't move yet."

I throw the cuffs to the side and shed my robe, tossing that, too. On my knees, I shuffle closer, in between his legs and press myself against his back. I skim my hard, aching nipples across his skin as I kiss along the line of his neck and trace the tip of my tongue along his shoulders and down his spine. When I can't go any lower, I work my way back up, making sure to kiss along the angry welt that crosses his back. My mark on him.

I wrap my arms around the front of his shoulders, holding him close and whisper, "I want you so much," against the skin of his neck. When I sink my teeth into the corded muscles, his back arches against me. He groans, grabbing my arms, digging his fingers into my flesh, not pushing me away. No. He's keeping me in place instead.

"Green," he whispers.

When I bite the hard curve of muscle between his neck and shoulder, his head falls forward, and he shudders against me. I move to the top of his spine and grab his flesh between my teeth. It will leave a mark, but before I can release him, he's telling me "Green," once again and I bite harder, sink deeper. I only stop before I break the skin.

I'm panting as hard as he is now. Knowing he's getting off on me biting him sends a thrill right to my core. I push my pelvis against his ass and slide my arms down until I capture him in my hands. I cup his sac with one and squeeze the root of his length in the other. He lays his hands over mine and begins to control the movement of my fingers, my palm, up and down his shaft.

His cock is dark and his balls even darker from the cock ring cutting off his circulation. I want it off him. And I want it off him *now*. I trace the rubber ring with my fingertip. "Take it off."

I fear he'll lose some of his hardness when he removes it, but it's worth the risk. I want to know he desires me and not just kinky play.

After carefully removing the ring, I'm pleased he's just as ready. I can touch him easier, more fully with nothing in the way. My fingers play along his hard shaft, the skin like velvet. I squeeze the head, milking a bead of precum onto my thumb and I swirl the silky fluid around the tip.

"You do it," I say, pushing myself to my feet and grabbing the bottle of Astroglide that's on the bed. I move in front of him again.

"Hold out your hand." He does without question. I pop the cap and squeeze a few drops onto his palm. "Show me."

He grabs himself and starts to stroke. Slowly at first. I watch the glistening skin slide with each pull. His eyes never leave mine as he fists his own erection. I think back to earlier in the evening when I caught him doing the very same thing.

His jaw tightens, and he reverses his grip, tugging harder, faster, his gaze still pinned to mine. I suck in air when I realize I stopped breathing. I can't look away. My eyes flick down to his quick movements and when I glance back up, he's grimacing and his eyes have closed. Still on his knees, his hips make minute movements in the same rhythm of his hand.

As I observe him, I touch myself. I brush my fingers over the diamond hard tips of my nipples, I sweep a hand down my belly and find my own wetness. I'm slick and hot, and I'm tempted to stop him from finishing because I want him inside me.

But watching Reid pleasure himself drives me mad. His whole body changes as he gets close. If I'm going to stop him, I need to do it now.

But I can't stop him. Instead, I plunge two fingers between my legs and into my wet core. I cry out because it'll take me seconds to climax. As his eyes pop open and he bears his teeth, I come standing up, while at the same time, the ropy strings of his release land into his open palm. A noise escapes from the back of his throat and he seems to lose all strength, reminding me of a rag-doll.

"Come here," he says and I step closer. He takes my hand, the one that was buried in my pussy and he slides my two slick fingers into his mouth, savoring the taste of my arousal.

Then he slowly and carefully pushes himself to his feet still holding my wrist so I can't back away. Before I realize what he's about to do, he kisses me.

The taste of my own arousal on his lips pulls a groan from me. "Touch me," I demand.

He raises his fist, the one containing his cum. "May I go clean up?"

I laugh. "Yes. Please." I tilt my head toward the master bathroom. "In there."

I can't help but watch him walk away from me. I appreciate the play of his muscles under his skin along his back, his thick thighs, and, oh, that ass. I can't wait to dig my nails into those muscular globes when he's pumping into me.

I shake my head and rub my eyes before looking over at the bed and seeing the rest of the contents of his box spread over the mattress. Yes, this is really happening. I haven't been imagining it. It's not one of my many Reid Turner fantasies.

But it seems too good to be true.

When he exits the bathroom, he's semi-soft, and the urge to take him into my mouth washes over me, because when he isn't aroused, I can take more of him at one time. But my desire to have him touch me instead overrules my instinct.

I've waited a long, long time for this man. I'm tempted to lock the doors and never let him leave again.

But that would make me no better than the woman in *Misery*. And I want him to be here because he chooses to be, not because he's forced.

I want him to touch me because he wants to, not because I make him.

As he approaches, his gaze caresses every inch of my body and he gives me a breathtaking smile that sucks the air from my lungs. His dark brown eyes appear almost black and he moves with a fluidity that reminds me of a dancer. Impossible. He's too solidly built to be so graceful. He's a powerhouse, a body made for strength. A man made for loving.

When he steps toe to toe with me, we end up only a breadth apart, but nothing touches but our breaths and our heat. He scorches my being, all the way to my bones.

My breath shallows as I die for his touch a little more with each passing second. If I shift even a little, I'll be seared by his skin. I fear those scars may not ever disappear, unlike the marks I left on his body. Those will fade, be forgotten. But I will never forget this.

This moment, this night, this man.

It's only ever been him.

I will relish every touch, every kiss I receive, in case this is the only night I spend with him.

"Sydney," he murmurs as he stares down into my face.

"*Reid Fucking Turner*," I whisper back.

His eyes flash and the corner of his lip curls up. "May I touch you now?"

"You fucking better."

I expect him to go right for the goods. But he doesn't. He sweeps his fingertips along my hairline, across my forehead, over my cheekbones, my nose, my chin… my parted lips.

It's a tenderness I didn't expect. It catches me off guard since it's a total turnabout of the earlier activities.

His gaze follows the same path as his fingers as they move down my throat and slide across my shoulders. My nipples are tight, painful, aching for his touch, especially as he gets closer.

But he avoids them, drawing a hiss from me. He ignores it and continues his journey, tracing the outer curves of my breast, my ribcage. When his hands span my waist, they circle around back and down my ass, he then smooths his palms over my hips before dropping to his knees once again in a submissive position. He draws circles over my thighs, narrowly missing a brush against my damp folds with the backs of his knuckles. I shiver at his light touches. When he gets to my feet, he starts his way back up, using his mouth, his lips, his tongue this time, worshiping my trembling body as he goes.

I clench my fingers into fists to stop myself from shoving him to the floor and mounting him right there. He presses butterfly kisses across my lower belly and I realize then this is simply another form of torture. The tables have temporarily turned.

His actions may not involve crops, or hot wax, or any discomfort at all. But it's painful all the same. Because I *ache deeply* for him. From my very core to every extremity. Every nerve stands on end, every sense becomes sharpened.

And just when I think I can't take anymore, he slides my thigh over his shoulder and presses his mouth to my sex. I grasp his head in my hands as he sucks my clit, then circles it with his tongue. My eyelids flutter closed as my fingers dig into his hair, pulling him tighter against me. He slides his tongue between my folds, stroking, caressing, until I cry out. When he slips two fingers inside me, I curse him. Because *Reid Fucking Turner* is going to make me come apart, but not quickly enough. With his mouth pressed to my sensitive clit and his fingers fucking me, I find myself on the precipice.

He finds my ass, his fingers playing along my crease, teasing me where no one has touched before. But before he can take it any further, my core ripples and clenches tightly around him, soaking him with my arousal. He makes a noise as he licks away all traces of my climax and when he sits back on his heels, I can't miss how my orgasm affected him. He's long and hard again, and I'm ready for him to put his cock where his fingers just were.

CHAPTER SIX

REID

I never knew she existed and now I can't get enough of her. She consumes me. When this night ends, there may not be anything left of me. She may own me completely. She my master and I her slave.

But I don't care, because my wrists are now bound to the upper corners of her headboard, my arms stretched wide. In one way or another, I will atone for never noticing her all throughout high school.

I will gladly grovel at her feet to make up for what a fool I was.

Naked, she kneels on the bed between my spread legs. Her face is flushed and her eyes sparkle as she holds up a latex toy. I can't get over how beautiful she is.

"What's this?"

I study the object, one of many I've added to my collection since my separation and divorce in the hope that I'd find someone to play with, to explore some new experiences. I think again on how lucky I am to have moved next door and to find Sydney. Her long, dark hair flows loosely around her shoulders and I want to feel its silkiness against my skin, over my cock.

"An anal plug."

She looks at it curiously. I'm pleased she hasn't found any of my toys distasteful so far. She's been open-minded all night. And she really seemed to get off on "punishing" me earlier.

"Is it for you or for me?"

My breath catches at the image of me coating it with lube and pushing it inside her, stretching her, filling her before my own flesh takes its place. I groan at the thought of how tight she would be. A place untouched by any other man. "Either," I finally answer.

"Have you used one before?"

Fuck. I see where she's going with her question and I almost wish I hadn't bought it. I may end up on the receiving end of the plug tonight. I don't know whether to be excited or worried. "No."

She meets my gaze and gives me a smile that makes my cock twitch. "Do you want to?"

"Do I have a choice?" I pull at the ropes binding me to the headboard to remind her that I really don't. She holds the power in her hands right now.

"No, I guess you don't. But you're not in a good position for us to try it."

I agree, especially since I'm sitting up in bed, bound to the headboard. But I'm sure she can figure it out. I question whether I should tell her that or not, since I'm still on the fence on whether I want her to try it on me. Though, if it came down to it, I wouldn't hesitate to use it on her. And, smart man that I am, I didn't get a big one. Luckily. My ass might thank me later.

"I guess I would need the lube," she says, searching the bedroom for the tube.

"I would suggest that. Otherwise, the neighbors might wonder why there's a man in your bedroom screaming *red* at the top of his lungs."

She giggles and hops off to locate the Astroglide. She raises the tube up in triumph when she finds it and a bead of sweat pops out on my forehead. I tell myself that I should be willing to do anything

I'd want to do to her. I tell myself again. And one more time for good measure.

Look at me being a pussy. Hot wax and being whipped with a leather riding crop didn't faze me a bit. But a little anal plug scares the shit out of me.

When she climbs back on the bed, she pauses to study me. I see the wheels turning in her head. "Bend your knees."

"I don't know—"

"Do it!" she shouts at me.

My eyes widen and my lips twitch, but I do what she asks—no, *demands*. I see what she's doing, exposing my *vulnerability*. AKA my ass. She squirts lube all over the anal plug.

"Do you want to put something down on the—"

"Quiet!"

Okay, then.

She shuffles on her knees across the bed until she's between my thighs. "Damn, I need an extra set of hands."

I certainly can't help. I'm bound to the bed. But I *am* curious why she needs assistance.

Then she does something I don't expect. She takes me between her lips again. I groan as she practically swallows my length into her hot, wet mouth. Her tongue plays along my cock as she sucks me. *Ah, fuck.*

As her amazing mouth pulls at my dick, I lift my hips slightly to meet her. She cups my balls and they tighten from the contact. She pulls them higher and then there's a finger playing with my ass.

Ah, fuck.

The more she teases my tight hole, the more I relax. So far, so good. Between her mouth working my cock, the finger action, and the little sucking sounds she's making, I'm in heaven. My eyelids get heavy and I find myself breathing quicker, deeper. Then my chest heaves as she pushes her index finger in to the first knuckle. She's driving me nuts. It's weird but great at the same time and I'm surprised. Pleased. And—

Aaah, fuck.

Her whole finger slips in and out of me. She's fucking my ass. *Holy shit.* She curves her finger and strokes my prostate, which makes me groan and I want to shoot my load down her throat.

Then her finger is quickly replaced by something larger, firmer. She presses the slippery plug but finds resistance. When she sucks me harder, faster, I fucking want to grab her hair and fuck her face. But I can't. I'm being punished. I can't move my hands. I have no control on the speed of her mouth, of her sucking me. And my cock gets even harder at the thought.

One hand squeezes my balls and the other— She shoves the plug past my sphincter and I cry out at the pinch and the slight discomfort. I feel full, stretched. It's an odd sensation. It's not so bad, I'm kind of liking it.

She raises her head with a look of victory in her eyes. "Success." Her lips are shiny and I don't want to do anything but kiss them right now. When she straightens up, I'm a bit disappointed. I was hoping she'd suck me to completion. But when I see a condom in her hand, my disappointment quickly disappears. Because I know what's coming next.

I am so fucking ready.

I've been ready for this moment since I stood watching her out of my window.

And here it is… hours later. And finally… *finally*, I'm going to be deep inside her, feeling her pussy squeezing me tight, milking me dry.

Unless… she's just teasing me. No. No. *Noooo.*

But no, she's rolling the condom on my cock and I lean my head back against the bed and watch her with hooded eyes. I drop my knees so she can straddle me. I suck in a breath as she lifts herself above me, lines me up, and—

Ah, mother fuck.

As she slides down my length, her eyes flutter shut and her mouth goes lax. My brain just shuts down to nothing. All I can do is concentrate on the tight, wet heat that surrounds me. My cock throbs inside her. It's like a little piece of heaven. When her eyes pop open, she plants her palms on my chest and begins to move. Slowly, oh so slowly, at first. I want to cry like a baby with how good it feels. The only thing that would make it better would be to scrap the condom and feel her directly against me.

But I know that's stupid and—

Ah, fuck.

She leans forward to kiss me and her puckered nipples brush against my chest. The next time I fuck her—or she fucks me—I want my hands free. I want to be able to explore her body as she rides my shaft like a dime-store pony.

Every time she lowers, the anal plug shifts deep inside and my mind is blown. I think I may not ever want to have sex without one in again.

Then she does something with her hips. A grind, a circle, whatever the fuck it is, it's amazing and I groan into her mouth. She nips my bottom lip, making me cry out.

I'm so ready to explode. My balls feel tight, by cock has never been so hard, and I swear her hips are double-jointed. Then she sinks down on me and stills for second. Only a second because then she makes small movements… she's rubbing her clit against me. I want to touch her there. I want to tease her until she comes around my cock. But I'm fucking tied up and I can't. I can't. I want to, but I can't.

"Fucking bite me," I cry out, surprising even myself at my outburst.

She sinks her teeth into my neck and I realize I may have made a mistake. Her biting me might make me lose it before she has even climaxed. But she whimpers against my skin and she's just as turned on as me.

"Green," I practically groan. My eyes squeeze shut with the intense pleasure that runs through me when she kisses my shoulder and then bites me hard. My hips jump off the bed, thrusting hard and deep into her. The anal plug shifts again and I'm done.

So done. Stick a fork in me.

"I can't…" I groan. Trying to tell her I can't go on any longer.

But instead of slowing down, she increases her pace as she rises and falls on my cock and she bites me again in the chest. I cry out from the sharp pain, but I'm almost there. If she doesn't stop, I'm going to go. With or without her.

She reaches between us and rubs furiously at her clit, throwing her head back with abandonment.

When I feel her core ripple around my length, I come like a geyser. My cock pulsates violently and I slam my head back against the headboard with a crack and a curse.

I see stars. I'm not sure if it's from the impact to my head or the mind-blowing sex with this woman. Sydney collapses on top of me, her arms around my shoulders and she rubs the back of my head.

"Are you okay?"

Okay? You can crack my head with a baseball bat if I get to have sex like that. But I keep that to myself. Instead I say, "Perfect."

She nuzzles her nose in the crook of my neck and sighs.

CHAPTER SEVEN

SYDNEY

No way! I just fucked *Reid Fucking Turner*. I should hire a prop plane with an aerial banner (like the ones at the shore) and have it buzz the neighborhood, the county, the state, hell, the country. Let everyone know that my mission has been accomplished. Not only did I get to fuck him, I got to shove an anal plug up his ass.

Who would have guessed that? Now the problem was, who was getting it back out?

Not me. I'm not raising my hand for that job.

When I return from disposing of the condom, I stop at the end of the bed and study Reid with his arms still outstretched. Marks from the wax and my teeth mar his chest and I almost feel guilty about them. But I shouldn't. I didn't do anything he didn't want me to.

I move around to each side of the bed, releasing the ropes that bind him. His arms drop to the bed and with a groan, he rubs his wrists.

He watches me and I him as the seconds pass without a word. Finally, I ask, "Well?"

"Well what?"

"You going to go remove that thing?" I nod toward that area.

He chuckles, but doesn't move. "Are you giving me an order?"

"No." I hesitate, but for only a moment. "You don't want to take it out?"

His eyes crinkle at my surprise. "I kind of like it."

I shrug. "Okay, leave it in then." I climb onto the bed and settle next to him. "What's it like?"

He cocks an eyebrow my way. "Do you want to find out?"

"Mmm. I don't know." I chew my lower lip. I'm not sure if I'm ready for that at this point. But this man may be able to talk me into anything. Especially if it keeps him from getting dressed and walking out my front door.

I glance at the clock and realize the night's half over. I wonder if dawn will bring a dose of reality and we'll go our separate ways.

Though, as I look at the various toys scattered across the floor and the two nightstands, I can't imagine he'll find anyone more convenient than his next-door neighbor to voluntarily play his sex games.

And anyway, who said I'm letting him leave? I got him, now I'm keeping him.

His arm curls around me and he pulls me into his side, nuzzling my hair. "I still can't believe I didn't know who you were."

"And you still have more making up to do."

When he murmurs, "I look forward to it," into my ear, I shiver and am relieved he doesn't feel the need to escape any time soon.

"What are the odds of you moving next door?"

"Karma," he says and drops a kiss on my shoulder.

See? That's what I thought. Some people were just meant to be together.

Though, I'm not saying that out loud, since we're not really "together" at this point and I don't want to scare him away before I even get a chance to formulate our future.

I clear my throat and my crazy thoughts. "So, what happened with you and Pam?"

He leans back against the headboard and blows out a breath. I wiggle in closer against him and lay a palm over his chest. I study his strong jawline until he says, "Pregnancy."

"What?" I shake my head, confused. "You didn't want kids?"

He glances down at me with what looks like pain in his eyes. "I didn't want someone else's kid."

"I don't understand."

"Yeah. Don't feel bad, I didn't either, until it smacked me in the face."

He pushes a strand of my hair behind my ear and gets serious. "She was pregnant with someone else's baby."

My mouth makes an O. I'm sure my eyes do, too. Finally, I whisper, "Damn, that had to hurt."

"And you know, she was going to try to pass it off as mine."

What a bitch. "How did you find out?"

"I caught the two of them in bed together."

"Damn."

"Did I mention it was my bed? In my house? Yeah."

"Well, at least you didn't kill him. Or her."

"She wasn't worth it. All those years wasted…"

"We learn from our mistakes," I say, trying to put a positive spin on it. Though, apparently, I'm not successful since he snorts in response.

He tucks a finger under my chin and lifts my face to his. "I'm done making mistakes."

I really doubt that's true, but I keep my mouth shut.

"My biggest one was with you." He continues in a rush when he sees my frown. "No, not tonight. I meant in high school."

Oh yeah. *That* mistake. I pat his thigh. "You'll make it up to me."

"Sure will."

I squeeze the hard muscle of his thigh and then trace the contours. His thighs don't jiggle like mine do. "You still active in sports?"

"I play on our department's baseball team. I run. I fuck my neighbor."

I glance up in surprise and laugh. "I'm not sure you can consider that a sport."

"Well, you wore me out, and you've been a good sport."

"Oh, I'm not done with you yet."

His voice becomes low and husky. "That sounds promising."

"I'm sure there's some toys we missed."

"Yeah," he says softly. "But we can't get to everything tonight."

"So, another night," I suggest and hold my breath.

"Yeah," he answers, running his fingers up and down my arm.

Both his answer and his touch has goosebumps breaking out all over me and my nipples hardening into points all over again.

"There was something you said earlier that we need to circle back around to."

Oh shit. Dare I ask? I try to deflect. "About how fucking sexy you are?" I run a finger over his six-pack (a freaking six-pack!).

He grabs my hand and holds it still. "No. You said something about only wanting me and no one else."

"Oh. You caught that?" I try to pull my hand away, but he tightens his grip.

"I'm a cop. I don't miss much."

"Is it creepy?"

He finally lets me go and rubs his hand over his face. "I don't know. Is this—" He waves his hand between the two of us. "Going to be like *Fatal Attraction*?"

Ugh. An old movie reference. Maybe I should tell him I referred to *Misery* earlier and perhaps we need to be on the same page. But then, maybe I shouldn't share that either. "No, not at all."

"Is what you said true?"

My mind starts to spin and I'm not sure how to answer. At least, without making it sound worse than it already does. I mean, I only stalked him in high school. And now we're in our early 30s, so that was a while ago. Though, I never did forget about him. And I've truly only wanted him. "I just had a silly high school crush."

"Is that all?"

The fucker sounds disappointed! *What. The. Hell.* "Well..."

He turns my face toward him. "Well, what?" he asks, his lips just above mine. Okay, he's not playing fair, and he knows it.

I meet his dark brown eyes and my breath escapes me in a rush. "It's only ever been you, Reid. I've only ever wanted you. No one else ever compared."

He blinks and his eyebrows furrow. "Why?"

I stare at his lips. I want him to kiss me. "I don't know," I murmur. "If I knew why, I wouldn't have tortured myself like this. Maybe I would have found a nice guy and settled down by now."

"You want to settle down?"

I lift a shoulder slightly. "I don't know. I don't know if I could've been happy with anyone else. I'm not sure if I could have been satisfied."

"You want to be happy." He wasn't asking me, he stated a fact.

"Of course. Everyone wants to be happy. Don't you?"

"Of course," he echoes. He brushes a knuckle down my cheek. "Are you happy right now?"

"With you in my bed? Hell yes."

He finally kisses me, his lips moving softly over mine. He keeps his mouth closed and makes the kiss almost chaste. His tenderness makes my heart melt as quickly as the candle did earlier.

CHAPTER EIGHT

REID

Do I find it a little weird that the woman stalked me throughout high school? Yes. Do I find it strange that she thinks I'm the only man for her? Absolutely. Although, I'm flattered. Besides the so-called "high school crush," she seems perfectly sane.

Besides, who can turn down that luscious body of hers. Curves in all the right places, a mouth that could make a grown man cry. Super responsive during sex, and none of my kinky desires so far have made her bat an eye. And did I mention? She lives right next door.

Right. Fucking. Next. Door.

She may be the perfect woman for me.

I'm making a lot of assumptions, though. Like she doesn't have kids, she has gainful employment, she's not on any psychotropic medication, and she won't stab me in my sleep. Simple things like that.

Maybe the next time she hits the head, I'll check her nightstand drawers for weapons.

I snort and she looks at me with curiosity.

"What?"

"Nothing," I answer. "Just thinking about that karma thing. It's laughable."

"Coincidence, karma, whatever. I'll take it."

Me, too. This has been a helluva night so far, and it isn't over yet. I glance over at her clock. I haven't stayed up this late since I was out partying in my early 20s. I can't believe I haven't passed out yet, but the woman lying next to me is keeping me energized it seems.

Could I do this every night? Hell no.

"Do you mind if I raid your fridge?"

Sydney shifts, starting to get out of bed. "What do you need? I'll get it."

I grab her arm to stop her. "No. You stay. Let me." Although I need fluids to revive my drained body, I have other nefarious reasons to go down to her kitchen.

Not to spy, even though it did cross my mind. Since we're neighbors, I'll have plenty of other opportunities to do a little digging if I need to.

I shoot her a smile. "Want anything?"

"Water, please."

I give her a nod and tromp downstairs all naked-like. Not caring if I have everything hanging out.

I grab a couple bottles of water out of the refrigerator door and my eye catches something colorful. And my mind goes south. See? I said I had nefarious reasons. I grab it and then stare in the fridge's interior, my mind spinning with other possibilities.

I dig through the freezer next. And, lo-and-behold, I get an even dirtier idea. I chuckle to myself, gather my loot, and jog back upstairs.

Okay, that's a lie. I don't have enough energy to jog, so I *drag* myself instead. That couldn't be me doing the groaning every couple of steps, could it?

As I come around the corner into her bedroom, I see her on her side, her eyes closed. Yeah, so it isn't only me who's exhausted.

I clear my throat and her eyelids slowly lift. Then widen when she sees my goodies.

"Whipped cream and ice pops? Do you need a sugar fix?"

I toss her one of the bottles of water (I'm impressed with how well she catches it), then glance at the frozen pops. "They're sugar-free."

"Oh yeah. But you brought up the whole box."

So I did.

"Are you hungry? I could have made you something with a little more substance than frozen colored water and a topping that's made with corn syrup."

I frown. "You're turning up your nose at shit you had in your own kitchen?"

She shrugs and laughs. "Yeah, well. It might be in my fridge, but it doesn't mean I eat it. I do have a couple of nieces."

"Well, I didn't bring it up for us to eat." At least, not in the usual sense.

"Oh, well then, that's different."

And, holy shit, this woman seems to be up for anything. I feel like jumping, punching my fist into the air, and screaming "Hell yeah!" But I don't, I need to save my energy because I have every intention of fucking this woman—or her fucking me—again before dawn. Once wasn't enough.

I have a feeling one night won't be enough, either.

I could see this becoming a very slippery slope where I can never get enough of her. It surprises me but worries me, too.

I shrug it off because, you know, I'm a man, and no woman will ever own me. Right?

Right.

I have to do something with the popsicles soon before they turn into Kool-Aid.

"So, what's your plan there, pop boy?" she asks me.

"Just you wait," I tell her, like I have this all thought out. Which I don't. But we can wing it. No big deal. It hits me then that the stuff probably stains, so we need to put something down on the bed. Oooooor…

Move to the bathroom where things are washable, and then we can get as messy as we want.

It also may be a good place to take out the anal plug which, by the way, is still up my ass. Not that I was going to forget about it, going up and down the stairs certainly reminded me.

"Bathroom?" I ask her, tilting my head towards it.

"Really?"

"Yeah, unless you don't care about destroying your sheets and possibly messing up your mattress."

"Okay, but you still haven't told me your plans."

"Come with me and you'll find out." I head into the bathroom to put the stuff down and check out her shower. It's average size and might be a little tight but it's a tub/shower combo and having somewhere to sit may be an advantage.

Sydney comes up behind me and brushes her fingers down my spine, between my crease, and flicks the ring on the anal plug. "Not yet?"

"No. After. When we shower."

She presses herself along my back and I can feel her hard nipples against my skin and just that alone gets my dick to wake back up. I'm proud of it. It hasn't let me down once tonight.

As her body hugs me, she reaches around to play with my cock and it doesn't take long for it to come to full attention. But she releases me too quickly and grabs the box of ice pops, pulling one out and ripping it open. I find myself cemented in place when she slides it slowly into her mouth and acts like it's the most delicious phallus in the whole wide world. I'm jealous.

It's hot watching her work the frozen treat in and out of her mouth, suck and lick the tip, and close her eyes in ecstasy.

My cock twitches and I grab it, stroking it a couple times. She takes two steps toward me and lowers herself to her knees at my feet. And, oh shit, this was not a part of my non-existent plan. But I hurry and pencil it in.

Her mouth makes little slurpy sucking sounds around the slippery pop and then she pulls it out, takes control of my hard-on to slide her cold mouth right over me.

Holy popsicle. It's a crazy feeling but—

A groan escapes me.

She alternates from sucking the pop to sucking my dick and the semi-formulated plan to use the popsicle on her disintegrates. At least for the moment. Her lips become a bright red from the cherry-flavored coloring, and she works the tip of my erection like a champ.

Every time she takes me into her ice cold mouth, it's shocking until we both heat up again. From freezing cold to burning hot. I realize what a genius I am for bringing the whole box upstairs.

As she holds the melting pop above my cock, it drips on me and she licks it away. And, fuck me, do I want to come all over her face. You'd think the cold would make me shrivel up to nothing, but no, I'm as hard as a rock. (Yeah, I did say I'm proud of myself, right?)

The floor is starting to get slippery and we need to move into the shower. So, I grab her under her arms and haul her up. She throws what's left of the stick in the sink and smiles at me. Her lips are coated with the red sticky mess and her chin needs a good wipe down. But fuck that. I jerk her to me and lick her clean. I slide my tongue over her lips and then kiss her hard until she grabs at me for balance.

Yeah, I kissed her that hard.

"Sit on the edge of the tub, feet in." I think that's the first order I've given her tonight, and she doesn't hesitate. When she settles on the edge of the tub, I grab the whipped cream canister and another pop and follow her, barely squeezing in enough to face her. "Spread your knees." She does. My cock jerks in anticipation. "That's it," I whisper and stare at her pussy. It's pink and smooth and looks so much more edible than the dessert in my hand.

I drop to my knees between her legs and squirt some whipped cream into my mouth. Then I kiss her again. I open wide and invite her in, her tongue scooping the sweet cream from me.

Fuck, the intimacy of that makes me want to come.

I pull away and squirt some on her lips as an excuse to suck on her bottom lip. Then I move to her breasts and cover her nipples completely with the sticky topping. I draw a pattern over her belly and down to her hips. Then follow it with my lips, my tongue, and my teeth as I nibble along her skin, making sure to uncover those perky nipples of hers.

"You are the best dessert I've ever eaten," I murmur. And it's true.

Her answering chuckle makes me want to fuck her right then and there, but I didn't bring the popsicles upstairs to just let them melt. Though, I'm quickly bored with the dessert topping and put it to the side to concentrate on the grape ice pop in my hand. I push her knees open even wider.

"Open yourself up to me. I want to see you."

"Like this?" she asks, her eyes shadowed and her breathing shallow between her parted lips.

"Yes, like that," I whisper, pressing the slick end of the frozen pop to her clit. She jerks and cries out at the shock of cold. I pull it away and replace it with my hot mouth. I do it again and again. Cold then hot until her fingers dig into my shoulders, her back arches, and she throws her head back. Before the pop can melt down too far, I slip it into her, slowly fucking her with it. I suck her clit, working the popsicle in and out of her as it drips down her thighs, the side of the tub, and pools at my knees. When that's gone, I grab another out of the box and continue until she's about to explode. As long as I don't explode first.

I remove what's left of the pop from her and press it against her nipple, watching it pucker into a hard peak. Her body breaks out in goosebumps and she shivers. She takes the pop from my fingers and circles both nipples with it, leaving trails of orange flavored liquid behind. The drips run down the curves of her breasts and over her belly, collecting in the narrow patch of hair above her pussy.

She reminds me of a piece of art, with orange, purple, and red colors painted over her body. My ex-wife would never have allowed herself to look like this, to be so messy. But not Sydney, she takes it in stride. She's having as much fun as I am. As the pops melt, the discarded wooden sticks end up stuck to the bottom and sides of the tub.

She unwraps the last one and stands. It's another grape. She starts to draw over my body so I'm just as sticky and messy as her. She giggles as she writes her name across my back. She decorates my face with "war paint." She turns my nipples just as hard as hers, but she laps the grape flavoring away and holy hell, I knew I liked my nipples played with but her sucking and flicking them with her tongue makes me want to spin her around and fuck her from behind.

I must have made a sound, because she says, "Mmm. You like when I suck your nipples."

Hell yeah, I do, but I can only grunt an answer and dig my fingers into her hair to hold her in place. She sucks them harder, scraping her teeth over the tiny tips. I drop one hand down to cup her ass, pulling her tighter against me to thrust against her belly. I don't want to come yet, but I just might not be able to stop myself.

Especially when she squeezes my balls at the same time she nips my nipple. *Fuck.*

"I'm buying Fudgsicles next time I'm at the store," she murmurs against my chest. I want to laugh but I can't, because I'm too busy picturing myself fucking her with a fudge pop. Or watching her fuck herself. It's fucking weird, true, but it's hot, too. There may be another place on her where I want to stick a Fudgsicle. Which quickly brings me back to my dilemma.

The anal plug. But I want to fuck her once more with it in first. And though I brought the freezer pops and the whipped cream canister into the bathroom with us, I forgot the most important thing. Condoms. They are still in the bedroom and even though they are only steps away, it seems like a trek to Siberia.

"Get the condoms," she orders me, like she's reading my mind. I can't say no to her command, so I climb out of the tub, quickly find them and hurry back to the bathroom, and I almost blow my load right there.

Her back is pressed to the shower wall, her feet propped on the edge of the tub and one hand is busy between her thighs, the other squeezing a breast. Holy fuck, I want to remember this sight forever. I lean against the door jamb and take a mental picture of this moment. Her eyes closed, her lips parted, and the sounds that escape her as she brings herself quickly to orgasm, drives me just about out of my mind. Damn, I'm jealous of her hand right now.

"Don't move," I tell her when she opens her eyes and smiles at me. "Stay just like that."

I rip open a condom with my teeth, sheath myself, and step into the tub between her spread thighs. I take some of her weight into my hands by cupping her sweet ass and she guides me inside her.

Oh, holy hell. Holy motherfucking hell. Her hot pussy encases me completely. When she ripples around my cock, I fucking grit my teeth to keep from coming right away. Every time I pump into her, my ass clenches around the plug and it feels like a sex train, where I'm fucking her and someone is fucking me. And it's absolutely glorious.

My cock can't get any harder, or my balls any tighter. As her thighs squeeze me, her hands loop around my neck, her fingernails dig into my back. When she sinks her teeth into my throat, I slam her even harder, faster, making her cry out against my skin. She bites me harder and I grunt, stilling within her.

When I'm finally able to slow my out-of-control spinning, I make the tiniest of movements within her. I need her to come before I do. And she needs to do it soon, so I furiously work her magic spot and she clenches around me, squeezing. Her teeth scrape along my shoulder and finds purchase in the muscle above my collarbone. I jerk as pain shoots through me, but my cock hardens even more. I'm so close. I want to spill inside her so badly, but she needs to come first.

She needs to come first.

When she releases my skin, she cries out, "I'm coming!" And... *fuck,* she climaxes around me, her body squeezing me like a fist. I want to collapse to my knees, but I can't, I'm holding her up against the wall and I'm about to blow my load. I release a curse and my cum explodes from me with a force that I swear makes me see spots. I empty myself inside her with a shudder. In an attempt to catch my breath, my chest heaves as I gulp air. This definitely wasn't a marathon session, but I was already exhausted and my body can't take much more of this long night.

Sydney's eyes remain closed, her head leans back against the shower wall, and her lungs pump oxygen as fast as mine. I doubt she can last much longer, either.

I don't want to pull out because I want to stay a part of her as long as I can. I have a feeling we're going to end up in a crumpled heap once I do.

"That was fucking amazing," she says without opening her eyes. "Crazy, but amazing."

I second that, but haven't recovered enough to be able to stitch two words together yet. I simply nod and press my forehead against hers, closing my eyes for a moment.

When she drops her feet down to the bottom of the tub, she dislodges me and I'm overcome with disappointment at the sense of loss. After I toss the condom into a nearby wastebasket, she twists and pulls at the shower faucet, and when the cool water hits us we both shout in shock and then laugh as it warms up and soothes our tired muscles.

She grabs the poof hanging off the shower head and I take it from her. "Let me." After squishing some shower gel into it, I lather her body gently, as if it's made of delicate crystal. I take my time washing away the stickiness and the mess from her luscious body.

Which, again I admit to myself, I can't get enough of. Though, my cock isn't having any of it, and hangs flaccid as if on strike.

After she's clean, I shampoo her long dark hair and she groans in pleasure. While conditioner soaks into her tresses, we switch spots and she takes the poof from me and soaps me down, making sure to get into every crack and crevice.

Damn, showering together seems so intimate that my chest squeezes. If you don't count high school, I haven't even known the woman twenty-four hours yet, but I'm addicted already.

The tables might be turning... she was obsessed with me during our teens, I may be obsessed now that we're adults.

I can only hope she'll want more than this one night.

When the shower spray rinses off the last of the suds, I realize it's time to get down to business. It's time to pull the plug. (Literally.)

I wonder if I should ask her to step out and do it in private because I don't want to embarrass myself. But I also think it may be cool if she's willing to help. She's the one who shoved it up my ass in the first place, anyhow.

"Do you... uh..."

"Yes," she answers, anticipating my uncomfortable request.

"Okay, well..."

"Turn around," she demands and I smirk before I do what I'm told. "Brace your hands on the wall."

I spread my legs and plant my palms like she says and it feels like I'm about to be patted down before being arrested.

Hmm. Role-playing. We may have to try that one night in the future. I shake the thought out of my head and concentrate on the task at hand.

"Squat down and relax your... muscles," she tells me and I look over my shoulder at her. Really? She acts like she's a pro at this and I know she's not. But, hey, I don't have a better idea, so I bend my knees and sink down a little bit. I feel a tug and a wiggle and a pull, and I'm not sure if I actually like the feeling or if I should be mortified that I'm in this position with a woman who, by all intents and purposes, I really "just met."

Someone who I'll have to wave to daily when I check my mail. As I laugh at my stupid thought the plug pops out, although certainly not as easy as going in. And, damn, it hadn't been easy going in either.

But I can't say I didn't like the experience, so it's staying in my goodie box for future use.

If I'm lucky and Sydney is willing, I'll be adding to my collection as well.

And, hopefully, I end up being one lucky son-of-a-bitch.

CHAPTER NINE

SYDNEY

R*eid Fucking Turner* actually toweled me off and dried my hair. Dried my hair! (With a hairdryer and everything.) The man I wanted my whole life (well, almost) is eating out of my palm. How the hell did this happen?

Not that I'm complaining. But I still keep thinking I'm going to wake up from a dream and find out he didn't really move next door, and I imagined having him tied to my bed earlier.

Boy, would that fucking suck.

The best part is he isn't an asshole either. He's freaking hot, sexy, great in bed, and he's… nice! So yeah, any moment I'm going to wake up and be disappointed that I'm alone in my bed and the only thing I got fucked with was my trusty vibrator.

Watch it turn out my new neighbor isn't Reid, it's some fat, hairy Italian guy who smells like pepperoni and garlic.

That would be more my luck.

But if it's a dream, it's an awesome one, I think to myself as I watch Reid gather the sex toys that are scattered all over my bedroom floor. As he tosses them in his "old photos" box (isn't he clever) I can see the ripple of his muscles under his skin. Ooo, baby.

If I wasn't so tired, I'd jump his bones. Again. But as it is, I think I'm going to need a wheelchair to get around tomorrow. I glance at the clock next to the bed. Or later today.

Sadness creeps over me as I realize dawn will arrive soon and Reid will have to put his clothes on. When he's done hunting and gathering his sex toys, he stands by the bed with his box of goodies. My heart skips a beat because I think he's about to leave.

"You going?" I ask him, keeping my expression blank.

Unmistakable disappointment crosses his face. "I... uh... Do you want me to?"

"Fuck no!" I want to scream. But I don't, I grip the sheets in my fingers and fight that urge. "Not really. You might as well stay the rest of the ni—morning."

He sets the box down by my bedroom door and I can't resist staring at his muscular ass as he does so. He turns to face me and I smile innocently.

"Well, I can take you to breakfast in the morning... if you want."

Really? Is *Reid Fucking Turner* asking me on a breakfast date? I run my fingers through my hair. "I probably look like shit."

He puts a knee on the bed, snags my hand, and kisses the knuckles. "You look beautiful."

"And freshly fucked?" A smile twitches at my lips.

"Definitely well fucked."

"I don't want this to go to your head or anything, but... tonight has got to be the best night I've ever had. The sex with you was everything I ever expected."

He drops my hand and climbs onto the bed, walking on his hands and knees until he's directly over me, staring right into my face. I blink when he asks, "You thought about having sex with me a lot?"

Look, we're both naked. We've both seen each other in various positions (naked). The man's been inside of me (naked). So really there's no reason to hide the (naked) truth. "Reid, you've been my masturbation material since the ninth grade."

He cocks a brow. "That long, huh?"

"Oh yeah. That long."

"And is the real thing better than the fantasy?"

Damn. The fantasies were pretty good, though. "The real thing is better than my own fingers."

"Or a vibrator?"

All right, now he's gone too far. "Well…"

"Damn, that hurts." He smacks his lips against mine then falls to my side, gathering me into his arms and pulling me tight to his side.

"Well, I did name my favorite vibrator Reid."

He turns his head to face me. "Yeah?"

"Yeah."

"Is that the one you were using when I saw you through the window and you called out my name?"

"Maybe."

His low chuckle makes his chest rumble and I can't help but smile at the sound. Why the hell did his wife fuck around on him? I don't get it.

It's only ever been him for me. Now that I have him, I'm not letting him go. No way. I think of all the wasted years we spent apart. All those years he was with Pam to have her only screw him over in the end.

I, Sydney Ryan, solemnly swear to never screw *Reid Fucking Turner* over.

I reach over and pinch him.

"Ow!" He jerks his arm away and rubs it. "What was that for?"

"I just want to make sure I'm not dreaming," I tell him, turning my head away so he can't see my smirk.

"If you're going to pinch me, at least pinch me somewhere good." Now I jerk when he pinches me back. "See? You're not dreaming."

I roll onto my side and study his face. He studies mine. "I'm glad. Now about that breakfast…"

Before I can finish, his eyes slowly slide shut from exhaustion. I end up watching him sleep until the dawn's sun peeks through the drawn curtains. And I have to say...

Reid Fucking Turner is one man I won't avoid a morning meal with.

~The End~

An Obsessed Novella

NEEDING *Him*

Jeanne St. James

This is not just a love story, it's an obsession...

Grace:

The same week every year he comes to my little resort in Maine for five days, then disappears. His darkness, his demons, intrigue me and I need to know his story.

I hope he shows up again this year, because I'm determined to talk to him, make him see me and not look through me like I don't exist. Make him realize I'm not just some anonymous person who hands him a key.

No, this year will be different.

I haven't gotten laid in a long time. So, *tag*, he's it.

Nick:

For the past three years, I've come up to this remote area to forget, to bury my grief. But this year, I don't need a trip to this run-down resort, this little cabin on the lake, to survive this week. However, there's one thing I've left behind each year when I head back to reality…

Her.

I've found the right woman who'll fill the emptiness deep inside of me, the hole that's lurked there for years. I can't get her out of my head. Funny thing is, I don't even know her name. I never asked.

This year that's going to change. And I hope she's willing because I'm taking complete control.

Note: All books in the Obsessed series are standalone novellas. They are intended for audiences over 18 years of age since they include explicit sexual situations, including BDSM.

CHAPTER ONE

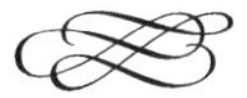

Grace:

Every year he shows up. He comes for five days and then disappears. Same week, every year, for the past three years. Arrives on a Sunday night and leaves Friday morning.

He hardly says a word to me. He picks up the keys to his cabin with a couple grunts, then locks himself in for the duration. I don't know if he sleeps, eats or what. All I know is I'm not to disturb him in any fashion. He made that perfectly clear in a surly manner the first year.

I'm just glad I have an occupant. He never quibbles about the price of the cabin, never asks me for anything. Never complains.

The best part is, he comes during the off season when it's so slow I think I'll become destitute. Be homeless and starve.

But, I watch him. He intrigues me and I want to know his story. Why this small town in Maine? Why this time of year?

Why?

And, last but not least, why is my tired little lakeside resort his choice? Yes, the area is beautiful, but it's remote. Though, it's not like he goes out hiking, or mountain biking, or even boating on the large lake.

Maybe that's what he needs. Quiet. Peace.

Me? I get too much peace and quiet. This town bores me to death. Anyone with any ambition escapes as soon as they can.

Though, I can't get myself to run away. I can't even walk away.

This was my father's resort. When he died, he left it to his only daughter. Hell, his only child. He took pride in this place, he built it with his own hands. So, of course, I take pride in it, too.

Even though it bores the fuck out of me.

And the dating scene?

Non-existent. If I'm lucky, I get laid when tourists come to moose watch in the summer. If I'm lucky, I get laid when the snowmobilers blow into town and take over the frozen lake and the nearby trails. If I'm lucky, I get laid when mountain bikers come and ride through the woods when the leaves are changing colors.

But, let's just say, I haven't been very lucky lately. Not in a long time. I swear I've converted back to a virgin, if that's even possible.

Fortunately, I'm not uptight and can take care of my own needs. Though, that gets lonely and boring, too. Batteries and my vibrators have become my best friends.

Honestly, I really just need to get the fuck out of this town.

I sigh and look at my reservation book. Yes, book, because even the Internet sucks up here. And cell towers? Yeah, right. You may get a signal if you stand on your head and face North while singing *Yankee Doodle Dandy*.

Every cabin is still equipped with landline phones and the only television comes from a satellite dish, which only works when it isn't cloudy, raining, snowing, or the birds aren't chirping.

My heart races as I see his name written in my unreadable scribble. But, I know it's him. I've reserved his regular cabin.

Not that any of the other cabins are booked since it's the shoulder season. No one in their right mind is here. The leaves are now brown and falling, the lake too cold to swim in, but too warm for winter activities.

He made his reservation for this year before he left last year.

I hope he shows. Even at the deep discounted rate I've given him for coming at this time of year, every penny counts.

That's not the only reason I hope he comes. No, this year I'm determined to talk to him, make him see me, and not look completely through me like I don't exist. Make him realize I'm not just some anonymous person who hands him a key and makes him sign a receipt.

No, this year it's going to be different.

I haven't gotten laid in a long time.

So, tag. He's it.

***Nick*:**

Once again, I'm making this fucking long-assed trip to the middle of Nowhere, Maine. And I have no idea why.

No, I know. I just don't want to completely admit it to myself. Or think about it too hard.

I don't need this place anymore.

I'm almost back to normal.

Whatever that means.

For the past three years, I've come up here to forget. To bury my grief. But, this year, I'm sure I don't need this trip, this run-down resort, this little cabin on the lake, to survive this week.

Not this year.

So, that's not the reason I'm taking this six-hour drive to a place that has shitty TV service, no cell coverage or Wi-Fi, right?

Not that I can't use a break from my hectic schedule at work. I can. But, I could do that somewhere better. Like Aruba, not

Bumfuck, Maine, where it isn't warm, and the water is too cold to swim.

But, there's one thing I've left behind each year when I head back to reality.

Her.

And she's the reason I'm making this long trek again. Only a mere six hours from the city, from my everyday life.

Though, wouldn't that just suck if she hooked up with one of the locals in the past year? Got married, is barefoot and pregnant, gained fifty pounds, and now wears a mu-mu and slippers around the place.

Damn.

If so, I would turn around and drive another six hours home, repack my bag, and jump on a flight to somewhere else.

Maybe not Aruba, maybe South Beach. Where the women are bangin' and I may get a little banging myself.

It's been too long.

Way too long.

And I'm so ready.

But I can't get her out of my head.

And I don't know why.

Funny thing is, I don't even know her name. I never asked.

My bad.

CHAPTER TWO

GRACE

When his car pulls up, I not only hear it, but see it. And for good reason. I've been waiting on pins and needles for him to arrive. My German Shepherd, Magpie AKA Maggie, lets out a wimpy bark and gives me a look.

Thanks for letting me know the hot stud just arrived, dog. Like I hadn't noticed myself. Does my dog even know my nefarious plans? She might be ashamed of me if she did.

My breath catches as I hear his car door slam and his heavy footsteps approach the office. Soon his big body will be in this tiny office with me.

When the door swings open, my heart thumps all the way into my neck and I freeze as Maggie gives him a soft woof and wags her tail. Yeah, she's no guard dog, that's for damn sure. But she's good company, even though she has no choice in the matter, since she gets paid in kibble to live here.

My gaze raises from Maggie to the man patting her on the head and pushing his way past the sixty-five-pound useless security system.

I open my mouth to greet him and I squeak.

Actually. Fucking. Squeak.

I frown for a second, then quickly recover my nervous smile, and try again. "Welcome back, Mr. Landis," I get out this time like a normal person.

One side of his mouth turns up. And, *oh fuck,* it's sexy as hell. "Thanks. Good to be back."

Wait. What?

The man actually answered me? I didn't just get a bunch of grunts?

As he stands there smiling down at Maggie, petting her, she's looking up at him in adoration and I'm jealous. His hands are on her. Her eyes are on him.

I'm jealous of my freaking dog.

What a bitch.

"What's her name?"

Wait. What?

Uh…

"She has a name, right?"

"Yes… It's Magpie."

His eyebrows twitch. "Magpie?"

"Maggie."

He smiles again, not at me, but *at my dog.* "Hey, Magster, good to see you again."

What. The. Fuck.

However, as I think about it, he's not only saying words to me, but he's talking to my dog. So, I wonder if he's now on medication. He's never been this talkative nor this openly friendly.

Weird.

With a last pat to Maggie's head, he takes the two steps (yes, that's how small my office is) to the counter, and stares right into my eyes.

I blink. Then blink again. And when he gives *me* a smile, I just about come in my pants.

(I said it's been that long. Don't judge.)

But instead of having an orgasm, I stutter. "I… I… Uh." I shut my mouth, spit the marbles out, and try again. "I reserved the same cabin as last year. I hope that's okay."

"Perfect." His low, deep voice makes me quake in my boots. A rush of warmth lands between my thighs.

What happened to the broody man that had been here three times before? I almost don't recognize this new guy.

Although, I'm not complaining. Like I hoped, he's actually *seeing* me. And I hope he likes what he sees.

I'm wearing my best-fitting jeans, a soft maroon V-neck sweater (the only one I have that shows any cleavage), the only push-up bra I own, and my only pair of unpractical boots (and by unpractical, I mean it has a small wide heel). So, it isn't going to get any better than that.

I study his face. The hollows under his cheekbones have disappeared. He's filled out, but then the first couple years he'd been super thin, had dark circles under his eyes, and seemed moody.

Not that he ever looked bad, even then. But now, he looks even better.

Oh so much better.

His flashing grey eyes study me back and I realize how rude it is of me to stare. I wonder how he'll react if I brush my fingers over his tight beard, or his short dark hair. The beard is new, the short hair is not.

The facial hair fits him, though. He looks more rugged, like an outdoorsy man, not one from the city where I know he's from.

Who cares where it looks like he came from, I can't wait to see him naked.

If he wants to go for the rugged look, being naked holding a carabiner in his hand will work.

If he wants to go for the slick city look, wearing a necktie around his wrists when I tie him to the bed will work, too.

I won't be picky.

However, I will be demanding.

Because I did say it's been a long time for me, didn't I? (I'm pretty sure I did.)

Right.

The man wears a soft grey, cotton button-down shirt which matches his eyes (completely unbuttoned) with a white T-shirt underneath it.

Aaaaaaand… I'm still staring like a sex-starved woman (which I am).

I drop my gaze to the reservation book and clear my throat.

Then I hear a chuckle which makes heat rush into my cheeks. Without looking up, I ask, "Would you like daily room service?"

"Absolutely." The way he makes that one word sound, it might as well have been a dirty word he whispered into my ear. I quickly look up and see the crinkles around the corner of his eyes as if he's amused.

He's never wanted anyone to bother him or his cabin before when he's visited. This year he does.

Interesting.

I slide the key across the counter and before I can pull my hand away, he covers it with his.

"What did you say your name was?" Now it's his turn to look embarrassed because he's never asked and probably just realized it (though, you better believe I'm well aware of that).

I swallow hard. "Grace."

"Grace." My name comes out of his mouth like a whisper and something low in my belly heats up, perks my nipples, makes me want to leap over the counter and shove my tongue down his throat and other places.

But I don't. Instead, I pull at my hand. Not hard, just enough so he'll release it. He doesn't. Instead, he curls his fingers tighter for a moment before finally letting my hand go. I stare at it like it will never be the same again, then shake myself mentally.

"That's a beautiful name."

Uh… "Thanks, Mr. Landis."

"Nick."

"What?"

"I'm Nick."

"Yes, I know." I point to the reservation book and my horrible handwriting. "I have it written down."

"Please call me that."

Uh… "Okay."

"Nick," he says again.

"Okay… Nick."

When he smiles at me, I just about melt. This man is not the same man who first arrived four Octobers ago.

I'm not saying I don't like this new Nick. I do. But he's different, which makes me suspicious. Not that I can help that, it's just my nature.

But, look, I need to get laid, and I already tagged him to do the job, so I'll take Nick anyway I can get him. New Nick, Old Nick, Nick on his back, Nick sitting, standing, doing the hokey pokey. Don't care.

Finally, he turns to leave and I sigh quietly. Not in relief because he's leaving, but because his ass in his Levi's looks absolutely spectacular (with a capital S).

"Do you need help with your luggage?"

He stops and glances at me over his shoulder, once again appearing amused. "Do you have a bell boy?"

He knows I don't. "No."

"Then I got it. I'm good. But, thank you anyway."

"Sure," I say and watch with disappointment as he walks out the front door and closes it behind him.

Sagging behind the counter, I peer down at Maggie. "You lucky shit, you. He had his hands all over you. But I'm next. So, keep your paws off him, you hear?"

Maggie sits with a thump, her tail swishing across the floor, as her tongue lolls out the side of her mouth.

"Okay, girl, now that he's here, I need to formulate a plan."

I hear Nick's car start and pull away from my small log ranch home that houses the office. He always stays in the farthest cabin from the house so he has privacy.

Again, not that there's anyone else on the property except for me and him.

However, this year, he's not getting any solitude. Though, I hope he doesn't mind, I'm not sure I care if he does. I've got one mission. And that's...

Operation End Dry Spell.

And he's been recruited.

For some reason, I missed his phone call last night, but he left a message on the office answering machine.

"Grace, can I get some extra towels delivered?"

Towels. *Delivered*. Apparently, last night while Maggie and I were busy formulating Operation End Dry Spell, I missed the biggest (not to mention, easiest) opportunity to get into his cabin (and possibly his pants). With his permission, at least.

I look at the clock. Seven AM. It's early, he probably hasn't showered yet and I certainly can be accommodating by bringing him an extra towel or two. I grab a laundry basket, throw in some clean towels, an extra wash cloth, and a couple homemade muffins I made the day before.

Because, you know, food is a way to a man's heart. Not that I want his heart, I need something a little stiffer than that...

I ask myself if I should bring him some fresh brewed coffee to go with the muffins, but that might take too much time and I'm anxious.

Not to mention, a little bit excited. To say the least.

I wonder if I should take some condoms with me (just in case). I could always tuck them in between the towels until they're needed.

Then I realize, *dummy me,* I forgot to buy them. I threw my other box out because they expired.

Yes, *expired.*

Because that's how long it has been since I've needed condoms.

So now what?

Go with the flow. Operation End Dry Spell was under way and a little thing like being unprepared isn't going to slow me down. If it doesn't go as planned, I'll make a trip into town later this afternoon and stock up. Well, as long as Mrs. Sanders isn't working the cash register, because if she is? Everyone in Greenville will know I'm trying to get laid.

Not that they'll know by who. But they'll wonder. Even start guessing. And the next thing you know, they'll have me sleeping with Floyd at the Test 'N' Tune garage. Even though Floyd is about one hundred years old (not really, but he kind of looks it). Then Floyd might have a heart attack if he hears that and it'll be all my fault.

For just buying a box of condoms.

Shit.

As I throw the basket in the back of the golf cart I use to putt around the property, Maggie jumps into the passenger seat and off we go down the dirt lane to the very last cabin.

With the golf cart, it only takes a couple minutes and I pull up next to his black Infiniti SUV which is parked in the grass in front of the log cabin. The moose themed curtains are pulled closed across the wide, lone window (which I admit needs replaced). I suck in some oxygen in an effort to soothe my nerves. But that's a fat ol' failure.

Instead, I give myself a little pep talk. Not loud. No. Like under my breath, but apparently, Maggie can hear me muttering, since she's watching my face and tilting her head, probably thinking I've gone off the deep end.

"Don't look at me like that. You eat poop. No judging."

Maggie practically smiles at me, jumps out of the cart and sniffs the SUV. Then tracks the ground following Nick's scent to the faded stained front door where she whines.

I get my ass moving before the dog actually knocks on the door and Nick lets her in. For some reason, I can picture both of them having a wonderful time together while I'm outside looking in.

Tucking the laundry basket under my right arm, I approach and hesitantly knock, then listen for any sound of movement.

Nothing.

I knock a lot harder this time and…

Still nothing.

I glance around, wondering if he went out for an early morning walk. But there's no one around but me and Maggie, so if he's out for a stroll, he's far enough away where I can't spot him. I transfer the basket under my left arm and knock one more time, not quite pounding but close.

"Mr. Landis?" I call out. "Nick? I've got the towels you requested."

Not a peep. I look down at Maggie, she looks up at me, sneezes, then looks at the door like she's waiting for me to open it.

Hmm.

Yes, I can just let myself in, drop off his towels, and come back later.

Good idea, Maggie! My dog's so smart.

I tentatively turn the handle, checking to see if I need to use my master key, but the knob turns. Wherever he went, he left his door unlocked.

Not that this isn't a safe area. It is. But still…

The hinges creak a little when I slowly push the wood door open. WD-40 is my first thought. Then as I peer into the dark interior of the small cabin, my second thought is…

Holy fuck.

Nick Landis sprawls across the bed on his belly from corner to corner, his head turned away from the door, the sheet barely covering his long, naked body, one teeny-tiny corner of it crosses over his hips. And there's clearly nothing between him and the sheet which is wrinkled like he'd slept restlessly. He's completely bare.

Yes, bare.

And not the bad type of bear (which we have in the area), but the good type of bare (which I haven't seen in way too long).

Yessssss.

Frozen in the doorway, I clear my throat, hoping he'll turn and see me. I get nothing. His back rises and falls like he's now sleeping soundly. Maggie's nails clip along the wide planked floor as she heads to the bed to check on the sleeping man. (Did I say he's totally naked? Because he is!)

"Maggie!" I whisper in a bit of a panic, then freeze when she nuzzles his armpit with her nose.

I make a low noise, one that means, "Oh fuck me. She's going to wake him up, and he'll catch me staring at him while he slept and think I'm a weirdo stalker." And being considered a weirdo stalker will not get me laid.

I think about dropping the basket on the nearby table and rushing out of the room before he catches me, but Maggie's having none of that.

She shoves her muzzle deeper under his arm. Did I mention that she's an attention whore? She probably just wants his hands all over her again.

I slide the laundry basket onto the table and almost knock over a half-empty bottle of whiskey.

Fuck.

Apparently, he didn't fix his problems. In the past few years, after he's checked out, he's left behind a bunch of empty bottles in the trash. And by a bunch, I mean more than one person should drink by himself.

I figure since his attitude seems changed this year that maybe it won't be the same. But it appears it is. Maybe he isn't over whatever he comes up here to escape from.

That being said, he's probably passed out in bed in an alcohol-induced stupor and not really sleeping.

Damn it, I'll never get laid if he stays in a drunken/hangover/passed-out stage all week.

I move closer to the bed, stepping tentatively in case he really *is* sleeping.

"Nick?" I whisper. "Are you okay?"

At least if he hears me, then he'll think I'm only checking on him, concerned about his well-being and not planning on jumping his bones.

"Nick? Mr. Landis?"

Still nothing. However, no one sleeps that heavily.

I approach the bed on the side nearest the door, opposite where Maggie is. Opposite of where his face is turned.

I bravely poke at his shoulder.

All of a sudden, he moves. I don't (since I'm now frozen in place once again). And he groans. Which makes *me* want to groan because I can imagine him doing that while he's inside me.

Fuck. I squeeze my thighs together.

I shake myself mentally because maybe he's hurt and needs assistance. It's been a while since I've been CPR certified, but I'm sure I can administer mouth-to-mouth to Nick without a problem. He may enjoy it, too.

Give him a little slip of the tongue and—

His hand snakes out with super human speed and snags my wrist. Before I can react, I'm twisting through the air and landing on my back with a soft *oomph*. Suddenly, I find myself pinned to the bed with a heavy weight on me.

Not surprisingly, that weight is one hundred percent Nick.

His face is only a few inches from mine and I'm breathing heavily. Probably due to the fact I was just knocked off my feet, and maybe a little due to the fact that the man is now very naked and very hard against my thigh.

Damn.

Nah.

Hot damn!

Both of my wrists are encircled tightly within his fingers and my arms stretch over my head. When he nudges a knee between my thighs, it presses against my very needy pussy.

Let me just say, I think I tagged the right man. (Go, me!)

"You bring my towels?"

His voice sounds rough from non-use and goosebumps break out all over my body, including my two biggest ones, my nipples. I'm wearing a stylish, purple long-sleeve thermal T that fits snuggly enough that he won't be able to miss them. Especially since they press into his chest.

Did I mention he's naked?

Yeah.

I kick myself into action. Operation End Dry Spell is a go.

"Yes. Sorry I missed your call last night." My voice is so breathless that I sound like I just orgasmed. Which I may have. Just a little bit. "I brought your towels... And a couple muffins, just in case you're hungry."

"Grace."

His deep voice saying my name stops my roll and I blink.

"I'm hungry."

Oh yeah, so am I.

"But not for a muffin."

How about that? Neither am I. "Well, there's a diner in town—"

"Grace," he stops me again and I meet his gaze. His eyes are dark grey now and burning into my soul. Though, I'll be glad to sell him my soul for a really, really great orgasm.

"Yeah?"

"I'm not hungry for breakfast."

"Okay," I whisper.

"You know what I'm hungry for, Grace?"

I'm hoping me. "What?"

"You."

Yeah. I was right. I'd high five Maggie right now if I could.

"You were supposed to show up last night," he murmurs, staring at my lips.

I lick them out of nervousness. "I—"

"Then we would have had all night. Now we need to make up for lost time."

We do?

Oh. We do.

Yes. I agree. One hundred percent.

"Okay."

One corner of his lips lift. He has a beautiful mouth. Stunning eyes. And from what I can feel, he's no slouch downstairs either.

"I've been waiting for this," he murmurs a hair's breadth from my lips.

"You have?" I also murmur, wishing he'd kiss me.

"I have."

"Me, too."

"Good to hear that."

"Why?" I ask and then curse myself because he pulls back a little bit, going the exact opposite direction I want him to go.

"Why what?" he asks, looking somewhat confused.

"Why me?"

"Because I haven't stopped thinking about you since I left last year."

Now I'm the one somewhat confused. "Oh."

He smiles.

I smile.

Then he lowers his head once again and asks almost against my lips, "Do you want this?"

"Yes," I hiss. I don't just want this, I need this.

"Is there anything you won't do?"

What? Uh...

But before I can ask him to clarify what he means, he crushes his lips to mine and I sigh into his mouth. He kisses me like he's a starved man and I am his respite. I quickly forget his question as his tongue sweeps over my lips and explores my mouth. He tilts his head slightly to bring us tighter together. And now I'm moaning into his mouth.

I usually don't kiss the guys I sleep with... the mountain bikers, the snowmobilers, the fall leaf peepers. None of them. Because they're one-night stands and kissing is an intimate act for me.

But, I like Nick kissing me and realize at that moment that, no, there won't be anything I won't do with Nick.

Because it's Nick.

And I feel like after the last three years I know him better than any other man I've been with. Even though that might not really be true because I really don't know him at all. But I feel I know him deep down inside, deep in my bones, deep in my psyche. Nick is mine. Even if only for the next few days.

There's always been something about him that's intrigued me, even when he was moody and seemed to be in a deep funk. I liked him then. I like him now.

Now that his weight presses on top of me and he's kissing the shit out of me, making me wet, making my pussy pulse in need, I like him even more.

How can I not? I'm all systems a-go in Operation End Dry Spell.

He breaks the kiss and his eyes appear dark and stormy as he meets mine. "You're not resisting."

"No." Of course not, this may be the smoothest operation in history.

"Do you like to play with toys, Grace?"

Fuck, I love when he says my name with his deep, gruff voice.

He cocks an eyebrow at me and I realize he's waiting for an answer. "Yes," I say, thinking about the battery-operated boyfriends I have in my drawer. BOBs, as in plural. Like potato chips, you can't have just one. "Should I go get mine?"

"I brought my own."

Oh. He has toys. Then I start to wonder what kind of toys a man has. But, I think I'm going to find out.

"I'll ask you again, is there anything you won't do?" As he asks me this (quite firmly, I might add), he tilts his hips and his hard length slides along my inner thigh. It's a question that makes me more curious about these toys of his. A thrill runs down my spine.

In my limited experience, I've never come across anything I didn't want to do. However, I'm getting this feeling that Nick has a lot more experience than me and he's not thinking along the same lines as I am.

Which makes my mind spin. "Can you give me an example?"

He spits them out like a machine gun, not giving me a chance to answer. "Spanking?"

I...

"Anal play?"

Uh...

"Being restrained?"

Oh...

"Blindfolded?"

Yes...

"And more."

There's more? "I've never done any of those things," I finally whisper shakily, excited but anxious at the same time.

"Are you willing?" When I hesitate, he adds, "With me, Grace?"

Hell yeah! Because who knows when the next opportunity will come along for me to get laid.

But instead, I say (like I'm coy), "I would be willing to try."

He smiles again, his eyes crinkling at the corners. "I had a feeling you would. I won't do anything you don't want to. You can trust me."

My muscles relax as a little bit of the tension leaves my body. I'm a woman alone in the woods with a man I've only seen a few times, never really had a real conversation with, and I'm well aware he's been fighting some sort of demons every time he's come here to stay.

I don't know what kind of demons, so I may be putting myself into unknown danger.

However, this will be the most excitement I've ever had in my life in this boring town and I'm not going to pass up the opportunity to get naked with Nick, even if it means the possibility of a few rope burns and bruises.

As long as the only thing he's stabbing me with is his cock, I'm good.

Foolish, maybe. But, I'll have my trusty German Shepherd to guard me. Right?

Sure.

I turn my head slightly and can't see her. Maggie's probably asleep in the corner already having doggy dreams.

Sigh.

"If you don't want to do something, just tell me," he says, releasing my wrists and pushing up and away from me. His words make me wonder if I'm making the right decision.

But, then I get an eyeful of his cock, which I already knew was hard, but now I can see its beauty. Long and thick, his sac hangs heavy beneath it. A light dusting of hair covers his leanly built chest. A dark strip continues down his belly and then thickens around his groin and lightens up again down his muscular thighs. He's still a little leaner than I like, but, damn, he looks good. When he turns away from the bed, I take in his broad back and the dimples right above his round, muscular ass.

He doesn't bother to cover up. (And, *oh lordy*, he shouldn't.)

I study him as he moves toward an open suitcase tucked into the corner of the cabin.

"There's going to be rules," he informs me, still facing the suitcase, his back to me. I push myself up to my elbows, watching him, listening, wondering if I should get undressed.

"Don't touch yourself. I will touch you. Don't ask. Don't beg. I will let you know when and if you can. You wait for my permission. Do you understand?"

Okay, then. "Yes."

"I tell you to do something, you do it. No complaints, no hesitation. You do it and you'll be rewarded."

I've never had anyone this bossy during sex. My sexcapades usually only consisted of wham-bam-thank-you-ma'am hit and runs, though without the thank you. Not that I was buying them a Hallmark card afterward either, but still…

Was I that sex-starved I'd let any man boss me around?

No, not any man… Nick.

Yes, I might be a bit desperate for an orgasm (not self-induced), but this bossy shit admittedly turns me the fuck on.

This man's voice, his manner, controls me. Owns me. Drives me to the edge.

No one has ever done that before.

And I can imagine no man will ever do it again.

Only this one.

Only Nick.

CHAPTER THREE

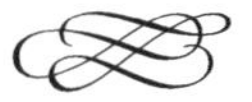

NICK

My blood rushes, my heart thumps in my chest. I've needed this. I've needed her.

I started planning this two years ago. I thought I was ready last year.

I was wrong.

But this year… this year will be different. I had another year to get myself together. Gather my thoughts. My desires.

And hope that Grace would be willing to play.

Could I have found another woman to play with me? Yes. Did I want another woman? No.

Don't ask me what it is about Grace. Because I don't have that answer.

Maybe she doesn't seem jaded like lot of women from the city. Maybe I think she'll appreciate everything I'll do to her.

There was something in her eyes every time I checked in. Every time I checked out. The first year I hardly noticed her. The second year, I did, but I couldn't pull out of my darkness enough to recognize it. Last year, I noticed, and I tried. I really did. But I just wasn't there yet.

But now I'm ready.

And she's willing.

I study the contents of my suitcase. I didn't bring much. Just enough to teach her the pleasures of my preferred type of play. Just enough to please. Just enough to punish.

And she will enjoy both. For now, I only take out the lube, condoms, and the silky black blindfold.

When I turn, she's watching me with those beautiful dark eyes of hers. She hasn't moved from the bed and I'm relieved she doesn't look scared or worried.

However, she's still dressed.

I approach the bed (stepping over Magster, one ear twitching in sleep) to place the lube and condoms on the nightstand. Grace's eyes follow my motions, so I slide the silky fabric between my fingers slowly, sensually, letting her see what's to come.

Though, what she doesn't know yet is I'll want complete control. Yes, I've told her in so many words, but until I show her, she really won't understand.

"Should I get undressed?"

I fight back a smile at her eagerness. "You don't ask me questions, Grace. When I want you to do something, I will tell you. Is that understood?"

Color blooms in her cheeks and I see her eyelids lower just enough I know my commands turn her on. I can see the pulse pound in her throat, and her nipples press against the snug shirt that needs to go.

"Yes," she answers softly.

"Stand up."

She rolls to her side on the bed and quickly pushes herself to her feet.

"Stand in the middle of the room."

Without hesitation, she does so. Once again, I find myself very pleased at her willingness to follow direction. When she reaches for the top button of her jeans, I give her a sharp, "No," and her hands jerk, then fall to her side.

When she bites her bottom lip, it pulls heat into my stomach and down to my cock. Soon it'll be my teeth she'll feel in that exact same spot.

"Shoes and socks off."

She bends over and removes one boot, then the other, pulling off her socks and tucks them inside her boots. She puts them neatly to the side. Then she straightens and looks to me for further direction.

Right now, I'm so hard that I'm having a difficult time not grabbing my dick to stroke it.

I remind myself that I'm the one who's in charge, so I need to remain in control. Of her. Of myself.

"Now you may remove your jeans. Leave your panties on."

She does as she's told and then straightens once more. Her panties are red and I can see the outline of her pussy through them. I can't wait to get up close and personal.

"Remove your shirt." As she begins to tug at the hem, I add, "Slowly."

She makes a show out of removing the purple top and placing it over a nearby wooden chair. She moves back to the middle of the room and waits for her next command.

She's perfect. I can't be any luckier. Her ivory skin glows, her curves are luscious, her thighs look welcoming. Her long dark hair curls around her bare shoulders and covers the soft, pale mounds that push out of her bra.

I debate whether I want to remove her undergarments or I want to watch her do it. A split second later I'm moving forward, my body deciding for me.

My need to touch her is stronger than my need to bend her to my will.

She stands stock still as I move behind her and her shoulders tense. Just slightly.

Since we hardly know each other I'm not surprised by her natural reaction. As I stand behind her, I study the curves and planes of her back, the roundness of her ass in her little red panties. Her ribs expand and contract with each ragged breath.

"So beautiful," I murmur as I sweep a finger from one shoulder to the other, pushing her long, wavy hair over her shoulder so I can see the clasp of her bra. I trace a fingertip along the back of her bra, causing her to shiver. With a twist, I unclasp it and it falls to the floor in a whisper. Her fingers twitch, as if her instinct is to cover herself, but she pins her hands to her sides.

This pleases me.

"Arms up. Yes, that's it. Hands on your head. Perfect." I run my fingers along her sides, over her ribs, and around to cup the weight of her breasts. I haven't seen them yet, but I want to touch them first, and I follow their curves until I find her nipples, pebbled, peaked, waiting for me. Waiting for my attention.

"Do you like me touching you?" I ask, pressing my lips against the silky skin along her neck.

"Yes," she says so softly I barely hear her.

My thumbs brush over the hard peaks, back and forth, until I hear a noise escape her lips. I roll each nipple between my thumb and forefinger, plucking and twisting until my cock flexes as she releases another sound. A whimper? Maybe.

The tip of my tongue finds the top of her spine where I sink my teeth gently into her flesh. Her back bows as she presses her neck toward my mouth and her breasts deeper into my hands.

"Exquisite," I tell her. Because that's what her reactions are. When I release her breasts, I let my hands slide down her belly to the top of her panties. I tuck my thumbs under the elastic and slide her red underwear down, down, down, until they are partway down her thighs. I release them and slide my hands back up to cup her mound.

She's hot, damp, responsive, as I slip a finger between her folds, testing her wetness.

Yes. She's slick, welcoming, her thighs part ever so slightly. Enough to give me room for a second finger.

I shift until my cock nudges the cleft of her ass and I feel her push back against me, encouraging.

She doesn't realize it won't be that easy. Nothing today will be easy.

She moans as I thumb her clit and work two fingers in and out of her.

"Ah, that's it. You want to come, don't you?"

"Yes," she hisses, her head pressing back into my collar bone, her back arched.

"You can't come unless I say you can."

"What?"

"Don't speak unless I ask you a question, or I tell you that you can speak freely."

She releases a loud breath, her body tensing slightly.

"While you're in this cabin, you'll be naked. While in this cabin, you will not come unless I tell you to. There's only one word you can say without permission. That's your safe word. Let's establish that now."

She nods and once again I am deeply pleased. I press my lips against her ear. "I'll give you a word and if at any time I do something that is too much, that you aren't comfortable with, or you just want me to stop, you simply say that word. Tell me you understand."

"I understand."

"That word is pineapple. Remember that word, Grace. It's important."

I slip a third finger inside her, but only for a moment. When I draw them out, they're slick with her arousal.

"So wet, baby," I murmur, my dick now painfully hard. I need a release as much as she does. I drag my fingers across her lips, then dip them into her mouth. "Taste yourself."

She groans, as do I, while she sucks my fingers clean, her tongue playing along my digits. I can't wait to bury my face between her thighs and taste her myself. But instead, I release her and back up a step.

"Remove your panties. Do it slowly."

She hooks her fingers in the panties that are now almost to her knees and slowly bends over taking them all the way to her ankles.

"Stop there. Grab your ankles."

With her panties and her fingers wrapped around her ankles, she's bent over in front of me, showing me all her glory. Her pussy is pink and slick, her ass soft and round. And I finally must touch myself.

I grab my cock and squeeze hard before stroking its length from root to tip. "Pretty, baby. So pretty. You're already ready for me."

She says nothing, and it thrills me she's following my rules. So far, she's the perfect playmate.

Her pussy isn't the only thing I plan to own.

"Your mouth. Your pussy. Your ass. They're no longer yours. While in this cabin, they're all mine. Whose are they, Grace? You may answer."

"Yours."

"What's my name?"

"Nick."

"Who do you belong to, Grace?"

"You, Nick."

"That's it. Does that please you?"

"Yes," she says on a breath.

"Finish removing your panties and get on the bed. On your hands and knees. Face the headboard." And with that, I slap her ass.

She gasps, finishes ripping her panties off and without even a look my direction, she hurries to the bed into position.

My cock twitches in my palm and my balls tighten. I might have to fuck her quick before continuing with our session. Because I can't wait much longer to sink into her sweet heat.

Fuck. For someone who loves to be in control, mine is quickly unraveling.

CHAPTER FOUR

GRACE

I don't look at him as he approaches the bed because I'm not sure if I'm allowed. Whatever game he's playing, I'm not sure of all the rules, only the ones he's told me so far. And I doubt that's all of them.

I have a feeling this game has rules he'll omit just so I can be punished.

Is that fair? I don't care. So far, everything he's done and everything I hope he'll do is play I'm willing to take part of.

Although he's given me an out, a safe word, I hope not to have to use it.

I'm sure he hopes the same thing.

Pineapple. Odd, but effective.

I knew his soul was dark. I knew he had demons. I did not expect any of this from him, though.

I'm not disappointed. Not at all.

This is something new to me. Something exciting. I'll take this day, this night, these next few days to do something that will cut through my boredom, my every day hum-drum life.

Operation End Dry Spell has veered off into something else. And I can't wait to find out just what it's become.

I keep my eyes pinned to the headboard as the bed dips behind me. His weight shifts the mattress as he moves on—what I can only imagine—is his knees.

"Grace, with intimacy, communication is key. Whether it's using body language, words, or even a look. I want to give you what you need. Build a trust, a closeness. But to do that I need you to listen carefully to everything I say. I need you to obey."

Obey.

I draw in a shaky breath. I'm tempted to look over my shoulder, to see what he's doing. But I want to obey. I want to be what he needs.

I want him to be what I need.

The heat of his body touches me, along my legs, my ass. He's right behind me, close. My heart pounds faster as I now think I'm going to finally get what I want, what I need.

When he strokes my back with his long fingers, I sigh. His touch is soothing but stimulating at the same time. My nipples long for those fingers, my pussy clenches for his cock. He continues to brush his fingers along my skin, down my spine, over my ass cheeks, up the cleft of my body, only lightly brushing my labia, my anus, as he moves up all the way to the back of my neck. Then he snags a handful of my hair and pulls my head back, bowing my neck. He leans over me as he sucks on the skin at the side of my throat. His teeth rake gently against my flesh, his erection presses against my slick, plump lips. Just a shift...

A shift and he'll be inside me. I'm tempted to push and press to encourage, but again... I want to obey and he has not given me permission... yet.

Not yet.

So, I remain in place, I remain where he wants me as he tugs on my hair, traces the curve of my ear with his tongue, back down my neck, down the center of my spine, until he reaches the cleft of my ass again. He doesn't stop there.

No.

With a shock, he circles my tight rim with his tongue, flicks, teases me there and I can't help but groan. My former encounters have been boring, nothing like this.

I have never had any man approach me there.

Not there.

But, the more he licks and kisses, and prods, the more I relax, appreciating his skill. Until he releases my hair abruptly and separates my ass cheeks, and I hear him make a noise. One of appreciation.

"Beautiful," he whispers.

He makes me feel just that. Beautiful. Even in this vulnerable position.

He's right about intimacy and communication.

His words make me trust him, make me open to him. His touches, as well.

"Do not move your hands. Separate your knees a little more. Not too much. That's it. Right there."

And then he's quiet... because his mouth is against my mound, pressing against my clit, his tongue plays with me, circling, flicking, stroking my sensitive nub. I struggle to remain still. To keep my hands and knees in place.

I want to drop to my back, grab his head and hold him in place as he eats me until I come. With or without his permission.

But I don't. I play his game.

I wait.

His tongue, his mouth, then his fingers, draw me to the edge. I'm close to coming and I can't. Not yet. I haven't been told to come yet.

I hope it's soon.

My nipples are hard and aching, my anus clenches, almost in need, and my pussy throbs as he tastes all of me, savors it, savors me.

He groans against my swollen flesh and the vibrations make me whimper. I bite my lip to contain it.

I'm on the edge of orgasm but he hasn't told me to let go yet and I struggle to convince my body to behave. To wait.

"Not yet," he says, as if he can read my mind. But he can't, he's probably just reading me, my body. "Soon, but not yet."

He shifts and reaches for the items on the nightstand. Within seconds, I feel the cool gel of the lube against my heated flesh. It dribbles down the crack of my ass, and with his thumb, he massages it around the rim. More drips, more circles made. And then pressure.

Not his mouth this time. No. A finger, long, strong, determined to take my virgin ass.

Slowly, he works the digit to the first knuckle, past the tight ring. Then the second knuckle and I'm blown away by a sensation I've never felt before. One I never thought I'd ever want or need.

But I want this. I need this. It's like this man knows everything I need. Everything I crave.

Then he's moving inside me with a rhythm that could very well drive me mad. And when he buries his mouth against me again, sucking my flesh between his lips, his teeth, I almost scream "pineapple." Because I can't take any more and not climax.

His torture is not allowing me to come. And I can't ask him, I can't beg.

I'm not allowed.

He must allow it.

I need him to say it.

But his mouth is full of my sex, my sensitive flesh, and he's not saying anything.

I want to give up.

I want to scream for mercy.

I'm done.

I'm done.

I'm done.

"You may come," he says so softly that I almost think I imagine it.

And when his mouth finds me again and now two of his fingers fuck my ass, I no longer care if I'd imagined it.

I let go.

My mind spins. My body convulses.

I clench around his fingers and a sound I've never heard before escapes me.

A wail. A cry of release.

Finally.

And before the last of the orgasm ebbs away, he's inside me. Taking me hard, deep, and rough, slamming his hips against my ass. The slapping of our skin, our ragged breathing, and sounds of ecstasy filling the small cabin.

With one hand still working deep in my tight canal, his other grabs my hair again, pulling my head back roughly until my neck can bend no more.

"That's it, Grace. Ride my cock. Feel me deep inside you. That pussy's mine. That ass is mine. Your mouth will soon be mine, too. You do not come until I tell you to. Tell me you hear me."

"Yes, Nick. Yes, I hear you."

"You fit me perfectly. Like you were made for me. Were you made for me, Grace?"

"Yes. Only for you."

"Who do you belong to?"

No hesitation. "You, Nick. I belong to you."

"Do you want to come?"

"Yes," I hiss. Because it's true, even though I just came, I'm ready to come again. His words, his smooth like butter voice, turn me on like nothing ever before.

It's insane. But I love it.

This is how I'm meant to be fucked. I'm not meant to be pushed off the cliff, I'm meant to be thrown.

"Are you ready to come again?"

"Yes," I force myself to say, because thoughts are difficult, words even more so.

"When I say 'now,' you will come."

His fingers curl inside me, stroking, and his cock slams me even harder, deeper until there's nowhere else for it to go.

He tenses, his body hiccups. Then he groans, "Now," and I fall with him. Over the edge, into an endless space below. I can't tell who is throbbing. Him, me, both of us.

I only know one thing...

This was the man I was made for.

Him. And only him.

~

Jesus. I feel like I'm losing myself. How could this man have become my everything in the matter of under an hour?

"How long has it been?" he asks. His arm is curled around me, holding me tight against his side.

We lay naked on top of the sheets, the seasonal chill drying the sweat from our bodies, cooling our heat. I shiver and he gives me a little squeeze.

"Too long." I should be embarrassed by my answer, but I'm not. I've got nothing to hide. "How long has it been for you?"

"Too long," he echoes me.

His answer gives me some satisfaction. Especially since he chose to break his own dry spell with me. I press my cheek harder into his chest.

A thought hits me, making me shift my eyes to his face. "Did you plan this?"

"Yes."

A small smile curves my mouth. "So did I."

His wide-eyed gaze pins mine in surprise then he throws his head back and laughs. His laughter sounds deep and masculine and it makes me want to throw my arms around him and squeeze out whatever demons he has left.

Because I think they're still there. Lurking.

I want to ask him about it, but the timing isn't right. I've known him for a long time, but I really don't know him at all. And I certainly don't know him well enough to ask what haunts him.

If he wants to tell me, I'll listen.

If not, I'll respect that decision.

But my curiosity about other things, more intimate things, gets the best of me. "I thought you were going to tie me up."

"I said restrain, Grace. Not tie you up."

I'm confused and he must read that in my expression.

I love how observant he is. Like he said, communication consists of more than words.

"You need to listen to my commands carefully. I will tell you once. If I need to tell you again, you'll get punished. If you follow my commands, then you'll get rewarded."

He piques my interest. "What kind of punishment?"

His hand cups my jaw and his thumb brushes idly over my cheekbone. "You might like the punishment and push me to do so. You might not like the punishment, but if you don't, I'll make sure you're taken care of afterward. Is that a deal?"

"But you never said what kind of punishment."

"Test me and see."

He's not threatening, instead he's challenging me.

I've always loved a good challenge. They help push away the boredom, help pass the time in a place where monotony and the slow movement of the clock rule my days.

My attention slides down his body, down his belly to his groin. His cock, spent from our actions not long before, lays quiet, soft amongst trimmed, dark hair. My fingers follow my gaze, but skip his dick, and instead, I cup his warm, full sac in my palm. I feel its weight and squeeze slightly.

His thighs tense. Maybe because he knows that if I clasp him any harder, it will become painful. I roll his balls along my fingers. I'm tempted to take him right now into my mouth. When he's soft like this, I'll be able to take him fully.

My body automatically moves, slides down his, and I settle between his legs, which he spreads farther to accommodate me.

I press a kiss to the spot where his root meets his sac, then I suck him into my mouth.

He stays soft long enough so that I can swirl my tongue around him, tasting him fully. And then he begins to grow, to lengthen, to harden. I circle two fingers around the base and squeeze, my teeth scrape along the crown, my lips suck along his length.

His fingers slide into my hair, curl, and pull so hard my scalp begins to burn. But I continue my machinations of coaxing him into an erection, even so soon after his release.

"I didn't give you permission to do that," he says firmly, but his voice isn't as powerful as he'd like, I'm sure. My mouth weakens his reserve, his power. The harder he tugs, the harder I suck, lick, scrape.

"Grace," he warns.

I don't care. For the moment, I want to disobey. I want to challenge him. To discover what punishments he will mete out when I'm obstinate, when I don't follow his rules.

"You will get the tawse," he warns again, his fingers clenching and unclenching in my hair, though not relenting on the pull of my scalp.

Once again, I don't care, since I'm ready to take whatever punishment he sees fit. Though, I have no idea what a tawse is. It sounds medieval. Wicked.

Maybe I should be worried. But I'm not.

While in this cabin, I am his and he can do to me what he likes.

CHAPTER FIVE

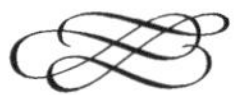

NICK

She's relentless with her mouth. I fight to not groan and thrust deeper, harder.

I am supposed to be the one in control. Not her.

This cabin is my domain. For as long as I'm here.

She is to be mine. For as long as I'm here.

I can't lose control so quickly.

My threat about using the tawse on her does no good, and that excites me. I was planning to use it anyway and now I have a good excuse.

My cock hardens even more when I anticipate showing her what a tawse is and how it will be used.

I decide right then and there, what she's doing is unacceptable. Not allowed.

Because I haven't given her permission.

Letting her hair go, I snag her wrists instead. I sit up and tell her firmly, "Release me."

She does. I shouldn't be surprised, but I am.

Her lips are shiny and her eyes unfocused. She enjoys taking me in her mouth. She's probably wet and ready from giving me pleasure.

But I'm not pleased with her disobeying me and must teach her a lesson.

"On your knees in the middle of the room." The tawse will have to wait. When she doesn't move fast enough, I assist her by pulling her wrists and taking her to where I want her. She drops to her knees before me in the center of the room and looks up at me silently, calmly.

Her eyes aren't subdued; they snap with excitement. Though, she keeps her expression blank, unreadable.

"Cross your ankles, hands behind your back, your wrists crossed, also."

With only a slight hesitation, she does as I say. "That's it. Like that. You do not move no matter what. If you move, you only add to your punishment. Tell me you understand."

"I understand."

I cup her jaw in my palm and tilt her head higher, studying her. I smile. "Good. You took it upon yourself to take me into your mouth without permission. Is that correct?"

"Yes."

"Yes what?"

"Yes, Nick." A shudder runs through her. Her nipples bead to the point of hard pebbles. I want to suck them into my mouth, score them with my teeth.

But I, and she, will have to wait.

Right now punishment, then comes reward.

I flick both nipples with my fingers and her body jerks back slightly, but her eyes never leave mine. They don't even flinch.

Fuck, she is perfect.

I've met my challenge, my match. She's it.

If she takes everything I give her today, tonight, and beyond, I may never want to leave.

And what I'm about to give her is what she wanted but not in the way she expected.

I slide a thumb between her lips and open her mouth, then step forward. "This is my mouth. Keep it open. I think you forgot yourself and thought it was yours. You need a little reminder."

Raking my fingers through her hair, I grip her head and as I pull her toward me, I thrust into her mouth, her lips automatically close around me. And she's not the only one who needs a reminder.

I do, too.

Her mouth is warm, wet, and as her tongue slides along my hard length, I feel my knees start to buckle. I gather my wits and tighten the muscles of my legs, keeping me on my feet.

"Suck me harder," I demand, and she does, her cheeks hollowing out. I hold myself still and let her control the rhythm for a moment. But only a moment. Because this is for my pleasure, not hers.

"With your mouth full, you can't say your word. But after your punishment, comes the reward. Don't forget that while you do as I tell you. But if you must relent, then uncross your ankles. I will take that as a sign you're unable to finish your punishment and are willing to give up your reward."

My fingers curl into fists and I still her movement. I begin to move instead. I control the rhythm. Now it's up to me how deep I go, how fast, how long.

She struggles slightly as I push deeper, push her farther, probably farther than she's ever gone. But she keeps her ankles crossed, her hands behind her back.

She groans around me and doesn't whimper. So, I go even deeper, and her eyes find mine again as if she's telling me she's up for any challenge I give her.

So, I push her even more.

My eyes drop from hers to her ankles, which remain crossed, then they flick back to her mouth which is stretched but still closed tightly around my length. Her face has become flushed, and her eyelids have closed.

As I bump the back of her throat, I feel it convulse then relax once again. Christ, she pleases me. She's almost taking my whole length, but not quite.

I slow the roll of my hips and push slowly forward, going as deep as possibly allowed. Her lips circle the root of my cock and she's struggling to breathe. With two fistfuls of her hair, I hold her head still.

"Look at me."

Her eyes are shiny when she opens them, but she does as I ask. I check one more time, her ankles remain in place. I'm relieved at her willingness to do what I tell her.

A tear escapes the corner of her eye. Not because she's upset, but because I'm so deep inside her mouth, she can't control it.

I release one hand from her hair and brush the lone tear away. I back off slightly, letting her breathe easier, then trace her stretched lips with my thumb.

"So beautiful, Grace. This is what you wanted, but it had to be on my terms." I tilt my hips forward again, giving her all of me once more. I go slow because I don't want to hurt her.

She's too precious to me. She has given me herself like a gift, and I must take care of her like she is one. I must take care of what's mine.

And in turn, she will take care of me.

Just watching her take me fully makes my balls tighten, my dick harden even more. I'm there at the point of no return again. This time I will release down her throat. Give her a part of me.

I pull back and then tilt my hips forward once more and close my eyes as I spill inside her, along her tongue, down the back of her throat. She groans and her eyes never leave mine. But I see satisfaction there. It's unmistakable.

She enjoyed what I gave her and I enjoyed giving it to her.

When my cock stops throbbing, I pull from between her lips and tell her, "Lick the head clean."

I give her a smile when she does. When she's finished, she smiles up at me.

"Speak freely," I say, stroking a thumb along her jaw.

"May I stand?"

"Not yet. But you may uncross your ankles and drop your arms."

She does so with a relieved sigh. Her muscles most likely ache from holding that position.

"Did you enjoy that, Grace?"

"Very much."

"Let me take care of you."

I see her eyes widen for a split second at my words, then she quickly schools her face. "I would like that very much, as well."

CHAPTER SIX

GRACE

I took care of him. Then he took care of me. After taking Maggie outside for a break, he had me sit at the small table in the cabin while he fed me a muffin and he ate the other. Then in the small kitchenette, he cooked us a large cheese and vegetable omelet from the items he brought along in a cooler. He placed it on one plate and used one fork. One bite for me, one bite for him, alternating feeding us both until the plate was clean.

Once finished, he wiped my mouth gently with a napkin. I didn't have to lift a finger. Before I could push away from the table, he rose and came around, massaging my shoulders, my neck, my arms since they were a little sore from holding them pinned behind me.

He did this all while murmuring compliments in my ears. He called me lovely, beautiful, gorgeous, and more. Descriptions I've never been called before. I don't know if any of them are true, but as long as Nick believes those things, that's all that matters.

At first, I figured this was my reward. My recompense for accepting my punishment.

But it wasn't.

I found out later that this is just Nick being Nick. Open. Kind.

Caring. No sign of anything dark or haunting. He seems to appreciate me and my willingness to play with him.

Afterward, he took my hand gently and led me to the bed, me on my side and him curling himself around me. As we laid quietly, I listened to his steady breathing until I fell asleep.

Hot lightening shoots down my belly and lands in the apex of my thighs. Another pull at my nipple brings me to consciousness and I blink up at the ceiling until I realize where I am. In the cabin. With Nick.

A relieved sigh escapes me.

I thought maybe this all had been a dream. But it isn't. He has one of my nipples sucked deep into his mouth and his eyes are on mine. He smiles around my nipple and then sinks his teeth into the soft flesh.

My back arches off the bed and, instinctively, my hands reach for him. Then I remember again that this *is* Nick and stop myself from touching him without permission. My fingers curl into my palms.

"This is your reward, Grace. You may touch me if you'd like."

Oh, yes, I want to touch him.

Sweeping my fingers through his dark hair, I push him back to my nipple. He chuckles against my skin and I can't help but smile.

When his lips snag my nipple again, he sucks it hard before scraping his teeth over the beaded tip.

He rolls the other one between his thumb and forefinger before pulling it away from my body. When my skin won't stretch anymore, he pinches harder.

"I should've brought some clamps," he murmurs against the outer curve of my breast.

Yes, he should've.

"Next time," he says and I still.

Next time.

Will he make me wait a whole year for a next time?

Suddenly a million questions fill my head, but I sweep them away. Now is not the time.

No. Now is for my reward. Plenty of time later for other things.

He nibbles a path from one breast to the other until he clamps his lips tightly around my nipple and flicks the tip with his tongue.

"Nick..." I groan.

"Are you enjoying your reward?"

Oh, hell yes, I want to scream. But I don't. I murmur, "Oh yes," instead.

My neck bows as I tilt my head back and suddenly he's there, nipping along my throat, tickling the hollow with his tongue. When he sinks his teeth in a little harder at the junction of where my neck meets my shoulder, I gasp.

"No?" he asks.

"Yes," I encourage.

Again, he chuckles softly, deeply, and suddenly I'm covered in goosebumps. His voice alone can make me wet and wanting.

The evidence is making my inner thighs slick. I throb for him. *Actually throb.* That has never happened to me before. To need someone so much that my body cries out for him.

But there's no doubt I want him, need him. All of him.

He works his way down my chest, biting the upper curve of my breast, nipping the tip of my nipple, softly kissing the skin of my belly. He doesn't stop until he reaches the top of my mound. His hot breath beats against my flesh and my pussy clenches. He's not touching me anywhere, but can make me react with just a breath.

Simply a breath.

"Open yourself to me, Grace. I want to see all of you."

I slide my hand down my belly and separate myself.

"Beautiful," he murmurs. "Once again you're ready for me. But that's not your reward..." His voice drifts off as he strokes along my center with his tongue, the tip of it finds the tip of me, teasing my clit, making my hips dance off the bed.

"That's it, Grace. You taste so good. I can't get enough of you."

He's quiet, but I'm not, while he works me into a frenzy and takes me to the edge several times but won't let me fall. Instead, he pulls away to nip my inner thighs or blow gently on my sensitive clit. Though, even that almost makes me come.

I find the more I whimper, mew, or cry out his name, the harder he sucks, licks, flicks, so it becomes a new game. One where I'll clearly be the winner.

I mindlessly chant his name, begging him to let me come. This is supposed to be my reward; I shouldn't have to beg. At first, I don't think he's trying to be controlling, but only trying to extend my pleasure. In one way, I appreciate it, in another I want to curse him.

Until there comes a point where I can't take anymore; the tension in my body needs to be released. I'm tempted to shove his face closer and grind against him.

But I don't.

I wait.

I trust him to know what he's doing... Which, I realize, is learning my body, my reactions, what I like, what I love, what creates a slow build, what takes me there quickly.

I have a feeling he'll use this to his advantage later. Though the thought is electrifying, to have someone end up knowing your body better than yourself, it's also intimidating.

It hits me that it's another form of control. He'll be able to play me like a fiddle. I'll be putty in his hands. And every other cliché that bounces around my addled brain.

"Tell me what you need, Grace," he says against my swollen folds.

"I need to come," I almost snap at him because I'm at the point of breaking but also teeter at the point of frustration.

I'm ready.

So, when he chuckles against my clit and slides two long fingers inside me, curling them to stroke that secret spot of mine, my hands slam down on the mattress, grip the sheets, and I wail as my body bows and then ripples around him, throbbing against his mouth.

He's saying something. I don't know what. My head's foggy, my gaze unfocused from the most intense orgasm I've had in a long time.

I hear his words but can't make out what they are. With a last gentle kiss to my clit, which still makes me jerk against him, he slides up my body, careful to keep his weight off me.

When he's face to face, he takes my mouth like he owns it, because he does. My body still shakes, my pussy quivers, my fingers curl around his biceps while my nails dig into his flesh to take purchase as he tips my head back from the force of his mouth against mine.

And, holy shit, it's fucking glorious.

The best damn kiss I ever had.

He whispers to me how good I taste. I agree, because I discovered my own essence during his kiss.

Even though he's hard again, he slips to my side, lays a heavy arm over my waist and plants a hand on my hip before tugging me tight against him.

"How old is Maggie?"

It's the last question I expect him to ask. But besides his erection, the rest of his body is relaxed against me, so maybe he wants to learn more about me. Or my dog, anyway. Of course. She always draws the attention.

"Eight."

His hand sweeps the hair away from my face and, with his fingertip, he draws a line from the top of my forehead down to my chin by the way of my nose.

"That's old for a dog that size?"

I shift one of my shoulders. "More like middle-aged."

"She looks good for her age, then. She's well-behaved. I like that."

He would.

Since we are speaking freely, I would love to know more about him. Especially what I've always been dying to know. But once again, I wait.

"My father trained K9s in the military. He taught her a lot of commands, both verbal and hand signals, but I don't put her through her paces. She's just my companion."

"You live here alone."

Not a question. He knows. He's just affirming a fact that doesn't need stated, because I'm well aware that I live here alone. It was one of the reasons I was so desperate to catch his attention. So, I don't respond.

"What happened to your father? Did he pass?"

"Yes, the year before you started coming up. I'm an only child, so this all got handed down to me."

"How do you keep up with this place? There has to be at least a dozen cabins."

"I'm used to it. I hire local help when I need it." And can afford it, I add silently.

I shiver. I think about the fireplace and how nice it would be to start a fire just to get the chill out of the air. Unfortunately, I don't have any firewood stacked near the cabins yet.

"Cold?"

"A little."

He leans away from me enough to grab a blanket that's folded neatly on the bottom shelf of the nightstand. He pulls it over us both.

"Better?"

"Yes."

"You can wrap your arms around me, Grace. I bite, but only during sex." His eyes twinkle as he tells me this.

I have to say I enjoyed his nips and nibbles as well as the couple times he sank his teeth into me a bit harder.

One more thing I have never done before.

He studies my face when he asks, "Did you like it?"

"Yes, I did."

"Good." A slight smile curves the corners of his lips and I can't help but brush the tips of my fingers over them. He opens his mouth and snags one between his teeth playfully, then lets it go.

I continue my exploration of his face, follow the strong line of his jaw up and around all the way to his brows. His eyes follow mine.

His voice sounds husky when he says, "Tell me how long it's been."

I stop my exploration and drop my hand. "I told you, too long."

"Be more specific."

"Months."

"How many?"

Why does he insist on knowing this information? I'm not comfortable telling him about my sex life. Or more like the lack of one.

"Nick…"

"I asked you a question, I expect an answer," he insists.

"Does that work both ways?" Because if so, I have a lot of answers I'd like to hear from him.

He shifts a little under the blanket, drawing a leg over mine. Now with his arm and his leg crossing my body, I'm pinned to the bed. Another type of restraint without using actual ropes or cuffs.

Interesting.

"I'll make a deal with you. I'll only ask you a question I'm willing to answer myself. Deal?"

"Deal," I say.

But wait.

I frown, regretting my quick decision. Does that mean only he can ask the questions? If so, then I may never find out what I want to know.

CHAPTER SEVEN

NICK

The last thing I want is to turn our limited time together into a game of twenty questions. But I'm curious about her, about her life, and why she remains in a remote area of Maine by herself.

Because of our deal, I word my questions carefully.

"Why don't you sell this place? Seems a lot to handle by yourself."

"I could, but I'd feel guilty. My parents put their heart and soul into this place. Then, when my mother died, my father kept this place because it was a piece of her. Now I keep it because it's a piece of them."

"There's more to it than that, Grace. Tell me."

I watch her face as she hesitates, uncertainty peeking through.

"I wouldn't know what to do, how to live, how to make money. This is all that I've ever done, ever known."

Her parents created a business, a home, but in a sense, they painted their daughter into a corner by doing so. The world is so big, but I have a feeling Grace never had a chance to explore it.

Which is a shame, not only for her, but for the world, too.

"You've never married." I try to make it a statement and not a question because it's something I don't want to answer myself. However, I'm curious.

And we all know curiosity killed the cat, though for me, it may become more of a slaughter.

"No. You?"

"Yes," I answer and her eyes widen.

"Yes, you *are* married? Or yes, you've *been* married?"

I clarify. Only because I don't want her to wonder if I'm still married and am cheating on a spouse. "Was."

Her body relaxes against mine again. I leave it at that, but I know she'll want a follow-up. And I'm right.

"Messy divorce?"

Messy. Yes. Divorce. No. Heartache and pain all the same, though. If not worse.

Even though she's asking a question I haven't asked of her myself, I don't have to answer, but I will. "No."

When she opens her mouth to ask another question, I put my finger against her lips. "You forget yourself. I will only answer questions I ask you."

She frowns against my finger, and I quickly replace it with my mouth, kissing her back into a smile. I like when she smiles at me.

"What would you want to do with your life if you could do anything?" When she tucks her bottom lip in her mouth, I touch it and shake my head. "That lip is mine. Only I get to bite it."

She releases it immediately and smiles again. "I like it when you bite me."

"I know. I plan on doing it some more."

Her body jerks just slightly. I assume it's from excitement or anticipation. Because I like when I bite her, too.

Very, very much.

I smooth the pad of my thumb over her lower lip, following it with my eyes. Her mouth parts and I can feel her soft, warm breath sweeping over my fingers. Her eyes darken and the tip of her tongue darts out to touch my thumb.

"Do you like taking me in your mouth, Grace?"

"Yes," she whispers, her eyes hooded. She should be sated, but she's not. She wants more. "I enjoy it."

And I like that very, very much, too.

"Did you like when I came down your throat?"

"Yes." This time her answer is so soft, it's more like a breath.

"Why do you like it?"

Her throat works up and down, like she's swallowing hard. "Because you're giving me a part of you."

Her answer brings my cock to attention. I can't believe my luck. To have found the right woman, one able to fill what's missing inside of me. The hole that's been there for years. My instinct about Grace was right. Every time I saw her, even if only for a split moment in the past few years, I knew she might be the one. And I am quickly finding out I was right.

I just needed time to get to the place where I'm currently at. One where I could offer myself to her. One where I could comfortably ask her to give herself to me.

So far, she's been nothing but open, honest, and hasn't hesitated to do anything I request. Or tell, more like it.

When my life spun out of control a little over four years ago, I realized I never wanted that to happen again. So, I will never let it.

The more control I sought, the more I realized how much I like it. Even during sex.

Especially during sex.

"Why do you come here every year at this time?" she asks. Then she pins her lips shut and her eyes widen again.

She couldn't help herself. It's a question she probably has been wanting to ask.

"Every question you ask me out of turn, you will get one strike of the tawse. And I won't guarantee that I will answer. You've already broken our deal. So, this is the new one. Do you accept it?"

"I don't know what a tawse is," she answers.

"Ask me."

Conflict crosses her face. She knows if she asks, it will add one more strike from something she has no idea what it is.

No matter if she stops asking questions, she's earned herself one strike at least. My cock thickens at the thought of using it on her ass, making it red.

"Do you want to know enough to ask me?"

"No," she says, her voice a little shaky.

"I will never hurt you and you have your safe word," I remind her.

When her expression becomes determined, I fight back my smile of triumph. She likes a challenge. And she's finding this a challenge she may want to participate in.

I'll give her a little information to whet her appetite to want to know more. "I come up here every year to get away."

"Why?"

Strike two. Her cheeks darken as do her eyes.

"It's an anniversary I want to forget. I leave everything behind once a year at this time to cleanse my soul."

"What kind of anniversary?"

Strike three. Her lips part and she blows out a ragged breath. So do I because the anticipation is beginning to grow inside of me to epic proportions.

"An anniversary of a major loss."

I'm only giving her enough so she must ask more.

"A loss of what?"

Strike four.

"A loss of loved ones."

She bites her bottom lip and I give her a pointed look. She releases it, but I can see she's dying to ask who, how, and when.

Though it's somewhat easier to talk about now, it's still not something I like to discuss. I came up here and drank myself into oblivion year after year to forget. Even though the loss of memory was only temporary. I needed to get through this week in a stupor until the pain became slightly bearable. But it's still not completely gone.

And it never will be.

"You want to know the details," I finally say.

She nods and says softly, "Yes."

"Then ask." I'm not letting her off that easily.

"Why here?"

Strike five. My cock twitches against her thigh. I close my eyes for a second to gather myself, not because I'm having a hard time with the memory, but because of my anticipation of giving her her punishment.

"Because no one would know to look for me here. I'm completely out of my element. I live and work in the city, Grace. No one would think I would hide in the middle of Maine."

"Who are you hiding from?"

Strike six. My balls tighten and I get even harder.

"Friends, family. Anyone who would hover, anyone who would worry about my mental state this week every year."

"Tell me what happened."

Ah, she didn't ask. Smart.

I may give this one to her because six strikes are already a lot. Though can alternate light and hard. I think she may enjoy getting this punishment as much as I will enjoy giving it to her.

"First your punishment, then the answer might be your reward," I decide.

My heart beats a little faster, my breath speeds up a bit as I slide off of her and out of bed. I can't wait anymore. I'm looking forward to this and I brought the tawse with me planning to use it one way or another, whether in punishment or play.

I will let her see what it is before blindfolding her. As I head toward my suitcase, precum beads at the tip of my cock.

And I can't wait to fuck her once her ass is pink from my efforts.

CHAPTER EIGHT

GRACE

I suck in a breath when he turns. He's holding a long strap-like object in his hand. It's flat and looks wicked. The thick, brown leather is split up the middle and on the other end there's a hole with a leather cord running through it that would go around his wrist.

Now I wish I hadn't asked so many questions.

He smacks the tawse lightly against his palm as he approaches the bed. The snap of the leather against skin makes me jump. Every time he slaps his hand, his erection bounces.

There's no doubt he's looking forward to meting out my punishment.

My gaze lifts from the instrument to his face. His eyes appear bright and his lips curve slightly. He doesn't look evil. No, he's excited. And he looks exactly that.

"On your hands and knees and come to the edge of the bed. Face me."

I do as he says and turn to face him. As he steps up to the edge of the mattress, his cock is level with my face. "Open your mouth."

I do so.

"Stick out your tongue."

Oh, fuck, he's not going to strike my tongue, is he?

I tentatively do so.

But all he does is slide the crown of his cock down it, leaving behind his silky, salty precum.

"Does that taste good?"

I close my mouth and swirl his essence around. "Yes."

"Do you want more?"

"Yes, please."

"Soon," he answers and moves away, leaving me there at the end of the bed, naked, on my hands and knees. Vulnerable.

I don't let my gaze follow him, I stare straight ahead at a spot on the wall. My nipples are peaked and needing his attention. The inner walls of my pussy clench tight.

Then he's there again, at my head, pulling the blindfold over my eyes.

The cabin goes dark. Now that I've lost one sense, I need to use my hearing to follow what's going on next.

He strokes my hair, then my cheek, before running his thumb over my bottom lip.

"Can you see me?"

"No."

"No what?"

"No, Nick."

"That's it, baby," he says softly. "I love my name on your lips. Especially when you cry it out while you come. Do you want to come, Grace?"

"Yes, Nick."

"That will be your reward. But first, we have other business to attend to. Six strikes, Grace. But, once I start, you may ask me for more."

I don't answer. My mind spins with both anticipation and trepidation. I both hope he holds off and also hope to get it over with so we can move on to the reward.

Suddenly, his hand cups my chin, and he's gently pulling me up.

"Baby, you're so beautiful, your body responds perfectly. You have a flush running up your chest into your cheeks, your nipples are as hard as diamonds. I see a sheen on your inner thighs. Come, stand up."

Since I can see nothing, he helps me to my feet and guides me around to face the bed, away from him.

"Bend over and lock your wrists together on the bed."

I do so, pinning my wrists together as if they're bound.

"You feel the rope on your wrists, Grace?"

It's crazy. With simply his words, my wrists really do feel like they're bound with rope. He's playing with my head. My pussy throbs at the thought of being tied up. Of being unable to escape. "Yes, Nick."

"Is it too tight?"

I test my imaginary binding. "No."

"Does it feel good?"

"Yes," I hiss. Because it does. His voice, his presence, controls me, everything about me.

I am his to do with what he wants.

I never realized how much I needed him, needed this, until today. I had only hoped to break my long dry spell. But now, this is so much more.

I never imagined it would be like this.

And I hope it only gets better.

"Your pussy is pretty, Grace. It's wet with need. It's all mine, is it not?"

"Yes, it's all yours, Nick."

I feel him move around the room. It's strange that I can't see him. But my hearing seems more acute now that I'm blindfolded.

I may not be able to see him, but I can sense his heat behind me and cannot wait for him to touch me.

Even though this is supposed to be some sort of "punishment" for my transgression of asking questions, I'm looking forward to what he's about to do. I lay my trust in his hands, for I'm sure he won't hurt me. His punishment can't be any more than a torturous pleasure.

I will accept what he gives me. Whatever it is.

Then his hands are around my ankles, pulling them wider, placing my feet where he wants them. My legs are spread, my ass in the air, my elbows and wrists on the bed.

I wait.

And wait.

Until I don't want to wait any longer, but I curb the need to demand him to hurry.

I know I'm already getting six strikes of the tawse and until I know what it's like, I don't want to add to the number.

He's quiet, so I wonder if he's staring at me, studying me. I feel exposed, bent over the bed, everything on display.

Do I feel self-conscious? No. Maybe I should, because anyone in their right mind might. Especially with someone they don't know so well.

But it's Nick, I remind myself.

And I need this more than anything.

I close my eyes behind the blindfold and imagine him standing behind me, stroking himself as he looks at my pussy, which must be dripping at this point. I'm melting for him and I wouldn't be surprised if I leave a puddle on the floor.

Though ridiculous, the thought makes me smile. He would probably like that... especially knowing that was all because of him.

He finally speaks, "Where you are right now, I don't want you to move from. Tell me you understand."

"I understand, Nick."

"Good, Grace," he says softly.

Yes, because I'm good. But I also want to be bad. However, I won't move. Not until he tells me to.

Suddenly, he grabs a handful of my hair and yanks back, making me gasp, more in surprise than anything. My head rests on my back, my neck stretches tight, and I'm breathing hard. I quiver as his free hand strokes along my back, over my shoulder blades, down my spine. He reaches underneath me, tweaks my right nipple, and I gasp again. I want to tell him to do it again, but I can't speak unless spoken to. I can't answer unless asked.

So, I breathe deeply as he cups my breast within his hand and twists my pebbled nipple between his forefinger and thumb. I try not to wiggle, but it's difficult to stay still.

I enjoy what he's doing to me so very, very much.

I try not to whimper a complaint when he releases me and slides his palm over my ribs to my waist and then rests for a moment on my hip. When he lets my hair go, my head falls forward.

"Rest your forehead on your arms."

I do.

"No matter what, keep your ass up as it is now. Understood?"

"Yes."

"Yes what?"

"Yes, Nick."

"That's it, baby. If, at any time, you need to say your safe word, you do so. What is your safe word?"

"Pineapple."

"Do you want to use it now?"

"No, Nick."

I picture him smiling at my answer, which makes me smile. I am making him happy and have this driving need for him to be just that. It seems like he hasn't been happy for a long time. And I really like this new Nick. This verbal, non-grunting Nick.

If I can help him, I will.

Just as he is helping me. Giving me what I need. What I crave.

He squeezes my ass cheeks together and lays a gently kiss on each one. "You're giving me a gift, Grace. And I appreciate it." Then his warm hands are gone, the cool air taking their place along my skin.

He slides a finger through my soaked folds and he murmurs

something I can't quite catch. His finger dips inside me for only a split second and then it's gone. It just makes me want him more.

But that's the point, I guess.

He wants me to not only enjoy my reward but my punishment.

I take a deep breath through my nostrils and clear my mind as the leather strap slides across the curves of my ass.

I bite back a groan as he slides it around again. The leather is smooth against my skin and now I'm looking forward to whatever he will give me. Whatever Nick thinks I deserve for asking questions out of turn.

But I need him to get on with it.

He's toying with me.

And it's driving me mad.

He taps the tawse along my skin. Not striking, no. Soft taps to waken my nerve endings, to make me aware of the instrument in his hand. To remind me of who's in control.

Tap, tap, tap along my buttocks.

Goosebumps break out all over my body and I bite my lower lip even though I'm not allowed. I know he can't see it from where he stands.

Plus, I'm sure his attention is focused elsewhere.

Then the air moves with a suddenness and I hear the sharp smack of the leather against my skin before I actually feel the sting. My body shifts forward even though I fought my reaction. I can't help it.

And he's not going to like that.

But he says nothing and pulls my hips back into place.

Then I wait.

Finally, he says, "Every time you move it doesn't count. Do you understand?"

"Yes," I hiss. Then I quickly add, "Nick."

I swallow hard and tell myself to stay still, to be ready this time. And when the tawse comes down on my other ass cheek, I do as he says. I remain in place and accept what he gives me.

I make a noise and so does he. This affects him as much as me.

I'm pleased with that.

And, surprisingly, I'm not finding the leather strap unpleasant. It makes me feel alive.

His fingers gently trace what I can only imagine is the welt that the tawse left behind.

"What is your safe word, Grace?" he asks again.

"Pineapple."

"Are you going to use it right now?"

"No, Nick."

"Good," he breathes, sounding relieved.

Once again, he strikes my right cheek in a different spot than the first time. The bite of the leather making my skin come alive. I open my mouth but no gasp comes out. Nothing but silence escapes me.

And it's crazy, I know, but I like it.

Never in my life would I have thought I would enjoy something as forbidden as this. Something I tried to avoid as a child. And now, I can't get enough of.

I want to feel. Really *feel*. Experience that rush from my ass to my core, making me wet, making me want him more than humanly possible. I want him to do it again.

He does.

And again.

He does.

I want more. But I can't beg him for more. I can't even ask or suggest. So, I stay quiet.

"Do you want to use your word, Grace?"

"No, Nick."

He blows out a breath and I feel it against my heated skin and I get wetter, my pussy seems so swollen, ready. I actually hope he smacks me there instead.

He doesn't.

He pauses and nothing touches me but the cool air that surrounds us.

But then something slick, smooth, drips over my anus, down the cleft of my ass.

"Whose ass is this, Grace?"

"Yours, Nick."

"Has anyone ever had you here?"

"No."

"So, it *is* all mine."

I don't answer because he didn't ask a question. It's true, no one has had me there, but I've always wondered what it would be like.

If I'm going to find out, I want it to be with Nick.

He presses me there, pushing slightly, circling, and I can't believe how good it feels. No matter what he does, he always makes me want more.

However, he doesn't press too hard, just teases along my tight rim. My instinct is to push against him, but I quell that. And I wait once more.

He presses a finger, maybe a thumb—I can't tell—at the opening. And when he brings the leather strap down on my ass, his finger (I know this now) slips inside of me at the same time. I can't help it, I cry out.

"Tell me your word if you need to," he says, sounding a bit strained himself.

I like the effect I have on him. He thinks he's in control. But my reactions really control him. Though he'd never admit it.

I don't say the word and when he strikes me again on the other ass cheek, he slips a second finger in and stretches me.

With my stinging ass in the air, he fucks it slowly with his fingers and it's glorious.

I never, ever imagined sex to be this good. It's unexpected that I would like these things I would have considered debauched with any of my other lovers.

But with Nick, it feels right.

I don't think there's anything he can do to make me not want him.

But let me just say... If this is punishment, I want to be a bad, bad girl.

CHAPTER NINE

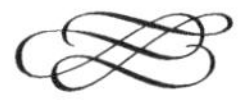

NICK

Grace impresses me. She excites me.

My Grace.

She has taken the strikes of the tawse, one of my favorite toys, like I thought she would. She likes a challenge, and this is certainly one she's never had before.

She has kept her wrists tightly together as if they were bound, she hasn't moved her feet. Besides the movement forward when I first struck her, she's done as she's been told.

I can't get any harder than I am at the moment. She *wants* to please me. And because of that, I want to please her.

But I still owe her two more strikes of the tawse. The skin of her ass already shows the effects of the leather strap. Red, pink, and a little puffy. I kiss each place I've landed a blow, thankful she's allowed me this.

Because she could always have said no.

She could have always stopped me mid-strike. She did not.

And I know now she'll take the last two as she did the first four.

What's even more exciting is that she likes ass play. And it's one more reason I can't get enough of her.

Out of appreciation, I hand over a little of the control to her.

"For these last two... On a scale of one to ten. Ten being hard, one being just a light tap... What number, Grace?

She's silent for a moment, most likely judging her own tolerance. "Six," she finally says, her voice breathy.

Six is about what the last couple I gave her were. I give her a six again, which makes my balls tighten painfully.

"Last one. Number."

"Eight."

I hesitate. "Are you sure, Grace?" I need to be sure. I don't want to hurt her, but I want to give her what she asks for.

"Yes, please, Nick. An eight."

I give her an eight and she whimpers before blowing out a shaky breath, but she didn't move. Not an inch.

I toss the tawse out of the way and concentrate on stretching her tight canal with my fingers as much as possible. I'm not sure if she'll be ready for me to take her there today. Or even tonight. But by the end of the week, maybe. It's something to look forward to.

When she groans, and squeezes my fingers, I say, "And now, the reward."

"I think I like the punishment better."

I throw my head back and laugh. Not surprisingly, I haven't laughed like that in a long time. It's an incredible feeling.

"How do you know? You haven't received your reward, yet. Though you talked out of turn. Are you purposely pushing me to punish you again? And who said the punishment next time will be the same?" When she doesn't answer me, I add, "You can speak freely, Grace."

All this time, I'm sliding my slick fingers in and out of her ass and as soon as I tell her she can talk, she lets out a loud moan and her spine bows. She rocks her hips back and shoves my fingers deeper.

I grab my cock with my free hand and spread the precum around the head before stroking it to the same rhythm of my fingers.

Watching her move against my hand turns me on to no end.

"Do you want me inside you, Grace? Is that what you want for your reward?"

"Yes," she hisses. "I need you... right now."

"Pull off the blindfold, grab a condom." As she does what I ask, I continue, "Open it up and hand it to me." She rips the package open with her teeth and passes the condom back to me, turning enough so she can watch me roll it on one handed.

"I'm so ready for you, baby," I murmur as I press the crown of my cock between her swollen lips.

"I'm ready for you, too." She sighs as I press slowly into her.

I'm surrounded by hot, wet silk as she accepts me fully. I pause. Mostly because I need to gather my wits. I don't want to come immediately and that may very well happen, especially with my fingers deep inside her, also.

She groans and pushes back against me. "Nick..."

"Yes, baby, I hear you. I know what you need. I need it, too," I reassure her. "Let me tell you how beautiful your ass looks right now, striped from your punishment, stretched from my fingers inside you. It's perfect. You're perfect."

I close my eyes and bite back a groan when she squeezes me tight, both my fingers and my cock. Then I have no choice but to move; I can't hold myself back anymore. I try to keep control, keep it slow, steady. All the way in, all the way out. Her body hugs me and the need to move faster, harder pulls at me.

"Fuck me," she groans.

"Faster?"

"Yes."

"Harder?"

"Oh...yes."

I give her what she wants until I lose all sense of time, all my thoughts float away until there is nothing left but her. Only her. Only me. Just the two of us connected as we climb to a higher plane together. Her cries come steady and when she calls my name, I struggle not to lose it. I want this to last.

I've waited a long time for someone to come along and fill that hole deep inside me. And now that I have her, I don't want to let her go. I don't want to let go of myself.

But I must. My body can only take so much, my mind spins out of control. I need to find release.

And as she ripples around me, groaning, moaning, gripping the bed sheets, shoving her ass into my hips, I let myself go. I let *everything* go.

But I also let her in. I let her fill that emptiness deep inside me.

If only for a moment, I feel whole again.

Wanted.

Needed.

Loved.

Complete.

CHAPTER TEN

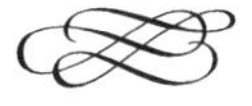

GRACE

It's getting late. Poor Maggie has been patient with me. With us. But now it's time for her to eat and she needs another break outside. I don't want to leave the bed. I don't want to leave the cabin. I don't want to leave Nick's side.

He's only here for a short time and I know the time will go by too quickly. Any moments away from him will feel like a loss.

I run my fingers over his short beard, testing the short, prickly hair. His eyes are closed, his bow-shaped mouth slightly parted, and his chest rises and falls in a steady pattern as he sleeps. His arm wraps tightly around me, holding me close, like he's afraid to let me go.

If I can slip quietly away, I can go take care of Maggie's needs, grab some food for us while I'm at it, and come back before he even realizes I was gone.

I eyeball my clothes on the other side of the room and begin to gently lift his arm off me, carefully, slowly, until I have enough room to slip from underneath him. I shimmy across the bed and then roll until my feet hit the floor.

A groan escapes me when I stand. My body is stiff and sore, plus my backside hurts from more than one reason. But I'm satisfied. Hell, I'm happy. So, it's all good.

As I pull on my clothes, I face the bed, watching Nick sleep soundly. Maggie whines a little when she sees me pull on my boots. She really needs to go out and I make a face at her to shush.

She wags her tail and I can see her excitement building as she was probably bored as hell since Nick and I have spent the day in bed.

The problem is, when she gets excited, she tends to bark. Loudly. Not to mention, often (believe me, it's annoying). And I don't want her to wake Nick.

I hurry to open the door and she runs out, taking off without me. Since I know where she's headed, I don't worry. There's only one thing she likes as much as tummy and ear scratches… food. She knows where her bread's buttered. When I climb into the golf cart, she doesn't even bother to wait for a ride. She's stretching her legs, relieving her bladder, and racing me back to the house.

Dusk is upon us. The lake and surrounding woods are quiet as I drive down the lane, shivering, since the temperature has dropped. I make a mental note to wear a sweatshirt on my return trip.

My smile grows as I think about bringing more than a sweatshirt back to the cabin with me. Nick may have brought his own toys, but I have some, too.

In October, it doesn't take but a minute to go from dusk to dark. And when Maggie and I head back to the cabin, darkness has moved in and I need to use the headlights on the golf cart. I'm surprised when I notice through the crack of the worn drapes that the interior of the cabin is dark, also.

I've only been gone about an hour. Just long enough to feed the attention-hogging dog and scrape together us humans something to eat, too.

I hope Nick isn't picky because I had to raid the cabinets to throw something together that was, at minimum, fuel for our bodies, since I figure our activities will continue throughout the evening into early morning. At least, I hope so.

Who needs sleep, right? I can sleep when I'm dead.

I shut off the golf cart and study the cabin for a moment, while Maggie sniffs the bottom of the door, wagging her tail.

Huh.

I gather the basket of goodies and head to the cabin. When I quietly open the door, Maggie rushes by me, just about knocking me over. Before I can catch my balance, there's a hand wrapped around my throat, the door slams shut behind me, and I find myself with my back pinned to said door.

Even though my eyes haven't adjusted yet, I can feel Nick's warm breath against me and know his face is close to mine.

"You left." His voice sounds low and grumbly, which excites me more than scares me.

His grip on my neck is just enough to hold me still, but doesn't hurt. No, instead I get this perverse pleasure out of him doing it.

It makes me wonder if I'm fucked in the head.

The heat from his body sears me, even though I'm fully clothed and even wearing a heavy sweatshirt.

"Yes," I whisper. "I had to go back to the house."

"You were gone a long time." Not an accusation but a statement of fact.

"I—"

He cuts off my explanation by crushing his lips against mine, opening my mouth with his tongue, and then exploring the inside.

Damn, this man knows how to kiss.

I try to melt against him, to fit my body along his like two pieces of a puzzle, but I'm holding the heavy basket. Instead, I show my approval by moaning into his mouth and letting my tongue war with his until he twists his head enough to bring us even closer together for a moment.

Then he pulls back. Just slightly. His breath mingles with mine. He inhales me, and I him, for a few long moments.

"I woke up alone," he murmurs, my eyesight has adjusted enough now that I can see him staring at my mouth. I lick my lips slowly and he notices.

"Sorry. I didn't want to disturb you."

"When I woke and found you gone, I worried."

Why would he worry? I live on the property. If he thought I was running away to escape him, I couldn't get too far.

But there was no way I was leaving him alone for the rest of the week. He's mine as long as he's here. And, anyway, he told me he owns my mouth, my pussy, my ass. So, there's that.

I bite my lip, trying not to giggle at my crazy thoughts.

"Don't bite *my* lip. Leave that to me." And with that, he leans in just enough to snag my bottom lip with his teeth and presses down gently. Enough for me to feel the tug and pinch but not enough to break the skin. My pussy clenches because I want his mouth on me again. But not on my mouth (though that's acceptable, too).

"Nick," I breathe when he releases my lip.

With his hand still on my throat, his fingertips press a little harder into my skin. Not enough to make me panic, since he isn't restricting my breath at this point, but enough to make me wetter, make me want him even more.

He takes the basket from my hands and without letting me go, he sets it on the floor at our feet, then straightens.

With one hand, he unsnaps and unzips my jeans, tugging at them enough to make room to squeeze his hand in and find my slick center. He draws a long finger through my folds, circles my clit, and I groan, closing my eyes.

"Did you shower?" he asks.

"Yes. I made us something to eat, too."

He nods slightly, but doesn't answer. He's concentrating on playing with my sensitive nub until my hips buck against him. I'm suddenly desperate for him to make me come. I'm right there.

Right. There.

When I mentioned earlier about him learning how to play me like a fiddle, he's doing just that. Every movement of his hand, his fingers, are precise. He knows how to take me *right there*. To that edge but not over it.

"You're so wet, Grace. I'm honored that it's all for me. You're squeezing my fingers. You want to come, don't you?"

"Yes." The word turns into a gasp. Just a few seconds more... Just...

He pulls his hand out of my panties and steps back causing my suddenly boneless body to collapse against the door.

Shit. Now *I* want to shove my hand down my own pants and make myself come.

My thoughts go to the two vibrators I threw into the bottom of the basket. If only...

"Take your clothes off. When you're in this cabin, you're to be naked. Remember my rules, Grace?"

I rip the sweatshirt off me. My shirt quickly follows. I'm kicking my shoes off frantically as I'm wiggling my jeans down my hips at the same time. I lose my balance and fall against the door (ass first, luckily).

He stands back, watching me, amused. I wish I could see him more clearly, but the lack of light is a handicap, because what I really want to see is his smile; it's important to me. I doubt he's smiled enough in the past few years. If at all. And to think that *I* can bring a smile to his lips thrills me.

When I'm finally free of any clothes, I throw my hands up in the air and sing, "Ta-da!" which draws a chuckle out of him.

"Wanna eat something?" I ask, because I assume I'm allowed to speak freely at this time. If not, oh well, I'll just have to put up with whatever punishment he sees fit.

Which will not cause any heartache on my part.

"I do, but I'm thinking of something different from what you're thinking."

Oh, I'm not going to say no if he'll put that skilled mouth of his on my pussy once again.

I'm all for that. Food can wait. I can't. I look forward to him finishing what he started only moments ago. Fingers, mouth, cock. I won't be picky about what he uses to make me come. I'll even tell him about the toys I brought along if he wants to break them out.

Though, if I must choose, I prefer the real thing.

"Where do you want me?" I ask in my excitement and, of course, that makes him chuckle again. Hearing him laugh warms my heart and makes me smile, too.

Even in this short time together, I'm changing his life. Maybe not in a huge way, but if I can bring a little light into his darkness, I'm pleased.

He hits the switch by the door and the cabin floods with light. He's naked, of course, and his cock is ready once again. No surprise there. This man seems to be the Energizer bunny.

"I brought something… actually some *things*," I admit, because I can't keep it to myself any more.

He cocks an eyebrow. "What did you bring, Grace?"

I lift a wait-a-minute finger and dig in the basket, pulling out my two favorite toys.

I hold them up triumphantly and he nods his head in approval. He puts out his hand and I hand him both, watching as he inspects them, turns them on and off, checking their variable speed and movement. As he does so, I squeeze my quivering thighs together in anticipation. Then his eyes meet mine. His eyes are dark and search my face before he says, "Ah."

Ah. That's it?

He points to a nearby wooden chair with one of my vibrators. "Stand behind that, hands on the chair back. Eyes forward. Don't turn and look at me or what I'm doing. Do you understand, Grace?"

Oh, yes. We're back at it again. Playing his games I like so much.

"I understand," I say, having a hard time hiding my enthusiasm.

How am I going to go back to my normal, boring life once he leaves?

I push the thought away. Time to play, not ponder. So, I do as told, gripping the top of the chair and bending over, though he didn't instruct me to do that. I just assume the position, thinking that's what he'll want.

I can't see him, but I can hear him walk across the cabin toward the bed. But he quickly returns to stand behind me. I have to admit, I'm a little giddy with anticipation. I need this week to be as full of orgasms as possible. It needs to hold me over until next year...

Next year...

What if he doesn't come back?

If his demons disappear, he may not need to return next year. Am I hurting myself by helping him chase them away?

Damn it.

Before Friday, I need to convince him that he can come up here for other reasons. To see me. To do things like this. I need to show him I could be the sole reason for him to return.

He's doing something behind me and I don't know what. I resist the temptation to peek at him, but it's difficult. Then he's dragging another chair behind me and now I'm really curious. The possibilities bounce around in my brain.

The way the air shifts, I know he's now sitting in the chair. He wraps his hands around my ankles and I jerk slightly at the unexpected contact. He traces his fingertips up the backs of my legs, along the backs of my thighs, over my ass cheeks. I shudder under his warm fingers. His touch makes me aware of every nerve ending in my body. I concentrate solely on his touch for a moment, blocking out everything else... like my own ragged breathing.

"The marks are gone," he murmurs, sounding a little disappointed as he strokes my skin slowly, gently. "Though, you're beautiful with or without them."

He trails his fingers along the cleft of my ass before teasing them along my wet folds, parting me there, too. Then he works back up, separating my cheeks, circling my tight rim.

I know he wants to fuck me there. I want him to also, however, I just don't know if I'm ready yet. But with him sitting in the chair, I don't think that's what he's planning at this moment.

And I'm right.

His light kisses follow his fingers' path, until he's stroking me with his tongue, nipping me here and there, and finally…

Finally…

Fuck.

Finally, he tickles my tight hole with the tip of his tongue and I lose all the breath in my lungs, my knees just about buckle, but I steel myself to keep standing as he does something to me that's incredulous. Now I know why he asked if I'd showered.

As he kisses, licks, and teases in the place I never expected, my head spins. In one way, I tell myself it's so *wrong*, in another, I tell myself it's so *right*.

The hum of the vibrator brings me back to reality for a moment and he slides it between my folds, gathering my arousal for lubrication. He presses it to my clit for a second, then two. I cry out, so ready to let go.

But, once again, before I can, he pulls it away and slides it inside me instead. I go completely mad with the vibration of the toy deep inside while he dips his tongue into my forbidden place. Again. Again. And again until I can hardly hold myself up anymore. I want to drop to the floor, grab him and scream at him to fuck me. Fuck me as hard and as fast as he can.

Because I need him. I need him right now.

But I can't beg, I can't ask, I can't demand.

I must remain quiet and in place and let him do to me what he will.

When he pulls back, I feel a sense of loss. "Fuck, Grace. I want you there." He blows out a breath. "I want you there, but you're not ready."

No.

But now I want him there even more than ever. He slides the vibrator from my pussy and I hear the snap of the lube cap. Suddenly, I know what his plan is. And my heart thumps harder, faster in my chest.

"Relax, Grace," he murmurs.

Doesn't he know to never tell a woman to relax? It always causes the opposite reaction.

I close my eyes and try to do just that, though, while inhaling long, deep soothing breaths.

When the lube is dribbled over my ass and down my crack, I suck in a breath. My body starts to shake and I swallow hard, forcing my muscles to release. Then I hear both vibrators start. He slides one between my folds, presses it against my clit, then I feel the blunt, lubed end of the other one at my rear. I hope he picked the smaller of the two. The vibration against my clit and my anus at the same time is insanely erotic. And, even though he doesn't give me permission to come, my body gives him a big "fuck you" and I gasp as an orgasm rolls through me.

"Grace," he says in a low warning tone.

I don't care.

I don't care.

I don't fucking care.

He presses the vibrator past my rim until it stretches me beyond anything I've ever been stretched before. The sensation is strange. But the vibrations stimulate every nerve ending in that erogenous area and beyond.

Another unexpected climax makes my eyes roll toward the back of my head and I cry out.

"Grace," Nick repeats, but he doesn't sound as in control as I'm sure he would like.

My clit is so sensitive right now, I don't think I can take the other vibrator there anymore. As if he read my mind, he moves it between my wet, swollen folds and slides it slowly forward.

Ah, fuck.

The sensations are so exquisite they are on the brink of torturous. And, once again, I can't wait for his permission to come. My body has a mind of its own as he works both vibrators in and out of me in alternating rhythms. Playing me like that fucking fiddle I knew he would.

He's whispering something. I have no idea what because all I hear is the blood rushing in my ears, my heart beating frantically, and I don't think I can hold myself up any longer.

My knees buckle, but I catch myself before collapsing, gripping the chair back even harder, my nails digging into the painted wood. The vibrator slips from my pussy and I almost sigh in relief. I never knew that pleasure could get to a point where it's actually too much to bear.

"Turn around, Grace. Face me."

I open my eyes and slowly straighten as he carefully holds the remaining vibrator deep in place. He's sitting in the other wooden chair, his eyes hooded and dark. His erection strong, thick, the crown shiny with precum.

I want to lick it clean.

"Grab that condom… and put it on me." He sounds as breathless as I feel. I snag the foil wrapper off of the nearby table and rip it open. He twitches in my hands as I roll it down his length.

"Now, straddle me."

I climb onto his lap, hold him in place, and then sink down slowly until he's as deep as he can go. With both him and the vibrator inside me, I feel full, stretched, complete.

Wrapping my arms around his neck, I hold his gaze as I push up and down, using my toes on the floor as leverage.

His one arm is snaked around my hips, still holding the vibrator in place, and the other cups my face, his thumb brushing over my cheekbone.

"Don't come until I tell you. I want us to come together this time."

Unable to speak, I simply nod my head slightly. I heard him, but I'm not sure if my body will cooperate.

Fuck. Sex had never been like this for me before. Never like this. Never this good.

Only with Nick.

I realize I will never be satisfied with quick fucks again. It'll never be like this with the snowmobilers, the hikers, the moose watchers.

He's ruined me for anyone else but him.

I keep my pace slow, steady. All the way up, all the way down until I'm panting, grimacing, trying to keep from letting go.

Trying to wait like he wants.

Because he hasn't said to come yet.

Though he's struggling himself. And I take pleasure in seeing his gritted teeth, his tense jaw, his muscles tight.

"Kiss me... Grace." My name is nothing but a breath crossing his lips.

I lean in enough to press my lips to one corner then the other of his mouth, before taking him completely, letting him in to take over.

He breaks off quickly. His body tenses beneath me and I know he's about to release deep inside me. And I'm so ready for it.

"Get ready, Grace," he murmurs against my lips. "Get ready. Are you ready?"

Hell yes, I'm ready. I release a noise that sort of sounds like a yes and feel the wave rushing up to sweep me away.

"Come with me," he demands as his hips rise. And I do, pressing my cheek to his, whimpering in his ear.

He pulsates deep inside me, making me squirm on his lap. I rest my forehead on his shoulder as he slips the vibrator from my body and turns it off, letting it fall to the floor so he can wrap me in his arms and hold me close as I attempt to catch my breath, gather my thoughts.

"Fuck, Grace, you were made for me. I knew you were the one."

"The one..." I repeat softly, wanting him to continue.

"The one to bring me back."

"Back from where?" I want to ask. Instead I stay quiet and nuzzle my nose along his short beard.

Gripping my hips, he stands, bringing me with him, keeping us connected. I wrap my legs around his waist and my arms around his neck, burying my face in his neck. He takes us over to the bed and he places me in the center, finally letting me go. He disposes of the condom and returns to the bed, climbing in beside me, pulling the blanket over us.

We're both on our sides facing each other when he breaks the silence. "Fate is a funny thing."

I agree.

Nothing has ever felt so right as being in this cabin, in this bed, with this man. Within one day, this man has wiped away all the loneliness I've ever felt living in such a remote part of Maine with no one but my dog for company.

And I don't want him to leave.

Or I need to leave with him. But I know that's impractical. Impossible. And he might not even want that.

When I don't respond to his last words, he prods, "You can speak freely, Grace. Please... tell me what you're thinking."

No, I won't admit my most recent thoughts, but I'm dying to finally know the answer to my lurking question…

"Nick, I need to ask you something…" I drift off, wondering if he'll answer me openly and willingly.

With his fingertips, he brushes my messy hair away from my face. "What?"

"How did you wind up here and why? What's the whole story?"

CHAPTER ELEVEN

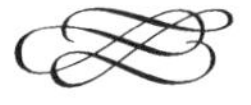

NICK

I should have known that's what she'd ask. It was only to be expected. But my tranquil, contented mood had caused me to let my guard drop. Not something I allow to happen very often.

However, being with Grace made me forget for a little while. When I originally planned this, I'd hoped she'd be willing to take me to her bed.

She was.

I'd hoped she'd be willing to play my games. To give me what I needed.

She was.

I'd hoped she'd be as sensual and sexual enough to be open minded.

She was.

She is.

She's exceeded my expectations. And, now, leaving on Friday may prove difficult.

That's something I hadn't expected. Not at all.

We've only spent hours together, but it feels like an eternity. Though, not in a bad way.

I feel that ache I couldn't shake for so long finally leaving me, that emptiness filling in little by little as our time passes together.

I didn't expect to leave here after this week and leave anything behind. But what I may leave behind might be an actual part of me. That new part. The part that's currently growing and blooming into something I never expected.

But it's not like I can stay at this point. I can't. Life still waits for me back at home. Too many loose ends that would need to be tied first. Tied or conceivably cut.

Though, I'm crazy for even considering returning to this area ever again.

No matter what, I can't imagine not seeing Grace again. I know that now. So, I need to answer her question honestly and as thoroughly as I can manage.

"I need you to listen and not ask any questions. At least until I'm done. Can you promise me that?"

Her eyes widen slightly, but she whispers, "Yes."

I take a long, shaky breath and begin. "I was working late one night..."

I was supposed to pick them up to go to my daughter's dance recital. I made sure I cleared my calendar of any meetings so I wouldn't be late. But, fuck, if at the last minute I didn't get snagged at the office. I was determined to not miss the recital, but I told my wife to go on without me. My plan was to head directly to the school and meet them there.

I arrived with ten minutes to spare, but I couldn't find them. No one had seen them. They never arrived. I even asked around because I began to panic. The dance instructor even questioned me about where they were. My daughter only had five minutes until she needed to be on stage.

My wife wouldn't answer my calls, my texts.

And with dread, I knew something was very wrong.

I decided to backtrack. Head toward home, taking the route my wife would have taken. Only six blocks from the house, I...

I close my eyes because I'll never forget what I came upon. That horrific scene at the intersection. The lights were blinding, the sirens deafening. And the tractor trailer driver, whose brake system failed and had T-boned them, sat on the curb with his head in his hands as he answered questions by the responding officers.

Fuck. I just knew... I just knew...

I almost threw up as I dragged myself out of my car. I forced myself to run, even though my legs felt full of lead. I could barely recognize the car, but I knew...

I lost everything.

I had nothing left.

If I'd only picked them up, a difference of seconds could have changed the outcome.

I'd still have my family. My wife. My baby girl.

"And so, every year on the anniversary I come up here to forget, to get away from it all. My fucking job that made me late. My family. Her family. Every year it gets a little easier. But it'll be with me forever. That scene etched in my mind. The anger is lessening, and so is the pain. It's more bearable now."

I stop talking for a moment, refocus on the cabin, on Grace. On the here and now.

"I found this place in the most unorthodox way. I closed my eyes and pointed to a spot on the map. And I found you, Grace. Fate found what I needed to heal."

When I look at her to see her reaction to my words, my confession of sorts, she's not focused on me at all. Her eyes are closed and I wonder if she's even listening at all, is she hearing what I'm saying? Understanding the meaning of my words?

"I almost didn't come back this year. But something pulled at me. Grace," I whisper, needing her to look at me. I cup her jaw and she opens her eyes, which are shiny with unshed tears. "You pulled me back here, Grace. I don't know how, I don't know why. I'm not going to question it because I won't understand it."

"I only hoped you'd return so I could get laid," she says softly, amusement now in her eyes, chasing away the tears.

I laugh. She has made me laugh more in this day than I have in years. "I know. I gave you what you needed, didn't I?"

She gives me a wide smile and wipes at her eyes. "Yes. You certainly did and then some. I gave you what you needed also?"

"You absolutely did. And I'll be forever grateful. I feel whole once again. It's been a long time." I press a light kiss to her forehead, the tip of her nose, and then her lips. When she parts them, I deepen the kiss, gently exploring her mouth, teasing her tongue.

I'm feeling the same pull that made me drive up here this year, but now it's making me hold her closer and our bodies tangle like our tongues, fitting together perfectly.

As her nipples tighten, harden, press into my chest, I harden as well, ready to take her once again, to make her mine.

Though, I don't want to think about the end of this week, I need to know something before we get distracted "When I leave Friday, I want you to wait for me. Can you do that?"

Her brows raise in surprise. "For a year?"

I shake my head. "No." No, because I can't wait a year, either. "A month. I'll be back in a month. And then we'll see where this goes, where we need to go. Can you accept that?"

"Yes."

"No one else, Grace. Promise me. I need to hear it." For my own sanity, I do need to hear it. Now that I have her, I'm not letting her go.

"I promise."

The relief I feel is overwhelming, and it warms my insides. I slide my fingers into her hair and make a fist, before leaning close and whispering against her lips, "I promise, too."

Her lips curve against mine.

I think I'll let her choose how we play this time…

~The End~

An Obsessed Novella

LOVING *Her*

USA Today Bestselling Author

Jeanne St. James

It's not just a love story, it's an obsession...

Noah:

I've loved Bree my whole life. We were each other's firsts when we were young and inexperienced, and I totally screwed up. I disappointed her, causing her to cry and run away. But over the years, I've learned, I've perfected, and I've dreamt of one day getting another shot with the love of my life.

When I finally get the chance never in my wildest dreams did I think Bree was like this. The girl who used to wear yellow sundresses is no longer Bree, she's Brianna, my new mistress. I'll do whatever needed for her forgiveness, even go to my knees and grovel.

However, there's just one thing... I want Bree back, not Brianna. Once I get Bree, Brianna can do to me what she will.

Bree:

Maybe Noah doesn't realize it, but he's been mine ever since we were teens. I tried to apologize for disappointing him our first time, but never got the chance.

Now, when he approaches me at the bar, I can only think about all the things I want to do *to* him and *with* him. I plan to show him the skills I've honed over the years.

Little does he know what's in store for him because I know his secrets, his desires, his needs. And I plan on giving it all to him.

However, just when I think I'm in control, he turns my world upside down.

Note: All books in the Obsessed series are standalone novellas. It is intended for audiences over 18 years of age since it includes explicit sexual situations, including BDSM.

YOU NEVER FORGET YOUR FIRST...

CHAPTER ONE

Noah:

I've loved her my whole life. At least since I can remember, which is all the way back to when she was in kindergarten and I was in first grade. I'd chase her through the backyard and around the jungle gym, trying to catch and kiss her.

If I'd succeed, she'd curl her little fingers into a fist, sock me in the gut, then run and tell her mother.

Yep, I had no game.

And, apparently, I didn't leave an impression. Because now, at thirty, she's still avoiding me.

Even though she can't go very far at the moment since I'm her brother's Best Man, and she's the Maid of Honor.

Let me tell you, I hate weddings.

I hate them even more when I'm forced to stand across from her and can't touch her, drag my fingers through her long, dark hair and run my lips along her delicate neck.

The only time I *can* touch her is when I escort her up the aisle. I've done it twice so far. However, she won't meet my eyes, she feels stiff on my arm and she's hardly said two words to me. And now I stand here while the wedding planner drones on and on about what's expected of us during the ceremony tomorrow.

Yawn.

Look, Ms. Wedding Planner, it's easy. Put one foot in front of the other, walk (without tripping) up the center aisle (can't get lost while staying in between the rows of pews and aim for the front of the church), then stand to the side (no picking noses, asses, or adjusting your junk).

Simple.

Oh, and don't pass out. Otherwise, the video will go viral across cyberspace.

One more thing... the rings. Can't forget to put the rings in my tux pocket.

Got it.

Yawn again.

It isn't as if I'm not happy for my buddy, getting married to a great woman (although, not quite as stunning as his sister) who makes him happy, but I'm not thrilled with being a part of it. But I have his back. And I'd love to have his sister on her back.

Again. But in better circumstances.

We lost our virginity together at seventeen in her parents' pool shed. I was in love with her then, too. Her with me? Not so much.

And in those forty-five seconds of bliss, I fell in love with her even more. I don't think she thought it was even close to bliss, though. In fact, she had run out of the shed crying while pulling down her sweet yellow sundress.

I was devastated, and that was a major blow to my seventeen-year-old ego.

I'll admit it, I had a lot to learn.

However, I had to learn it elsewhere since she was no longer game. In fact, she avoided me (just like at this rehearsal).

But I did learn. I was determined to improve, to not make her cry next time. But, unfortunately, there never was a next time.

Eventually, Mrs. Callahan down the street was kind enough to take me under her wing. Teach me the ins and outs of women. Of pleasure. Of discovering what I wanted and what I wanted to give in return.

Mrs. Callahan.

Yeah.

She made me call her that, too. And I did (when I wasn't calling her Mistress).

I learned.

I perfected.

I dreamt of one day getting another shot with the love of my life.

Now here we stand, across from each other. My eyes on her. Her eyes on everything but me.

I want her.

I need her.

Still.

Even after all these years.

As I stand across from her, I'm mesmerized by her unforgettable, stunning beauty.

I love her.

But I can't have her.

And that fucking blows.

~

Bree:

At dinner, I watch him over the rim of my wine glass. My eyes narrow as he leans over to say something quietly into the ear of one of the bridesmaids. The single one with the big boobs that made sure she snagged the chair next to him. She throws her little blonde head back and laughs. He smiles in response, his golden-green eyes sparkling. They have a secret. Apparently a funny one, too.

She can laugh with him all she wants, but she needs to know... he's mine.

He's been mine ever since we lost our virginity together all those years ago.

Maybe he didn't realize it then. He doesn't realize it now.

Maybe, just maybe, he needs a lesson.

One different from what that whore Mrs. Callahan taught him.

Yes, I know all about Mrs. Callahan and Noah.

And what she did to *my* Noah.

Days later I followed him, trying to catch up with him to apologize for running out crying after he popped my cherry. I even called out his name, but he didn't hear me. Or maybe he was ignoring me. Probably because I disappointed him that day in the shed and he didn't want anything to do with me anymore.

But then he went to *her* house. I watched (in shock) as the door opened and he was pulled inside. He had just turned eighteen. Barely legal. That bitch was like a hundred at the time.

Okay, probably the same age as we are now. Though, back then, it might as well have been a hundred.

She opened the door wearing some sexy almost see-through nightie. One I would have killed to own (and fill out like her). Her eyes flicked up to me and I froze. She smiled like a predator at Noah, snagged his arm and dragged him inside. Then she aimed that smile at me as she shut the door behind him.

I ended up following him more than once. More than twice.

I'm embarrassed to admit how often it truly was.

But what he learned, I did, too. I watched them.

And one day when I was hidden, I saw it happen.

She had her husband's belt. And she whipped him with it while he was on his knees, his head to the mattress.

I watched him twitch with every strike. His ass getting redder with every blow. And she wasn't gentle. No. She struck him hard, often, but I couldn't hear if he made a noise. If he cried out, if he asked her to stop.

Though, it didn't appear so.

He could have escaped, gotten away. He wasn't tied in any fashion, he wasn't restrained. He moved into position willingly with, from what I could see, his eyes showing excitement.

A smile curled that witch's lips as she did it.

I got scared while watching her hit him.

Not for him.

No.

But for me.

Because I realized what she gave, what he willingly accepted, did something inside of me. It lit a fire in my belly, caused goosebumps to break out all over my body, tightened my nipples, made me slick between the thighs.

What Mrs. Callahan was doing should have disturbed me. It didn't.

It excited me.

I wanted to switch places with her.

Now, I not only wanted Noah, I wanted to do things to him I never expected.

CHAPTER TWO

Noah:

At fifteen, Bree and I kissed for the first time (or the first time without me being punched in the gut) when we played Spin the Bottle at a party she tagged along to with some friends. Our kiss was quick, wet and warm. Totally fucking glorious.

When it was her turn again, I watched with dismay as it spun to a stop in front of Donnie Carson. Their kiss lasted a lot longer than normal, so let's say I was relieved when she finally pushed him away and made a face, wiping the back of her hand across her lips.

My relief was two-fold. First, because I thought I would have to kick his ass (and that would ruin the party) and second, she hadn't made that face when she kissed me (which made me hope I kissed better).

Since a couple of the guys had stolen some booze from their parents, we were mixing vodka with Kool-Aid. By the time the clock turned ten, we were pretty much smashed out of our gourds and Spin the Bottle had turned into Seven Minutes in Heaven. There were only a few of us left sitting in the circle, so my odds were good.

I held my breath the whole time when she spun it, because if it landed on someone other than me, there would be a problem.

It was bad enough watching her kiss other guys (and girls), but being locked in a dark closet with someone other than me for seven minutes… that was a big fucking *N-O.* I wouldn't stand for it. No, I would not.

Did it land on me? Fuck no. I couldn't be so lucky. However, it did land on Mary Jane Pavlovich. I watched in fascination as both of their eyes widened, they giggled, then MJ grabbed Bree's hand and dragged her into the closet, slamming the door shut.

I have no idea what they did in there, but there sure was a lot of laughing mixed with long periods of silence.

Yeeeeaaaah. Talk about a teenage boy's wet dreams. That was it right there.

When someone finally forced the door open, their hair was messed up, and they both wore a wistful smile.

Now, as I approach her at the hotel bar, I know no matter what, I want to see that wistful smile on her face again.

And I plan on putting it there.

I'm done fucking around, playing this game with her where she won't look at me, won't acknowledge that I even exist.

No. Stick a fork in me, I'm done.

Time to step up my game.

Bree:

I take another sip of my Merlot and give the sloshed man next to me at the bar a polite but dismissive smile. He's been talking my ear off for the past five minutes and I need to get away because he's starting to lean toward me and I'm well aware of what comes next. Hand on my thigh. An "accidental" brush of my boobs. Plus, I need to go home before I drink too much (like him) and can't drive.

That wouldn't be good. Although, it would be the perfect excuse to go knock on Noah's door and crash in his room. I know he's staying here because he had to fly in from out of town—

A hand lands on my shoulder interrupting my thoughts and at first, I think it's the toasted schmoe next to me. Then I realize it isn't because his glazed eyes are glued to someone standing behind me.

The hand squeezes my shoulder, and my eyes widen as a deep, oh so fucking deep, masculine voice murmurs in my ear, "Need an excuse to escape?"

Without turning around, I know who it is. *Noah.* His name whispers through my mind.

About. Fucking. Time.

Nodding, the pounding of my heart radiates through my whole body and lands south where it turns into another type of throbbing.

I slide my wine glass away from me and turn in my seat. He looks so fucking delicious, I lose my breath.

A lock of his dirty blond (and too long) hair has fallen across his forehead and I want to sweep it to the side with my fingers. Since it's late, a five o'clock shadow graces his jaw. It fits him. If it was up to me, he would never shave again (trim, yes, shave, no).

I had to fight staring at him at the church (and again at dinner), forcing myself to look at anything but him. Otherwise, I might have pulled him right down in the middle aisle of the church and fucked his brains out on the marble floor. By the way, that would be *after* I rode his face.

I think Jesus (who's nailed to a cross above the altar) might frown upon that.

Not to mention, my brother, Rob and his fiancé, Barb. That could have put a little kink in the rehearsal.

In more ways than one.

As he grabs my elbow, he leans close again. "Nightcap?"

"Sure," I answer. Because I'm not a fool.

And I'm tired of the "let's pretend it never happened" game.

"Your place or mine?" His question sends a shock of lightning down my spine.

I'm getting the feeling that he's not suggesting a little chat about old times and he's decided to get right down to business.

Direct. I like it.

I'm all for this new game.

However, I must think about his question. His "place" is a hotel room upstairs. The pro is that it's close and convenient.

The cons are that it's in a hotel which is full of people, I don't have any of my stuff with me, and our nightcap will be limited by whatever's in the room's minibar. Which most likely isn't much and is probably all bottom shelf crap.

On the other hand, my place is only about ten minutes away, it's fully stocked with the basics (though quality) when it comes to alcohol, it's private, and I'll have my own stuff.

And by stuff, I mean my toys.

Which I would love to introduce Noah to. And, not to mention, have waited a long time to do it.

My knees wobble for a second and his fingers dig into my arm to steady me.

"You okay?" he asks softly.

"Yes," I answer just as softly. The love of my life is leading me out of the bar… And I'm thrilled he's giving me a second chance.

"So?"

So? Oh, yes. "My place." For sure.

"You close?"

"Yes."

"I'll follow you in my rental."

"Yes," I repeat, because apparently that word is the only thing I can say since I'm giddy with excitement and anticipation. Not to mention, my brain is only focused on one thing…

Noah with the five o'clock shadow.

My body quivers as he steers me through the lobby and out to the parking lot, his fingers tight on my arm as if he's afraid I'm going to cut and run. He asks me where I'm parked and I can only point because my mind spins with what I want to do to him and how I want to do it.

On the drive back to my house, I keep checking my rearview mirror to make sure I don't lose him. Otherwise, I'll have to turn around and hunt him down.

He's not going to slip from my fingers this time. Even if I have to tie him down… Or up.

~

He didn't get lost. He didn't veer off. He followed me closely and parked behind me in my driveway.

And now as I hand him his whiskey on the rocks, I study him. This time I don't hide my interest. I feel a twinge between my thighs and a rush of heat as he watches me take stock of him.

He's taller now. He's matured well. His shoulders are broad under the white button-down shirt he wears. The neck is open and a white undershirt peeks out. He's in some sort of shape, that's for sure, but how much… I can't tell until I get him naked. His torso appears trim, though, down through his hips. His thighs fill his jeans and what I saw of his ass, that's very nice, too. No pooch, no beer gut, and his legs are longer than I remember. The longish blond hair is "dirtier" than when he was younger. Though darker, some streaks of light remain as if he spends a fair amount of time in the sun. Maybe he still runs like he did when he was a teen and ran cross-country.

No matter what, he's definitely different since I last saw him before we both left for college.

He doesn't drop his gaze as mine comes back to his face. No, he meets my eyes directly and steadily. Almost as if a challenge.

I like that. I don't like weak men, and he gives me no sign of softness. But he also gives me no smile, not even a small one. No indication he likes me checking him out. But he does. I know this because it's apparent by the tightness in the crotch of his jeans.

I like that, too.

Responsive. Eager.

I tilt my head slightly as he lifts the glass to his lips, taking a healthy sip of the expensive whiskey. It's so smooth he doesn't even wince slightly as it slides down his throat. My gaze drops from his eyes to his long fingers wrapped around his drink.

Fingers I have plans for. My nipples tighten in anticipation, my breath shallows in need.

He lowers the glass slowly. "Bree…"

My brain barely registers that he's spoken. "Hmm?"

"I'm sorry."

"For what?" I murmur, still distracted by the beauty that is him. I thought he was striking when we were teenagers, but he's only become more so with age.

His lips tighten a moment before he says, "For being a bumbling idiot all those years ago."

Me, too.

"We were young," I say as if it's in the past and the past isn't important.

Though it is. The past defines who we are today. Who I am now. Who he is.

"I know. But I made you cry."

What? No.

What he says takes me out of my reverie. I blink, letting reality rush over me.

This is Noah standing in my living room.

Noah.

"You thought…" I shake my head. "I didn't cry because you were a bumbling idiot." Just the opposite. It was me, not him.

"You ran out—"

"Yes, I ran out because I thought *I* disappointed *you*. I was…" I hesitate. Do I really want to admit this? Now? "Embarrassed."

"Fuck," he breathes. "I thought I disappointed you."

"Well…" Less than a minute wasn't anything to write home

about. But I didn't need to rub that in.

He must have read my expression because I know I didn't confess that out loud. "I know… It was bad."

Well, since he admitted it... "Yes."

He scrubs a hand over his face. "For both of us."

I lift my shoulder and a small smile pulls at my lips. I can't help it. We had been young and inexperienced. But then, wasn't everyone at one point?

"I promise I'm not like that now."

I'm well aware of that. But now is not the right time to tell him. Because then he'll discover I know his secret. And then I'll have to reveal mine.

Later.

"Why are you here, Noah?"

"Because you invited me back to your house."

"No, I didn't."

His eyebrows lower and he hesitates. "No?"

"No, you made a suggestion."

Clarity crosses his features. "Yes, your place or mine."

"Yes, but why?"

"Why not?"

"Noah," I chastise him softly.

His fingers tighten on his glass as he lifts it again, downing the rest of the contents, then staring at the empty glass. He swirls the remaining ice, then his gaze meets mine. Confident, but with a touch of anger. "I couldn't watch another man touch you."

Ah, like Mrs. Callahan touched you. I endured that. "The man at the bar?"

"Yes."

"He didn't touch me."

"He wanted to."

"Maybe."

"No maybes about it."

I tilt my head in question. "Why do you care?"

His gaze drops to his glass again and his shadowed jaw tightens. "Because you're mine." He turns away and places the glass on the sideboard.

Just like that. I'm *his*.

Damn.

My knees weaken with his statement and I hide the surprise from my face before he turns back to me.

I keep my voice steady as I ask, "Since when?"

A small noise escapes him. Impatience? "You know when." No, the anger in his words are unmistakable. He knows I'm playing with him in an attempt to draw things out from deep inside.

"Tell me," I demand, but gently.

"Since forever."

I suck in a breath. "Forever is a long time."

"Yes." He tilts his head and narrows his eyes. "Why are you playing this game, Bree?"

"This isn't a game." Not quite.

"What is it?"

"I just want to make sure this is what you want."

"I want you."

"How do you want me?"

"Any way I can have you."

I fight the urge to ask him why. Why me? Why then? Why now? Why our whole lives we've danced a dance that never brought us closer together but only farther apart? Something that started even before we could understand it. We were always drawn to each other. Obviously, we still are.

"If I ask you to get down on your knees, would you?" He doesn't want me to play games, so I won't.

Something unreadable crosses his face and his eyes darken. But he takes his time answering, weighing my question. "Yes."

"Would you do anything I ask of you?"

He blows out a breath. "Do you know what you're doing?"

Of course, he wouldn't know that I do. He couldn't know I

honed my own skills over the years with some of the best. Not only in hopes that I would someday get this opportunity before me, but because I needed it for me also.

"I do." I lick my lips because I can't wait to taste his skin against them.

His gaze lifts from my mouth to my eyes. "How do you know what I want?"

"I'm not asking you what you want. I'm inquiring about whether you'll do anything I ask. Simple."

"Not so simple."

"It can be," I shoot back.

"If I allow it."

"Will you?" I ask, trying to keep the hope obvious from my question.

He hesitates, then murmurs, "Fuck, Bree." He shakes his head. "What happened to the girl who wore yellow sundresses?"

Good question. "She grew up."

A smile finally lifts the corners of his lips. "That she did," he agrees.

"Do you like what she's become?"

His eyes rake over me, causing things to quiver low in my body.

I know what he's looking at. I've matured over the years, too. My curves have become more pronounced, my breasts heavier, my thighs softer. Full. Womanly. No longer a teenager. I would fill out a yellow sundress much differently now.

"I love what she's become."

I give him a smile, too. "Then you will do what I ask of you." Not a question because it's time to stop asking and start telling.

"Bree, you can bend me however you'd like."

"Bend but not break," I assure him.

Suddenly his eyes flick to mine and hold. Clarity is now behind him. He understands what I'm expecting of him. He understands that what he needs is what I need as well.

And I need to touch him.

CHAPTER THREE

Noah:

My mind spins as I sit on the couch. First, because I have a hard time believing I'm actually in her living room. Second, because I know my fantasies with Bree are about to come true. Third, I'll finally get a chance to make up for that horrible time we had losing our virginity. And fourth, if I'm reading her right (and I'm pretty sure I am), she is going to rock my fucking world.

She told me to wait out here. My cock is hard and aches for her. Fuck, my chest has an ache, also, and I slide my palm over my heart down my stomach to my groin.

I assume she's freshening up since she went down the hall with a purpose. The whole way my eyes were glued to her curvy ass in her black dress pants. I haven't even kissed her yet and I'm dying to do so. I should have taken the opportunity before she disappeared.

In the meantime, I need more bourbon. To fortify me, at least. So, I push myself to my feet and head to the sideboard, grabbing the bottle of Japanese whiskey and pouring myself two more fingers worth. She knows her liquor. She likes quality. Her house isn't huge; it's a good size for what I assume is someone who lives alone.

Though, I hadn't even asked if she does.

But the furniture and the décor appears to be quality as well. Everything is done in primary colors. Blacks, reds, white, a touch of yellow here, blue there.

Classy.

I take a sip of the Yamazaki and appreciate how smoothly it goes down. It heats my gut.

Like Bree does.

Just when I think she might have forgotten about me, I hear clicking down the tiled hallway. No mistaking the sound of a woman in high heels. And here I thought she would have gotten more comfortable.

With the glass halfway to my lips, I turn my head and...

Lose my breath.

Fuck. Me.

The girl I love who used to wear yellow sundresses has definitely grown up.

As she closes in on me, not only do my balls tighten, my asshole puckers. My heart skips a beat before it begins to thump wildly.

Bree is no longer Bree. No, this woman before me is Brianna.

And she is my new mistress.

Now I know why she asked if I'd go to my knees for her.

As I watch her get closer, I decide right then that she wouldn't even need to ask.

Her long, silky, almost black hair is still up in the tight bun that she wore all afternoon and evening. Not a hair out of place.

Her eyes are darker now, smokier. Makeup, maybe. But the glitter in her coffee-colored eyes is unmistakable. Determined. No nonsense.

Her lips are a deep red, her cheeks hold some color. A rush of blood from excitement, possibly, but I'm not sure.

But. Fuck. Me.

She's wearing a black leather corset with a bone-insert waist that pushes her tits up and out from the cups. The pale skin of her breasts glows softly. The front is cross-laced from her cleavage down to the bottom with a hint of skin peeking through. The bottom curve of the corset doesn't quite meet the leather skirt she wears. The skirt is not short, but it's tight, hugging her hips and luscious thighs. It stops a couple inches above her knees. And those legs... She's wearing sheer black stockings that make them look long enough to wrap around my hips while I'm fucking her.

But those fucking heels. Damn. Black leather to match the rest of her outfit with a wickedly high stiletto heel. The height of her heel makes the curves of her calves look absolutely delicious.

As my eyes roam back up, I notice she's holding something in one hand. I'm hoping a whip, a crop, something, anything she can use to take me to task. But it's not. It's a circle of black leather with a buckle and a D ring.

Then it hits me what it is.

A fucking collar. Attached to the metal D ring is a thin leather leash curled up in her hand.

She's going to make me her slave.

Fuck. Me.

"On your knees." She says it softly but firmly. And there's no ignoring the authority behind the words.

I hesitate too long. I think it's because I wasn't expecting this. I had no warning. A hint, yes, but that was it.

"Don't make me tell you twice."

I quickly place the glass on the sideboard and fall to my knees, hitting the hard tile with a grunt of pain. I tip my chin down, my eyes falling to the floor, aiming for her shoes.

I will not challenge her in this. I'm dying to see where this goes.

Actually, I *live* to see where this goes because I can't get any harder than I am right now. Seeing her dressed like that, hearing her demand, I know my fantasies of her were never this rich, this perfect, this colorful.

She's totally blown my mind.

"Chin up."

I lift my face obediently, but keep my eyes pointed to the floor. She struts (and the woman can fucking strut with those heels on) around behind me and I hear the metallic clink of the buckle. The leather circles my neck and she tightens it until it's snug. A reminder of who now owns me. I hear the click of a tiny padlock and the hairs on the back of my neck rise.

Then there's a sharp tug as she steps back. "On your feet."

I push myself to stand but don't turn around. I keep my eyes down and my body loose.

I had no idea she was like this.

She had no idea I was, either.

How did she know I would accept her collar without fighting it? Without at least some words of concern?

She didn't. She couldn't.

When Brianna steps around me, I discover that in her heels she now comes to my chin instead of my shoulder.

When the collar jerks against my neck, my cock jerks, too, and I follow her down the darkened hall.

I don't know what to expect. A bedroom. A playroom. But it's the not knowing that makes my blood rush, my heart beat faster, my limbs tremble.

All the things she could possibly do to me floods my mind, and when we reach her bedroom, I quickly take note of everything in there. Especially, the king-sized bed in more blacks, reds and whites. Sharp, bold colors.

She jerks the lead and, once again, I follow her willingly. This time to the center of her large bedroom. "Stand there."

She unclips the leash and tosses it onto the bed, then turns to face me. "I'll ask you again, Noah, are you willing to do whatever I ask?"

"Yes," my voice holds a tremor from the excitement that slides through me.

"You have a safe word?"

I nod but don't answer.

"Noah," she says in a low warning tone.

I smile. I like when she admonishes me. It makes my cock twitch in my jeans. She steps closer, close enough that her heat sears me. She trails her fingers over my lips, her eyes following.

"Noah," she says softly. "Tell me your safe word."

She knows I have a safe word. She knows me, she knows what's inside of me. I don't know how, but she does. "Mississippi."

With a sharp nod, she accepts that and steps back. I feel the loss of her heat, her closeness. I don't want her to go.

"You know the drill," she states as she steps behind me.

Yes, I do know the drill. I know to use my word when I'm pushed beyond my limit. It's only happened a handful of times in all these years. It had been when things had gotten very rough or out of control, mostly because I was with the wrong person for the wrong reason.

"Unbutton your shirt."

Her voice, husky but firm, comes from over my shoulder. My fingers immediately find the buttons, pushing them through their holes. Working my way down, I get to my waist and pull the shirt from my jeans until it hangs open.

Then I feel her hands on me, tracing the edge of the leather collar, traveling down my neck, under my shirt, over my shoulders, shoving the shirt down my arms and off of me. As she runs her palms up my back, she snags my undershirt and pulls it up and over my head, tossing it to the side.

Her hands are on me again, this time she's digging her nails into my skin and raking them down my back. I arch against the pain and huff out a breath. Not hard enough to score my flesh but enough to make me very aware of how long her nails are.

Fuck. Me.

She reaches around me to unbuckle my belt and the overflowing mounds of her breasts press into my back and I can't help but groan. I want my face buried in them; I want her nipples in my mouth. I want to test her wetness with my fingers and tongue. And then ultimately my cock.

Heat rolls through me as I wonder what she's wearing underneath the skirt, if anything.

Her fingers play along my zipper, along the hard bulge in my jeans. She unfastens them, unzips, then she's gone again, moving around to the front of me.

"Kick off your shoes."

I do, sending them flying into the corner of her room.

Sliding her hands into the waistband of my jeans, she shoves them down with my boxer briefs at the same time. And she goes with them, bending over as she pushes them lower, over my knees until they fall to my ankles. She drops down and taps my right leg and I lift it automatically. She pulls the leg of my jeans, my sock and my underwear off one side and repeats with the other.

When I stand before her totally naked, my erection bobs in the air, beading with precum as I stare down at her crouching at my feet.

She gazes up my body, her eyes coming to my cock and she licks her lips. And don't I just feel that deep in my balls...

As she comes up, she drags her tongue along my length, capturing the precum with the tip, then tastes it.

"Beautiful, Noah."

Yes, I have to agree, what she just did was absolutely beautiful.

"You take care of yourself," she murmurs as she straightens with a smile that cuts right through me.

"Yes."

"I'm pleased."

"I'm here to please you."

"I'm glad to hear that. Now, move to the doorway."

I glance over my shoulder to her open bedroom door, that's when I notice the eyebolts in the corners of the jamb, top and bottom. And next to it on the floor is what looks like Neoprene cuffs. Nothing hardcore since they fasten with Velcro. Something used on the willing.

And I'm certainly that.

Brianna:

His body is amazing, still a runner's body. Trim, hard, sculpted. And it's all mine. At least for tonight. My heart thumps in my throat with my barely contained excitement, but I must remain in control. For me. For him.

I have so many things I want to do to him, do with him, and so little time to do it. So, I've picked a few of my favorite toys to play with. Ones I know will not invoke his safe word.

As he moves to the doorway as I asked, or demanded, more like it, I watch the play of his muscles under his skin in the soft light of my bedroom. His ass though... the indentations in the glutes makes my mouth water. I can't wait to feel the flex of those muscles under my fingers and calves when he's pumping into me.

But we're not there yet. We must play first.

I must give him what he needs to make this extraordinary. I must take what I need in hope of redemption.

When he reaches the doorway, I bark out an order. "Face me. Arms and legs spread-eagle. Touch the corners of the jamb."

He turns, his dark blond hair falling across his forehead, reminding me of when we were young and so innocent. I can see the gleam in his eyes as I approach him. Luckily, he's tall enough that the doorway will work perfectly to place him in the position I want him in. But he's not too tall where I can't reach him comfortably while wearing my heels.

When he's where I want him, I murmur, "Don't move." I gather the Neoprene cuffs and carefully strap his ankles wide, then I stand and restrain his wrists above him. "Pull," I order and he does. They hold fast. "Good, my pet." The nickname slips out before I can stop it but I'm thrilled to watch him shudder when I call him that. *Perfect.* It will remain.

I leave him for a moment to pick up two things from the side table that sits along my wall.

As I slip the wide blindfold over his eyes, I'm almost wondering whether I should forego it. Shame, really, to cover such beautiful, expressive eyes. Maybe later I will leave it off. But for now...

"Can you see me, my pet?"

He releases a long breath. "No."

"Do you want to see me?"

"Yes," he hisses, which makes me smile. Now, to begin...

I check the Wartenberg pinwheel in my hand. One of my favorites. Unlike pinwheels from when we were children that spin in the breeze, this pinwheel is oh so adult. It reminds me of a cowboy's spur. The handle is made of metal, with twenty sharp needle-like points radiating from its wheel. It could be used twofold... to bring pleasure or to bring pain, depending on the pressure, depending on its use.

But for now, I want my pet to be hard, ready for me for when I'm ready for him. I want him to be driven to please me after I please him.

Give and take. I will give and I will take. He will come along for the ride.

"One Mississippi," I murmur as I roll the wheel along his skin from his pelvis up his belly to his chest. He sucks in his stomach and blows out a breath, his cock twitching, leaking between us.

"Two Mississippi." I lightly direct it over his right nipple.

"Ah fuck," he mutters, his jaw tight.

"Three Mississippi." I roll it to his left nipple, over the very hard tip and he jerks in his restraints.

"Bree," he breathes.

I love my name on his lips when he's engulfed in pleasure, it makes my pussy clench. I want to take him there and squeeze him tight, feel him fill me up and make me orgasm mindlessly.

But it's too soon. We've only just begun.

I roll the pinwheel along the tender underside of his arms which are exposed as they stretch before me. I roll it down his chest again, over his stomach, pushing harder this time, leaving marks behind.

"Yes?" I ask him.

"Yes," he groans.

Not that I'd change my course of action if he'd said no. He knows what he needs to say to stop me.

I continue my path along his waist, over his hips, down his thighs, his muscles tightening, clenching, twitching. Then behind his knees, down his calves, around his ankles. If I didn't have him bound, I'd do the bottom of his feet and drive him mad.

I'm disappointed I can't. Maybe next time.

Now on my knees in front of him, I roll it along his inner thighs, coming to the apex of his legs. I study him, the pinwheel gripped tightly in my hand. He's stunning. His cock is no more than average length, but the girth is remarkable and his balls hang heavy just waiting for my touch.

I don't know if I should give him that just yet, because I find myself fighting my own urges. And if I give in to them, I'm no longer in control.

No matter what, I don't want to disappoint Noah again. Not now, not ever.

I rake my nails over his length, then over the tip and a noise escapes him that turns my nipples into even harder points. Lightly, I roll the pinwheel down his length, just missing the delicate skin of his sac.

"Ah, fuck," he cries out, his chin dropping to his chest.

"You like that, my pet?" I ask him out of courtesy but nothing more.

He says something that sounds like a yes, but isn't a fully formed word. I smile.

Tonight, neither one of us will be disappointed, unlike all those years ago. I will make sure he leaves here fully satisfied. I will make sure he leaves me in the same way, as well.

I run the sharp wheel over the crown of his cock and circle the head. "You like my instrument of torture?"

"Not... torture."

No, clearly it is not.

I run it back down, once again stopping before I touch that delicate skin. Maybe another time I will test him there. But not tonight.

I draw my nails over him again, then follow the same path with the tip of my tongue, and he groans loudly.

"More..." He drifts off. He doesn't know what to call me. I will let him figure that out. That will be another lesson learned.

"What do you want more of, my pet? The wheel, my nails? Or my mouth?"

Not that I'll give him a choice. He will get what I give him and nothing more.

"All of it."

Though, I have to admit that answer pleases me. I cup his sac and lightly squeeze as I suck the tip of him into my mouth, tasting his salty precum. He's delicious and I savor his taste. His essence on my tongue makes me want him even more. The wetness between my legs grows, causing me to squeeze my thighs together. I'm on the edge of coming and it wouldn't take much.

In fact, I want to do just that. While he's blindfolded and tied up, I want him to hear me come.

But I'm not there yet, I need more to get me right to that point without his touch.

With a last lick to the slick head of his cock, I stand and inspect his chest. His small dusky nipples pebble amongst a smattering of hair. Not a thick patch, but just right. His skin looks tan, as if he spends a lot of time outdoors, which would make sense with his sun-kissed hair. He has no marks or scars I can see. Not a single tattoo.

He's almost flawless. Almost. Because sometimes the biggest flaws are hidden on the inside.

Even so, I would love to see his nipples pierced. If he becomes my regular pet, I would insist he do so.

I suck on one of his nipples and flick the other with the tip of my nail. He jerks against me, his chest heaving, his breathing ragged. The long line of his cock presses between us. His hips tilt as he rubs it along the smooth leather of my skirt.

He will make me come if he continues along that path. And I need to torment myself and him a little longer before I allow myself that release.

When I step back, his body bows in the doorway. He either craves my touch or he's relieved I've let him go.

My hope is the former and not the latter.

I go to my side table and grab the next toy. I eyeball it, wondering if it will even fit. If anything, it may be a little snug due to his girth. But he'll manage. He'll certainly endure.

This is a toy that will benefit both of us in the very near future.

I move closer to him and sit on my heels, taking him into my palm. I slide the silicone cock ring over his engorged head and down his length, pulling his balls none too gently into the second ring. He's already jerking in my hand, but has no idea what's next.

And when I turn it on, his body turns solid, his lips open and he lets out an "Ah, fuck me."

"Are you complaining, my pet?"

"No," escapes his gritted teeth.

I stroke his thighs and the cock ring isn't the only thing vibrating. His muscles tremor under my touch while my pussy throbs between my legs. "Then I assume it's not too tight and you enjoy the sensation you're getting."

"Fuck yes," comes out on a ragged breath.

"Would you like to fuck me with that on?"

"Fuck... yes. *Please.*"

I smile, then take him into my mouth.

CHAPTER FOUR

Noah:

I just about lose my mind when she encompasses my dick almost completely. Between the wet heat of her mouth and the powerful vibrations of the cock ring, I put more weight into the cuffs that hold my wrists high.

My body has become hers and no longer belongs to me. And I want to dig my fingers into that hair of hers and fuck her face hard. But I can't.

She won't let me.

And that makes me even more determined.

I don't want to come down her throat; I want to come inside her. She has been mine forever. She might not know that, but I do. And I need to claim her.

Although I love that I'm her pet and she knows how to make my body react in just the right ways, I need to show her that I can please her. I need to make up for my former mistake. My inexperience. The reason I made her cry.

As her tongue strokes along the underside of my cock and her mouth surrounds me, my knees weaken and I lock them tight to stay on my feet. Otherwise, I will be hanging from my arms, and I'm aware these restraints aren't made for that.

I don't understand why she has them. I don't understand why she's like the way she is. I'm not complaining. Fuck no. This is my fantasy. And never in my wildest dreams had I thought Bree would be like this.

It makes being here with her all the sweeter. But the sweetness can only go so far.

Normally, I don't mind a blindfold; however, right now I hate it. I hate not being able to see her lips stretched wide around me, her cheeks hollowing as she sucks me hard. Her teeth graze the tip of my dick and instead of pulling away I push deeper into her mouth, encouraging the scrape of her teeth along my whole length.

Fuck. Me.

It's fucking outstanding. My balls are already tight from being shoved into the snug ring, but now they pulse, wanting to empty. But I refuse to come without seeing her face. I get a sudden urge to dig my fingers into her flesh, while pounding her hard, fast, watching her lips part, call out my name, ask me for more, tell me she's coming. Not once. Not twice. But as many times as she'll allow.

I usually love this play, these types of sessions. Like the blindfold, though, I'm suddenly despising it. Hating the fact that I want Bree in a different way and this is not it.

I can't get the picture of her out of my mind from all those years ago. Her yellow sundress pulled up, exposing her sweet thighs, the damp curls between her legs. She was offering something to me that she could only give once. Just once and it was to be mine.

I was the one she was giving this special gift to. Me.

And I fucked it up.

I fumbled. We knocked teeth. I was too rough because I couldn't control my urges. My brain could no longer function because my body had taken over, wanting only one thing... release. And it found it way too quickly. I rushed ahead and left her behind.

My inexperience, my youthful eagerness, destroyed that precious offering she wanted me, and only me, to have.

I let her down.

I let myself down.

And, although I never thought she'd let me touch her again, here I am. Tied up, blindfolded. And, *fuck me,* I'm not allowed to touch her.

I'm unable to right the wrong I did to her all those years ago.

And normally, I'd love this. Revere in this. But not right now.

Not like this.

I loathe it.

I want Bree, not Brianna.

Once I get Bree, Brianna can do to me what she will.

Brianna:

As his body tenses beneath my fingers, a low wail escapes him that makes me break out in goosebumps.

It's not a cry of pleasure, no. It's a sound of pain and frustration. I quickly rock back on my heels, releasing him.

Before I can figure out what's going on, his muscles flex, his hands fist, and he rips his arms from the restraints.

I fall back on my ass and watch in shock as he tears off his blindfold, his nostrils flaring, his face in agony.

Did I hurt him somehow? My actions flash through my mind. No, I did nothing he didn't like. I didn't miss him saying his safe word. I would never continue if he had.

The rip of the Velcro is deafening as he tears his ankles free, but his eyes are only on me. Intense. Hot. Almost frightening.

Fuck.

We've hardly even begun. I have so much more planned and he can't take the wheel, my nails, my teeth and my sucking him?

Can't be.

Before I can crab walk back away from him, he's on me, grabbing me under my arms, pulling me up, throwing me over his shoulder. The air whooshes from my lungs, making it impossible to scream at him to stop, to explain.

As he throws me to the bed, his fingers snag my bun, and my hair pulls free, falling around me. An *oof* rushes from me as I land on my back.

Then he's on me, over me, dominating.

This was not how it was supposed to be. My lips part to tell him this, but my words disintegrate as he grabs my ankles and rips me down the bed.

"Noah," finally falls from my lips as I manage to suck in a breath. I'm shaking with confusion. He's not saying anything, not explaining.

I've never been dominated like this before. I can't say I don't like it, because it's never happened.

He flips me over and unzips my skirt, but he doesn't pull it down. Instead, he loosens it just enough so he can shove it up around my waist.

I'm drenched, my breath comes with difficulty, my nipples ache painfully against my corset.

He has reversed this session, and this is not the actions of a sub. Not at all. I thought he was a submissive.

Maybe I was wrong. Maybe along the way he changed.

I gasp as he fists my hair, yanking my head back, arching my throat. Then he's on me. His weight, his heat. His erection is hard and heavy against my inner thigh.

Putting his lips to my ear, his voice is low, gruff. "Somehow you know I like this, live for this. I don't know how. I don't know why. I don't give a shit at this moment. This is *my* moment, then I will let you have yours. And I will let you do it because I need it. Just not yet. Right now, I need to do this because I've waited over thirteen years for it. This time we're doing it my way, then you can do to me what you need to do to take it all back."

His words make me quiver, send a shock deep through my soul.

I shouldn't allow this. I should fight to take back the control. Punish him for doing something unacceptable and out of turn.

I try to twist around to face him, but his weight keeps me pinned in place.

"Let me up," I insist.

"No."

"Noah."

"No."

"You will be punished," I warn him over my shoulder. Though, even to my own ears, those words don't sound harsh enough.

"Yes."

He rakes his teeth over my neck and then sinks them into my shoulder, drawing a gasp, then a moan from me.

I work my hands from underneath my body and as soon as I do, he has my wrists circled within his fingers and stretched over my head, held tightly to the bed.

"Release me," I try again.

"No."

In all honesty, I'm relieved he won't. I'm surprised how this excites me. Him taking control, acting the alpha, taking what he thinks is his.

But no matter what, at this point, I can't let him know I'm enjoying it, he wants the battle.

Because he wants to win it.

I see that. And I know how to play that game, too.

I squirm underneath him and he sits up, straddling my thighs, pulling my wrists to the small of my back, still holding them tightly.

With his free hand, he snags my thong and rips it from me, my body jerking with the force of it.

Fuck. I'm dripping wet. My breasts have fallen out of my corset from being thrown around and now my nipples rub against the stiff edge of the leather, stimulating them, making them even harder.

I groan, once again shifting under the heavy weight of his thighs.

He smacks my ass and the sting makes me cry out and squirm harder.

"Noah," I breathe.

"Right now you're mine. Then I'll be yours. Not a moment sooner."

Fuck. I don't like dominant men, that's what I've always told myself. But my body is betraying me. Maybe I don't like it from others, but I'm liking a forceful Noah.

He grabs a pillow from beside my head and shoves it under my hips, then he bites my ass cheek.

Fuck.

He slides his body down my legs, his tongue tracing my cleft. The bed shifts and his knees are between my thighs, spreading them roughly. Then his tongue is there again, slipping between my ass cheeks, teasing all the way down, tasting my wetness, separating my pulsing, swollen lips, dipping, nibbling, scoring me with his teeth. He presses a finger to my throbbing clit and I jerk, unable to control my own reactions.

"Noah," I moan again. I should be discouraging his actions, taking him to task.

But I don't want to.

I'm finding this current turn of events to my liking.

And I never got to come yet. I had been so close when I had him in my mouth. Suddenly, I'm back there, at that edge, teetering.

He sucks hard at my slick folds, and I feel that pull all the way to my center.

"Fuck, these stockings," he groans against my pussy and my breath escapes me in a shudder.

He sucks me harder, tweaks my clit and I lose it. Totally lose it. My core clenches around nothing. Not his fingers, not his cock. It's empty but still throbs as a climax rips through me. And it's amazing.

Then his hand digs in my hair again, pulling my head back until he can grip both my hair and my wrists in one hand. With a knee, he nudges my hips up higher, higher, then he sinks into me. Fast, hard, his hips slamming my ass. The vibrations from his cock ring bring me to a peak again almost immediately, then I tumble over that bittersweet edge once more.

Twice in seconds. There will be no tears tonight, no running away in shame. I know my body now; he definitely knows his.

He snakes an arm under my hips and pulls my ass even higher as he thrusts deeper, slamming me harder. The sound of our skin slapping melds with the words he's mumbling, the encouragements I'm crying out.

I'm not telling him to stop, I'm demanding he give me more, all that he has. All that he can be.

I tilt my hips more as he slaps my ass again and groans out a "fuck."

"Again, Noah," I demand. He smacks my flesh with his palm once more, and I cry out, "Yes. Again."

He does it.

"Fuck, Bree."

"Again. And make me come. Now."

He does both. A crack against my bare ass. A third orgasm. And a complete switch. He's doing what I'm telling him and he doesn't even realize he's given up the control.

He's lost in the moment, his own pleasure and mine.

He thinks he's doing what he wants. But he's doing my bidding.

"Noah, fuck me."

"I'm fucking you," comes from what sounds like gritted teeth.

"You can't make me come again."

"I can. I will."

I smile, but I quickly lose it as my body rocks forward with the force of his thrust. His hand under my hip, holding me up, slides between my legs and his fingers drag through my wetness, touching us where we connect so intimately. And when his thumb strokes my sensitive clit, I clench around him, squeezing him as hard as I can then my body takes over, pulsing intensely.

"Fuck," he groans and his body curls over mine as he drives deep one more time and stays there, the root of his cock pulsating against my flesh as he spills inside of me. The cock ring is pushed so tightly against my pussy that the vibrations take me over the edge once more.

"Five," he murmurs against my neck.

Five fucking orgasms in a matter of minutes.

And not one tear shed.

He's proud of himself. As he should be.

He releases my hair, my wrists and I press my forehead into the mattress, gathering my strength, sucking air into my lungs.

Then he shifts and the vibrations stop but he stays deep inside me. His fingers brush over my ass, and I'm assuming my skin shows the mark of his handiwork.

"Fuck," he murmurs. Then he repeats, "Fuck," in a sharp bark.

He slips out of me and is gone. I feel the loss tremendously.

I try not to groan as I turn over to see where he went. The light to the master bathroom is on and he's inside but I can't see him since the door is almost closed, although not completely.

As I sit up my hair falls around me in a thick mess and I sweep it away from my face, run a shaky hand over my damp forehead and drag my fingers over the bite on my shoulder to test its tenderness.

He marked me.

As his.

On my shoulder. On my ass.

These are not the actions of a sub.

CHAPTER FIVE

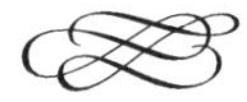

Brianna:

I haven't moved an inch before the light extinguishes in the bathroom and the door opens.

Noah strides confidently across the room. I think he's coming back to the bed, back to me. To tell me that I was wrong, he's not a sub. He's a complete alpha, taking his woman, making her his.

But then my breath hitches as, without ever meeting my eyes, he drops to his knees in the middle of the room, sits on his heels and curls his body forward until his forehead reaches the floor.

He's groveling.

Jesus Fucking Christ.

The man is begging my forgiveness without even uttering a word.

Now I do want to cry because his actions are beautiful and simply breathtaking. He is offering himself to me.

I push to my feet, pull down my skirt and zip it closed, tuck my breasts back into my corset and say fuck it to my hair. There's no way I'll get it back into a bun without a lot of fuss.

And right now, I have more important things to do.

Like take care of my precious pet.

I move to stand before him, watching his ribs expand and contract with each breath he takes. His skin appears flawless, the curve of his neck delectable as he grovels at my feet.

This is not the man of minutes ago.

I can't say which I like better.

Both, perhaps.

"Speak," I tell him.

His hands slide closer until his fingertips touch the toes of my shoes. I could take him to task for touching me without permission. Since it's barely a brush, I'll let it go.

"I'm sorry, Mistress."

Mistress.

Though, it only makes sense that he'd call me that, that he would *think* to use that title, I won't tolerate it. Not from him.

As the title echoes through my mind, my body quivers as something dark and sad runs through me. "Don't call me that," I snap before I can contain my irritation.

His head jerks up, his eyes meet mine, questioning, curious. Confused.

"You called *her* that."

"Her," he repeats on a whisper, his eyebrows furrowed, his eyes searching.

"*Her*." The woman who took him from me.

I circle him, there on his knees in the center of my bedroom in a very subservient position. Waiting for his punishment.

"I saw you. You broke my heart." Then turned it to steel.

I can see him working out my confession in his head. A look of shock flashes over him, but it vanishes, his expression quickly becoming schooled. His lips part as if he's about to say something but can't.

"Did you like what Mrs. Callahan did to you?"

His lips part again but it takes a few beats before he asks, "What do you know?"

"More than you think. I watched you, Noah. You and her. At first, I thought she was just sick. Depraved. Then..." I trail off.

"Then?"

"Then..." I shake my head slightly. "Then I realized you liked it."

"Yes," he says simply.

"And you kept going back for more."

"Yes."

"And as you learned what you liked, what you needed, what you *craved*... so did I."

Once again, confusion crosses his expression. "What do you mean?"

"I realized I wanted it to be me in there doing that to you. Not her. *Me*."

I barely hear him say, "You should have said something."

"Right. Because that's how honest we were with each other at the time, at that age."

He closes his eyes. "All this time..." When they open they look different. Pained. Sad. "If I had known."

"It wasn't the right time," I murmur. Because it's true. We were too young, too confused. Too embarrassed.

"I hated her," I admit, because that's true, also. "But I'm also grateful to her. She made you true to yourself."

"Yes. She made me find something deep inside me that I never knew existed. I thought I'd outgrow it. I didn't. I embraced it. But you still should have told me."

My nostrils flare and my jaw tightens as I stop in front of him. "Right." I try to keep the bitterness out of my tone, out of my words, but it's difficult. "And then what, Noah? I was no match, no comparison, for a woman with that level of maturity and experience. She could read you, figure out your needs. I knew nothing at the time except how the parts fit and even then..." I drift off, hardening my resolve, not trying to let this affect me, affect our limited time together. I shake my head. "So, don't ever call me Mistress. I am not her."

"Bree—" is all that escapes him before I cut him off.

"Now you need to stop talking," I demand.

"Bree," he starts again, a little more firmly. A small step toward taking back control. I can't let him have that. Not again. Not now.

"Stop. If you want to remain in this bedroom, in this session, just stop talking, Noah."

His eyes close and a shudder runs through him, strong enough I can see it but I steel myself against his reaction. And when he opens his eyes again, his golden-green eyes are no longer soft, they're dark, determined.

He wants to continue to play. He's ready to hand over the reins again. But I think he struggles with it also.

As do I.

"Ms. Brianna?"

"Just Brianna if you'd like."

"Do I have another choice?"

"I'll accept Ma'am."

"As long as it's not Mistress?"

I've accepted it from others, but I can't from him. "No."

He nods and lowers his eyes, no longer challenging me.

Surprisingly, I find myself a little disappointed.

"You removed your cock ring."

"Yes, ma'am."

"To the floor, as you were."

He plants his palms to the floor and drops his forehead down.

"What would be a good punishment for my pet?" I step forward until the tips of my shoes are within his line of sight. "You removed your cock ring without permission. You touched me without permission. You challenged me. You planted your seed inside me without a condom."

At the last, his body twitched.

"I did not give you permission to do that, and you didn't ask, did you?"

"No, ma'am."

"I did not give you permission to remove your cuffs and your blindfold, did I?"

"No, ma'am."

"So many infractions. You disrespected my authority, did you not?"

"Yes, ma'am."

"What am I going to do with you, Noah?"

"What you will, ma'am."

"I should send you away. Back to your hotel."

His body tenses at my words. I imagine he wants to sit up, to plead his case, perhaps, but he doesn't. He remains.

"I should put an end to this. Should my pet be rewarded when he has been nothing but naughty?"

"No. Please, ma'am."

"No? You don't want to leave?"

"No, ma'am."

"But is it your choice?"

He hesitates. "No... ma'am." His answer is so low I almost don't hear him. His fingers, once spread wide, now curl into fists.

I am pushing him again. He is being reminded of his place.

If he doesn't want to do this he could get up, get dressed and walk out. That easy.

He doesn't.

He won't.

He needs this as much as I do.

"Hands and knees," I order.

Immediately, he pushes into position, keeping his eyes to the floor. I weigh my options.

He needs to be punished but I want us both to enjoy it. I leave him there to go to my dresser and dig in the top drawer, pulling out a wide, round leather paddle. Another of my favorites. The one with the flat metal rivets that outline the edge. For the inexperienced, it would be intimidating. However, Noah is not inexperienced.

I approach him, tapping my palm with the paddle with each step I take. I stop in front of him.

"Look, my pet. Do you approve?"

I do not need his approval, but I want to see his acceptance.

When his gaze lands on the instrument in my hand, his lips part and his eyes darken. "Yes, ma'am. I approve."

"How many times should this touch your flesh to make up for all your transgressions?"

"As many as you deem necessary, ma'am."

Good answer. He's no longer pulling at the control, but instead accepting that it's held in my hands... just like the paddle.

"I've seen you paddled before, Noah. I've seen how hard it makes you. I've seen that paddling alone can make you lose yourself. Will you give me that gift tonight?"

A hesitation. Though, I know why. He's only just come, and he's no longer eighteen. It takes longer for a man our age to recover. I'm asking something of him he may not be able to deliver.

He may be willing, but it may not be possible.

But, *God*, I want to see it. I want to be the one to bring it about. I want it to be me and no one else that's in his mind when he feels the sting of the hard, flat leather against his skin.

I want to wipe all that I've seen through Mrs. Callahan's open window out of my memory and his.

I want this to be ours instead.

I need this to be ours, because if it's not, we will never work. She will always be there between us. And the woman needs to be cleansed from our past so we can work on our future.

If we decide there is one.

But that's not a concern right now. Right now, I must mete out Noah's punishment, remind him of his mistakes.

"You haven't answered me, my pet."

"Brianna, I will do my best."

"That's all I can ask." I move behind him, slide the paddle over his ass cheeks and watch the muscles flex underneath his taut skin.

Anticipation is a powerful tool.

"Head down," I tell him.

He drops his head once more, his ass high in the air. His thighs are tight, the muscles strained, his hands are still in fists on either side of his head. His hair is long enough that it covers the sides of his face. Once again, I think that's a shame that any part of his glorious body is covered. But that's just the way it must be.

His sac hangs heavily between his thighs and I'll have to watch I don't hit him there. I don't want to hurt him; I want to excite him. I want to see if the strikes of the paddle will bring about another erection, another release on its own.

The dampness between my thighs grows as my body clenches in its own anticipation.

"Are you ready, my pet?"

"Yes," hisses from him as I step to his left and raise my right arm. And as I do so, his whole body jerks.

As I said, anticipation is a powerful tool. It can fuck with your head.

"Mississippi?"

"No."

I nod, pleased, even though he can't see it, and bring the paddle down with as much force as I can. The sharp sound of leather meeting skin fills the room.

"Fuck!" he yells, his whole body moving forward from the impact. His fists are no longer that. He now has his face buried in his hands. And I fight back the panic.

"Mississippi?" I ask, trying to keep the tremor from my voice.

He groans but says, "No, ma'am."

Fuck.

His ass is already turning a pretty shade of red with just the first blow. And, fuck, just looking at that makes me want to ride his cock.

I glance but he's not hard yet, so that won't do.

"Are you ready, Noah?"

His curse is muffled within his fingers. "Don't ask me, don't warn me... *please.*"

He doesn't get to set the rules. If he doesn't like them, he can walk away.

Though, I hope he doesn't.

"Are you ready, Noah?" I ask again because I must.

"Yes... *fuck.*"

I strike him again, but this time not quite so hard and it lands on one cheek instead of both. Though the smack of skin still fills the air, after which I hear him blow out a relieved breath.

"You like that, pet?"

"Yes, ma'am."

"Another?"

He hesitates. "If you want me to get hard, ma'am."

I smile. I certainly do.

I smack his other cheek. These last two only pinken his skin, not redden it like the first one. But it's still beautiful.

He's beautiful.

And, *God,* how I love him. I love him even more at this moment because he's doing something I've asked of him. And he's doing it willingly.

He wants to please me.

"Again?"

"Please, ma'am."

"Yes," I murmur, "that's my pet."

I strike his ass again and again until he's hard and the precum beads on the crown of his cock as it hangs low and heavy like his sac. It twitches with each strike, though I've softened them immensely because I'm enjoying this and want it to last.

After a number I think is sufficient, I ask, "Enough?"

His face is no longer buried in his hands, his palms are again flat on the floor, his fingers spread on either side of his head. "Not if you want me to come," he says quietly.

"Do you need to assist?"

Again, a hesitation before admitting, "Yes."

I will allow him this, because I want to watch him come and I don't want to have to take this paddling to the extreme, to the point of where he must ask for a reprieve. I still want it to be pleasurable for him. Not just me.

"Touch yourself."

He wraps one of his broad hands around his dripping cock and he tugs on it, the glutes of his ass flexing with each stroke.

That alone is enough to test my willpower.

My fascination turns from the desire of making his ass red to what's between his legs. Without even a second thought, I toss the paddle aside. "Sit up."

He does as he's told, sitting back on his heels, his cock hard and long in his palm, though his motions have stopped.

"Continue," I tell him and he does.

Watching him palm his own cock, watching the drop of his eyelids over unfocused eyes, watching his back bow as he brings himself to a point where I almost can't watch his beauty anymore... I realize he's art.

I have living, breathing art in the middle of my room.

He's exquisite. Precious. And mine.

When he squeezes the head of his cock until it's dark before sliding his fingers back to the root, I can't take anymore. I move to directly in front of him, facing him, though his gaze remains lowered.

My fingers find the small zipper at the back of my skirt and I unzip it. "Look at me."

His gaze lifts but his jaw is tight, and he wears a grimace. He's close. I must hurry.

"Slow down, Noah. Save yourself for me."

His chest rises and falls at the same pace as his hand. But eventually he slows.

I let my skirt drop to the floor and I step out of the circle of leather, kicking it out of the way.

I can't get any wetter than I am right now. "Sit."

Without releasing the hold on his cock, he shifts forward to bring his legs around until he's sitting cross-legged.

"Hold steady."

His hand stills, the head of his cock so slick and shiny from his own arousal. I move over top of his crossed legs and with hands on his shoulders, I lower myself to my knees and then slowly sink myself deeply onto him. Finally, his hand moves away and to my back, his other hand joining it, sliding up into the hair at my scalp, digging in, pulling, as I lift and lower myself on his length.

"Take off my corset," I say much more softly than intended. His fingers find the zipper at the top and slowly slide it down, down, down until it falls away, releasing my breasts. He tosses it to the side and drives his fingers back into my hair.

"I've always loved your hair."

I give him that, his speaking out of turn since I haven't asked him a question. However, nothing has gone as it should so far tonight.

I fear I'm losing my touch.

But I'm gaining another... Noah's.

Though he wears my collar, I feel I don't own him. Instead, he owns me.

Once again, the undercurrents in the room have shifted and he controls me.

And the rush I feel from that thought could be from trepidation or excitement.

With one hand still gripped in my hair, he drops the other to my ass, holding tight, squeezing every time I post on top of him.

The need to come, to fall apart, overtakes me, making me arch my back. But I'm afraid if I let go, he will, too, and I want this to last a little longer this time. I want to appreciate all that is Noah as we sit face to face. Eye to eye. Our lips parted, our breaths mingling.

And I realize... we haven't kissed. We haven't done the most intimate act. Something we did so long ago that we loved to do. One thing we discovered we were good at before that fateful fuck up.

Back then, his kisses alone had made me wet, wanting. The reason we took it to the next step.

The misstep.

As I stare at his lips, remembering how they used to feel, his middle finger sweeps down the cleft of my ass and presses inward. And when he takes me there, I take him, too, capturing his lips, groaning into his mouth, tasting his tongue as we tangle together.

I rise up then land hard on his lap, grinding my hips as he fucks me with his cock, fucks me with his finger. I'm no longer fucking him, it's just the opposite. Once again, he's gained the upper hand.

He's taken before he's asked.

He's a naughty pet, my Noah.

But, suddenly, I don't care.

He can do to me what he will.

I will be his slave.

He can be my master.

I will do anything he asks.

I will grovel at his feet.

I just want him to continue to do what he's doing.

Kissing me.

Fucking me.

Loving me hard and fully.

He doesn't release my lips until we both come moments later.

CHAPTER SIX

Noah:

My forehead rests against hers as we catch our breath, wait for the slowing of our heartbeats.

"That was our first kiss tonight," I murmur, a hair's breadth from those gorgeous lips I just tasted.

"Yes," she answers as if that's completely normal.

"You normally don't," I state.

"No."

I understand why she doesn't. I hardly ever kiss anyone I'm with. My mouth is used for everything but. Funny how a kiss seems more intimate than actual intercourse. To me, the person you're kissing should mean something to you, not just a body you are getting a sexual release from.

Maybe it's the same with her.

"If I asked, would you kiss me again?"

"You haven't asked," she says simply.

True.

I can ask or I can take. I wonder which she prefers. No matter how much she's determined to be in charge, that control clearly slipped several times so far tonight. And in those moments, my need to take over, be something I haven't been in a long time, something I hadn't needed to be in over a decade, has grown to epic proportions.

And, honestly, I have a feeling it's only because it's her. Having her in my arms gives me a burning desire to protect her, take care of her, make her mine.

I decide not to ask, and just take what I want, brushing my lips softly against her red ones once, twice. Then tilting my head, I take our kiss deeper, my tongue dipping inside, exploring, hers doing the same. She groans into my mouth as I drive my fingers into her long, silky hair, gripping it hard. I hold her in place and take her mouth like it's mine.

Because *finally* it is.

My cock remains buried deep inside her when she shifts, tilting her hips, pressing her clit against me. I drop one hand between us to tease her clit with my thumb. I circle it, pressing, and she grinds hard against me, squeezing me tight.

Then I feel it, her body rippling once again around me. Our mouths are joined, our bodies connected and I don't want to let her go.

That last orgasm was solely for her since I'm lucky to have just stayed hard enough to remain inside her. I know that will change very quickly. But she doesn't shift off my lap and I hold her hips tightly, wanting to keep her close.

She buries her face into my neck and breathes deeply. I nuzzle my nose into her hair near her ear.

"Bree..."

"Hmm?" she murmurs against my skin.

"You feel so fucking good."

Her spine straightens, and she sits up, her face too serious for just orgasming for the millionth time tonight. Okay, maybe that's a bit of an exaggeration. But this woman is no one hit wonder.

"Things haven't gone the way I expected," she admits.

I find myself pleased with that admission and need to press my lips together to keep from giving her a big, goofy grin. Finally, when I have it under control, I ask, "Is that so bad?"

"When have multiple orgasms ever been bad?"

At this point, I can't fight it anymore. I smile and press a kiss lightly to her lips. "Never. And I'm glad I can give you that."

"That you can," she says on a sigh.

Finally. It's only been about thirteen years, but yes, I can finally give her that.

With regret, I tell her, "As much as I love you being on my lap, my legs are falling asleep."

She touches the leather collar around my neck, sliding her fingers along the upper edge. I still. A subtle reminder.

"Are you asking or telling me to get off of you?"

"Asking."

She nods, and, with her hands on my shoulders for balance, she pushes to her feet. "I need to clean up anyway since you haven't used a condom yet."

"Is that a problem?"

She arches a perfectly shaped eyebrow at me. "Is it?"

"Not on my end," I reassure her.

"Not mine, either. However, it's not something I normally do."

I want to respond with, "That's good to hear," but I keep that to myself. But it certainly is something worth noting. The kissing, the intimacy, the lack of complaint with not using a condom. It proves to me that I mean more to her than anyone else she's normally with.

Not that I want to delve any deeper into how many men she's been with. I'm not into self-castigation. The thought of any man having my Bree is disturbing, though I'm realistic. And it's not like I've been saving myself either.

Because I certainly haven't.

My life's been a sexual journey of discovery. All the way from stolen backyard kisses until right this minute.

And during every one of those many minutes, every one of those partners made me a better lover, as well as more appreciative of a woman's body and the power she can wield with it.

So, now I stare up at my ultimate partner. The person this journey began with and the one I want to end it with.

She stands over me, wearing black thigh high stockings, stiletto heels and a questioning look.

I slip back into my place. "How do you want me, Brianna?"

Instantly, her eyes darken and the slightest curve appears at the corner of her lips. Not quite a smile, but more like a look of satisfaction. A kitten who just finished a bowl of warm milk.

"I will clean up first, then you. Then I want you in my bed."

And I want to be there. Preferably with Bree, but for now, I will take Brianna.

Brianna:

He's breathtaking. I can't bear to cover his stunning golden-green eyes with a blindfold again so soon, so he watches me intently. His well-developed arms stretch above his head, not in Velcro Neoprene cuffs, no. This time his wrists are bound tightly together in leather, attached to the hook on my very strong headboard, the one made specifically for this type of play. He would have to do some major damage to break loose this time. And, most likely, it would cause more damage to himself than anything else.

I could sit here all night, studying him. I did it for months all those years ago. Through that window. Into that bedroom. With that woman. Watching his body react to everything she did to him, everything she said to him. Though it excited me, it churned my stomach all the same.

At the time, I didn't understand why he no longer wanted me and seemed to prefer what she offered. But maybe it was for the best. Maybe he needed to discover all his true desires.

And I needed to discover mine.

The problem is... now, I want something totally different between the two of us. I don't want what they had.

I want something that's our very own.

I've waited a long time for him. He says he's waited a long time for me.

Maybe we need to rediscover ourselves. See what works for us.

Normally, I don't like kissing men.

I love kissing Noah.

Normally, I don't yearn for soft moments with my toys.

I love being held by Noah, who is clearly more than a toy.

Normally, I don't let any man dominate me. Not ever.

Surprisingly, I loved being dominated by Noah.

But I need to make sure. I don't want to give up what I've worked so hard over the years to achieve to only find out he actually wants what I have to offer, the skills I've developed over the years with the experts I had sought out. But the moment he broke free of his cuffs earlier and took over... I hadn't felt a rush like that in a very, very long time.

It made the orgasms even more poignant.

They actually meant something to me, more than a bodily function, which I could get from almost anyone if I worked hard enough.

He made it easy.

Too easy.

I could get used to him taking over, making my body ache for him, cry out for him.

Is that going against my grain? Maybe.

Is that going against his? Possibly.

It's a conversation we'll need to have if this continues on after this one night.

However, I'm not sure if that's possible, or even realistic. Tomorrow is my brother's wedding. Then Noah returns to his life. Though, I have no idea what that involves since I never asked my brother. I only know it's a plane ride away. And I only know he came to the wedding alone. But everything else is a mystery. One that will eventually need solving.

"Bree..." His voice is soft, almost a whisper.

He must have seen something in my expression. I blink myself back to the here and now. "Brianna," I correct him.

Because that's where we're at, at this moment. Here. In my bed.

"Brianna. Sorry, ma'am."

When he calls me Bree, I melt. When he calls me Brianna, I harden.

With his prior actions, I find myself curious. "Do you switch?"

"No."

"Never?"

"No."

"What was earlier then?"

"Me needing you desperately."

Jesus. This man knows how to take me to my knees with his words alone.

Oh, wait. I'm already on my knees, straddling his hips and he's underneath me, waiting to see what comes next.

And for the first time ever, I'm at a complete loss. I want this man. I do. I'm just not so sure I want him in this way anymore.

But I also want him to be happy. I want to fulfill his needs and if this is what he desires, then I want to be the one to give it to him. No one else. Not again.

I draw a nail lightly down his chest, over the tip of his nipple, his eyes darken as they hold mine. I scrape the other nipple before I draw a line down his belly, stopping just above his pelvis.

He's still soft, but that doesn't bother me. I know he needs a little bit of time to recover.

I'm patient.

There are plenty of other delicious things I can do to him, or he can do to me, while I wait.

However, there's one thing he hasn't done yet. Hence, the way he's tied up. Arms overhead, body stretched long on the mattress, ankles lashed wide at the foot of the bed. Vulnerable. Delectable. Like earlier, his runner's body, trim and tight, reminds me of living art.

Normally, I'd force a man to his knees, stand over top of him to remind him of his place, then I'd crop or cane his back while he did my bidding.

But again, for some reason I want things to be different with Noah and me.

I want this to be ours.

And maybe that's simply ridiculous. But I don't care.

My pussy pulses at the thought of his mouth on me. I move to my hands and knees over top of him, reach for a pillow and tuck it under his head. I want to ensure he can see me without difficulty.

After adjusting him just right, I dig through my nightstand drawer and bring out one of my tamer toys.

A woman's best friend.

I get off the bed, move to the foot of it and again pause to appreciate all that's laid out before me. I'm swept away by the trust he's put in my hands by allowing me to restrain him once more.

I settle myself between his spread legs, draping my own over his thighs, opening myself to his view. With the angle of his propped head, he doesn't have to strain to see what I'm offering and I can't miss when his eyes drop from mine. I'm still wearing my thigh-highs, but that's it. I've abandoned my heels and left the skirt and corset where they lay from earlier. His eyes follow the lacy top of my stockings to my center.

When he licks his lips, I feel that all the way to my core before the heat radiates out to every part of my body. My nipples pucker and I brush my fingers over the tips before cupping their weight in my hands and squeezing them together.

He watches my every move, especially when I roll both nipples between my thumbs and forefingers.

"You like nipple clamps, Brianna?" he asks, his voice a bit broken. He's already affected and I've barely begun.

"I do."

"On you?"

I don't answer him. So, he bravely continues.

"Do you like the bite of them on your nipples, Brianna? That pull you get through your body when they pinch tight?"

My lips part and a puff of air escapes. I tweak my nipples harder, imagining the sharp sensation clamps can provide.

"Do you want me to clamp them on the tips and pull them on a long chain with my teeth until you beg me to fuck you hard?"

He's doing it again. And I yank him back.

"Stop talking," I demand. I love how he's making me hot and needy. But, he's trying to turn the tables, and I'm curious to know why.

"You want it," he murmurs.

And I do. But now he's talking out of turn.

"You're a disobedient pet, you know that, Noah?"

He doesn't answer me, but I see that gleam in his eye. He's determined to undo my control.

I may allow that, but not yet. "You liked that earlier paddling?"

Again, he doesn't answer me.

"Apparently, it wasn't enough to teach you to behave."

Again, nothing.

"You may speak," I tell him.

"Yes."

I arch a brow at him. "Yes?"

"Yes, I liked the paddling. But, no, I don't want to behave with you. So, you may paddle me until I'm black and blue, but I will give as good as I get."

"You've had Mistresses who have put up with this type of behavior, this insolence?" I ask in surprise.

"No."

"You normally don't challenge?"

"Never."

I open my mouth to ask, "Why now?" But I don't because I know why. It's a turn-on to me. Although, only with him. He recognizes this and is attempting to use it to his advantage.

"Are you disrespecting me in this fashion?" I don't find myself angry with it, more like amused.

"No. Never."

I give a sharp nod, finally release my breasts, drawing my hands down to my labia, separating the folds, stroking a finger between them.

"You can't escape this time, my pet." When he doesn't answer, I become concerned. "You understand that, right? I'm sure you've worn similar cuffs and please be aware my bed is specifically made for this type of restraint. You can't escape without hurting yourself. If you absolutely need to be released, use your safe word."

I wonder if he's even listening. And I must make sure he hears me.

"What's your safe word, Noah?"

His eyes flick up to mine and then back down to what my fingers are doing, which are slowly trailing between my plump, slick lips.

"Mississippi," he says so softly I almost miss it.

I grab my favorite red vibrator and twist the top until its hum serenades us. He whispers something else, but I don't catch it.

With two fingers in a V, I open myself up and press the vibrator to my clit. My thighs tense and so do his. His body gets tight as I circle and tease myself to the point of having to part my mouth to release my rapid, ragged breath.

Heat rushes through me as I observe him watching me closely. With a finger pressed to my clit, I move the toy lower, sliding it slowly deep inside. The tone of the vibrations changes as I squeeze it tight, sensations radiating through my core, bringing me to a peak, but not quite over the top yet.

Not quite.

I work it in and out of me, over and over, my hips twitch, my thighs clench, my fingers moving faster against my clit. Normally, I can make myself come very quickly. But I want it to last just a little bit longer this time, I want him ready to take me with his mouth. I want him to be *hungry*.

"How badly do you want to taste me, my pet?"

His eyelids heavy, his mouth parted, his chest rises and falls at a quick pace. He jerks on the cuffs at his hands and feet, almost bucking me off.

His cock is long and hard again, a drop of precum glistening at the very top. "I want you now, Brianna."

"You don't get to demand things, my pet," I say calmly, desperate to keep myself together.

"*Now*, Brianna," he shouts like he's losing his mind.

He swallows hard and his Adam's apple jumps, drawing my attention to his throat. I'm dying to sink my teeth there while he cries out my name.

His eyes snap and become wild when I murmur that I'm about to come.

He shuts his eyes. Which is unacceptable.

"Watch me," I demand.

His chest heaves and he jerks again at his restraints. The bed doesn't give, not even the slightest. "Fuck," he groans.

"Open your eyes, Noah," I tell him more firmly.

He blows out a breath but opens them, his gaze burning me.

"Watch me come."

My hips shoot up as a climax rolls over and through me, curling my toes as I throw my head back, gasping.

His legs jerk beneath me as he strains against his restraints. As if almost from a distance, I hear him growl, "Fuck."

The vibrator slips from me and I toss it aside as my head lowers to look at him.

His jaw is tight, a muscle ticking fiercely, his arms bulge as he continues to fight the restraints.

"Fuck," he barks again.

But he doesn't ask me to release him, he doesn't say the word which would stop his torment.

"Did you like that, my pet?"

"Fuck," he repeats again, slamming his head back into the pillow, rocking it back and forth.

Walking up his body on my hands and knees, I go face to face with him, trailing a finger down his cheek, over his lips, the ones that will be on me shortly. His mouth opens, and he sucks my finger in between his lips, playing along my digit with his tongue. That's when it hits me that he's tasting my arousal still on my fingers.

A second later he releases it. "Sit on my face," he orders.

That was my plan, but now he just demanded something of me he shouldn't have. "That sounded like a command, my pet. Surely, I misunderstood."

His eyes flash as he struggles to say calmly, "Yes, ma'am... Please...forgive me."

I slide a thumb over his other cheekbone. "I don't know if I can let that slide, Noah. You're awfully disobedient."

His lip curls almost as if in a snarl. "I am. Punish me by sitting on my face." He jerks his arms again. I raise my gaze to where the cuffs are hooked. Everything remains where it should be... still secure.

I pin my lips together in an attempt not to laugh at his impertinence. He's determined, if nothing else.

I slip my fingers into his hair and push it off his face. "My pet," I whisper. "My Noah. What am I going to do with you?"

"I don't care what you do with me as long as I have you."

My heart squeezes, some of my resolve melts. I dig my hands into his hair on both sides of his head and shift to my knees on the bed above his shoulders. Then I take his mouth as mine when I lower myself. My fingers curl tightly in his hair as his tongue nudges me apart, and he eats me like a starved man. Gentle can't describe his actions and I love every second of it. His teeth, lips, and tongue work me into a frenzy. My hips rock above him as I grind myself against his face, wanting more, wanting everything he's giving to me. He sucks my clit hard, scrapes it with his teeth, making me whimper. I yank his head up by his hair, keeping him pressed tight, and he groans against my soaked pussy. The stubble on his face scores the delicate skin high on my inner thighs.

Fuck. He's going to make me come again at any moment. My body goes tight, my back bows, my neck arches, and I cry out his name. But he continues to flick, nibble and suck me as I come back down.

When I unclench my fingers, his head drops back to the pillow, but I follow him down, capturing his lips with mine, tasting myself on his tongue. He makes a noise at the back of his throat and I break the kiss.

"Mississippi," slips from him on a breath.

What? Now? Why?

That makes no sense.

CHAPTER SEVEN

Noah:

"Mississippi," I say louder and more firmly this time because she's not moving fast enough. In fact, she's not moving at all. And that's unacceptable.

She needs to hurry, let me go, because I can't take anymore. I'm at my limit and I'm done.

Completely done.

Annoyed concern crosses her face. "Don't fuck with me, Noah," she warns and I get what she's saying... this better not be a trick.

I'm not going to explain my actions. I won't. I can't. *Fuck it.* "Mississippi," I say again, determined that she recognize my wish.

Like snapping out of a trance, she hastily shifts down the bed, unbuckling my ankles first. All the while, my head spins like a Tilt-a-Whirl and I need it to stop. I need to right my world.

Once my legs are free, I bend my knees in anticipation of release, of freedom. Of being able to make decisions for myself.

I can't take my eyes from her as she moves to my wrists, leaning over the bed in an attempt to reach them. Her breasts hang inches from my face, my mouth, tempting me and I groan, which makes her eyes flick down to me, now more worried than displeased.

She thinks I'm suffering. And I am. But not in the way she may think.

As the tension eases on my wrists, I can taste it right there... my freedom. And suddenly, I'm just that... no longer restrained. Before she can pull away, my hands circle her waist and flip us over, so I'm on top and she's not.

I rake my hand through her hair and grab a handful, pulling her head back to expose her neck. Shoving my face into her throat, I sink my teeth in hard.

"Noah," she gasps. "What—"

I quiet her by taking her mouth, forcing my tongue between her lips, and a noise vibrates up her throat and I swallow it. It's mine. Any words she utters now belong to me, and any noises she makes are mine. Her breasts, her pussy, that ass of hers, all mine.

I don't want to be her pet. I want to be her man. She needs to belong to me as much as I belong to her. And I need to prove that to her. Show her how important that is.

I move down her body, nipping, kissing, licking, teasing a nipple, sucking at her navel, down farther, grabbing the flesh of her mound between my teeth until she cries out. Then going even farther, I shove her thighs up and out, burying my face where I was at when I previously couldn't touch her with anything but my mouth.

Now I can touch her as I'd like. Now she can't do anything about it.

This is my time.

This is for me.

And this is for her.

But nothing I do is gentle. Right now I'm not trying to woo her. Instead, I want to satisfy her and I need to prove to her that I can do that without any gimmicks, without any toys. No whips, no chains, no cuffs, no vibrators.

She's getting just me.

Just Noah.

Just Bree.

Just us.

The way we were meant to be back in that fucking shed, in that moment that changed everything. That time and place that altered our lives.

Something so stupid, so simple and so easily laughed off, wasn't. It was taken to heart by two people who didn't know how to communicate.

It can never be like that again. Not if we want to survive as an *us*.

Her hips dance around, grinding against my mouth as my tongue slides in and out of her, my fingers follow the dance along her clit.

She looks beautiful. She tastes beautiful. She *is* beautiful. Inside and out. That hasn't changed.

My mouth and fingers switch places and I suck hard at her clit and curve my fingers deep inside her knowing exactly where she needs me to be, what she needs me to do.

She pulls at my hair, tearing at my scalp as she screams when a climax rips through her. But I don't let up. Not for a moment.

I will make up for every orgasm I should have given her throughout these years. They may not be all tonight. That's impossible. But eventually... Eventually I will make up for the chunk of our lives where we could have been together, loving each other, curling up together, talking, sharing... creating a family.

Everything we missed because I made her fucking cry.

Now I need to hear her cry in a different way.

Her hands drop to my shoulders, her nails raking my skin, and I smile against her flesh as she orgasms once again.

"Let up. Let up," she chants, breathless. "I need a break."

I surge forward covering her body with mine. "No break, baby," I grunt as I thrust deep inside her. Her arms snake around my neck, her stockinged legs curl around my hips, her heels dig into my thighs as I ride her hard and fast.

Her head slams into the pillow and her neck arches as she moans, "Ah, Noah... Noah..."

"That's it, baby, say my name."

A whimper escapes her then she rises up, grabs my hair to pull me down into a deep kiss, but we both have to break it quickly because we're breathing too hard, too fast. I slide my hands under her hips, lifting her, tilting her and I touch her as deeply as I can.

"That's me inside you, baby, that's me. Noah. Not your pet. Not your toy. Not your sub."

"Noah," she cries. "Fuck me, Noah, fuck me."

"I am, baby, I'm fucking you like you were meant to be fucked. By me and only me. There's nobody else for me but you, Bree. Only you. Do you feel this between us? Do you feel it like I do?"

"Yes... I feel it."

"Is it yours?"

"It's mine."

"Is it mine?"

"It's yours."

"It's ours, baby. All ours. Fucking come for me, Bree. I want to feel you throb around me. I want to come with you. Do it, come for me."

"I... I can't... I can't... Oh, fuck. I can't..." she whimpers, her eyes rolling back.

I press my lips to her ear. "You can. Do it. *Now*."

"Fuck, Noah... Fuck!" she screams.

Her chest slams into mine as her body bows beneath me and I feel what I'm looking for. Her muscles squeezing my cock hard, fast, and that's when I spill inside her, meeting her on the other side.

Breathless. Boneless. Fulfilled.

I push my face into her damp neck as the energy rushes out of me, as I struggle to control my breathing, to suck in badly needed oxygen. I inhale her scent and a calm moves over me.

Her fingers wrap around the back of my head, smoothing my hair down, and I remain quiet, listening to her breathing which is slowing as well.

I reluctantly slide out and off her, collapsing to her side and place a palm over her heart, feeling its strong beat under my fingers.

Then it hits me again, this time more sharply. I never wanted any of this with her. Not with Bree. The only thing I ever wanted from her is beating under my palm.

My chest squeezes and I rise up onto an elbow, looking above her. "We're done here. Done with this." I indicate the cuffs still hanging from the headboard.

With eyes wide, she blinks up at me. "What's wrong?"

"Everything. Everything's wrong."

"I hurt you earlier?" she asks, the surprise evident in her voice.

"You hurt me when you ran out of the shed crying. It hurt when I didn't get the chance to apologize. I know you didn't do it on purpose and it happened. It's life. I grew a set and moved on. I'm aware I hurt you, too. With my inexperience, with what you witnessed in that fucking house, a place I only escaped to in an effort to make sure I never made a woman cry again for that same reason. But now, Bree, this shit has to stop."

With shaky lips, she whispers, "I'm sorry. I thought—"

"I know what you thought. And I know why you thought it. Everything you thought is true. But not with you. I can't be like this with you."

"I thought this is what you wanted."

I shake my head. "No. This is not what I wanted." I close my eyes for a moment to gather my torn thoughts. "Okay, it's what I needed to figure out what I wanted. But, baby," I cup her face in my hands, "this is never what I wanted from you."

"What did you want from me?"

"Just you. Sweet. Yellow sundresses. Pink cotton panties. Smiles. Laughs."

It's all clear to me now.

"You don't like the leather?"

What I don't like is the insecurity in her voice. It doesn't belong there and I don't want to be the reason it's there. "I like the leather. I like the fact that I become rock hard with you wearing that leather get-up. I like that you drive me crazy while wearing those freaking stockings as you're paddling my ass or sucking my cock. But I love Bree, baby, *Bree*. Brianna is great but not for every day. I like Brianna very much, don't get me wrong. But, baby, I *love* Bree. I've always loved Bree. I've loved you since the moment I saw you. I knew you would be mine the first time I kissed you in your backyard and you punched me in the gut."

"You've loved me since then?"

"Yes. I've loved no one but you."

"But—"

"Don't mistake this... There have been other women. And I've had other Mistresses. But none of them has ever lasted because deep down inside I knew I was meant to be with you. Only you, Bree."

"Noah," she whispers, her voice catching.

"No regrets. Now it's time to bury them. Move on."

Bree:

"I don't know where we go from here," I say, because I honestly don't know. Our lives split into two separate directions on that fateful day.

"Do we need to know where we're going? Does a path need to be set in stone? Or can we discover it as we go?"

I know I'm willing to do whatever I need to do to be with this man. However, logistics may be an issue. That and the fact that we only knew each other as children, as teenagers, not as adults.

"You're thinking too hard," he says, brushing a lock of my hair away from my face.

It's true. "I know. There's so much to consider."

"Like what?"

"Time. Distance. The fact that I don't know if I can be just Bree anymore." And that's true, too.

He wraps a lock of my hair around his finger and he studies it for a moment. Then he meets my gaze, a determined look in his eyes. "We can do nothing about the time. It's gone. We only have the time moving forward. We can only look toward the future. The distance? I'll work on. That I can promise you. And as far as being just Bree..." he hesitates, then takes a deep breath before continuing, "I'm not saying I want Brianna to disappear completely. I don't. There are times I will need your Brianna. However, most times I'll need my Bree. I can't imagine not having you tie me up and make me yours in all ways. But I'll need the same with you."

"I can live with that."

When the corners of his lips curl, I am blown away by the simple beauty of this man once again. He's offered himself to me tonight and now he offers himself to me... possibly forever.

He's right, we can't go back and fix things, and maybe it's best we can't. Maybe we both needed to head our own direction to find ourselves as individuals, to make ourselves better as a whole. We've become more well-rounded people with different life experiences under our belts.

All that has gone before has made us both better lovers at a minimum. And hopefully better people in general.

In all these years he could have found someone else. He didn't. And neither did I. So maybe, in the end, we were meant to be.

A love lost and then found.

Back then, I hated that woman for what she stole from me. But now I realize at the time he wasn't mine to steal.

His low voice brings me out of my thoughts. "Know this... I look forward to waking up next to you, rolling over and taking you in my arms, kissing you awake, bringing you breakfast in bed, making love to you slowly, gently, sweetly. And I will love every minute of it. Then there will be the moments where I will come home and you will put this collar on me," he fingers the leather still circling his neck, "and force me to my knees to do your bidding. Then we will fuck hard and fast until we are both out of breath, exhausted and thoroughly satisfied. And I will love every minute of that, too."

Oh, so will I.

Once again, this man makes me melt with his words. My steel-coated heart has become molten.

Noah:

She has not balked once at what I offer. And I will do everything possible to make my promise true.

I continue, "I don't fly out until Sunday evening. Tomorrow we have your brother's wedding. Then tomorrow night and Sunday morning, you have me. I will let you decide whether it's Bree or Brianna. But no matter what, I want to be with you. Can you give me that?"

"Oh, yes. I certainly can."

Bree mirrors my smile. That smile lights up her face and brings me back to when we were younger and had no clue as to the directions our lives would turn.

"I must thank my brother," she murmurs.

I need to thank him, also. "As much as I hate weddings, I'm glad he dragged me into this one. And if I have to walk down the aisle with anyone, I'm glad it'll be you on my arm, Bree." I brush my lips against hers. "It's where you were meant to be." And I believe that with all my being.

To make this happen, to finally be where I'm meant to be, I have a lot of work and planning ahead of me. If I have to move mountains, I will, because I know what's waiting for me on the other side.

They say you always remember your first. They (whoever "they" are) are absolutely right. I've always remembered her. She never forgot me.

I've loved her my whole life. This woman I wanted so much, amazingly, I now have her. And this time…

It'll be forever.

An Obsessed Novella

TEMPTING Him

USA Today Bestselling Author

Jeanne St. James

It's not just a love story, it's an obsession...

Skylar:

Every time my neighbor jogs past my house, I do my best to tempt him. Washing my car, watering my lawn, doing yoga in the grass with all my assets in the air. I'm not sure if he notices me, but I sure can't miss him.

Then one day he falls... into my arms and into my bed. Surprisingly, we're better matched than I would've expected. But when he reveals who he is, my world comes crashing down around me because if he finds out my secret we're finished before we've even begun.

Cade:

Three days a week, I put myself through hell by jogging through my neighborhood. I suffer through it simply to catch a glimpse of a woman I don't know. Every time I pass her house she's outside tempting me. Until one day I fall... over my feet, over my heart, over this woman and into her arms.

I know nothing about her, but I want to discover everything. Even her deepest, darkest secrets. However, little does she know, I have one, too. One that may sever the tie that binds us.

Note: All books in the Obsessed series are standalone novellas. It is intended for audiences over 18 years of age since it includes explicit sexual situations, including BDSM.

CHAPTER ONE

Skylar:

I watch as sweat drips one bead at a time onto my over-priced yoga mat. The sun is so freaking hot and here I am, like an idiot out in my yard, bent over in the downward facing dog pose for the past million years. Okay, not years... maybe more like a million seconds. But my body has decided it hates me (nothing new) and is cramping while my head spins. Even better, my over-priced yoga pants have clawed their way up my crack (as well as one other place). And still...

No neighbor.

What the hell?

Despite my eyeballs' attempt at bulging out of their sockets, I peek at my sports watch. He should've been by here two-point-five minutes ago.

Shit.

The man is usually like clockwork, jogging by my house on Monday, Wednesday and Friday afternoons every week. For the most part, anyway. Though, thunderstorms seem to discourage him from his cardio. (Not sure why.)

On those days, I would be willing to recommend another type of cardio to get his heart pumping. And maybe get his hips pumping, too.

Anyway... look at me! Doing yoga on my front lawn, on the uneven grass, waiting like a desperate woman. (I'm not, really, I promise! It just looks that way.)

But, damn, the man is fine and when he jogs past shirtless, he's shiny with sweat, which makes me want to drag him inside and give him a sponge bath with my tongue.

My thighs start shaking as I peek between my spread legs, because, of course, my ass has to be facing the street. I want him to get a good look at what I'm offering.

I may even wiggle it a little when he jogs by.

That is if I don't pass out into a heap first.

I sigh.

Then sigh again a little louder just for good measure.

Maybe it would be easier if I just took up jogging. Wear one of those sexy sports bras, put my hair up in a cute little pony tail, plaster a smile on my face and follow him around the block at a perky pace.

I'll die first.

Cade:

Why I ever started this shit, I'll never know. No, I lie. I know. I thought, "Cade, dude, wouldn't it be great to up your cardio game and start running?"

I answered myself with, "Yeah, man, that would be *great* and *fun*, too!" And then maybe I won't get so winded when I play basketball with the guys. I'll have more endurance, I'll look and feel younger, and...

Fuck that.

Running sucks. And I don't even think what I do can be considered as running. No, it's more of a jog. Or a lope. Or trotting like a donkey with a lame hoof.

Inhell. Exhell.

My chest burns, my leg muscles spasm, my balls feel like they're floating in a puddle of sweat, and the crack of my ass...

I'm not even going there. (Trust me, you don't want to, either.)

So, why don't I just stop the torture? (Good question!)

I've asked myself that for the past month.

And the answer has always been...

Her.

I sacrifice three days a week just to see a woman I don't know.

Not sure why, but she always seems to be outside at the same time of the day. For that reason, I make sure that's when I go running (jogging, trotting, limping) by.

Am I crazy to torture myself because I find someone attractive and I'd like to get her attention?

Eh. Maybe.

Why don't I just knock on her door and ask her out? (Another good question.)

Maybe I want to impress her with my physique and athletic prowess.

But honestly, something has to give and it has to be soon. Because this running shit sucks balls and I'd rather stick razor blades under my fingernails.

At least my slow trot is the right speed to observe her without being creepy. Walking would be too slow and obvious. Driving too quick and useless, not to mention dangerous when she's clearly a distraction.

And, of course, my pace always allows me enough time to enjoy the show she gives me.

On Wednesday, she was out washing her car, her top soaked, her nipples pushing through the thin fabric of her shirt, and when she bent over to scrub the hood of said car, my boner just about popped out of my shorts. You know, those little nylon running shorts. The ones with the mesh liner, clearly not made for sexual arousal.

But I digress.

The week before, she was out watering her lawn. And, once again, her top was wetter than her grass.

Here's the thing, the entire neighborhood has built-in sprinklers.

Maybe hers are broken.

It's possible.

I grunt as I turn the corner and try to push myself a little faster since I'm off my game today. I'm later than normal, and I want my running to look as effortless as possible. It needs to look as though I've got my shit together and I'm not secretly suffering.

My eyes swing to the left as I jog. She's the fourth house up. The brick ranch home with the two-car garage.

Two houses to go yet.

One house.

My eyes widen as I see her ass in tight black yoga pants in the air. My step stutters but I can't stop my momentum.

My mouth becomes an *O*, partly because I'm falling over my own two feet, the other because she's dropped to her knees and is now arching backwards grabbing onto her heels, her generous tits straining against her top.

Last thing I see is her blinking upside down at me as her head hangs down her back.

Suddenly, I'm staring at nothing but pavement (and my loss of manhood). The little bit of oxygen I had sucked into my lungs is now gone.

Then, what seems like seconds later, bare, cute, red painted toes come into view.

I want to just die.

So much for impressing her. That's been completely shot to hell. I just want to crawl away on my hands and skinned knees to go hide in a bush.

"Are you okay?" she asks, her hand on my shoulder, sounding

concerned. Which touches me. But, that's not the touch I need from her.

I raise my eyes from the toes I want to suck, up those snug yoga pants, and I hesitate when I get to the V of her legs.

I have a feeling she's not wearing panties.

"Can you stand?"

Jesus. I should respond. I can't just pretend none of this happened. Or could I?

"Yeah," I say, but it sounds more breathless (and unmanly) than I'd like. Like I'm out of shape or something.

Can't be. I run three days a week.

Right.

Suddenly, I realize I'm still staring at her crotch. Not cool. I reluctantly lift my eyes over the snug sports top she's wearing and hesitate for a brief, pervy second on the hard beads of her nipples. I finally continue on, no wait... one more peek. Okay, I lift my gaze to her face and notice she's biting her bottom lip and her eyes are crinkled at the corners like she's trying hard not to laugh.

Because me falling over myself is a laughing matter, right?

Maybe I should start laughing and we both can guffaw, and then I can go limp home and lock myself inside until I find my lost manhood again.

"Need a hand?"

A hand. A mouth. A...

"No, thank you," I answer and try to prove it by pushing myself back onto my feet. This time I want to stay vertical.

When her gorgeous sky-blue eyes travel over my body, I have to assume she's searching for injuries. And I stand there like a dummy as she studies my chest (which I'm hoping doesn't appall her), runs her gaze over my shorts (I hope my chubby is not detectable) and then down my legs, which are my best feature (if I say so myself) since I do a lot of squats (hey, at least it's not running).

When she gasps, I look down. Maybe she's impressed with my

monster cock. But no... she's staring at my knees. Without warning, she squats down and puts her hands on my thighs. "You're bleeding."

I stare at the top of her blonde head, which is way too close to my package. If she doesn't get to her feet and take her hands off my legs, she's going to get a face full of my unruly erection.

But she's right, my knees are bleeding, though it's nothing life-threatening. "It's nothing. I can go—"

She suddenly pops up, eyes wide. "Oh no, let me take care of that for you. I have a first aid kit in the house."

Suddenly, I picture her in this white, tight, short nurses uniform (the old style with the skirt – remember those?), with white stockings and everything. (Well, except for the matronly shoes. She's wearing three-inch stilettos in my little fantasy.)

Then *BAM*...

My half-mast becomes a full-blown hard-on.

"Come on," she urges as she lays a hand on my arm. I stare at her delicate fingers wrapped around my bicep and discover her fingernails are painted the same color as her cute little toes.

I realize how badly I want those nails to be raking my back and digging into my ass while she's encouraging me to fuck her harder.

Holy hell, I have just fallen into a deep well of depravity.

I follow her anyway. She's tempted me for weeks. And I finally have an "in," even if it's me being a klutz.

As she guides me toward her front door, she tosses her blonde hair over her shoulder as she says, "I'm Skylar."

Skylar.

It fits her and her sky-blue eyes.

I clear my throat, because when I answer her, I want to sound much manlier than earlier. "Kincade."

She smiles over her shoulder at me and I just about trip again.

Now, why did I just give her my full name which I never use? Ah, because all the blood in my brain has now pooled in my cock, that's why. "Please... just call me Cade."

"Cade," she murmurs as she pushes open her front door and,

letting go of my arm, she steps inside and moves out of the way enough to let me pass.

It takes my eyes a moment to adjust to the change in lighting, but while I'm doing that, she shuts (and locks!) the door behind me.

When I glance around the foyer, I discover her house is set up just like mine, as is probably most of the houses in this neighborhood since they were all built around the same time, by the same builder.

Because of that, I know exactly where her master bedroom is. Which doesn't help the blood flow to my cock. Not to mention, the lack of vital blood to my brain.

Then I realize neither of us have moved. I glance over my shoulder and she's leaning against the door, eyeing me up like I'm a medium-rare filet mignon at a Ruth Chris steak house.

"You've got a really nice ass," she murmurs.

I slowly turn to face her, trying to keep the shock of her comment from my face.

Ah fuck it... "So do you."

"Do you like ass play?"

I blink. "Sorry. What?" A pain shoots through my brain as it explodes.

"Ass play."

Holy shit. Am I hearing things? I shake myself mentally, and it seems maybe I need to clean out my ears.

I try to swallow, but my Adam's apple sort of sticks in my throat. "Ass play," I repeat, trying to keep my cool.

"Yes."

Here I thought she was going to clean up my skinned knees. However, ass play sounds so much better than alcohol wipes, antibiotic ointment and Band-Aids.

She's waiting for my answer.

"I... uh... I don't *not* like it," I respond, wondering where she's going with this conversation.

"Giving or receiving?" She pushes off the door and I

automatically step back. Though, I have no idea why. She *looks* harmless...

"I'm not sure why—"

She tilts her head toward my shorts. "You must be having the same thoughts that I am since you're as hard as a rock under those silky short shorts of yours."

I stop my hand from heading in that direction since I don't need to feel it to know how hard I am at that moment. I don't need to see it. And, apparently, I can't hide it, either.

No matter what, my first thought was not the same as hers. Ass play certainly hadn't entered my brain until she mentioned it.

However, I must admit, now it's stuck there.

"Come with me." Her words come out so huskily that I'm suddenly willing to do any ass play she wants. Even if I'm on the receiving end.

CHAPTER TWO

Skylar:

My luck couldn't be any better right now. Him falling in the street was my ticket to not only talk to my neighbor, AKA Cade, but invite him into my lair (I mean house).

I figure getting right to the point and mentioning ass play would be a good test to see if he scares easily. He didn't run out of the house screaming, so that's a good sign.

As I move down the hallway, I hear him following me (willingly) and goosebumps break out all over my body.

I've been watching this man for the past couple of months and my appetite for him has grown to epic proportions. (But again, I'm not desperate or anything, I swear!)

Oh, wait. I forgot something important...

"Have a family, Cade?"

"Should I be worried that you're luring me farther into your house to murder me, bury me in your backyard and now you want to know whether anyone will come looking for me?"

I stop abruptly at the entrance to my kitchen and he runs into me, his erection (by the way, he's definitely not lacking in that department) smashing into the small of my back. He quickly backs away and mumbles, "Sorry."

"No, I was just trying to get to know one of my neighbors," I say as I turn around to confront him.

"Sorry," he says again and it looks like he means it. "I have family, but no one nearby."

I hope that means he's single. My gaze drops to his left hand. He lifts it and wiggles his ring finger, which is empty, thankfully.

"You?" he asks.

"Nope, it's just me and my pussy."

His mouth opens, then snaps shut and I smile at his reaction.

I clarify. "My cat. Meowsers."

"Meowsers?" His expression tightens as if he's trying to hide his thoughts.

"Yes, I know. Ridiculous, right? Unfortunately, it was the name he came with when I adopted him. I just call him Brat to keep it simple."

"Ah."

Cade might be thinking I'm a little off my rocker at this point. With a last look at him, I turn and head into my kitchen, grab the first aid kit from under the sink and then head right back out.

"Are our houses set up similarly?" I ask him without waiting to see if he follows.

"Yeah."

Surprisingly, Cade is still on my heels as I head toward my master bedroom. Now I'm thinking he may be the adventurous type. I sure hope he is. No matter what, he's a brave soul.

"So you know where I'm headed?"

"Yeah," he responds softly.

My smile broadens as I enter my bedroom, and head straight to the master bathroom.

I close the toilet lid, then point to it. "Sit."

He sits. His dark hair is still slightly damp from running and I want to brush my fingers across the short, bristly cut. Military-like.

Hmm. I've always appreciated a man in uniform.

He's not wearing dog tags, though. So, he may not be active duty. Even so, he'd probably look good in camo, and my nipples harden even more at the thought.

I realize he's staring at me and I'm staring at him. His dark brown eyes are heated, his lips full and certainly kissable. His bare chest rises and falls at a rapid pace, even though he should no longer be winded from his run.

Could it be possible he's as affected by me as I am with him? Has he been watching me on his runs as much as I have him?

I drop to my knees and open the first aid kit. Time to get down to business. "You're pretty consistent with your running schedule." I dig through the kit for the alcohol wipes, find two and rip one open.

"Need to keep in shape."

"Why? What do you do that you need to keep in shape?"

"I... uh... work for the government."

My eyes flick up to his. He's watching me intently. "This is going to sting," I warn him, though he probably knows that since he's most likely around forty and not four.

He jerks under my fingers as I start to clean off his left knee.

I drop my gaze back to his leg to concentrate on my task. "Since when do government workers need to keep in shape?"

"Most don't."

"But you're special."

"Not really."

His voice is so much deeper now than it was when he first fell. He's gathered himself. I like his voice. It fits his physique, his square jawline, his broad cheekbones, his wide shoulders.

I unfold another alcohol wipe and carefully clean up his right knee. "Do they hurt?"

"What?"

I glance up. "Your knees."

"Not much."

I give him a small nod. "Good. Wouldn't want you to be out of commission from your government job." After a few more swipes over his knee, I ask, "Federal?"

He hesitates. "Yes."

Nothing out of the ordinary around here. Our community in Virginia is full of federal government workers.

It wouldn't even surprise me if he was FBI or Capitol Police.

"Are you a cop?" I ask, throwing the used wipes into the small trash can tucked behind the toilet.

"Law enforcement."

I smile at his knee as I rub an antibiotic cream into his brush-burned skin. His knees aren't bad, but I find myself enjoying taking care of him. And it's a good time to learn more about him.

"You must have a cushy schedule if you can run by my house at the same time three days a week."

"So you notice," he states.

"I do." I have both hands on his thighs right above his bent knees and I squeeze gently. A little sign he'll pick up on. Law enforcement officers tend to pick up on subtle hints more than other people. Though, I really can't say I've been subtle. (Remember the ass play question? Yeah, there was that.)

"I noticed you, too."

I sit back on my heels and consider him. "No bandages needed. The cuts aren't deep or excessive. You'll live without total amputation of both legs, officer."

"Not an officer." He says that as if it's important that he corrects me. He doesn't want to be considered an ambiguous "officer."

"Then what?"

In the short time we've spent in each other's company, he hasn't smiled once. Not once. I find that odd.

"Secret Service."

With a gasp, I fall backward onto my ass and he instantly jumps up off the toilet, reaching for me.

"Skylar."

My brain has stopped functioning causing my thoughts to swirl. And I stare up at the tall man holding his hand out to me.

"Skylar, are you all right?"

I blink a few times, trying to clear my head. "I... Yes, sorry." I take his offered hand and it's warm, broad, and strong as he helps me to my feet.

My master bathroom is a decent size but not big enough for the both of us to stand in front of the toilet and not be pressed against each other. Especially with his size, which now being so close, he seems to be taller and broader than I first realized.

He's staring down at me as his hand sweeps the hair out of my face and his fingers brush along my jawline until they hook my chin and tilt my face up to him. "You okay?" he whispers, concern obvious in his eyes.

I shiver and breathe out a "yes." Then I shake my head to clear it, plant my palm on his warm (and still bare) chest, and say louder and with more conviction, "Yes. I'm fine."

I feel his heart under my hand, beating quickly, strongly.

"What was that about?"

"Nothing..." (that I want to admit.) "I just got lightheaded for a second there."

His eyebrows dip low. He doesn't believe me, but he doesn't know me well enough to call me out on my bullshit.

Although, I can read it in his face.

I can easily see he is a man who likes direct.

Well, I like direct, too. But not in this case.

I quickly do a mental scan of my house to see if there's anything still out that will reveal to him who I am. Or who I used to be, more like it.

Because if he finds out, he may just walk out the door and all my planning will have gone to shit.

CHAPTER THREE

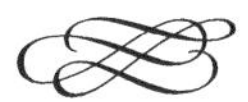

Cade:

I find her reaction to my career interesting. Maybe I'm reading too much into it and she really did become lightheaded. But my gut instinct says otherwise.

I should probably just leave...

But it's hard (literally) to step away. Her back is pressed against the wall and my hard-on is pushing against her soft belly. When her hand flexes on my chest, her nails dig into the skin over my heart.

As I stare down into her eyes the color of a cloudless sky, her eyelids drop, her pink mouth parts and her breath puffs from between her lips. Her nipples are as hard as diamonds beneath her yoga top and I'm tempted to brush my thumbs over the nubs just to test how hard they actually are.

I force my mind to work, but really there's only one thing on it. "Do *you* like ass play?"

Her breath hitches and she practically melts against me. It feels good, really good. I've missed this, this kind of intimate contact.

"I love ass play," she answers, tilting her chin up, beckoning me to kiss her.

I drop my head until my lips are barely above hers. "Biting, spanking, licking, fucking?"

"Oh, yes," she whispers, her eyes pinned on mine.

I exhale a burst of air. "Can I kiss you?"

"You better," she answers.

The last of her words are lost as I take her mouth. I don't need to force my way in, she opens her mouth, invites me in, teasing me with the tip of her tongue. Grabbing her wrists, I raise them above her head and pin them to the wall. I use my skinned knee to part her thighs with barely a wince.

I swallow her groan and she swallows mine, as I can't help but thrust against her. My cock has a mind of its own, that's for sure.

Breaking free from the temptation of that hot mouth of hers, I nuzzle the soft flesh of her breasts as they mound out of the top of her yoga gear. I've wanted to do this for almost two months, ever since I first laid eyes on her at the beginning of my running kick.

Transferring both of her wrists into one of my hands, I finally brush my thumb over those pebbled peaks.

Ah, fuck. I want them in my mouth. I want to squeeze her breasts together and fuck them with my cock until I come all over her. But I also want to come inside her, her pussy, her ass, her luscious lips.

With so many options, I hope we can get to them all. I have a feeling she'll be willing to do anything I ask of her.

And I am certainly willing to do anything she asks of me.

That thought makes my cock throb.

"Shower," she murmurs.

Without lifting my head, my nose buried between her generous, soft tits, I ask, "What?"

"Shower. We were both sweaty."

Fuck the shower. I need to bury my dick in her first.

"First we'll fuck, then shower, then after that I'm going to eat you until you scream."

A hiss sounds in my ear as she arches against me, but I don't think she's complaining about my plan.

I know if I don't knock one out quickly, I won't have the stamina to take my time with her. So, here's the plan... knock one out to take the edge off, then take my time and work on giving her the best orgasms of her life. (I'm not putting too much pressure on myself.)

The last two months of her tempting me three times a week have been like an extended foreplay and now I'm ready to get down to business.

But first...

"Condom?"

She blinks at me, her brain probably as cloudy as mine. But birth control is something I don't ever forget about. Not ever.

She tugs on her bound wrists, but I shake my head. "Tell me. I'll grab them. When I let you go I want you to get naked, lean over the sink, forearms on the counter and I want you to stick that sweet ass of yours in the air. Are you wet?"

"Yes," she says, a slight smile curling the corners of her mouth.

Ah, yes. "How wet?"

"You'll have to find out."

"That I will." I give her a wide smile back because I like her spunky attitude. She's not shy at all, which was clear right from the get-go when she asked me about ass play. Can't get bolder than that.

"Condoms?" I ask again. She tilts her head to a narrow closet next to the shower.

I release her, but she only drops her arms and doesn't move.

I don't move, either. "Get into position," I demand.

Suddenly, she's ripping her top off, her breasts bouncing as they're pulled up with her top and when the built-in bra finally releases them, they drop. Damn, they're flawless. Rosy nipples that are the perfect size for my mouth. They're not small and perky, hell no, they are heavy and full, squeezable. Kiss-, suck- and bite-worthy.

I can't keep standing there staring. I need to move. Especially when she starts to peel down those snug yoga pants, the ones that hug the curve of her rounded hips. This woman has plenty of flesh for me to grab onto when I'm pounding into her and, damn, that does it for me. When I enjoy a steak, I want the meat, not the bone.

I hesitate long enough to confirm my suspicions of her not wearing panties. (I was right, so I high-five myself mentally.)

I finally unfreeze my feet and open the narrow closet door, scanning the shelves for condoms. I find them way in the back on the second shelf. *Way* in the back. Which makes me wonder just how long it's been for her.

It might be rude of me to ask, so I'll wait to see if she volunteers that information first. I check the expiration date on the box. Relief floods me when they're still good. Otherwise, I might have to throw her luscious, naked body over my shoulder and hoof it back to my house.

Look at me, pretending like I can throw a woman over my shoulder and haul her two blocks away.

Nice fantasy. Let's just say, I'm thankful the condoms are still good.

After I dig one out, I rip it open with my teeth and turn, ready to roll it on.

She's done what I've asked. She's bent over the sink and watching me in the mirror.

Oh holy shit, her ass... shaped like a heart, teasing me, tempting me. I can see her plump pussy lips beckoning me. I can't wait to spread them, see if they're slick with arousal.

I know they are. I just know it.

Jesus.

I definitely need to keep it together long enough to make sure she's satisfied with this first go-around, then we can take our time and play.

The good news is that I don't need to be at work until Monday. I have all weekend to explore this woman before me.

"Touch yourself," I demand and capture my cock in my own

hand, sliding along the length, finding the crown slippery with precum. I'm not ready to put the condom on; I'm not ready to lose that sensitivity.

In the mirror, her eyes drop to watch me stroke myself. As she does so, she tucks her hand between her legs and slides a finger through her folds.

Jesus.

My balls tighten painfully and another bead of precum escapes the tip of my cock. With my thumb, I spread the silky fluid around the head.

I have to have her.

I have to have her *now*.

But, I like to make myself wait, too.

I like the anticipation. The speculation of how she'll feel around my cock as I bury myself deep inside her. The wonder of how she'll sound as I work her to a climax.

When she spreads herself open, I can see how shiny her pink center is.

"Tell me what you want," I say, hardly recognizing my own voice. It's deep, husky, thick with need.

I definitely know what I want. I'm a healthy forty-year-old with an insatiable sexual appetite. And I haven't explored my sexual wants and needs for a great while. It has been a year. At least. Maybe more. Though, I'm a fool for denying myself.

But I have.

I just didn't want the complications. The mess of a relationship. My job is steady now, but for the longest time before I moved up in rank, it wasn't. I would be gone at the drop of a hat, flying here, driving there. Hotels. Resorts. Anywhere I was needed, depending who I was assigned to.

Political heads of state tend to be demanding, needy. Just like a woman can be. I didn't want that in both aspects of my life... professional and personal.

Then things changed on that fateful day. Now...

I shake myself mentally. No point in dwelling in the past, it will just make me bitter and what I'm looking at is quite the opposite.

It's sweet. Skylar is very, very sweet.

"Tell me what you want," I repeat softly, rolling the condom over my hard length.

"You."

"Be more specific."

"Inside me," she tells the mirror as she continues to play with herself, to tease me. One finger, then a second, slips inside her and I bite back a groan.

Stepping behind her, I stare at the two of us. She is completely naked, exposed. In contrast, my shorts are shoved down only far enough to give me access to my cock and I still wear my socks and running shoes.

Since I don't want her to think I'm going to fuck her and run, I kick my sneakers off, peel off my socks, yank my shorts down and kick them away. Then I step closer until I'm tight against her ass as she moves her hand away and plants it back on the counter.

Rubbing the head of my latex-covered cock through her folds, I shut my eyes for a moment because I can't believe I'm in this woman's house, in her bathroom, ready to actually do what I've fantasized about doing to her for the past couple of months.

For a second, I actually wonder if I'm dreaming.

I force my eyes open and take my hand (the one not full of cock) and trace my fingers down her spine. She feels real enough. Smooth and tan, not a mark or a mole mars the perfection of her skin. I lean over, pressing my cock into the cleft of her ass as I skim my tongue back up her spine. Her moan encourages me, so I nip her shoulder blades, then along her ribs, her waist and finally I nibble the top curves of her ass.

"Do you have lube?"

She stares at me in the mirror for a couple of seconds before answering. "Yes. Now?"

"No, for later."

No, definitely not now. If I sank into that sweet, tight ass right now, it would be over before it began. Again, I just need to take the edge off.

I adjust my cock so that the head presses against her entrance and before I can press forward, she rears back and impales herself on me.

My eyes pop up from where we're connected back to the mirror. Her eyes are squeezed shut, her mouth is open and I fill her completely.

I intended to take it slow.

Apparently, she didn't. I can live with that.

She plants her palms flat on the counter and begins to rock against me, slamming her ass against my hips.

That won't do. Not at all. I need to control the pace or she won't experience the pleasure I plan to give her.

I need her to want this again and again.

"Stop," I yell, then smack her ass cheek hard. Her eyes pop open, her gaze is hot and dark as she looks at me with a question in her eyes. "Let me," is all I can say, hoping she catches my meaning.

Her cheek is turning slightly pink where I spanked her. And, holy hell, that doesn't help my endurance.

Later, I'll spank that ass until it's red. Later, I will tease her tight hole until she's begging for me to take her there.

Right now... I just need to take the edge off, I remind myself (again).

"Watch," I tell her as I begin to move, slowly at first because her pussy is like melted butter. It burns my soul. It draws me in.

It fucking feels tremendous. Abso-fucking-lutely spectacular. Why have I gone so long without this? Why did I deprive myself this feeling of luxurious heat that surrounds my cock?

CHAPTER FOUR

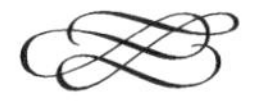

Skylar:

I suck in a breath as he takes his time, slowly moving in and out of me. I've missed this feeling of fullness, completeness, not only being physically connected but having a mental connection with another human being.

I've been empty, lonely.

I'm not sure why this man caught my eye (beside the fact that he's hot), but he did. I'm glad I seemed to have caught his eye, too.

Maybe it was meant to be.

Fate.

I shake that ridiculous thought out of my head. It's nothing but a physical attraction, I remind myself. The only "connection" we have is sexual.

Even that's questionable since we've only really met each other within the last half an hour.

I raise my eyes to the mirror. Not to watch him fucking me (and he's doing it very well, if I say so myself) but to look at myself.

I haven't even known this man for a half an hour yet and he's inside me.

I should be ashamed.

But I'm not.

This is what I've wanted for almost two months. And I'm the type of woman who usually goes after what she wants. I just haven't seen anything I've wanted in quite a while.

His eyes are on me in the mirror and whatever he sees makes him hesitate, messes up his rhythm.

We can't have that. Because I need to come and so does he. This way we can move on to bigger and better things.

A shower. A bed. A chance to discover what he likes, needs, wants. What turns him on, what turns him off (hopefully, not much).

How open minded he is.

His limits.

And just how far he can push mine.

With that thought and a smile, I clench down on him and his hips stutter again. His chest rises and falls as if he's sucking in a deep breath, and his eyes become hooded. I do it again, this time I'm not smiling, though. This time, as I hold his gaze, I can't help but breathe just as hard.

The oxygen slides in and out of my lungs at the same pace he slides in and out of me.

I need to encourage him to go faster. "Fuck me harder."

He shakes his head, his fingers digging into my hips. "I will. Not yet."

"Don't wait. Now."

"I need to—"

"You need to fuck me harder."

"Fuck," he mutters and slams me hard, pushing me forward.

He stops deep inside me and squeezes his eyes shut. I clench around him again, trying to encourage him to move.

"I just..." His words fade off. He tries again, "I just... *fuck*."

Then he's slamming me over and over, my hips jammed against the counter, the slapping sound of our skin filling the small room.

His eyes open. Dark, heated. His jaw appears tight like he's gritting his teeth.

"Yes, just fuck," I tell him. "That's it. Fuck me."

Cade drops his head and blows out a breath. When his head rises, he studies me, and I see what looks like determination cross his face. He's gotten his shit together and he's ready to take it to the next level.

"Up on your hands."

His demand shoots a shiver down my spine.

Yes.

This.

I straighten my arms, bringing my chest higher, and within seconds he's cupping my breasts, squeezing, kneading. He rolls both nipples between his fingers and my back arches, my lips part.

The words "that's it" barely escapes me. "Yes, Cade. *Yes.*"

He mutters a curse, the cords in his neck bulge, and I watch the play of muscle along his shoulders and chest.

Cade's a beautiful man. He appears put together but not harsh. Fit but solid, not built like a runner at all, but still athletic enough to make my mouth water.

He's hitting the end of me with every thrust, and as much as I love his hands on my breasts, I need them elsewhere.

Leaning all the weight on one hand, I grab one of his and shove it between my legs. "Touch me," I whisper.

He rolls my clit the same way he rolls my nipple and the blood rushes through me as I slam back into him. "Yes, Cade, yes. *Yes*!"

His other hand finds my hip again, gives it a squeeze, but doesn't remain there, instead he smacks my ass, then trails his fingers over to the crease.

I suck in a breath before letting it out in a long, low groan as he circles my tight hole. I force myself to relax, even though it's a struggle since he's still slamming me hard at the same time. My brain doesn't know where to concentrate: his fingers on my clit, his cock deep inside me, or his finger circling and teasing my anus.

"I need to..." he drifts off, pressing harder against me.

"Yes, just do it," I encourage him. "Just—"

I lose my thought as he pushes a finger inside me. Would it be better if we waited for the lube?

Yes.

But it's still good and glorious and everything I need from Cade. He works me with a sense of gentleness, though as I study him in the mirror, he's showing anything but on his face.

His expression has become tense and dark. He quickens the pace of his finger to match his hips. And watching him move, seeing him on the edge, drives me to mine.

"I'm going to come," I groan, desperately trying to keep my eyes open, to hold his gaze.

"Yes, baby, come all over me."

Yes, baby, come all over me, echoes in my head. And his words spur me to do just that.

My body clamps down on his and, finally... *finally* I have to close my eyes to just ride out the orgasm as it rolls through me.

Wow. Wow. *Wow.*

The intensity of it makes me lose my breath and Cade becomes still while I shatter around him.

As soon as I can, I open my eyes and see his squeezed shut while he's biting his bottom lip. He must be ready to explode.

"Don't hold back." My voice sounds raspy, low. "Look at me." When he does I repeat myself. "Don't hold back. Let go."

Suddenly, his finger is gone, and he's gripping my hips hard as he slams into me once, twice before throwing his head back and groaning.

Watching him in the thralls of both pleasure and release, turns me on like nothing else and as I feel him pulsating inside me, I can't wait for this rendezvous to continue after we clean up.

~

Cade:

Seriously, my balls are thanking me right now. They haven't had such an intense release in a long time. Jerking off just isn't the same. The jagged edge I was riding is now smoothed out and we can continue after our shower.

Or... in the shower.

Or on the bathroom floor.

Once I recover, though. At my age, my body tends to take a little longer to revive. Like more than the five minutes it took at say... twenty. Or, hell, even thirty-five.

When the day comes that I can't recover at all, it will be one of my darkest moments. But that's not today and that's all that matters at this point.

Plus, the day is early yet. As long as she's willing and patient enough to wait for me, we'll be golden.

So not only are my balls thanking me, they're now happy campers. And so am I.

As she leans into the shower to turn it on, it hits me that she has no body issues at all. She seems to love who she is and accept it. I appreciate that.

I've dealt with too many women in my life who have hid themselves, worried about what I would think about their bodies, had low self-esteem. Not Skylar.

It's refreshing.

Even so, I can't help but like what I see. I like a woman with some flesh on her bones, a fullness in her hips and breasts, a womanly softness to her. Not fat, but curvy, luscious. Sweet.

If I wanted bones and muscle, I'd fuck a man. That's not what I want.

As Skylar turns to me, her sky blue eyes running down my body, I can tell she likes what she sees, also.

"You don't like to run, do you?" she asks, catching me off guard.

I bite back a smile on how intuitive she is. "No, I detest it."

"Why do you do it? It looks like you work out doing other things."

"I do." Besides playing basketball with the guys, I play on a baseball team with my coworkers, as well as doing regular sit-ups, push-ups, and squats. I've got a pool I live in during the summer. Nothing better than swimming laps to stay in shape.

"So why torture yourself?"

"How's the temp of the water?" I ask, because we are two people who hardly know each other, standing naked in a bathroom about to shower together. Not that it's awkward. Okay, maybe slightly. But our conversation can continue in the shower. (I'm a multi-tasker.)

She swipes her hand through the spray, and when she turns back to me she says softly, "Perfect."

That she is.

"Get in."

With a slight smile she climbs into the tub/shower combination and with a hand to the small of her back, I follow her. The shower is tight but that just means we'll get to know each other better and quicker.

The warm spray hits my back and it feels good. But not as good as being inside Sky.

"Can I call you Sky?"

"Sure," she says as she turns and now we're face to face in that cramped tub.

I'm beginning to think that showering together may not work. I'm not a small guy. I take up a bit of space and she isn't a tiny thing, either.

I step back directly under the shower head and let the water rush over me, rinsing me off. Then with a hand on her hip, we do a little shuffle to switch places and I stand just outside the spray and watch the rivulets of water run over her hair, over her breasts, to cascade off her pointed nipples.

Christ, I never want to drink water from a glass again. I only want to quench my thirst from the stream that runs off her nipples. Like a sexy water fountain. One that only I can drink from.

That thought stops me cold.

I have no ties to this woman; there's nothing to bind us together. To suddenly have the urge to completely possess her and make her mine, keep her as my own, is so unlike me.

I blink the water out of my eyes and stare at the woman who may be my downfall, who may knock down my house of cards.

I hardly know her, I remind myself. Maybe I need to write that down and tack it onto my forehead.

I push these crazy thoughts away, since now I've only known her for about forty-five minutes. But who's keeping track?

"Turn around and hand me the shampoo," I say. And she does as I ask without a question. After squeezing a dollop onto my palm and handing the bottle back to her, I drag my fingers through her wet hair that clings to her shoulders and back. Her blonde hair is darker now that it's soaked. I work the shampoo through her strands and I hear her moan as I massage my fingers along her scalp. "You like that."

"Yes," she answers, her voice breathy.

"Body wash," I demand. She hands it to me over her shoulder, as well as a pink nylon loofah. I suds it up and, sweeping her hair to the side, begin to run the loofah all over her body, over each curve, in each nook, along the line of her ribs, between the cleft of her heart-shaped ass, down her legs and back up again. She doesn't move, she lets me take care of her like she did earlier with my scraped knees. But her head is tilted forward and she's very relaxed. I reach around her and with my chest pressed against her back, I make sure her breasts, belly and everything lower is clean, too. I'm thorough because I'm enjoying this closeness as much as she is. And I simply like touching her. (So shoot me.)

I hang the loofah on the spigot and help rinse her hair, then press my lips to her shoulder in a kiss before asking, "Why didn't I trip sooner?"

Her body shakes against me in a quiet chuckle. "I don't know. I'd have never known you existed if you hadn't run by my house. What a lucky girl I am."

"No."

She twists her neck to look over her shoulder at me. "Hmm?"

"Not a girl." I slide my hands down her sides and grasp her hips. "All woman."

"Ah." Her response comes out as if on a sigh.

Yes, I want to hear many more sighs escape her lips before we're through today, tomorrow or by the end of this weekend.

I remember this shower was an opportunity to get to know her better, so I ask, "Ever been married?"

Her body jerks slightly under my touch. I find that curious.

"Once," she says, her voice distant, tense.

"Ugly divorce?"

She shakes her head slightly. "No. Just ugly."

I wait but she doesn't explain.

"You?" she asks me in turn, over her shoulder, the one I can't resist kissing.

"No."

"Never?" The surprise in her voice is evident. "Ever been close?"

"No."

"Ah, one of those perpetual bachelors. Not letting anyone steal your heart. You keep it locked away, then."

"Not necessarily. I've just been always looking for the right woman." I shake my head. "Maybe I'm too picky."

"Maybe," she agrees.

Maybe I do have unrealistic expectations. I want a woman who likes to be dominated in bed, but equal everywhere else. She needs to be strong-willed and confident. Smart and sexy. Does she need to clean, cook and do laundry perfectly? Hell no. She needs to be my match, not my housekeeper.

So why haven't I found anyone in my forty years? Maybe I wasn't looking hard enough. Maybe I liked the search. But again, my career came first and I found that too many women got clingy too quickly and I was always on the go.

Maybe it would have been easier if I had a nine-to-five job. But I didn't and I don't.

At least now I have a sane schedule. And if I find the right woman... Quite possibly, she'll want to swim laps in my pool with me. Or let me bring her breakfast in bed after I've spent the night spanking her ass, fucking her hard, and even coming down her throat.

My cock starts to twitch, but isn't rising to the occasion. Not yet anyway. Soon.

Nothing like a beautiful, wet, curvaceous woman pressed against you to get your blood flowing.

"Turn around, Sky." I help guide her to face me so she doesn't slip. We already had one fall today. Once was enough.

When she does, she's biting her bottom lip in a sexy, but feigned innocence. Her eyes raise to mine. "Cade?"

I'm mesmerized. "Yeah?"

"I'm going to wash you now."

I can't hide my smile at her words. "Okay, Sky." Suddenly, my cock is struggling to wake up.

Soon, I reassure myself, soon. I just need a little patience.

I watch in wonder as she squirts body wash into her palm instead of the loofah and beginning at my shoulders, she begins to soap me up.

And down.

Down.

Down.

CHAPTER FIVE

Skylar:

My fingers dig into his wet hair, my nails into his scalp. The shower having been turned off long ago, Cade is now on his scraped knees, my legs are parted and his mouth on me is just...

Fucking glorious.

Two fingers from one hand separate my folds, while two from the other slide in and out of me. And I'm soaked. Not from the shower, but from what he's doing to me. The tip of his tongue flicks my clit, circles it, then he sucks it hard. My back arches against the damp shower wall and I'm struggling to keep on my feet.

My breasts feel ignored, though, so I take matters into my own hands. Cupping both breasts, I push them together and then snag the nipples with my thumb and forefingers, rolling them hard, twisting, pulling. And suddenly, it feels like there's a direct line from the tips of my puckered nipples to my clit, where he is still working his magic.

Wow. Wow. *Wow.*

Where has this man been all my life? Did he practice licking soft serve ice cream out of a cone? Did he discover this skill by licking the beaters from a mixer?

I push those thoughts aside because I don't care how he learned, I just know what he's doing is making me lose my mind.

"Cade," I barely get out.

He lifts his eyes but not his mouth and the second he notices where my hands are, what my fingers are doing, his lids get heavy, his eyes hot. He groans against my sensitive nub and I groan along with him.

Damn, I'm so close.

His cock is at half-mast now. He's not quite ready, but I know he will be soon. And I can't wait.

Before I can climax, he's pushing to his feet and I miss his mouth on me. He nudges one hand away from my breast and sucks the nipple between his lips, his teeth scraping the edges making me gasp from the sharp sensation.

I like that.

Yes, I do.

His fingers still work in and out of me, his thumb taking over where his tongue left off as he draws my nipple deeper into his mouth. Impossibly deep.

Fuck.

Yes.

Then he buries his hand into my damp hair as he straightens, pulling my head back. Now my breast misses him, too. He stares down at me, his lips shiny from both his own saliva and my arousal.

We haven't kissed again since the first time. I have a feeling that's about to change.

And... I'm right.

As he drops his head, my lips part and I tilt my chin up to meet him. He takes my mouth like it's his, like it's always been his and his alone.

Like it's unchartered territory that's his for discovery.

I love that.

It's like I've had no one before him. This is my fresh start. My new beginning.

It's starting right now. In this shower. With this man.

Cade.

Holy hell, I feel like there's been a complete switch inside of me. I feel like I've finally come alive again.

All from this man's mouth.

How can that be?

His tongue tangles with mine and I groan deep from the back of my throat. The grip on my hair tightens and my scalp tingles from the sharp pull.

Oh, God, I love it, though. It makes me feel more alive than ever. My pussy clenches hard around his fingers. And with a last tweak to my clit, I feel the ripples explode from my center and my eyes roll back in my head.

He swallows my gasp but doesn't let up, his tongue continues to plunder my mouth.

It's too much. Too much.

Ah, yes.

I clench down on his fingers even tighter as the intense ripples fade away.

He lifts his mouth from mine. "Sky, look at me."

I blink away my temporary insanity to consider the man who stands tall over me. I wonder what's next. What his plan is.

I know what I would do, but I'm going to leave it in his skillful hands.

I want him to take control, to be the man I need.

I want him to dominate.

To make me his.

And his alone.

Cade:

There's nothing more exquisite than a beautiful woman skillfully bound with ropes.

So I can appreciate the scene before me. Sky is bound with her hands behind her back in the center of her king-sized bed. But her wrists aren't the only thing bound. She's on her knees, which are tucked underneath her, her cheek pressed to the mattress. I've tied her so that her breasts are harnessed in a fashion that is similar to a bikini top. And it's connected to the rope cuffs.

Here's the thing...

She had the rope. She's the one who brought it into play. However, I know how to tie it, how to secure it. And I think her bringing out her hemp rope and my knowledge of bindings surprised us both.

We both recovered quickly and as I wrapped the ropes around her, tying the necessary knots, her eyes never left me. She has a habit of biting her bottom lip, whether to keep herself under control, I'm not quite sure yet.

What I am sure of, though, is that it's sexy as all get out.

I now sport a raging hard-on. Seeing her bound, especially in a submissive position, pooled all the blood to my cock.

Her long, but still damp hair falls loosely around her face and shoulders. And that heart-shaped ass of hers...

Exposed. A gift for me to do with what I'd like. I considered gagging and blindfolding her, too. (Surprise! She had those, also. Where has this woman been all my life?) However, we can always bring that into play later.

Or tomorrow.

Or the next day.

My gaze traces along the rope that follows the line of her spine down to the small of her back. The rope is wound three times around each wrist and a special knot is used.

Her safe word is lollipop. After learning she had the rope, a ball gag and a blindfold, I wasn't surprised she had a safe word. I do wonder what other toys she has and if she will share.

Even though she does have her word, I hope she doesn't have to use it. I know it's weird to put trust in a man you really don't know and I really do appreciate the chance, but I'm not sure I would put myself in her place right now. Trussed up in front of a neighbor who you've only seen running past your house.

If it was anybody other than me, I'd worry about her safety. But it is me, and I am lucky.

Very lucky.

Back to her toys... It's one of the reasons I didn't gag her. I don't know where her stash is (and I'm sure she has one) and I'll need to ask her questions. Like...

"Lube?"

I don't miss it when her ass quickly clenches, but relaxes immediately. She's already anticipating what's to come.

Anticipation is a great aphrodisiac.

"Closet. Top shelf. There's a blue box..."

I spot the closet she's talking about and head that direction. Inside, there's a fairly large decorative box on the top shelf like she indicated. I pull it down and set it near the bed. Lifting the lid, a smile crosses my face.

Yes.

I wonder at what point in her life she realized she enjoyed these types of things. For me? It was a long, long time ago. I was barely twenty-one, still in college, and waiting to hear back from the Secret Service about my application. I had stumbled across what I thought was a college party, which turned out to be anything but.

And it changed my life.

Staring down into her box of surprises, I ask, "When?"

Even though I'm not looking at her, I feel her gaze on me. "What?"

"When did you find yourself?"

When she doesn't answer, I raise my eyes to her. She switched cheeks on the bed and now watches me.

"I haven't," she answers softly.

"Haven't what?"

"Found myself."

I wonder if she's being coy with me, but her face appears open and honest. I believe her.

She's still searching.

Nothing wrong with that.

I ask in a different way. "When did you head this direction?"

"A long time ago."

"And you still aren't sure?" I ask, surprised.

"I put it aside for a while."

A long time... "During your marriage?"

"Yes."

"Why?"

I could imagine her shrugging if she wasn't bound on the bed. "I had to."

"Why?"

Her brows knit together. "Things needed to be kept at a normal level."

A normal level. *Strange.*

"And you don't consider this normal?" I ask her.

"I do. He didn't. Things could get out of hand. It ended up he wasn't..."

"Wasn't what?"

Her eyes squeeze shut as if she's blocking a memory. I suddenly regret my line of questioning. She's not being interrogated, so I tamp down my instinct to do so. This is supposed to be pleasurable for her, not painful.

"Sorry, let's drop it," I say. At my apology, her eyes blink open and her face appears more relaxed.

"Thank you," she whispers and my chest squeezes painfully at the sadness or hollowness behind her eyes.

Jesus. Now I really want to know her secrets. She's keeping something buried. I'm curious now to know what it is.

I only have one thing that really haunts me and, unfortunately, it's not really a secret. But it's something I avoid discussing whenever possible.

I want to explore everything that's held in that large, blue box with her, but for right now, I dig out the bottle of lube and toss it onto the bed next to her. I don't want to keep her tied up for too long, especially in that position. Before I straighten, I spot something I can't resist.

It's a beaded glass dildo. It reminds me of anal beads (but on steroids) and I know exactly what I'm going to do with it.

I grab it and climb onto my knees on the bed. Before I do what I'm dying to do, I shift in front of her. I move until her head is practically in my lap, I spread my thighs, brush my thumb across her bottom lip, then grip her hair tightly in my fists.

"Open," I command.

Her eyes flick up to mine and her lips part, her mouth opens wide. Then those pink, full lips of hers wrap around me and she sucks me deep. My fingers convulse in her hair and she moans around my cock.

Fuck, yes. Perfect.

She's in a position where she isn't as free to move as she'd like, so using my hands in her hair, I guide her up and down my length. Her cheeks hollow out and she makes a noise as I hit the back of her throat. I realize she can't say her safe word and being bound she can't tap out. I certainly don't want her to bite down if it becomes too much, so I tell her, "Two blinks for a signal."

She understands, but continues on, her tongue stroking the underside of my cock as I move in and out of her mouth, giving her everything I have, my whole length and she doesn't give me the signal.

I'm impressed and in awe as I watch a tear escape the corner of her eye. A natural reaction to just how deep she's taking me.

Still no signal.

The hard suction of her hot, wet mouth, makes me fight the urge to come down her throat. There's so much more I want to do with her than just this and I don't want to have to recover again. Not yet. Not now. Not while she's bound and in my control.

What I can't fight is my eyes rolling back into my head. The sensations, the sounds of her taking almost every inch of me makes my balls tighten, and takes me right to that dangerous edge.

I'm right there. So ready to release. Instead, I let go of her hair and pull back. I'm amazed to see the disappointment in her eyes.

"You like taking me in your mouth."

"Yes," she answers, her lips shiny and wet. A little bit of saliva dribbles from the corner of her mouth, but she doesn't lick it away. Instead, I capture it with my thumb, then slide my thumb into her mouth. She sucks my digit clean, causing my cock to flex in reaction.

Damn.

I'm so ready to be inside her again.

"Are you still okay with your bindings?"

She gives me a *fuck-me* smile. "Yes."

I'm relieved. I brush a knuckle over her cheekbone, then sweep my fingers down her jawline. "Face down."

She immediately drops her right cheek back to the bed. She's an obedient lover. I like that, too.

I move behind her and let my gaze slide over everything she is offering me, openly, unabashedly.

It's quite beautiful, stunning even.

Her pink, plump pussy and the tight, puckered rosette calls to me. Tempts me. Begs me for attention.

I take the beaded dildo into my palm and feel the coolness of the glass. It won't take much to make it warm. I know exactly where to put it to make it so.

I run the tip of it from the top of her spine down, all the way to the crease of her ass, then back to where her hands are bound together. I rub it over her fingers.

"You've used this before?"

"Yes."

"Where? Here?" I ask, sliding the cool glass over her slick folds.

"Yes."

I press it lightly against her anus. "Here?"

"No."

"Why not?"

She hesitates. "I just haven't."

"But you're not against it." Not a question because I know what the answer will be. Because she likes ass play (hard to forget that).

"No."

I brush the round tip of the dildo down her crease again, this time all the way to her clit and back up. "Good," I finally say and she shudders visibly.

I separate her folds and slowly slide the dildo inside her, starting at the widest end. Her spine rounds, the rope along her back becoming taut, and she cries out, but it's muffled as she turns her face into the mattress.

As I slide it in and out of her slowly, gently, the glass becomes warmer between my fingers, capturing the heat of her. The slick heat that will soon surround me.

I can't take very much more. Her reactions are precious and her sounds like music.

Now I wonder how long she's lived here, how long we've been this close but never discovered each other. By dumb luck I decided to begin running. If it wasn't for that, I may never have found her. Never have even known she existed.

But I did.

I did.

I'm so fucking glad I did.

I slip the dildo from her and she makes a small noise that sounds like a protest and I have to smile at that.

She's greedy and needy.

I'm one hell of a lucky bastard.

CHAPTER SIX

Skylar:

The sound of the lube being opened is unmistakable and a thrill shoots through me. My legs are starting to cramp from being tucked so tightly underneath me. But I don't care.

I really don't.

It's been a long time since I've played like this. A long time since I've had a willing partner. I'm not going to waste one moment, not one second, complaining about a little discomfort.

The ropes binding my breasts rub against my skin, making me well aware of who is in control at this time.

Cade is.

He holds me at his mercy.

My breasts ache against the sheet; my nipples pucker painfully. I can't wait to have them back in his mouth, between his fingers, or even within my own. I'm willing to wait for that right now, because I know what's coming first.

Oh yes, I do.

Cade dribbles lube down my crease and the shock of the cool gel against my heated skin makes me gasp and clench hard, though I have nothing inside me to squeeze. I'm empty. No fingers, no cock, no tongue, not even the dildo.

But it's coming.

It is.

I wait. But not for long. His thumb circles my rim, spreading the generous amount of lube around and he dips it quickly inside. Just enough to be a tease.

Then it's there. My new favorite toy. I was disappointed when it first arrived. I had ordered it on impulse, and once I unwrapped it, I didn't think it would ever satisfy me.

However, today has changed my opinion. He used the wide end in my pussy, I wonder if he'll do the same this time.

When I feel the pressure of the rounded glass, I can easily tell it's not, it's the narrow end. One by one, the circular beads of the dildo are pushed inside me. The glass is slippery with lube and I relax to allow him to push farther, deeper.

"Are you okay?" he asks softly.

I smile and turn my head to the side. I'm moved by how caring he is. "Yes."

"More?"

"Oh yes." I groan as the beaded dildo works its magic the deeper it goes. I might even be able to come from simply that and, if my hands were free, from me touching myself.

Yes, we may have to experiment with that. Later.

Not now.

Before he's inserted the whole length, he's pulling it back out and a whimper escapes me. I've used anal beads before (or more like I've had them used on me with a partner) but this, this glass beaded dildo, is even better. I gasp as he pulls it out, one bead at a time.

Before it slips from me completely, with a little pressure, he slowly slides it back in, again one bead at a time, from the smallest to almost the largest. Then he stops. I hear his ragged breathing, even over the thumping of my own heart in my ears. I feel it beating against my skin.

"Do it again," I encourage, and close my eyes to enjoy the journey this single, simple toy is taking me on. Well, the toy and Cade.

It wouldn't be the same without him.

"Are you ready for me?"

"Yes. Please."

The tear of the condom wrapper perks my ears, and in my excitement, I clamp down on the dildo.

"Easy," he murmurs.

No. I don't want it easy. I want everything he can give me. Who knows when I'll have this opportunity again. Who knows when I'll have a willing and skilled partner at my fingertips, in my bed.

I feel the smooth crown of his cock against my labia, sliding up and down, nudging gently. My eyes roll back even before he enters me, because I just know how good this is going to feel. I know how great it will be to be filled completely in both places at the same time.

He pulls the glass toy back out until just about the end, then slowly, oh so slowly, he presses his cock inside me at the same time he does the dildo. Little by little he fills me until there's nothing left to give. I have it all.

"Cade," I moan, rolling my head back and forth on the bed. "Cade." My voice catches.

"I'm here, Sky," he says, his voice so low, so rough, it sounds painful.

He curves over my back so that the fingertips of my bound hands can brush against his belly, feel his hot skin.

Suddenly, I don't want to be bound, tied up, trussed for his use. I want to touch him. Everywhere. I want to explore his body, his mind. Discover his secrets, his thoughts.

I want to touch him inside and out.

"Cade," I cry out.

"Yeah, baby?"

Baby. I love that. "Fuck me."

"In a second." His voice sounds strained.

"Fuck me, please."

"In a moment, Sky." At this point, he's probably wishing he gagged me.

"Now, Cade."

This time he only grunts as he drapes farther over my back and presses his mouth to my ear. "I'll fuck you when I'm ready."

I shiver as his words fill me up like his cock. Like the dildo.

"I'm ready," I press.

"Sky," he says in warning.

"Now, Cade."

"You're pushing me."

"Yes," I hiss. And I am. I'm pushing him to get a reaction. I don't want it slow. Not right now. Now, I need it fast and hard and I need to come.

I know what he's doing. He likes the anticipation, the tease, the thrill of holding out.

"I saw you have a flogger."

My breath catches and then it escapes on a whimper. "I do." Many use the flogger as punishment. I prefer it used as a reward.

I won't reveal that just yet.

"Keep pushing then," he warns.

I press my face into the mattress to hide my smile. Once I get it under control, I twist my head toward him. "Cade," I begin again.

"Sky."

"Fuck me," I demand.

"If it was in reach, I'd flog your ass right now."

I suck in a breath, then blow it out. Blood rushes through me, every nerve stands on end. My nipples are now so tight that they cause a pull all the way into my belly.

"Make me come."

"When I'm ready," he says firmly, pulling away from me, going back to his knees.

I miss the weight of him across my back. I miss his voice directly in my ear. He now seems so far away.

"Please," I urge.

Finally, he moves, thrusting deep inside me while his hand remains on the dildo to control the movement.

Ah, fuck.

He's driving me out of my mind. He's going to make me come before he's really even began.

Again, he slams into me, doing the same with the toy. I cry out at the exquisite pleasure.

"Lift your ass higher."

Without hesitation, I rise to my knees causing my face to press harder now into the bed. But I see what he wants. He wants more of me.

Leaving the dildo deep inside me, he wraps one arm around my hip, his fingers finding my clit. The other snakes around my ribs, his hand cupping my breast. He tweaks one nipple then the other, before tracing the ropes that frame them.

A noise escapes him which makes me wish I could see his face. It's easy to figure out the ropes turn him on. There's no doubt that he's experienced with bindings. He knows how to tie the correct knots. He knew the correct tension and tightness so I wouldn't be injured. It's safe to say I'm impressed with his knowledge.

It's also encouraging. If this continues after today, we might be able to explore many, many options.

Not just ropes, but other things. Those possibilities make me tingle from the top of my head to the tips of my toes.

My excitement ratchets up by the thought of him using the flogger on me in the very near future. Like today. In fact, I won't let him leave until he uses it.

My smile disappears as his thrusts get faster, harder, and I have to struggle to keep to my knees, to keep from sliding up the bed. Though, that's difficult since I don't have the use of my hands.

My shoulders are starting to ache, but when he pinches one nipple hard and then the next, I quickly push that ache aside.

"More, Cade."

He pulls my nipple as far as it will stretch then twists until I don't think my skin will give anymore. It's exactly what I meant when I demanded more.

"Yes," I hiss. "Yes."

Two fingers circle my clit, press, tweak and even pinch. Every tease is felt deep within my core. I clench down around him and the dildo, and I hear another moan escape him. It's low and long, that sound alone drives me to the brink.

"Cade, I want to come."

"Tell me what you need."

"You. Just you." And, surprisingly, that's true. We have some uncanny connection. Something I can't explain. Him being inside me suddenly makes me feel complete. It's never been like that with anyone else.

Maybe I'm just making up these strange thoughts in my head.

I swore I wasn't desperate, but maybe I am.

For attention.

For contact.

For intimate interaction.

"You have me," he finally says, his hips now pumping hard, his breath ragged.

Yes, I have you, but for how long?

For just today? Tomorrow? This weekend? Until we get bored of each other? Until you find out who I am?

I push that thought away. Why ruin a good thing, even if it's only temporary?

"Sky, I'm going to come... I need you to be there with me."

I agree, I need to be there with him, too. I close my eyes, shut out the outside world, and bask in the incredible sensations he's pulling from me, from my body. He releases my nipple and with two fingers still on my clit, he slowly works the glass dildo in and out of me, but at a much slower pace than he's moving.

"I want you to come when I tell you."

"Yes." Yes. I want that.

I do.

I do.

I...

My breath catches when he says, "Come for me, Sky."

And just like that, it's so easy. He pulls a climax from me and I explode around him, my eyes squeeze shut to hyper focus on where we're connected. He has become still, so deep inside me, while his cock pulsates as he achieves his release. He doesn't move for a moment. His heated breath beats against my skin, making me shiver.

I groan when he slowly removes the dildo, then slips away from me so we're no longer as one. Now we're separate and distant. And I feel the loss of our closeness.

But we're not done.

Clearly not done.

We have so much more to give each other today.

He lays a kiss on each of my ass cheeks and one on each shoulder blade, then he curls over me again, his lips to my ear. "I'm going to start with your wrists."

Thc tip of his tongue traces the outer shell of my ear before he pulls away. Seconds later my wrists are released and he pulls me up on my knees, an arm circles under my breasts as he brings me against him. My back to his front. Both hands cup my breasts and he softly caresses them before, once again, tracing the rope that binds them.

"It's amazing how beautiful a woman bound in rope is."

"Why is that?"

He doesn't answer right away. He takes his time. Formulates his thoughts. "By making you helpless, the balance of power shifts my way. But that's not what the rush is for me. It's that you trusted me enough to do it. To put that power in my hands. Especially when you hardly know me... No. Hardly isn't even correct. You *don't* know me. I could have abused that power."

"But you didn't."

"No, I didn't. I wouldn't. But how would you know that?"

"I wouldn't know that. But I went with my gut." Again, I think about this uncanny but natural connection we have.

"That could be dangerous."

True. Because my gut instinct has been wrong before. Very wrong.

I don't think it is in this case.

"It must be your trusting face," I say softly, reaching behind me to cup his cheek. He grabs my hands, circles my body with his arms to hold out my wrists in front of me, inspecting for rope burn.

There's none. He was careful, which I appreciate. I also didn't struggle so there was no reason for the skin to break or get irritated. His thumbs rub the undersides of my wrists to help with circulation, but even that's not needed.

I'm amazed how those small movements, this caring of me, is erotic in itself.

I lean my head back to settle it along his collar bone and he presses his cheek against mine. "Hungry?"

"I think I could eat."

His thumbs move higher and he's now running his fingertips up and down my forearms. "I could run home and—"

"No," I interrupt him. I don't want him to leave, even for something as simple as takeout, even if it comes with the promise of him returning. Not now. Not yet. "I'm sure I have something I can put together in the kitchen."

"You don't need to do that."

"No, but I'd like to."

He skims his palms up my arms and over my shoulders, rubbing away any soreness from holding my arms behind me. I can't stop the small moan that escapes my lips.

He nuzzles my ear with his nose and then sucks on my earlobe for a second, playing with it with his tongue. "Sky," he murmurs against the skin of my neck.

"Hmm?"

"Do you want me to remove the rest of the binding before I go clean up and get rid of this condom?"

"No. Not yet."

The kisses he's peppering along my neck and shoulders stop and he lifts his head. "Very good. I'll go clean up and meet you in the kitchen."

He sounds pleased with my decision. I reach my hand back to wrap it around his head, pulling him forward as I lean back and twist to meet his lips in a brief kiss.

"Clean up and I'll get you fed."

He's fed my soul today, so it's the least I can do.

~

Cade:

Black silk or satin on a woman can be very sensuous. With a robe, a blouse or even a skirt, it clings to curves like a lover's hand. As undergarments, it emphasizes the simple beauty of a breast, an ass cheek, the angle of a woman's hip. And to watch Sky move around her kitchen in nothing but a black satin robe, hugging her generous curves, makes me hungry for more than just food.

It's not only the robe, though. It's what she's wearing underneath it. Not panties. No. I know she never pulled them on; it was hard to miss when she bent over to dig through a lower cabinet. The flash of ass cheek and peek of pink flesh made it obvious.

It's the outline of the rope she still wears that binds her breasts. Her nipples are hard like diamonds under the thin, slippery fabric, and just that knowledge of what awaits me when I get to unwrap that robe from her later makes me heady.

I blow the steam off my coffee as I watch her move around the kitchen from over the brim of my mug. Occasionally, she gives me a little glance over her shoulder and I feel that right down to my toes (not to mention, elsewhere).

Her blonde hair hangs loosely down her back and sways almost as much as her hips. The unmistakable sounds of classic rock surround us from an unseen stereo. Suddenly it hits me as I lounge in one of the chairs at the kitchen tables.

This could be us on any Saturday or Sunday morning. Her making breakfast, me drinking coffee, music softly playing in the background.

I'm just missing a Sunday paper, a pair of slippers and a Golden Retriever laying at my feet.

A strange feeling makes me shake myself mentally and I look up at the clock on the wall. Six o'clock. I began my run a little after four this afternoon. I tripped just a few minutes after that.

This little scene of domesticity before me suddenly sends a chill through me. I've never even lived with another woman. I've always liked my independence. And, of course, with my job, it would have taken the right woman to put up with my schedule. I wasn't willing to deal with sorting through them until I found the right one.

Suddenly, I feel like I should skip the meal she's preparing and go hungry. Play with her a little while longer, make sure I get to use the flogger and then get the hell out soon after.

Something soft weaves around my bare ankles and I tilt my head to see her cat Meowsers winding back and forth, rubbing his (or her) soft fur against my skin, head butting my calf, rubbing its whiskers along my toes.

Weird.

I've never had a pet. But, if I did it wouldn't be a cat. I love pussy, just not the four-legged kind.

Skylar's throaty laugh pulls my gaze up to her. She's watching her cat do its thing. "Brat," she calls. "I bet you're ready for dinner."

The cat's tail stands straight up and it lets out a loud *meow*. Sky disappears into the utility room off the kitchen for a few minutes then reappears with a small bowl in her hand.

Funny how the cat loses interest in me quickly and struts across the room to where Sky places the bowl. And once again, when she bends over, I get a perfect view of succulent, tempting flesh.

I try to picture those tan ass cheeks marked from my machinations, from my use of the flogger and my cock starts to stir in my shorts.

Food before fun.

Whatever she has on the stove starts sizzling in the pan and she hurries back to give it a stir.

"Smells good." And that's true. Whatever she's throwing together does smell very good.

If this woman can cook...

I might be a goner.

"Chicken stir-fry. I hope you like vegetables."

"Definitely, since I'm a vegetarian."

I keep my face as blank as possible as her mouth opens into an *O*. She quickly glances into the skillet then back at me.

"Just kidding," I say.

The relief is instant on her face and she giggles, which makes me smile.

After stirring the ingredients one more time, she leans back against the nearby counter, planting both palms on the edge. The robe separates just enough I can see a little cleavage and a bit of the rope.

"Fuck, Sky," I murmur, shaking my head. "If you're not careful, dinner might burn."

She follows the direction of my gaze and pulls her robe around her tighter before giving me a sultry smile as her fingers trail over the satin along the outline of the binding.

She asks me, "Are you sure you want to stick with coffee and not have a glass of wine?"

"I need to keep my energy up, wine may make me sleepy."

"Mmm," she murmurs as she snags her nearby wineglass and takes a sip of the red she poured herself earlier. "So..." she begins, tilting her head to study me. "When you said Secret Service, you meant agent, right?"

I take a sip of my coffee which has finally cooled down enough so it doesn't feel like I'm burning my tongue with the molten core of the earth. "Yes."

"Have you ever had to take someone out?"

I stare at her over my mug. I want to make sure I'm clear on what she's asking. Even though I know and I'm just delaying because this is usually a conversation I don't like to have. But most people are curious. They ask innocently not realizing the impact of such a simple question. Simple, only in the knitting of words together, not simple when it comes to real life consequences. "Take someone out?"

"Take down a threat, I mean."

"Do you mean hand-to-hand combat?"

"No."

I study her and wonder how she'll react to my answer. I carefully place my mug on the table. "Once."

The curiosity which was apparent in her face suddenly disappears, her face becoming a blank mask. "Did you think twice first?"

"No. Can't think about it. Lives could be lost."

"But... was a life lost?" The weight of her gaze on me feels heavy.

Taking a life is never an easy decision, but sometimes it's a necessary one. Having to take protective action is my job, but no matter what, someone will come out on the losing end. Whether it's the victim and everyone who loves and knows them. Or the person trying to take out the target. As well as everyone who knows and loves *that* person, criminal or not. It still affects them. That person has a family, has led a life.

It also leaves an impact on the law enforcement official who must dispatch the subject. It's something one never forgets. And shouldn't. But even if it's the right and legal thing to do, it leaves a mark.

No matter what, it's tragic all the way around. In that sliver of time, lives are changed forever.

Including mine.

Including the one and only person who was trying to assassinate a senator who was running for president. One who wasn't very well liked by certain groups. But still...

"Do you think about it still?"

"Every damn day," I mutter before grabbing my coffee and taking another sip.

With a nod, she turns back to the stove, fork in hand.

She spears something, then looks over her shoulder. "Come here," she says softly.

I move as if I'm on a string and she's pulling the end. She calls and I come. When I get to her she turns and lifts the fork toward my mouth, cupping a hand under my chin.

"Open," she urges.

Before she slides the fork full of stir-fry chicken between my parted lips, she puckers hers and blows. Then she does it again.

Holy shit. That was so hot. (And I'm not talking the temperature of the food.)

Before I can say a word, she shoves the fork into my mouth and I taste her "thrown together" stir fry.

Yes, this woman can cook.

I swallow, grab her hips and lean in close. "How are you still single?"

The corners of her eyes crinkle. "How are you?"

Touché.

CHAPTER SEVEN

Skylar:

Cade must have been hungrier than he realized. After scarfing down one and a half plates of my stir-fry, he released a long, satisfied sigh. I plan on releasing one of my own soon, too. But for another reason.

However, now it's my turn to sit at the table while watching Cade stand at the kitchen sink only wearing those little red silky running shorts. I was surprised when he offered to clean up the dishes. Of course, I was going to jump on that offer. But he had a stipulation...

For me to sit at the table wearing nothing but the rope binding while watching. His gaze seared me when without a word I slipped the robe off my shoulders and let it drop onto the back of the chair.

As soon as I did that, he wandered away only saying, "Stay seated until I tell you otherwise."

My brain starts spinning, wondering what he's planning. The anticipation makes my nipples bead into hard points, makes my clit ache for his attention.

"Can I touch myself?"

Without turning, he says, "Yes. It's expected."

Well now. Great minds...

I spin in my chair to face him, even though his back is turned and he's not paying any attention to me. He's concentrating on scrubbing the dishes with a sponge.

I want to call his name, but I resist.

I think he wants to imagine what I'm doing. I slide a hand between my thighs, stroking my center as I thumb my sensitive clit. I brush a palm over the tight beads of my nipples, one then the other.

As I stare at his back, willing him to turn around, I slip my middle finger inside of me causing a small sound to escape the back of my throat. I notice his hands still for only a moment before continuing with their chore.

I bite my lip, trying to avoid making any more noise, but eventually I have to blow out a shaky breath. I know he hears that, too, when the muscles in his bare back tighten ever so slightly.

Now it's a challenge and I'm determined to test him, to see how long he can resist. Can I make him break before he's finished with his task?

A low moan slides from between my lips as I tweak my nipples and insert a second finger deep inside of me. Teasing my own clit, I fuck myself, my hips rising and falling slightly.

"Yes," I hiss.

He grips the edge of the sink and his head bows forward, his back becomes tight, his biceps bulge.

I'm *oh-so-close* to making him break.

I'm also *oh-so-close* to making myself come. I twist my nipple between my forefinger and thumb, then pull it hard enough that I gasp.

I plant my feet on the floor and my hips shoot straight up. The chair bucks underneath me, making a clatter as the orgasm washes over me, takes over every muscle in my body, makes me convulse and close my eyes.

Because of that, I feel him before I see him.

I did it. I made him break. I hear something hit the table, but before I can open my eyes, his hand is under my chin pulling my head back, bending my neck until it can't arch anymore and I look up to see him standing over me. His face dark, his eyes flashing.

I have no idea what he tossed onto the table, but I'm sure I will find out soon enough.

Even so, it's the ice cube he slides over my stretched throat that makes me gasp. It leaves a cool trail down my skin, beads of water pooling at the base of my throat. But he doesn't stop there. He circles my nipples with it. One then the other, bringing them to painful peaks. His hot tongue follows the cube, first down my neck, then over my nipples as he flicks the pebbled ends with the tip of his tongue.

"Cade..."

"Quiet."

That low one-word demand makes me want to smile with satisfaction, but I can't. I can't. The ice between his long fingers is now traveling around my nipples once more before sliding down my belly to between my legs.

"Part yourself."

I lose my breath and can't answer him. So, I don't even try. I just do what I'm told and separate my folds to give him the access he demands. When the cold hits my hot, swollen nub, I jerk forward, but he tightens his grip on my chin, not letting me move, keeping me at a disadvantage, unable to watch or even pull away. The ice turns me numb, but before I can complain, he takes my mouth, plundering his tongue inside, tangling it with mine. I groan and he catches it, swallowing it down.

Then he releases me suddenly, and spins the chair around, the legs squealing along the floor. I almost squeal just as loudly because I wasn't expecting that. He drops to his knees, puts the remaining piece of ice cube in his mouth, and shoves my thighs open even farther.

He drops his head and this time I drop my head back on my own, my mouth gaping open as he takes me into his mouth, moving his tongue and the cube through my slit, over my clit, and back down again until only his mouth is left cold and wet, the ice cube long melted away.

Actually, his mouth isn't the only thing wet. I'm soaked. "I want you inside me."

He pulls away slightly. "Are you asking or telling?"

"Telling."

"Then you will have to wait," he answers and with a last lick to my pussy (even that quick lick makes me squirm), he stands up, grabs me under my arms and lifts me to my feet. "Over the table."

When I look over my shoulder at the kitchen table, I finally see what he threw there. A wooden spoon. Albeit the widest one I have, but still... *a wooden spoon*. My body quivers at the thought of it being used on me in what I can only assume is of a punishing nature.

And, honestly, I'm not sure if the shiver that runs through me is from fear, excitement or a combination of both.

Never having been struck with such an object, I try to imagine how much it will hurt. Or how good it will feel. It will depend on how hard Cade strikes me.

I always have an out.

Lollipop.

If I say it he would have to stop immediately.

Well, he wouldn't *have* to, but I need to trust him enough to believe he would. I meet his eyes and try to get a read on him, but I can't. His face is blank and I don't know him well enough to see behind that mask.

Finally, he says, "I'm heading into the bedroom for a minute. When I come back out, be in position." Dropping his head, he gives me a quick, but deep kiss, then murmurs against my lips. "I'll make it worth your while."

Oh yes. That sounds promising.

My gaze follows him as his long legs take him quickly out of the kitchen and out of sight.

I turn and stare at the table. Heavy oak, with four spindle chairs surrounding it. A location to eat. A spot to gather. And the place my next sexual adventure will he held.

I blow out a breath as I get "into position." Unfortunately, as I lay on the table the wooden spoon stares back at me.

~

Cade:

I glance around her bedroom, spot the lube that was tossed aside earlier and snag that along with another condom. But before rushing back out to Sky (and that sweet ass of hers which better be bent over the table) I stop and think. I'm not ready to break out the flogger yet, though I keep that in the plan. Instead, I look for something else.

I dig through her "toy" box and pull out a black silky blindfold. I could use more rope, but I want to switch it up. My head turns toward the partially open closet where the box was kept.

I'm wondering what else she has hidden.

Sliding open one side, I take a quick glance inside. Women's clothes are draped in an orderly fashion on the hangers, shoes stacked neatly on the floor on a shoe rack, and more boxes of various sizes are stacked on the shelf above the bar. I grab one that looks like a banker box, place it on the floor and remove the lid.

It takes me a second for my mind to process what's in the box. Papers, lots of papers haphazardly thrown into the box, mixed with newspaper clippings and photos. One catches my eye... a photo of Sky but with a man.

Probably her ex-husband.

I slide it out from under a document to see it more clearly, then I squint, blink and look closer.

Sky looks very young, maybe early twenties, staring up at the man who has his arm wrapped around her. They are both laughing, but it's the adoring look she wears that makes my chest squeeze.

She loved him. That's perfectly clear.

Then it's not the emotion that makes my heart squeeze. I lift the photo out of the box and tilt it toward the fading light from the nearby window.

He looks familiar.

Very familiar. I rack my brain. I know this guy.

I know him but can't place him. My brain spins when I try to put a finger on it.

I shake my head and toss the photo back into the box. I dig out another one. A photo of just him. Older, dark hair, but he's not laughing in this one. His face appears haunted, distant. He also looks more gaunt.

Something definitely changed during the years between the first and second picture.

I snag another photo. In it, the man wears tan fatigues. He's overseas in some sand-ridden country and surrounded by several other soldiers all posing with M4 Carbines. In this photo I recognize the brotherhood between the men, but not one of them is smiling. No joking. Nothing. They look burned out, finished with war games. They look like a group who has experienced loss and is ready to come home.

I throw the photo back in, feeling guilty about snooping. Maybe Skylar's husband came home with PTSD and they just didn't make it like a lot of couples do after their spouse comes home from being deployed.

But, again, the guy looks familiar and something is niggling at the back of my mind. Something heavy and disturbing. It's right there, bugging me, but it's not clear.

Maybe we'll get to the point where we can discuss her past marriage. It's too soon now, that's certain. But maybe...

Maybe if things go well... and we find out we're compatible and both of us want to explore whatever this connection is between us.

At this point, I can honestly tell myself that I want to give it a shot, see where this leads.

But, I also need to find out who this man is in the photo. As I start to rifle through the documents searching for a clue, I hear Sky call my name in a low moan.

Shit.

With a quick, regretful glance at the box, I cover it and throw it back on the shelf and slide the closet door shut.

Another time.

CHAPTER EIGHT

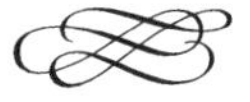

Skylar:

"Cade," I moan again and suddenly he's there next to the table, his hands full, but my eyes focus on the lube.

He has plans.

"Hey, beautiful," he whispers, his gaze running over me as I'm draped over the table, my bare ass in the air, my bound breasts pressed against the smooth surface. The rope has begun to dig into my skin, so after this, I'm going to ask for him to remove it. I probably could remove it myself as my hands are no longer tied together, but that wouldn't be any fun.

No fun at all. It would be like removing my own negligee.

"It took you that long to get those three items?"

He cocks an eyebrow my direction. "I was giving you an opportunity to think about your actions."

He's so full of shit. He loved my actions. This is all just a game. To him. And to me, too.

I bite my bottom lip until the smile that wants to spread is contained. "Of breaking your concentration on doing the menial task of washing dishes? I'm not sorry."

"*Ah*," he sighs. "I know you're not." He places the lube and the condom on the table, but within reach of where I'm artfully displayed. Then he lifts the blindfold up and stretches the elastic that will hold it in place. "For you."

Now I do smile. It's more out of satisfaction than glee. I wouldn't own a blindfold if I didn't enjoy using it.

He pulls my long hair away from my face and then slides the blindfold over my eyes. I reach to adjust it and he makes a sharp noise which makes me freeze mid-motion.

"Palms flat on the table in front of you unless I tell you otherwise."

Nice.

The bossier he gets with me, the more I like it. I'm not in any way a submissive person out in the real world, I demand on being an equal, but in the bedroom (or on a kitchen table) I want the man to take charge.

So far today, Cade has shown he likes to do so.

Perfect.

I flatten my hands on the table after stretching my arms out in front of me. I know the wooden spoon is in between them, laying there, waiting.

Again, a thrill shoots through me and I'm already imagining the sharp sting of the wood against my ass. My pussy clenches hard and my breath catches before rattling out of me on a shaky sigh.

"Tell me your safe word again, Sky."

By the location of his deep voice, I can tell he's moved behind me. "Lollipop."

"Very good."

Not so good for him if I use it. (Not so good for me either, if I have to use it.)

Now that I'm blindfolded, my world had become dark. I have to use my hearing and my sense of touch to figure out what he's doing. Though, it doesn't surprise me when his finger traces the crease of my ass.

My question to him earlier, "Do you like ass play?" floats through my mind. This man does not shy away from it, that's for sure.

"Hand me the spoon."

Ah. He's going to make me hand him the tool used for my punishment. Clever.

I feel around where I last saw it and my fingers find the narrow, long handle. I pick it up and swing it behind me to offer it to him.

I'm holding it out to him for what feels like minutes. But it's probably only seconds before he says, "Show me where you want me to use it."

Lowering the spoon, I let it brush my right ass cheek. "Here."

I startle when his hands suddenly grip my hips and his lips touch my skin where I had the spoon.

"Here?" he asks. "Where else?"

I move it to the left cheek. "Here."

He kisses that cheek, too. "Anywhere else?"

"No. Not now."

"Show me how hard you want me to spank you with it."

I hesitate. I've never spanked myself. However, I do love a good spanking, whether by hand, belt, paddle, crop. I'm not picky. Since a wooden spoon is something I've never experienced before, I'm not sure what I'll enjoy. *If* I enjoy it at all.

"Show me," he demands again, but more firmly.

I tap the spoon lightly against my ass. It's painless.

"That's it?"

"No," I breathe out.

"Show me."

"Cade..." I begin but drop off since I want him to take the spoon. I want it to be him to use it. "Please."

"Please what?"

"Please..." *Spank me, fuck me, make me come.* "Do what needs to be done."

"And what needs to be done, Sky?"

I hold out the spoon to him and he takes it from my fingers. "Palm back on the table."

I settle back into position, preparing myself mentally for what's to come.

But no matter if I thought I knew what was coming, it wasn't quite what I expected. The harsh sting of the flat wide spoon against my ass makes me suck in a sharp breath.

One of his fingers trails down my cleft again all the way to my clit and back up. And the crack of the spoon against my other ass cheek makes me curl my fingers, rise up on my toes and jerk forward in shock of how much it hurts.

The pain quickly dulls and the throb of my skin becomes pleasurable, making my core clench tightly. I want him buried deep inside me before he strikes again.

"Beautiful," he murmurs. "This is only the beginning of your ass being that color."

Only the beginning...

"Reach back and separate yourself."

Pressing my cheek into the table, I do as he says by grabbing my ass and spreading my buttocks wide.

"Fuck," he groans and I smile.

He taps the spoon softly over the top of both cheeks. I arch my back and encourage him to do more. But he doesn't. He stops and I hear him shuffling around behind me as well as a sound I recognize as him opening the lube. A shudder runs through me. There's no reason for lube if he's just going to fuck me. My pussy can't get any wetter than it already is.

As he works the lube around my tight opening, I hiss out a "yes."

Dipping in a finger to the first knuckle, he makes my entrance slippery, ready for him. I relax and enjoy the sensations of the push and pull of his finger as it goes deeper and deeper.

"Cade," I groan.

"Soon, baby," he assures me.

Not soon enough.

Suddenly, he's gone and I hear the tear of the condom wrapper and in my mind's eye I see him rolling it down his hard length then spreading more lube generously over his latex-covered cock.

Then he's sliding the crown of it across my anus, down my cleft between my throbbing labia and rubbing it over my clit. He shifts slightly, sliding inside me and I moan loudly as he seats himself deep within me, my fingers digging into my own flesh.

"Keep yourself open to me, Sky. I want to see all of you."

The scrape of the spoon against the table puts me on edge once again.

Because I know it's coming.

It's coming.

Now that he's inside me, it's going to be even better.

My heart pounds all the way up into my throat and I close my eyes, even though I'm blindfolded and can't see anything anyway.

As he thrusts slowly in and out of me, I beg, "Spank me, Cade. Do it."

"Are you asking or telling?"

Oh fuck. "Asking... *Please*."

His fingers trace the rope that runs along my spine then curves around my ribs and I shiver. The crack of the wooden spoon against my ass makes me jerk and whimper, but he grabs the stretch of rope along my back and holds me in place.

"Don't move."

I'd like to see *him* not move when someone's spanking his ass with a wooden spoon. Easier said than done!

"I want to spank your pussy with the spoon."

Shit. If he does do that I might be screaming "lollipop" (as well as some other choice words).

When he pulls out, I think that's his next move and panic. "Cade!"

He chuckles, leans over me and whispers in my ear, "I'm not going to hurt you. And, no, I'm not going to do it. You would need to beg me for it."

There's no chance of that happening. Hand, maybe. Wooden spoon, never. I'm not that much of a masochist.

I blow out a breath in relief.

I hear the cap on the lube again and then he's rubbing the head of his cock along my crease once more, and every time he does he pauses at my tight hole.

"Do you want this?"

Oh... "Yes." I certainly do. Though, I tense since it's been quite a while for me.

"Relax," he whispers, pressing forward, slowly stretching me open. "Say your safe word if you need me to stop, baby." Now there's no laughter in his voice. No, it's ragged instead.

I bite down on my bottom lip as he grips my hips hard, digging his fingers in to hold me still as he pushes past my tight ring and then slides gently inside. The stretch, the burn, makes me suck in a breath, but I don't want him to stop.

And I like him calling me baby. I not only like it, I want to hear it more from him.

My eyes roll back in my head as he drives himself as deep as he can go and stills. He leans over my back again, kissing my shoulder blades, my shoulders, my neck, then he sinks his teeth into the sensitive spot where my neck meets my shoulder. I cry out an encouragement.

I get off on biting as much as spanking.

"More," I groan.

Licking the bite mark, he moves back down my back, nipping my skin, gripping my flesh in his teeth, making my pussy throb even though it's empty and he's filling my ass instead.

Wow. Wow. *Wow.*

If he's skilled with a flogger, I may have to marry this man. I snort at my own thought and he hesitates.

"You okay?"

"Yes. Perfect," I say as he trails his fingers around my waist and wraps an arm around my hips to pull me back away from the table slightly. Just enough so he can find my clit and tease me.

"You're so tight," he groans against the skin of my back.

I'm well aware of that. When he slips a finger inside me while his thumb plays me like a fiddle, I let myself go.

"That's it, baby. Damn."

Baby.

"I'm going to fuck you harder," he tells me as he slips a second finger inside, working me into a frenzy. I've long since released my buttocks and have planted my hands back on the table to brace myself.

"Please," I beg.

"Please what?"

"Please fuck me harder. Make me come." A cry escapes me that's sounds like a wild animal when he slams me hard.

Then, before I realize what's happening, I'm moving backwards when he wraps an arm around my waist. I land on his lap when he settles into the kitchen chair I was in earlier.

I'm now on top, facing away from him as he's planted deep inside me, both his cock in my ass, his fingers in my pussy.

"Ride me." His growl in my ear draws a shiver from me.

Using the leverage of my feet on the tile floor, I rise and fall. His free hand pinches one of my nipples as he finger-fucks me and continues his assault on my clit.

Without warning, a rogue wave rushes forward, tumbling me over and over as I come around his fingers, clench down on his cock and cry out his name.

"That's it, baby. Give me all of you." He sounds out of breath, struggling to keep control. "One more before I come."

He nuzzles my neck with his nose, scrapes his teeth down my skin, once again sinking his teeth into my shoulder. But this time he doesn't let go. He bites harder as I rise and fall faster, encouraging him to take me back out to the surf to find another wild wave. I don't want a buildup, I don't want to know it's coming, I just want to be hit with it, tossed around, gasping for breath and struggling to right myself.

That's how I want to come.

It needs to be intense and all-consuming.

I land heavily in his lap and grind hard.

"Fuck, baby," he groans. "*Fuck.*"

Yes. Yes. *Yes!*

The more I hear him losing his shit, the more it drives me closer to that edge. I grind down again and he grunts loudly. I grind again and he curses.

Now I can tell he's hanging by a thin thread. One I don't want to break until I find my second release.

I cover the hand he has working my pussy with my own, guiding him, slipping a finger then two inside along with his, pushing him to move his fingers faster, more frantically.

And when he tenses, I know he's done. He's finished. He's losing himself and I whimper as my toes curl and the wave rushes through me once more, ripping a response from my center outwards.

As he's calling my name, I take him with me. Over and under before the wave spits us both back out. Breathless, panting, quivering with release.

Wow. Wow. *Wow.*

As soon as I catch my breath, I let out a long, satisfied sigh. He pulls the blindfold off me and tosses it onto the table, grabs my chin and twists my head to give me a deep, wet kiss.

When he finally pulls away, he whispers, "That was fucking awesome."

Why, yes, it certainly was.

CHAPTER NINE

Cade:

I study the silky blonde hair that's spread over my chest as I sprawl on my back across Sky's bed. Her ear is plastered over my heart, her palm slides mindlessly back and forth over my belly, her thigh pins mine to the bed, and her toe hooks around my calf.

My fingers rake through all that hair of hers as I separate the strands and wonder how she keeps the length from turning into a big knot. I'm glad she's not the type of woman who is afraid of messing up her hair. I like being able to touch it and relish the honey-like smoothness between my fingers.

Her breathing is slow and steady as her soft, full breasts press into my ribcage.

She's content.

So am I.

And what's really crazy is...

This feels so *right*.

I belong here.

She's supposed to be snuggled against me.

I'm complete. And I never realized I wasn't. At least, not until this very moment.

Now I know why I've never settled down with anyone else. They simply weren't right for me.

Sky is right. She's *the one*.

It's a ridiculous thought. To know something like this in such a unreasonably short amount of time.

What was to be only hooking up with a sexy, tempting neighbor suddenly has become so much more.

I can see the marks I left on her ass cheek, so I sweep my palm over her skin. "Good?"

"Yes," she says on a sigh.

I am, too.

"I didn't hurt you, right?"

Her eyes tip to mine. "No. Not at all."

"Good." I'm glad. I definitely want to do more things like that with Sky. And that flogger of hers keeps bouncing around in my brain. My fingers itch to try it out. To leave stripes on her tan skin over her breasts and over her ass.

Maybe not today. Maybe tomorrow. If she'll let me play with her this weekend.

Hell, even next week. Next month.

I have no idea how she's feeling about me, if she's even thinking the same way.

"Are you planning on spending the night?" she asks.

And there it is.

"Well, that flogger *has* been calling my name." I glance down at her draped comfortably against my side. "Would you like me to?"

"Yes, I would."

A sense of relief runs through me. Relief that she's not eager to kick me out after a few orgasms. Relief that she may desire to see where this goes, just like I would like to. "I don't have a change of clothes. I'll need to run home." I'll literally need to run home and grab an overnight bag that will last me for the weekend. Because, honestly, if she'll have me, I'll stay until Sunday night or even early Monday morning.

But I'll let her take it at her pace.

"Who said you'll need clothes?" She gives me a naughty grin.

I return it and trace a knuckle over her cheekbone. "True. But a toothbrush and some deodorant would be nice."

"Mmm. I see your point."

I laugh and her smile broadens, lighting up her face.

We both become quiet and enjoy the companionable silence for a few moments. I want to get to know her better. And it's not just the flogger that sticks in my mind. It's the photos I saw earlier.

I should approach this carefully.

"It's strange we don't know much about each other, but here we are, lying naked in bed together. We seem very comfortable with each other. Am I wrong?"

She looks at me in surprise with those beautiful sky-blue eyes. "No. I'm enjoying this. Enjoying you."

I try not to give her a big goofy smile. (Keep it cool, Cade.) "Ditto. But I don't even know your last name." A valid point to get this conversation rolling in the right direction.

She flicks at my nipple. "I don't know yours either, you know."

That's true. I haven't shared. Though, I hadn't found an opportunity to do so. Other than my career and my first name, she's in the dark just the same as I am. "Mine's pretty common. Harrison."

"Strong last name. Like your first name, too." She lowers her voice like a movie trailer announcer and says, "Kincade Harrison, Secret Service Agent."

Then her body jerks slightly and without lifting her head, her eyes find mine again and she studies me. I struggle to keep my expression blank because it's almost like she's attempting to look deep into my soul.

Something flashes behind her eyes and I become curious.

"Schaeffer," she murmurs softly.

Skylar Schaeffer. That last name doesn't raise any flags. "That's your married name?" I continue to lazily brush her hair with my fingers.

"No. I... I went back to my maiden name."

So, not the last name of the man in the photos. "How long ago did you divorce?"

She averts her gaze from mine and a prickle skirts up my spine.

I cock an eyebrow. "You're not divorced?"

She ducks her face into my chest, so now I can't even read her expression. "No, he passed away."

My breath becomes shallow in my chest. "I'm sorry to hear that. That must have been difficult. How long ago?"

"A couple of years now." Not a clear answer. I wait but she remains quiet.

"Long term illness?"

She hesitates for a heartbeat, two. "Complications from one, yes."

Now I'm *really* curious. But I'm trying not to sound like I'm interrogating her. I don't want her to not only shut down but shut me out.

I have to ask... "What was your married name?"

"Why?"

"Just curious."

~

Skylar:

Fear runs through my veins like a frozen stream. And that fear is because I believe my answer may be the end of us.

Done before it's ever really began.

I like Cade. I like wrapping myself around him in my bed. I liked when he had me draped over the table as he brought me to an exquisite orgasm. I love his voice, his demeanor, the power he has over me during sex. If I had to pick a man out on a dating site that would be perfect for me, Cade would be it.

We fit. Even in the short amount of time we've spent together, I recognize that. And from what I can see, he does, too.

And is it fate that we just happen to be neighbors?

Maybe.

Is it fate that he decided to start a jogging routine?

Possibly.

Is it fate that I happened to be outside working in my front yard when he ran by and caught my eye?

Most likely.

If I say my former last name he might recognize it, even though there are probably a million people with the same last name out there. However, it's a last name that might catch the attention of a Secret Service agent.

But lying to him will not give this tenuous relationship a solid start. A relationship, or even the possibility of one, built on lies will remain rocky and untrue.

A solid foundation is built on trust.

Can I avoid the question? Yes, for now, but sooner or later he's going to inquire again. He's a Federal agent. Law enforcement tend to be inquisitive by nature. As they should be.

No matter what, the truth will eventually come out. Better to rip a small Band-Aid off now than a large wound dressing later.

But still...

This churns my stomach and makes my heart beat wildly.

I start...

"My husband did a tour of duty over in Afghanistan. Like many troops, he saw things that would haunt him forever."

Cade says nothing, simply keeps stroking my hair, which I wish would soothe my nerves, and though it doesn't, it *does* encourage me to continue.

"And like many military members, he returned with PTSD."

Cade's fingers still. Even though it's only for a split second, I don't miss it. And now, his other hand is sliding along my bare back.

I suck air deeply through my nostrils and then let it go, hoping it'll bolster me. Unfortunately, it doesn't.

"It was hard. For both of us." Those words are simple, but they are so very true. "Our marriage struggled after that. He would close himself off. Get depressed, get angry, get violent."

Finally, Cade speaks, "Did he hurt you?"

I allow myself to meet his gaze, if only for a moment. "No. Never. Even throughout his own 'war' he fought after being overseas, he loved me. It came close several times when he would get out of control. But he never took it over the edge. Until..."

I close my eyes and press my face deeper into Cade's chest. The memories flood through me and I don't want to sob, cry, or lose myself all over again.

I can't lose myself because I've only just found *me* once more. And Cade. Who I hope will still give us a shot after I tell my story.

"The last presidential election..."

Cade moves slightly underneath me. Just a shift, but it's telling.

"I remember it well. I covered one of the candidates." His voice sounds a little monotone like he's trying not to give anything away.

And that right there gives it all away.

All the breath rushes from my lungs and now I'm this far in, I wonder if I can stop and we can move onto another subject.

I'm sure Cade won't allow me to simply change the subject. Not now. Not ever.

"Which candidate?" *Oh, God, please, please, please don't say who I'm afraid you're going to say.*

"The candidate who won."

My nightmare has returned. Though, maybe it never really went away. Maybe it lurked beneath the surface.

His fingers curl into my hair and still. His hand along my back disappears. "Your husband's last name was Williams."

Jesus.

He didn't ask, he stated that fact.

He knows.

He was there.

He witnessed the horror.

He now knows who I am. Even though I had no prior knowledge of my husband's plans or actions, I'm still tied to *that* person.

I was a victim, as well. But nobody cared.

"Landis wanted to reduce veteran benefits."

"And still does. He's not a popular person with vets."

"No. My husband snapped."

"I would say so." His hand curls around my chin and lifts my face to his. "Sky..."

I shake my head slightly, not enough to pull my face from his grasp, but enough to deny the sympathy in his eyes. The sadness that pulls at him. At me.

Shit. This is going all so wrong.

This was supposed to be a happy day, a day of enjoyment and of pleasure.

Will I never escape this? Will this haunt me forever?

"None of this was your fault. You had no prior knowledge he would snap like that and try to take out the senator."

"I should've known something... *something* was wrong. At least, more than normal."

"Don't blame yourself."

It's hard not to. I should've see some sort of indication. A telling sign that he'd finally gone off the deep end. His mind severely broken. And the decision he made to try to assassinate a senator was the final breaking point.

A fatal decision.

The end for him. The end for us.

I struggled for it not to be the end for me.

Eventually, I clawed my way back out of that black hole. And thought I was in a good place.

Then a Secret Service agent ran by my house. One who protected the actual senator who my husband tried to kill. How crazy is that?

Fate whispers through my mind.

We're all connected in some way. Some more than others.

"I assume you know the agent who shot my husband?" I ask.

His chest rises and falls as his eyes lock with mine.

In that moment, I know the answer without him ever saying a word. So when he does, it comes as no surprise.

"Sky, I have something to tell you... Please, please, forgive me..."

I close my eyes and let his deep voice wash over me. I never move until he's done speaking.

Suddenly, I realize... maybe this *fate* had a plan. Maybe we were brought together for a reason... To help us both heal.

To get over the past and move forward.

We'll see what fate has in store for us.

I, for one, want to know.

I'm thinking Cade does, too.

IF YOU ENJOYED THIS BOOK

Thank you for reading the Obsessed Novella Series. If you enjoyed these stories, please consider leaving a review at your favorite retailer and/or Goodreads to let other readers know. Reviews are always appreciated and just a few words can help an independent author like me tremendously!

ALSO BY JEANNE ST. JAMES

Made Maleen: A Modern Twist on a Fairy Tale

Damaged

Rip Cord: The Complete Trilogy

Brothers in Blue Series:

(Can be read as standalones)

Brothers in Blue: Max

Brothers in Blue: Marc

Brothers in Blue: Matt

Teddy: A Brothers in Blue Novelette

The Dare Ménage Series:

(Can be read as standalones)

Double Dare

Daring Proposal

Dare to Be Three

A Daring Desire

Dare to Surrender

The Obsessed Novellas:

(All the novellas in this series are standalones)

Forever Him

Only Him

Needing Him

Loving Her

Temping Him

Down & Dirty: Dirty Angels MC Series:

(Can be read as standalones)

Down & Dirty: Zak

Down & Dirty: Jag

Down & Dirty: Hawk

Down & Dirty: Diesel

Down & Dirty: Axel

Down & Dirty: Slade

Down & Dirty: Dawg

Down & Dirty: Dex

Down & Dirty: Linc

Down & Dirty: Crow

You can find information on all of Jeanne's books here:

http://www.jeannestjames.com/

AUDIO BOOKS BY JEANNE ST. JAMES

The following books are available in audio!

Down & Dirty: Zak (Dirty Angels MC, bk 1)

Down & Dirty: Jag (Dirty Angels MC, bk 2)

Forever Him (An Obsessed Novella)

Rip Cord: The Complete Trilogy

Damaged

Double Dare (The Dare Menage Series, bk 1)

Coming soon:

Down & Dirty: Hawk (Dirty Angels MC, bk 3)

Down & Dirty: Diesel (Dirty Angels MC, bk 4)

Daring Proposal (The Dare Menage Series, bk 2)

The Brothers in Blue Series

ABOUT THE AUTHOR

JEANNE ST. JAMES is a USA Today bestselling erotic romance author who loves an alpha male (or two). She was only thirteen when she started writing and her first paid published piece was an erotic story in Playgirl magazine. Her first erotic romance novel, Banged Up, was published in 2009. She is happily owned by farting French bulldogs. She writes M/F, M/M, and M/M/F ménages.

Want to read a sample of her work? Download a sampler book here: BookHip.com/MTQQKK

To keep up with her busy release schedule check her website at www.jeannestjames.com or sign up for her newsletter: http://www.jeannestjames.com/newslettersignup

www.jeannestjames.com
jeanne@jeannestjames.com

Blog: http://jeannestjames.blogspot.com
Newsletter: http://www.jeannestjames.com/newslettersignup
Jeanne's Down & Dirty Book Crew:
https://www.facebook.com/groups/JeannesReviewCrew/

facebook.com/JeanneStJamesAuthor
twitter.com/JeanneStJames
instagram.com/JeanneStJames
bookbub.com/authors/jeanne-st-james
goodreads.com/JeanneStJames
pinterest.com/JeanneStJames

Get a FREE Erotic Romance Sampler Book

This book contains the first chapter of a variety of my books. This will give you a taste of the type of books I write and if you enjoy the first chapter, I hope you'll be interested in reading the rest of the book.

Each book I list in the sampler will include the description of the book, the genre, and the first chapter, along with links to find out more. I hope you find a book you will enjoy curling up with!

Made in the
USA
Monee, IL